A RIVER
TO CROSS

BOOK TWO OF
THE STONES OF GILGAL

A RIVER TO CROSS

BOOK TWO OF
THE STONES OF GILGAL

C. L. SMITH

MOUNTAIN VIEW PRESS

Published by Mountain View Press, www.mountainviewpress.com, Toll Free (855) 946-2555.

ISBN 13: 978-1-68314-141-9 (Print)
　　　　 978-1-68314-142-6 (ePub)
　　　　 978-1-68314-143-3 (Mobi)

Library of Congress Catalog Card Number: 2016916739

DEDICATION

After watching my husband—my hero—face danger with courage, humility, integrity, and humor over the years, it was not hard for me to imagine Othniel, the first and most noble of the biblical hero-judges. The inspiration to tell his story grew into *The Stones of Gilgal* novels.

Thanks for the inspiration.
Thanks for all the adventures.
We've crossed a lot of rivers together—
Eden, this book is for you.

CONTENTS

ACKNOWLEDGMENTS

The powerful stories of Scripture have fascinated me my whole life. They have changed me, slowly transforming my self-centeredness to other-centered love. They have given me the courage and strength to triumph over my own troubles. I am grateful to the God who gave those stories to us. They are in reality one story, *his* story. Random, senseless, often violent, puzzle pieces of the universe fit together best when framed by the story of the Cosmic War between Good and Evil—the drama of that God of infinite love, betrayed and assailed by his own creation, but determined to save it. Thousands of voices are proclaiming the story through fiction, commentary, sermon or song. Their words have illuminated mine. I am grateful for them and humbled by the privilege of adding my small voice to that immense chorus.

The Stones of Gilgal storyline is not one that I plotted so much as discovered. I first noticed the kernel of a fascinating love story in Acsah and Othniel, two minor characters briefly mentioned in the first chapters of Judges. Then I realized they were contemporaries with Jonathan, another minor character from the back of the book—and the plot, as they say, thickened. Phinehas, Salmon, and Rahab jumped into the mix and the action began. I can't tell you how many times I found a scene not working or felt blocked because of a text later in scripture or a comment in a commentary, then awakened in the middle of the night to scribble down a conversation or a new twist in subplot directed by the characters themselves.

I could not have even conceived of doing such a project without the encouragement and support of my husband, Eden, and my four wonderful children. Beyond the close circle of support from my family is that of more professionals and friends than I can mention here. A few however, absolutely must be acknowledged by name. First, Inger Logelin, whose invaluable editing experience and efficiency gently corrected and perfected my original manuscript. Marcus Park beautifully captured the essence of the action-packed conflict of this story in a single image. And once again I must thank my friend, Marjorie Moran, for the beautiful map (updated for this volume) and the line drawing of the Gilgal, originally created for *Balaam's Curse*.

I have to admit that I am emotionally bipolar about this project. At times I am gripped with the sense that I have discovered an extremely exciting and underreported biblical story—then swing to near despair that no one will notice or like it. Positive comments and reviews from my readers (along with a sense of approbation from heaven) are the medicine that restores me to joy and well-being. A note from J. Paul Stauffer, the major professor of my college days, stands out as one of the most encouraging responses of the past year. My first book, *Balaam's Curse*, was dedicated to him. I was privileged to present a copy of it to him at the Pacific Union College alumni weekend this past spring and received this note a few weeks later.

First of all, let me thank you for your generous dedication. I am honored. Then let me congratulate you on the novel, which I have read with much interest and pleasure. You have developed your story from only a couple of chapters in Numbers, creating and elaborating events and characters that seem entirely persuasive and at home in the setting of the germinal text. The work and its proposed sequel reveal your fascination with the Old Testament and I wish you well as you continue your good work.

ACKNOWLEDGMENTS

Encouragement from readers means more than I can say. Thank you, thank you, thank you!

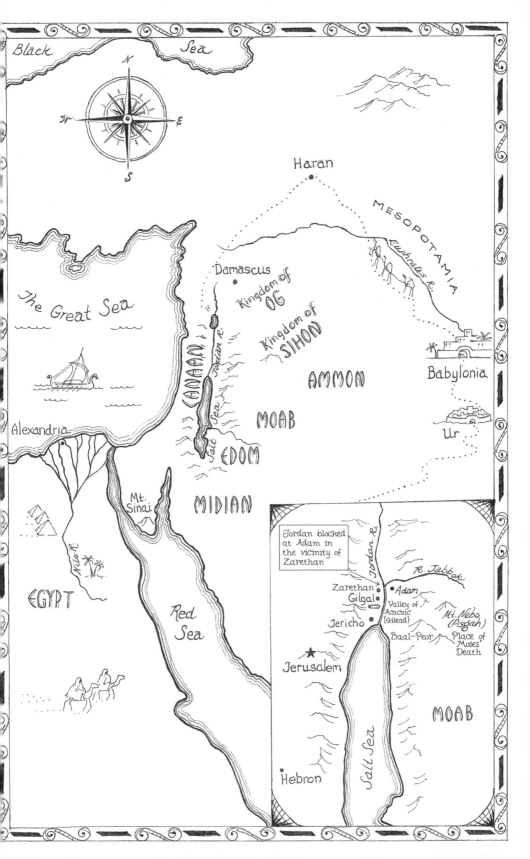

PROLOGUE

Remember, my people,
how Balak king of Moab plotted to destroy you,
yet I turned the curses of Balaam, son of Beor, into blessings.
Consider your journey from the sorrows of Acacia Grove
to the triumph of Gilgal,
that you may know the perfection of my mighty acts,
and my faithful love toward you.
—Micah 6:5 (KJV, author's paraphrase)

The steward clapped his hands. Two menservants, always at the ready when the king was in his private chambers, appeared instantly. "Take the king to the bathing room," he ordered curtly. "Wash him down in preparation for a good soak." The steward ordered a lower set of servants to bring water and hot stones for the bath while Nahari's personal menservants gripped the king from both sides in perfect synchrony, one hand hoisting from the armpit, the other stabilizing the arm, and set him on his feet with perfunctory efficiency.

Well trained, the steward thought smugly. *No reaction at all to the dead girl lying beside the bed, the stench of vomit in the room, or the blood and half-digested food befouling their lord and master.* Nahari seemed dazed, almost catatonic now. But he would remember and repay any response he considered demeaning. He always did.

The steward carefully masked his own irritation as the menservants escorted the king to the side chamber with its luxurious Minoan bathtub. This kind of thing happened too often. Just as he was settling down at the end of a long day in hopes of enjoying a peaceful spring evening, the king had turned luxurious order into stinking chaos. It would be hours before he could rest again.

1

He called for chambermaids to change the blood-spattered bedding. He called for a bevy of scrubwomen to cleanse stone floors, carpets, and walls. He called for the lowest servants, the refuse and sewage bearers, to haul the body out and toss it into the waste pit outside the wall.

The body . . . He regarded the girl for the first time. Reaching down to retrieve the king's favorite dagger from her belly, he charged the chambermaids with one more task. "Before you begin on the bed, remove the jewelry from this wench. See that anything of value is cleansed and returned to the house of the women." He looked down at the dagger in his hand. "Oh, and clean this and leave it on the bedside table."

That would take care of the room. But Nahari wanted the city cleansed. All remaining Midianite women in Jericho rounded up, exterminated. And he wanted it done tonight. The steward sighed and sent word for Ahuzzath, captain of Nahari's elite guard, to come to the king immediately. It wasn't concern for the health of his people. It wasn't personal fear of the plague. It was another of King Nahari's deranged swings from blistering rage to cold vengeance—only tonight he seemed to be assailed by both concurrently.

Normally, King Nahari barricaded himself within Jericho's unassailable walls until the dust of local conflicts settled, as his father and grandfather had done before him, but the invaders who conquered the land just across the river were unlike any other foe. They did not have a formidable army. They had little wealth. And their practices angered rather than appeased the gods of Canaan. Yet they swarmed in from the desert as unstoppable as locusts. Barbarian hordes. Hundreds of thousands of them. Hacking down the luxuriant worship groves of Asherah and razing the temples of Baal to the ground. Turning beauty to ashes. Annihilating all who attempted to stop them. First King Sihon's superbly trained forces in the Valley of Acacias. Then they turned north to the craggy, black heights of Bashan, where no other army dared go, and annihilated the Kingdom of Og, the last outpost of Rephaim giants east of the Jordan. The vast camp of Israel filled the eastern half of the Jordan

2

valley, and all that separated them was the river. For the first time the steward could remember, King Nahari had been truly afraid.

Against his usual practice, he formed a loose alliance with King Zur and the Midianite Five, the only regional power with a plan for defeating them. The Five had the manpower, but not sufficient camels or armaments for such a war. Nahari supplied the gold. Zur and his cohorts would supply the blood. But the Midianite army bled out. Dead as the girl on the floor. Nahari also provided gifts and a western base for the subterfuge suggested by the prophet Balaam—using Asherah's temple nymphs to lure Israelite men from their allegiance to Yahweh. That part of the strategy had failed as miserably as the war and Nahari raged over high expenditures that left him no more safe. The plague had not been severe in Jericho as plagues go, and it was all but over, but someone needed to feel the king's wrath tonight.

The steward could only hope the torture and slaughter of these women at Ahuzzath's hand would help calm the king. In the meantime, the steward had just the thing. Congratulating himself that he had convinced the royal physicians to stock the king's chambers with the potions that were needed most frequently and seemed to have the greatest effect on the king, he pulled a vial of valerian from the ornately carved *apotheca* chest and poured a double dose into the king's cup. By the time the steward entered the king's bathing chamber with the medicine, Nahari stood elevated on a block of limestone while the menservants splashed him with pot after pot of water. He looked every inch a king now, standing strong and manly, arms akimbo, with rivulets of fresh water flowing from his braided hair and beard, streaming over the rippling muscles of a perfect body. The steward crafted an admiring smile and met the king's eyes. "You are looking much better already, my lord." He raised the cup to his own lips and took a sip to reassure the king. "Drink this. Valerian to sooth any remaining disquietude from such an unpleasant evening."

He kept his eyes trained on Nahari's face, extending the hand with the cup toward the king, but also holding his left hand open and palm up. The king's magnificent stature, brawny, and at least a head taller than most other men, did not require armor or kingly robes to appear godlike, but he knew Nahari never felt more vulnerable than when unclothed and unarmed in this room, attended by a squad of sturdy men bringing hot stones, pots of water—and who knew what else?

The steward's feet sloshed through puddles of water that had not yet found their way to the drains in the floor, but he did not dare avert his eyes from the king lest he appear evasive. "I will see to your bath," he said quietly as the king accepted the cup.

The grand pottery tub, covered inside with sky-blue enamel and painted on the outside to look like a pool nestled in reeds, was already filled and waiting—the picture of pleasant rest and safety. But Nahari was so unpredictable. One unexpected move, one misinterpreted expression, one tiny suspicion of betrayal, and everyone in the room could expect their families to grieve at the sight of their heads, spiked and hanging as bird-pecked decorations beside the city gates.

The steward dipped a hand in the water, nodding his appreciation to the men who had executed this task. "Well done. Remove the stones and you are dismissed." He knelt beside the tub and nodded to the two menservants and the water bearers surrounding the naked king. "Dismissed. All of you," he said firmly. He stirred a handful of aromatic balsam powder into the bath, then dribbled a copious dose of oil of lavender over the top. He smiled up at the king. "The temperature is perfect, your majesty. Enjoy your bath."

Nahari moaned with pleasure as he settled into the water. He pulled the mixture of scents into his nose with a long slow breath. "Warm, wet, and more fragrant than a woman," he murmured, closing his eyes, and resting his head against the rounded rim of the tub.

The steward withdrew to a stool in the back corner of the room and relaxed for the first time in well over an hour. The swishing, rattling, and clanking bustle from the bedchamber was beginning to settle down as well. The palace peace had been restored, thanks to him. He smiled to himself, certain that Nahari could not find a more competent steward. The city had no idea of the skill required day after day to keep their king from descending into total madness.

The tranquil moment terminated all too quickly with a brief exchange of words from the guards in the hallway. Then Ahuzzath stormed unannounced into the room without even removing his brass-cleated war sandals. He slammed his fist against his chest in a hasty salute. "I came as quickly as possible, sire," he fairly shouted.

As the king raised his head in a groggy stupor, the steward leaped to his feet, hoping to intervene and allow the king to continue the soothing comfort of the bath. He fixed his eyes on the doltish captain and began to explain carefully and deliberately. "His majesty learned this afternoon that the women of Midian brought this recent plague on our city. They were not emissaries of Asherah and Baal after all, but emissaries of disease and death." He glanced down at the king. *Excellent.* His eyes had closed again and he was at rest.

"See to it," the steward continued. "Have your guards round up every temple wench that remains. The king wishes to have his city cleansed this very night."

Ahuzzath's eyes flicked from the steward to his king as he attempted to understand.

The steward rolled his eyes at the dullness of this man's mind. He elucidated his explanation with a simple command. "King Nahari wants every Midianite woman within the walls of Jericho tormented as you see fit and then exterminated."

"Tonight," the king added without opening his eyes.

The captain's grizzled face lit up. "I will send my men door to door immediately. Rest assured, my king. I will personally see that each pretty little filly pays for what she carried through our gates."

"Through our gates," Nahari repeated sleepily. Suddenly, his eyes flew open. A great swashing wave sloshed onto the stone floor as he sat up straight, gripping the sides of the tub as if he would leap out. "Through our well-guarded gates! These walls have prevented attack for centuries. Double in thickness; double in height. Built to withstand giants. Balaam and his coalition of kings assured us these women would bring about the end of Israel. Instead, Jericho

threw open its gates to disease. Bar those gates. No more allies."
His eyes rolled wildly, then fixed on his captain. "Ahuzzath, make
those whores suffer."

"Yes, my lord." Ahuzzath's eyes glinted with understanding.
He edged backward toward the doorway, not yet dismissed, but
impatient to begin.

"No quick and easy death for such deceit," the king ranted.
"No tenderness for treachery, no mercy for Midianites, no matter
how fine the girl. Go!"

"Exactly as you command, my king." Ahuzzath saluted once
more and was gone.

The steward's heart sank. One glance at his king, cheeks flushed
with rage, eyes smoking with ire, and he knew the man was on the
verge of madness yet again. How long would it take to calm him
so he himself could rest for the night?

CHAPTER ONE

PLOTS AND PROPOSALS

Acsah

Acsah sang snatches of the "The Dwelling Place" as her shuttle flew. It was a glorious new day.

> *Lord, you have been our dwelling place throughout all generations.*
> *Before the mountains were born*
> *or you brought forth the whole world,*
> *From everlasting to everlasting, you are God . . .*[1]

Moses had written this psalm after the appalling incident with the golden calf. Her people learned the song as they constructed the holy tent and its furnishings. They sang it during the Wanderings, sang it for forty years camped around that tabernacle, the Dwelling Place of Yahweh. Acsah had sung the song all her life, but never had it seemed as fitting as on this bright morning. Israel was at one with her God. The war begun by the schemes of the prophet Balaam was over. Abba was home again, and he had just given her this fine Midianite loom gleaned from among the items of plunder.

> *We are consumed by your anger*
> *and terrified by your indignation.*

You have set our iniquities before you,
our secret sins in the light of your presence . . .[2]

Teach us to number our days aright,
That we may gain a heart of wisdom . . .

Satisfy us in the morning with your unfailing love,
That we may sing for joy and be glad all our days.[3]

Acsah's spirits soared at the mastering of a new craft—and at the surprise she was creating for Caleb. She used the small loom they carried during the Wanderings to make an occasional mat, but there had been little need for new textiles, and the work on that small tool was tedious. This was pure joy.

Not only that, but today the need and the blessing came together perfectly. As soon as she welcomed her father home the previous afternoon, she noticed the frayed condition of his robe. War and seven days of purification washings had taken their toll. At just the right time, the Lord had blessed them with many baskets of wool, and her endlessly turning spindle had spun it into yarn during the long days of the Midianite War. Today, she could not keep from singing as her eyes carefully followed the movement of the shuttle through the warp shed, laying down row after row of filling yarns. At the rate her fabric was growing, she would complete Abba's new garment before noon.

Hesitant footsteps shuffled in the sand of the walkway. Could her father be returning already? No. A quick glance at the shadowy movement on the edge of her field of vision told her it was only Jonathan.

"Shalom, returned warrior," she said. "That was quite the storytelling last night." She hoped her smile was appropriately hospitable since she did not take time to look up or slow the pace of her work.

Jonathan cleared his throat with a short, nervous cough. "The best part is that I am alive to tell the story."

The ensuing silence became so long and awkward that Acsah stopped the shuttle at the end of the row and looked up. His face was as serious as death. "Father isn't here. You can find him down by our flocks, strengthening the new wagon we acquired. He is quite eager to cross the river now that the war is over."

"I already found him there, which is why I have come to see you."

Acsah guided the shuttle on another pass through the loom, feeling the intensity of his gaze as she waited for him to say more. She laid down two more rows. "This loom was part of Father's acquisitions from the war," she said at last, filling the silence without looking up. "What did you bring home?"

"Quite a lot, really. God truly blessed us." Jonathan began pacing.

Acsah stopped. She tucked the shuttle into the warp threads and gestured toward the cushion beside her. "Sit down, Jonathan, and take a deep breath. Why are you so anxious? You are making *me* nervous."

Ignoring her request, he thrust his hand into the bag slung over his shoulder, pulled out a gleam of gold and green, and held it out on his palm. "I brought this for you from my share of the Midianite plunder."

As she took the necklace and held it up in the sunlight, five emeralds flashed and sparkled, the very color of the sunlit meadows in this lush Jordan valley. "Beautiful!" she gasped in awe.

"But it does not come close to the beauty of your green eyes."

She laughed. "Jonathan, you flatter me. But this gift . . . it is too much. I can't take it." She held it up for him to take back.

Jonathan seized the outstretched hand with the necklace and enclosed it in both of his as he fell on his knees beside her. "In truth, it is not enough. You were named for a little ornament, that anklet you always wear, but you are a crown that would honor the head of any man who could claim you as his own. Acsah, I love you. Let me be that man. My father and I have already spoken to your father regarding marriage."

Acsah stared at him. "What did my father say?"

9

"He said that you were very capable of deciding for yourself."

His face was so endearingly expectant at that moment, she could hardly bear to crush his hopes, but those hopes were wrongly placed. "Jonathan, I love you dearly as a friend, but marriage . . . "

"All I could think about while I was gone with the army was you. Every dream, every waking moment, even when I thought I was facing certain death, there was only you. I will accept no answer but yes." Jonathan leaned close to embrace her, but she pulled back.

"That answer I can't give you—now or ever. Thank you for the honor of your request, but it cannot be."

Jonathan drew back, studying her eyes for some understanding. Suddenly, he leaped to his feet and began pacing again. "Don't tell me you love my cousin," he groaned.

"Cousin? Which cousin? What are you talking about?"

"Phinehas."

"Phinehas?" Acsah smothered a laugh. "He is a priest. He must marry a Levite girl. I can think of him in only one way—someday he will be my high priest."

"Well, it's fortunate you don't love *him*." Jonathan's expression reminded her of a petulant child. "If you married my cousin, I would kill myself."

"Jonathan, stop. You are talking like a mad man."

"Well, I was almost mad with jealousy the day Phinehas was introduced as the one God had chosen to command the troops for this war. Your admiration for him was . . . was . . . well, more enthusiastic than the occasion warranted." He began to pace again. "Who then? Salmon? Ethan? Surely not Igal or Othniel."

Jonathan's possessive arrogance was making Acsah angry. "I do not have to answer that question."

"But I need to know if there is someone—"

"One man has my heart, only one," she snapped. "He is the center of my life, and I do not feel obligated to reveal his name to you."

Jonathan's face went dark with despair. He raked his hand through his hair and his whole body slumped.

Acsah felt a stab of regret. She had to finish this unpleasant conversation immediately. *Stay calm, stay calm,* she continued reminding herself as she rose to her feet. She placed her hand gently on Jonathan's arm. "My father has my heart, Jonathan. Who can measure up to Caleb in courage or kindness? In righteousness or wisdom? I am quite content to remain only his daughter."

Jonathan swayed with a sigh of relief, and his voice took on a soft, reasoning tone. "Our love and respect for your father is mutual. Next to Moses, my own grandfather, I regard Caleb above all other men. But you cannot mean to reject *me* forever because of him. I don't want to wait to claim you as my bride, but I will, if that is what you want. Like Jacob, I would wait seven years for my Rachel and it would seem but a day."

"Don't think of waiting for me, Jonathan. This will not be."

"Your father is old, Acsah. You care for him now, as he cares for you, but who will you have when he is gone? The inheritance in Canaan will go to your brothers. Where will you go then?"

Acsah gasped out her rage. "Enough! Please leave." With a flash of green and gold, she flung the necklace toward him and darted into the tent.

"Acsah, please. I did not mean to make you angry. I just want you to see reality. I *will* wait for you. I could never love anyone else."

Acsah could see his shadow on the tent wall as he leaned toward the silence. She held her breath.

"Please . . . tell me I have a chance," he cried hoarsely. Never had she heard such desperate tears choke a man's words.

She did not answer or move—even after she heard his footsteps crunching slowly away. Her head was still spinning with images of his shattered visage when she finally emerged from the tent. She picked up the shuttle with shaking fingers. *Think of something else, anything else.*

An image of aged Miriam came to her mind and she began singing Miriam's song from the Red Sea story.

Sing to the Lord,
For he is highly exalted.

11

Both horse and driver
he has hurled into the sea.[4]

As her singing grew more vigorous, her fingers fairly flew.

Caleb

It was nearly noon when Caleb returned to the tent with three Midianite girls in tow. There hanging over the loom was a finely woven man's robe. He looked down at the one he had worn for forty years. He needed a replacement for certain, and there it was. Two new mats lay on the ground, and the entire basketful of newly spun wool was gone—as was Acsah herself. *How quickly she worked this morning. I suspect not out of joy. Now how am I to convince her that we need Midianite servant girls?*

"Hogluh and Hodesh, wait here. I have a perfect home not far away for Huldah. I will take her to live with my sister-in-law who is now a widow, and you two will live here with my daughter and me."

Acsah

At the same time Caleb arrived back at the tent, Acsah was on her way to the tabernacle. When she had come to the bottom of the wool basket, she felt a stab of panic. She glanced around in an attempt to find more mind-occupying work. That's when she saw the glint of gold and green on the ground, its gleam mocking her attempts at self-composure.

What am I to do with that? Why didn't he take it? She snatched up the necklace and dashed off to find Eleazar, one thought cycling through her mind. *Give it to the Lord. Give it to the Lord. I hope Eleazar melts it down. I don't want to see it again. Give it to the Lord.* When she reached the end of the tent row, she stopped. The shortest route to the tabernacle entrance would take her past Aunt Sarah's tent, past Igal's tent, past Salmon's . . .

She did not want to explain her mission to inquisitive friends, and she certainly did not want to encounter Jonathan again. *If I know Jonathan, he has gone home to sulk, so if I go down this row and cut through the middle of Judah, passing by Josedech's tent, I will emerge just south of the tabernacle entrance—far enough from his tent to be safe.*

"Acsah." Salmon's familiar voice hit her like lead.

She had just come around a corner and there were Salmon and Othniel walking directly toward her in this unlikely place. Obviously, Salmon saw her first.

"For Prince Nashon," he said, forcing a smile. "I could not forget your words and have worked at this smile until my face ached."

I have not seen Salmon for weeks. Why now?

Salmon's smile evaporated. "What is wrong? Your good counsel was not wasted. Aren't you pleased to see some improvement in your friend?"

"I am not pleased to see anyone or anything," Acsah snapped. "I do not have the heart nor the time for friends right now."

She glared at her cousin, looking as threatening as possible lest he toss out one of his famously droll retorts. "Othniel, don't even think of making a comment." Without another look at either of the young men, she rushed off.

Salmon

"What are we to think of that?" Salmon asked in dismay.

Othniel shrugged.

Salmon sadly tracked Acsah's retreating figure until she disappeared. Her friendship had become more precious than ever since the murder of his father. "I know Acsah better than my own family . . . but today it seems as if I don't know her at all."

"I don't try to understand women, not even my mother."

"My mother and sister are one thing, but Acsah is the one woman I truly want to understand."

Othniel pragmatically returned to their interrupted conversation. "Which tribes, did you say, hope to claim this valley? Manasseh and who?"

"Tribes? Oh . . . yes . . . " Salmon shook his head to clear his thoughts. "The tribes of Reuben, Gad, and half of Manasseh presented their case before the tribal council. They wish to remain here, claiming these plains and the heights of Bashan in place of land they would have received over the Jordan."

"It is rumored they have already begun to rebuild the cities."

"Moses met with them privately after the tribal council. That is all I know. I can barely manage the needs of Judah and our family."

Othniel looked thoughtful. "The flocks and herds of those groups far surpass those of the rest of the tribes. I can understand why they asked for this area."

"Yes, they have more livestock than the rest of the tribes, but they also have more skilled warriors. The whole nation worked together to clear this valley. And now they want to settle here and leave us to cross the Jordan and conquer Canaan alone. How fair would that be—nearly a third of Israel's best fighting men remaining behind to start their new lives here?"

"If they did, I suspect some of the other tribes would be fearful of crossing over. Might try to remain here as well."

"Or maybe they would choose to return to the desert as nomads since the lands of the Midianite Five are now vacant. What then?"

"Well, I know Caleb will help you lead Judah into the Promised Land—no matter what. He was forced to turn back once. God will not disappoint him now. I, for one, will gladly follow him."

"As will I, but what of the other tribes? What if they turned back into the wilderness again? Do you think Judah could take Canaan alone?"

"You worry too much." Othniel clapped his hand solidly on Salmon's back. "Rest assured, Moses will know how to handle this."

Acsah

Acsah was all askew. She tugged at her sash and slowed to a walk. Her chest pounded with a wild rhythm not entirely due to the sprint from the tabernacle. *Calm down, Acsah. If you look as if you are being chased by lions, people will ask questions. Take a deep breath. The necklace is where it needs to be. Jonathan will recover, and life will return to normal.* She was still admonishing herself when she looked up to see the tent entrance—her new loom to the left, Father's new robe flapping a welcome in the breeze above it—and two very young daughters of those despicable Midianites huddled on one of her new mats.

"Be gone! Go to your own tent." Acsah's stomach recoiled in disgust.

"Our master asked us to wait here," the older girl answered hesitantly.

"Not here. This is the tent of my father Caleb."

"We are at the right place. Master Caleb acquired my sisters and me with the spoils of war."

"That is ridiculous. He brought home tools, two cows, a pair of oxen, and an ox cart. He brought home a loom, a grinding stone, and some pots. Those things we want and can use. He did not bring home slave girls."

"He *chose* us this morning. He bargained with Achor for my two sisters and me. He gave Achor two cows for the three of us."

"I can hardly believe my father would do that without consulting me. I manage this household though I am merely his daughter. Our lives are settled, and we are quite content without servants. Go back to Achor."

"But Master Caleb already bought us."

"My father will get our cows back later."

"That cannot be. Mara made it very clear that Caleb could not change his mind once the trade was complete."

"Then we have lost the two cows for nothing."

"Please, mistress. Master Caleb is so kind." The little one sniffed back a tear. "Mara beat us when we didn't understand."

Acsah was not going to argue with two small children. "Shoo, shoo. I have work to do."

The girls moved a stone's throw away from the tent and sat down again. The smaller one began crying. "I want Huldah."

"Hush, Hogluh. I don't know where Master Caleb took our sister, but he told us to stay here."

"I want to go find her."

"We are slaves now, Hogluh. The whip awaits us if we disobey. We must wait here."

Acsah gave the little ones as compassionate a look as she deemed appropriate. "Go find your sister. Do not fear. I will explain to my father why you have gone," she said gently. Then with unquestionable firmness she added, "You cannot wait here. I cannot think with all your whining."

"We don't know where to go," the older child pleaded. Her shoulders trembled and her eyes filled.

Pity oozed up like honey through cracks in Acsah's self-righteous platform, but she refused to get trapped in it like some hapless fly. *Hmmm. Eleazar. I just rid myself of one unwanted object. What could be more appropriate? It's the middle road between becoming as cruel as Mara and letting sticky-sweet sympathy mire our household in compromise.*

She softened her fierce expression. The girls were obviously quite frightened. She stooped down close to them and spoke gently. "It was very kind of my father to save you from Mara's rod. I believe I understand now exactly what he intended. Come with me." She stood again and held out her hands.

"But Master Caleb told us to wait here."

"I will inform him when he returns. He will be quite pleased." Acsah smiled encouragingly as she grasped each of the little ones firmly by the hand and marched them toward the tabernacle. She pictured Eleazar suppressing a laugh when he saw her coming for the second time that day.

"Where are we going?" a little voice asked timidly.

Acsah responded tenderly. "I am taking you to our beautiful sanctuary and to Eleazar, the high priest. I'm certain my father meant for you to be a gift for the priests."

The trembling anxiety on the little faces morphed into silent screams of terror. With unexpected strength, the girls ripped themselves from her grasp. Long after they disappeared between the tents, the muffled wail of the youngest hung pitifully in the air. "Huldah, O Huldah, where are you? They mean to sacrifice us."

A short time later, Caleb shuffled up the pathway whistling.

"Just what are you up to, Abba? Don't pretend you are some merry little songbird and that this is a happy morning."

"What do you mean? It is past noon already, but I *am* happy. The wagon is ready for the crossing. We not only have a lot of goods, we have a pair of twin lambs just born this morning. It is a very happy day."

"And what of the plots you have been hatching this morning? First I had to deal with Jonathan, and then those two Midianite children."

"Poor frightened little things. I rescued them from Mara early this morning and they helped me work on the wagon. How could anyone who remembers how our people were treated in Egypt be so hard on the little captives?" He looked around quickly. "Where are they? Off fetching water or wood already?"

"Father, we don't need slave girls."

Caleb dropped his voice confidentially. "At first I didn't think so either, so I gave up my right to any. I changed my mind this morning, however, when I saw these little ones treated so harshly." He stroked his beard thoughtfully, "And I got to thinking about how much more work there will be for you if war breaks out in Canaan, as it surely will once we cross the river."

"I can handle whatever arises without slaves."

"What about me? No thought for your aging father, eh? It will not be long before you abandon my tent for that of a husband, and who will be left to help me?" He opened his eyes wide and gave her a look of feigned concern.

"You know better than that, Abba," she snapped. "Don't you ever again send a young man to inquire about marriage. It is a father's responsibility to make marriage arrangements, and I expect you to turn all suitors away. My answer to all is no."

"To everyone, always?"

Acsah rolled her eyes. "Until I tell you differently."

"Come, come, child. Surely, you are not rejecting every young man in Judah."

"Every young man in all Israel, if truth be known." She paused and looked directly into her father's eyes as the hint of a smile softened her face and voice. "Perhaps . . . if there were a young Caleb or Joshua in camp . . . but there is not."

"I see." Caleb coughed to cover a laugh. "Well, concerning the Midianite children: I simply could not leave those girls with Achor and Mara."

Acsah slipped her arms around her father's neck. "Abba, you can't buy every slave in camp who is treated a little harshly."

"No," he answered slowly as he patted her back, "but I can make a difference to these girls. Actually there are *three* sisters. I left the eldest with Sarah" He stepped back from her and looked down the tent row both directions. "Where did the two little ones go?"

"They ran away, and I don't expect them to come back," Acsah answered firmly. She spun on her heel and disappeared into the tent.

Caleb

Caleb left immediately to search for the runaways, within minutes finding all three sisters at Sarah's tent. As soon as Hogluh and Hodesh saw him, they threw themselves at his feet, sobbing. "Please don't sacrifice us. Please . . ."

"What are you talking about?" He took Hogluh up in a tight one-armed embrace while he stroked her sister's hair to calm her.

Hogluh stopped crying immediately and stuck out her lower lip. "That lady meant to sacrifice us at Yahweh's sanctuary."

"Master Caleb, don't beat us." Hodesh looked up with pleading eyes. "We tried to wait for you at the tent. But she was taking us to the priest."

Hogluh wiggled down from Caleb's arms, taking a defiant stance beside her sister. "We ran and ran and called and called until we found Huldah."

Caleb closed his eyes and shook his head in disbelief. "My precious little ones, you have so much to learn about our Yahweh—and about my daughter, Acsah. Children are never sacrificed in this camp."

The girls stared at him. "Never?"

"Never."

"But Acsah was mean, like Mara."

"She is not like Mara. It is just that she didn't know anything about you, and unfortunately, she has already had a disagreeable morning." Caleb gave the girls a reassuring wink. "This was probably not the best day for you to meet."

Sarah, his widowed sister-in-law, had been sitting side by side with the eldest Midianite sister sorting twiggy debris out of a basket of lentils. She looked up now, a rare smile flickering on her lips. "Thank you, dear brother. This girl is ever so quick to learn . . . and she is so young."

That smile alone was worth the high price Achor extracted from him for the girls. Caleb stooped down before the eldest sister. "So tell me, Huldah, besides helping to sort lentils, what have you learned this morning?"

"Mistress Sarah and I made soap from tallow and ashes. Tomorrow we will launder all the soiled linen and clothing at the river. I can hardly wait to try it."

Sarah snorted. "Her desert village did not have much water, so they never washed anything. She is excited about splashing around in the river."

"I may borrow her back when you do not have so much for her to do . . . so she can teach her sisters."

"But Acsah will have her own way of doing things."

"My daughter doesn't think we need or want help."

A dark look crossed Sarah's face. "She will—if and when we ever do cross over into Canaan. She will—if and when you men have gone to war. She will—if you should die in battle."

Caleb laughed. "Such happy thoughts, Sarah. I was hoping my daughter might be glad for help in less extreme circumstances."

Hodesh wrinkled her nose, "I do not know if I will be glad to help *her*."

Sarah's eldest son, Othniel, had returned to the tent during the encounter, silently watching and listening. When no one answered the little one's challenge, he said simply, "You will like Acsah once you get used to her and she to you."

Caleb laughed. "I think Acsah has the most 'getting used to' to do. She is quite opposed to all foreigners right now, but especially Midianites. We must give her time to adjust." He grinned at the confused little faces. "Be patient with her. Stick close to me until she adjusts."

Shua

A small oil lamp cast a golden glow around an otherwise cheerless room at the North Wall Inn, highlighting the worry lines on the brow of an old woman. She sat on the bed fidgeting with her robe, a battle of light and darkness playing a war game in the furrows of her brow as she waited. She felt tight . . . like a wire coiled and held fast, ready to spring as soon as it was released. The things that protected her also confined her—the walls of Jericho, the king and his army, even her family. She knew what she needed to do, but it wouldn't be easy.

She relaxed just slightly at the light footfalls in the hallway, glad that her granddaughter had arrived first. "Come in, my dear."

20

"What is it, Grandmother?" the girl said breathlessly. "Hannah said we should come up here. She said to hurry because you seemed so worried."

"That silly servant girl. The only thing that worries me is how your mother will react. I am . . . uh . . ." Grandmother Shua patted the bed beside her. "Sit here beside me. I will explain myself to both of you as soon as Keziah comes."

The girl laughed as she sank down and snuggled close. "Surely Mother's reactions no longer worry you. She is always hysterical about something."

Shua sighed. "My sweet Rahab." The girl was such a comfort and joy. The pain she had endured in this despicable place only served to make her more compassionate. She took her granddaughter's hand as she watched the door, finding renewed strength and resolve in the company of this child.

Keziah's sharp footsteps rang down the hall ahead of her. "Are you all right?" the words burst into the room along with the pinched face. "Hannah said—"

She frowned. "You look fine. Why on earth have you called us up here just before the evening rush? What are you thinking of, Mother?"

Shua looked up and announced gravely, "It is time for me to make a move."

"What are you talking about? From this room? From the inn? What?"

Keziah was always impatient when she had a lot to do.

"Surely, you can guess what I mean, my dear daughter. Weeks have passed since the Israelites settled across the river. It is time for me to go to them."

Keziah gave an exasperated sigh. "Don't be ridiculous, Mother. The presence of Israel has everyone else in this city on the verge of panic. The gates are guarded. Even if you could work out some ruse for leaving the confines of Jericho, you would be killed as a traitor if our guards caught you trying to cross the fords now. Israelite guards would just as likely consider you a spy if you made it to the other side."

The old woman glanced at her granddaughter. *Rahab understands.* "I would rather die trying then live out the rest of my life here."

"How can you say that? Jokshan has done everything he can to make you comfortable here at the inn."

Grandmother closed her eyes. "I appreciate it all."

"Then enjoy what you have and forget the impossible dream."

"Being safe—being comfortable—is far from being happy. How can I forget what has been my heart's desire for forty years?" She reached out for her daughter's hand. "When you were a small girl, you also longed to be part of such a blessed and righteous people."

"That was long ago, Mother. They were driven away and never came back. Now . . . I don't know anymore. Jericho's walls and the reputation of King Nahari's army protect us from invaders. The inn gives us a good living and I have a good husband who protects my family, including you."

"But a vortex of greed and violence swirls around this place. Can you be certain Jokshan will always be around to protect you?"

When Keziah didn't answer, Rahab snuggled closer to her grandmother. "I would escape from this city if I could." She smiled wistfully. "I love every story you have told me about Israel."

"Those are *stories*, child. Canaan has wondrous tales of its gods too. How many of them are true?"

"I believe the stories Grandmother tells us. She *talked* to the twelve spies. They were eyewitnesses of the plagues and miracles in Egypt."

"I heard their stories too that long-ago day. They said they were coming back, but they didn't."

"They are here now, and they miraculously defeated King Sihon and King Og. Even King Nahari was afraid of those two monsters across the river. He should be glad the Israelites annihilated them."

"But . . ." Rahab caught her grandmother's eyes with an impish grin. "The king is terrified of the monster slayers."

"We should be too," Keziah snapped. "We do not know what their intentions are. Will they attack Moab? Will they stay where they are? Will they cross the river and attack Jericho?" She paused and gave Shua a pointed look. "Or will the power of our gods drive them back to the desert again? No one knows."

Shua took a deep breath. Suddenly there did not seem to be enough air for three women in this small room. "That is precisely why I called you here." She understood the risks. Certainly, she could be killed. Worse, she could endanger her family, but what else could she do? She lived in a city that was evil personified. "I have a plan, and my mind is made up. I am not asking you for permission. I am declaring my intention."

Keziah ran her hand along her jaw and said slowly. "Give me a few days to think about this, Mother. I will discuss it with Jokshan."

"I must go *now*. In a few weeks, spring rains will make the ford unusable. Tomorrow morning early, when the caravans are jostling to get through the gates and the women are passing back and forth to the market center to get water from the well, no one will notice an old woman going out the gate. I am perfectly capable of navigating the fords by myself while they are still shallow. And, given the huge camp entrenched on the east side of the river, I won't have to worry about robbers and ruffians. I will contact the leaders of Israel and return before the day is over. Surely, I will find some of the twelve who remember me."

"No," Keziah shook her head. "Mother, believe me. I understand your dream, but I cannot let you do that. The guards are not so careless. King Nahari is more insane than ever over the danger Israel poses."

"Mother is right," Rahab said sadly. "We can hardly move about the kitchen now for all the water jars the king demanded we store here. Never mind that the springs feeding the fountain at market center have never failed in a thousand years."

"I can outsmart that fool. I have a devised a ruse that should get me out of the city quite easily." Shua gave a sharp nod to indicate her determination.

Rahab tightened her lips and frowned. "The fact that the king is a fool does not make him less dangerous. I could not bear it if harm came to you." She looked up at her mother. "Let me go with her."

Keziah's response came quick and sharp as a flashing bronze blade. "Absolutely not! The danger is greater than either of you can imagine—not for you alone. If King Nahari's guards caught you trying to slip over to Israel now, you would implicate our whole family in treason."

"I understand that, but what if I do nothing? The ancient prophecies assert that the Children of Israel will come to reclaim this land. If the time is now and war breaks out, Jericho may well be the first point of conflict. We do not want to get caught here in the city. On the other hand, even if they are not planning to cross the river into Canaan, I want to join their people. I would happily live on the plains of Moab or anywhere they go next. I will beg them to graft us into the trunk of Israel—not me alone, but any of our family who wish to join me."

"Oh, Grandmother. Your dream is mine as well."

"That dream is an empty mirage, Mother. If they are such a righteous people, would they allow Canaanites to live among them as equals? Would you have us give up the security of the inn to go to . . . to who knows what? Slavery? Life as outcasts?"

"I would risk alienation or slavery to live among such a people. I would rather die seeking that dream than settle for what we have here."

Keziah drew a deep breath and bit her lip.

"We need to let Grandmother go," Rahab responded softly. "She has prayed to the God of Jacob for forty years. Surely he will protect her. It is one thing for you, Mother. You have Father. The inn has been a good home for you, but not for Grandmother and certainly not for me."

"You enjoy your singing."

"Not when a houseful of lustful, drunken men ogle me."

"Would you rather be a slave?"

"Why not be a handmaid among the people of Yahweh? I am no longer suitable for marriage and constant danger lurks in these streets. We can never be sure we will live to see another sunrise."

Keziah responded with gentleness as well as authority, a tone intended to end her daughter's argument. "Jokshan has not let anyone touch you since he took over the inn. He watches over both of you now, as he watches over me. The inn is his life and wealth."

Shua broke into the dialogue. "But he cannot control evil men. Have you forgotten why *you* quit singing?"

Keziah colored. "Uncle Thahash was an evil man, but he is dead."

Shua cut her off. "My brother was a product of this culture. His greed was not simply the evil of one man. Thahash was *Jericho*, Keziah. Jokshan protects us through his wealth and position as innkeeper, but one thrust of a knife could change all that. We are all at risk every day that we live in this city."

Keziah looked away, tense, defensive.

Grandmother Shua knew that look well. It was clear these arguments were convincing and that her daughter did not want to be convinced. She stood and threw her arms around Keziah as she had done since her daughter was a toddler. "My decision is made," she said in as gentle but firm a tone as she could muster. "I will retire early so I can leave at dawn. I simply wanted you to know."

Keziah held herself stiff in the embrace and broke for the door without a word as soon as Shua relaxed her arms.

"I am no stubborn, credulous child, Keziah."

Keziah paused with her hand on the door latch. Everything in her stance shouted impatience, but she stayed to listen until her mother finished.

"I will take every precaution to avoid the king's guard so as not to endanger you. If I perish, may it be from an Israelite blade. If I succeed in my mission, I will return or find a way to send word back to you. I love you, Keziah. I love all of you so much."

Keziah's lips pulled tight as she opened the door. "There are customers waiting."

Grandmother Shua followed her out. "I'll help for awhile, but I won't stay up late."

Rahab

Long after her mother and grandmother left the room, Rahab lingered. All concerns about Grandmother's safety, all frustrations over her mother settling for the tenuous security of the inn, were drowned in a flood of long-repressed memories stirred up at the mere mention of a name—*Thahash.*

He was her uncle. Grandmother's brother. The previous owner of the inn. She could not remember anyone speaking his name in all the years since he died. Now, in the dim solitude of her grandmother's small room, she was shocked at how the mention of the name chilled her to the core.

To his credit, he did take his sister in when Shua ran away from her cruel merchant husband with little else but her daughter. That was nearly forty years ago. Grandmother more than earned her keep, working long days at the inn even while her daughter was very young. Then when Keziah was old enough to demonstrate her musical talent, she too began working for Uncle Thahash, playing her harp and singing. Shua and her daughter remained at the North Wall Inn even after Keziah grew up and married a kindhearted pot maker from Moab. Since Thahash had no heirs, Keziah's husband, Jokshan, sold his business and invested all his wealth in improving the inn.

That was the life Rahab was born into—father working like a slave for the greedy old man in order to own the inn someday. Grandmother cooking and cleaning. Mother serving as well as entertaining with harp and song. She could not remember a time when she was not a part of it, skipping through the large dining hall helping Mother bring food and drink to the patrons, giggling as she dodged pinches and pats on her little behind, curling up in a corner each evening, drifting in and out of foggy dreams to the rippling enchantment of her mother's harp and sweet, sweet singing. Uncle Thahash was always there in the background, but he had never noticed her, had never really spoken to her that she could remember until—everything came flooding back. She struggled for breath, a child again, helpless and hurting, reliving every harrowing detail.

With hugs and kisses and tears of separation, her parents left for a short business trip to Moab. Father went to acquire a cartload of fine pottery jars for the inn and Mother went along to find the harp maker who had made her own instrument. "You are nearly five years old," Mother said with a twinkle in her eyes. "Old enough for a small harp of your own. Be very good, and I will begin teaching you to play when I return."

A harp of her own. She could still feel the tingly excitement of standing at the city gate beside Grandmother, watching Mother clamber into the wagon, looking so beautiful sitting on the high wagon seat beside Father. "Mind Grandmother, and don't upset Uncle Thahash," Mother called as they rumbled away. Rahab did not even watch long enough for her parents to disappear down the road. She raced all the way back down the long narrow street to the inn. She didn't stop until she reached the low platform where her mother sang each evening. She plopped down on a cushion to pluck at imaginary strings, singing every song she could remember. When she finished, she leaped and twirled in a harp dance.

As business picked up toward evening, she did what she could to help, but she never quite stopped singing and dancing around the margins of the dining hall as she cleared tables. She danced up and down the stairs to the wine cellar getting beverages for Uncle. She danced all around the kitchen waiting for plates to take to patrons, being careful not to upset Grandmother as she cooked. When Grandmother made up a plate for her supper, she was too fidgety to eat. Remarkably, even Uncle Thahash shared her excitement. He tousled her hair and called her his singing, dancing Lily Bud. Long after Rahab snuggled under her soft coverlet that night, she lay awake. Her fingers would not stop plucking at her dream harp, and the songs continued racing through her head even as she fell asleep.

The room was dark as death when she awoke to a dull thump just outside her door. Every hazy shred of sleepiness vanished as the door creaked open. A hand, holding a flickering lamp, thrust itself into the room, sending wild shadows circling the room as it moved back and forth. Behind the hand, a massive black shape filled her doorway. He was searching for her, and she knew who it was—King Libni! She had eavesdropped on wild-eyed reports of the king of the Anakites who lurked in the Cave of Adullum. He was not a myth. More than one guest had actually seen him. Now he was here and it was too late to hide.

She held her breath as the lumbering black shadow followed the glowing lamp into the room. She pulled the covers over her head. She heard the shuffling feet come closer. And closer. The giant did not need the aid of that lamp. Her own heart betrayed her. Like a drumbeat leading soldiers to battle, the loud pounding in her chest was leading him straight to her bed. She felt the fingers grasp the protecting blanket, uncover her head, and gently fold it back around her shoulders. She couldn't look. She squeezed her eyelids closed lest they rebel and allow a peek at the giant. She waited for strangling fingers to tighten around her neck or for a cold, sharp blade to press against her throat, but there was only a soft rustling like a snake slithering through dry grass.

She opened one eye. Her visitor had crouched down to place the oil lamp on the floor. He was holding a cup. A cup she recognized from the dining hall. "Dance for me, Lily Bud," he whispered.

"Uncle Thahash! You scared me."

"Ha-ha, you senseless little bird." His sour breath puffed across her cheek. "I could not sleep for thinking about how lovely you looked today." The words were nice, but somehow his attention made her feel small and exposed. She pulled the covers close around her neck and held them there with tight little fists.

Uncle lifted the lamp and studied her face. "Perfect little Lily Bud. Come down to the platform in the dining hall and dance for me."

"Now? Is it morning?" With bleary eyes, she looked at the high window above her parents' bed. Not the faintest glimmer of light was shining there.

"It is almost morning." Her uncle's tone was hushed and very gentle. "In an hour or two, last night's guests will stir from their beds to break their fast and new patrons will come in the door, but we will have finished our fun by then."

Rahab sat bolt upright at the strange thought. "What kind of fun in the middle of the night, Uncle?"

"Just the kind you enjoyed yesterday, only better." He held out the cup and waved it under her nose, releasing wafts of the delightful fragrance of hot milk laced with wine and swirls of golden honey. "Drink this," he said. "Then we will go downstairs. I will teach you Asherah's dance."

The lamplight caught a strange glint in his eyes as she took the cup, but the warmth of the drink radiated through her body, comforting and delicious. She didn't stop until she had drained the last sweet drop. She felt braver now. Brave enough to dodge the hands that flipped her warm covers back. Brave enough to scold when he urged, "Up with you" and reached for her neatly folded clothes.

"I can get up and dress myself."

She pulled a woolen robe over her little tunic in a flash, but not before the night air chilled the flimsy undergarment. She shivered and her hands fumbled as she tried to fasten the sash. She had learned to tie it herself, but with Uncle towering so close, her hands could not remember how. He grabbed the ends impatiently, but when he finished tying it, he patted the knot with clumsy gentleness. "We need to hurry. Your parents will be back for the festival of the full moon, and I have planned a surprise for them when they return. But we must work hard to make our surprise perfect."

Her stomach flip-flopped. "What is the surprise, Uncle Thahash?"

He chuckled and playfully jabbed a stiff index finger in her tummy. "You will be the surprise, my little beauty." He poked and tickled her again until she wiggled and giggled. The next instant, his eyes narrowed and he clapped his hand over her mouth. "Shush, now. We must not awaken Shua. Promise me you will not tell your grandmother what we do tonight. I want it to be a surprise even for her." He held her shoulders firmly. Although he smiled as he talked, the fierce look in his eyes terrified her. "Do not spoil our secret. I will tell my sister when it is time for her to know."

Rahab hated the helpless feeling of being trapped in Uncle's grip. "I wish Mother was here so I could ask her about your surprise."

Uncle released her, and his voice became light and playful again. "Silly girl! We could not surprise your mother if you asked her, could we?" With an urgent signal for silence, he took her hand firmly in his, the light of his lamp illuminating the dark corridor and stairway as they padded barefoot down to the dining hall. When Uncle set the lamp on the floor beside the low platform, the light caught their shadows and flung them against the far wall.

Her own shadow was much bigger than she felt, but the gargantuan second shadow dominated everything else in the room. And it was reaching out both hands to seize the smaller one. Uncle laughed when she stiffened at his touch. "You're not afraid of our shadows are you?" He swooped her up and set her lightly on the platform, planting a wet kiss on her nose.

"Oooh, I could hardly do my work yesterday for stopping to enjoy my Lily Bud. Singing, twirling, looking so . . . so . . . perfect. Even when I finally finished my chores last night and crawled into my bed, I couldn't stop thinking of the sweet little flower blossoming right here in my inn. Did you know you could affect a man like that?" His voice was husky with emotion. "My little Rahab danced and sang through my dreams like a baby Asherah, a little goddess of delight. Have you seen her image in the temple?"

Rahab nodded silently. Lady Asherah was a symbol of everything beautiful.

Uncle Thahash chuckled. "You are the bud of Asherah's full-petaled glory. Just a few minutes ago, I awoke thinking about that, and I had a fantastic idea."

"Your surprise for Mother and Father?"

"And more. A surprise for everyone who comes to the inn on Asherah's Night. You will dazzle them with dance while your mother sings and plays her songs." He stroked Rahab's hair clumsily, letting his hand brush down the curve of her back before giving her a push toward the center of the platform. "Now dance." He dropped heavily to a floor cushion in front of her.

She stared at him. "I don't know what to do."

"I saw you yesterday. You are a natural."

"But I don't know what to do when you are watching me."

"Here. I'll close my eyes. Forget me. Hum one of your mother's tunes. Let it flow through your body like it did yesterday. Imagine little Rahab dancing for Asherah. Imagine a roomful of admirers delighted by your beauty."

Rahab suddenly felt like a grown-up lady. She began to sway as she hummed "The Song of Roses and Lilies."

"That's the way, Little Bud. Dance the silver beauty of Asherah's full moon." Uncle peeked at her through squinty, almost closed eyes.

Rahab closed her eyes and pictured the moon. She danced the loveliness of silver moonlight. She pictured the gilded statue of Asherah in the temple. She danced the beauty of Asherah's face, the bounty of her breasts, and the graceful curves of her folded arms and legs. She danced the glimmering gold and sparkling jewels. She danced beauty and love until everything else faded away.

"Oooh, little Lily Bud, you are a treasure for Uncle." The hoarse whisper was close to her.

Rahab's eyes blinked open. Uncle Thahash was on the platform, leaning over her with narrow, greedy eyes that sucked the joy from her soul. The liquid moonlight of her dance solidified into stone.

"Don't stop," Uncle grumbled, fumbling with a pouch hanging from his belt. "I have a reward for you. You please Uncle—" He seized her and pulled her close. "—and Uncle will please you."

Just as a little moan of fear escaped Rahab's lips, Uncle shoved a sweet, crumbly lump between them. She relaxed as the sweetness of palm sugar trickled down her throat.

"Uncle knows what little girls like," he whispered. He tousled her hair and then took her small hands in his, placing them on the leather pouch. "Feel the bulges in my sugar bag. Every one is for you. Please me and I will please you. Now dance for the sweet reward."

Rahab smiled. There was a lot of date sugar in that pouch. She hummed her mother's song again. She began dancing the sweetness of the sugar. Earning sugar would be easy. She would earn all Uncle's sugar, all the sugar in Jericho. The delightful thought oozed through her torso, diffusing to the tips of her fingers and toes in undulating waves of delight. Dancing for sugar was sheer joy.

When she glanced up at Uncle Thahash again, he grinned so broadly she could see all his dark teeth lined up like two rows of wet river stones in the middle of his scruffy gray beard. As with river stones in the Jordan, frothy foam had collected around and between his teeth. She closed her eyes again as he slurped back excess saliva. She did not have to look at him, but she would dance her heart out for the date sugar.

"Do you want more, Lily Bud? You must give me more. Dance the whipping of the wind on a stormy day when Baal sends the rain. Shimmy with your shoulders as you raise your arms, like this."

When she opened her eyes to look at Uncle again, he held a sugar lump in each hand and waved them in little pulses above his head. "You are a fruitful palm. You are the source of sweet dates and sugar. Dance like a palm in Baal's rainstorm."

She focused intently on earning both of those lumps. Stretching high like a graceful palm, she felt the sweetness within her. She felt the wind in her branches whipping her whole body faster and faster as she shimmied and swayed to the blasts of Baal's wind in Asherah's silver moonlight.

"You've got it, my sweet treasure," Uncle cried. He popped one of the lumps into her mouth.

It was sticky from his sweaty hands, but she didn't care. It melted wonderfully in her mouth. She crunched the crumbly bits and laughed at the intense burst of sweetness. Why had she been afraid of Uncle and his game?

"Sugar, sugar," she chirped, batting her eyelashes at Uncle's grinning face and opening her mouth wide.

After Uncle Thahash pressed the second lump onto her tongue, he toyed with the sugar pouch teasingly, flopping it lightly against her nose. "Maybe Uncle needs a little sugar for himself."

"I'm the one earning sugar here," Rahab retorted, grabbing for it with a laugh. "Your Lily Bud earned at least one more. I saw how my shimmies delighted you."

"More than you know." Uncle's hands trembled as he retrieved another treat and pushed it against her lips. She liked the way her dancing affected him almost as much as she liked the date sugar. She licked the sugar crumbs from his fingers before he pulled them away.

A froth of spittle dripped from the corners of his mouth. "So you like your Sugar Uncle, do you? Must I save your sweet sugar for Asherah's Night?"

"Save it? I want to earn all the sugar now."

"Sweet little bud . . . so innocent . . . so lovely." Uncle's hungry look and breathy tone suddenly frightened her. He planted a gigantic, gnarled foot between her tiny ones and pressed her body against himself in a confining hug. She stared down at the coarse black hair growing out of the tops of his toes and clenched her fists. *What would happen if I cried out for Grandmother?*

"Please, let me go, Uncle Thahash," she whimpered instead.

"You are right, Lily Bud. I must not squander a gift from the gods." He relaxed his hard embrace, rewarded her with another lump of sugar, and stepped down from the platform. "Dance. Dance again like a fruitful palm. Let your branches shimmer in the moonlight."

His tone had changed. His face and hulking frame were not so frightening from afar. Rahab closed her eyes, calming her trembling body as she resumed the dance of the palm.

"Sway in the silver light so all can enjoy your beauty," Uncle murmured. "That's it. Now feel Baal's response to you. Shimmer faster, shimmer at his touch. The god of the storm is enthralled with you."

Rahab relaxed. Uncle's gentle murmuring caressed her body from head to toe and awakened something new within her.

"The sensuous swaying of the palm arouses Lord Baal. Dance with him, sweet Lily Bud. Sense the change as his gentle breeze becomes a forceful wind. His thunder roars from the sky. Feel the wildness of his lightning flashing for you. Dance the pounding of Baal's driving rain. Tremble under the violence of the tempest. It is his response to your beauty. Yes . . . yes! Submit to his power. Bend like a palm. Let Baal embrace you with the fury of his storm. Arch back . . . back . . . like the graceful palm when the wind lays it down almost to the ground."

Rahab watched her shadow dancing on the wall in a frenzy of excitement like the beautiful temple dancers. No. She was not just a dancer. She *was* the thrashing palm, her fronds whipped by Baal's rainstorm, her trunk bent low in the wind. When Uncle moaned with pleasure again, she was not frightened. She was pleased. She flashed him a triumphant smile. No longer distracted by his greedy eyes, his ugly feet, his dark teeth, or the frothy saliva caught in his beard. She did not dance for him. She did not dance for sugar. Lady Asherah inhabited her body as she danced in the storm with Lord Baal himself, god and goddess joined together in dance. Her body throbbed with the thrill of it.

"Oh, oh, little Rahab," Uncle Thahash blubbered. "This is more than I hoped for." He covered his mouth, biting his hand as he fought to muffle his cries. "The gods possess you."

Suddenly, he was gone. The dining hall and the inn disappeared. Rahab soared high above earth and the storm. She was a star sparkling in the night sky, dancing on Baal's storm clouds with handfuls of other star jewels, dancing joyously around the silver moon. This was the way she would twinkle and dance for the Queen of Heaven on Asherah's Night. Let the patrons come. She would dazzle them with her beauty and delight them with her dance.

From far away she heard Uncle's voice, a faint awe-filled whisper. "You are a goddess." She smiled to herself at how surprised and pleased Mother and Father would be. Even Grandmother would be amazed that she could dance like this. Gods and humans alike would rejoice in the radiance of her little star, pulsing with the rapid shimmers of heaven's light, as Lord Baal plucked her from earth and placed her in the sky beside his Asherah.

"Stop! Leave the platform," Uncle suddenly ordered in a harsh whisper. He pulled her brusquely from the platform and shoved her toward the stairs. "Run back to your bed. I hear the servants."

Rahab was stunned. She had vaguely heard a rattle and rustle in the kitchen. But without even one more sugar lump, Uncle's scowl drove her from the room. Hurt and confused, she scrambled up the stairs to her parents' room and threw herself down on her little pallet. She was suddenly very tired. She pulled the coverlet close around her neck, hugging herself as she curled into a little ball and fell asleep.

A little later, Uncle was crouching at her bedside, shaking her gently. "You earned more sweets, my dear. Truly you did." He grinned as he shaped her hands together into a cup and shook the remaining contents of his leather pouch into them. "I thought I saw Asherah's beauty as you play-danced yesterday, but your dance this morning . . . You are a gift from the gods."

Rahab nibbled at the sugar he offered. She hardly knew what to think. One moment he was brusque, the next he flattered her with such pretty words. She closed her eyes and savored the sweetness melting on her tongue.

"Asherah's Night is almost here," he murmured. "When you dance on that platform, every man in the room will want to give you sugar." He poked her belly and winked at her. "Isn't this a fun game, Little Lily Bud?"

"How will the men know to bring sugar for me?"

"Don't be worrying about that. But only the lucky man who has enough gold for me will get to reward you."

"So my dance will earn gold for you *and* sugar for me?" she responded in wonder as she crunched another lump between her teeth.

Uncle Thahash nuzzled her with his prickly beard and grinned. He sat staring at her until the last of the sugar lumps dissolved on her tongue and she closed her eyes drowsily. "Sleep now, little Lily

Bud. We will practice our dance as often as we can until Asherah's Night."

Through the mist of a dancing dream, she heard him mumbling as he left the room. "Hee hee! You are a treasure for me, Lily Bud. The bees will swarm to the scent of nectar at my inn. They will return again and again to sip the sweetness, leaving their golden pollen for me. Oh, I will be rich!"

Rahab had never heard Uncle so happy. Singing and dancing was such joy for her. Who would have guessed it could bring such delight to a grumpy old man? As she slipped into a dream world filled with music and color and light, she smiled at the power of her dance. She would make every man in the room smile like that on Asherah's Night.

Rahab looked around with a start. She was still in her Grandmother's small room. She burned with shame at the memories. She felt again the searing pain of betrayal when the innocent joy of childhood ended with that celebration on Asherah's Night. "Mother is right," she whispered. "Dreams are not reality. The good people of Israel would not want me among them." As her lips uttered the words, her life-long hope of escaping Jericho shriveled and blew away like dust on the wind. Her soul was a desert, too dry for tears.

TRANSITIONS

Othniel

The first morning murmurings suddenly exploded into chattering expectancy. The long, low wail of a trumpet summons aroused the camp, but silenced the dawn bird chorus. Othniel gulped down the last few bites of manna porridge and smiled at the irony. *Those warblers have more sense than we do. They sing out their joy at first light, but know enough to stop and listen at the sound of the trump.*

"What are you snorting about now, Oth?" Seraiah asked with a grin.

Othniel blushed and shrugged. "Didn't know I was snorting."

"You always snort when you think of something clever. What now, older and wiser brother?"

"Just admiring the birds. They don't chatter about what they don't understand." He rose and began sloshing his bowl in the wash pot.

"What? You think I'm chattering?"

"Judge yourself. I was talking about the pointless palaver all over camp." He set his bowl out to dry and pulled a warm cloak around his shoulders. "Everyone seems bent on predicting what's going to happen. Better to wait and see." He ended the conversation abruptly by heading down the tent row toward the meadow southeast of camp.

"Wait for us, Son."

Othniel paused obediently while his mother and brother scrambled to catch up. Sooner than he wished, they walled him in on both sides with the Midianite girl, Huldah, trailing along behind with her younger sisters.

"Something extraordinary is afoot," Seraiah huffed breathlessly. "Don't you wonder what is going to happen?"

"Surely you want to know why we've been summoned to the meadow." It was not a question, but his mother expected a response.

Othniel continued tramping through the dewy grass into a stand of acacias. He was well aware of a churning expectancy in his belly, most likely similar to the emotions riling up all the others. Yes, it alerted him to the potential for great change. Something extraordinary was afoot, but there was no point in jabbering about it. He twisted his shoulders to dodge a drip of condensation falling from the acacias. Dodging the shower of questions from his family came just as naturally.

The elders made the instructions clear the previous evening: "When you hear the trumpets, assemble yourselves at the meadow of celebration rather than the tabernacle." But the purpose had not been disclosed—even to the elders. If Moses had wanted the people to know, they would have been told. Nonetheless, idle speculation buzzed through the air. Most expected Moses to announce they would be breaking camp and crossing the river. Othniel suspected there was more. A simple announcement like that could be made at the tabernacle entrance where Moses normally addressed the people, but his strong voice was often muffled or distorted at that location. This spot signaled something grand, an extended oration.

Othniel pictured the low promontory jutting out from the rocky bluff into the sea of meadow grasses. It had been nearly two turnings of the moon since Balaam used that stage to tell his story. A chill shivered down Othniel's spine at the memory of that speech. The evil prophet's slightest whispers tickled their ears. His bellowing declarations thrummed through their bodies. He held the entire nation captive to his every thought, the natural acoustics providing ideal support for the seer's bewitching elocution. It was high time to endow the place with better memories.

As soon as Othniel and his family emerged from the acacia grove and could see the rocky outcropping, he knew the transformation had already begun. The entire bluff was gloriously dominated by the figure of Moses, standing high above the crowds. The outline of his white hair, backlit by the first beams of morning sun, glowed in stark contrast to his dark, robed form. No longer a humble shepherd, on this notable morning Moses appeared with the majesty of a being from heavenly realms. Any lingering images of the posturing false prophet would be outshadowed forever.

The sight of Moses framed in fire instantly throttled the conversation between his mother and brother. It silenced the chatter of the Midianite children trailing behind. Othniel noted with satisfaction the hush spreading over all the crowds that were pouring into the open meadow. This would be one event where Moses would have no difficulty quieting the tribes. The setting, the crowds, the whole world, it seemed, grew dim in contrast to Moses and his halo of glory.

In contrast to his appearance of kingly authority, Moses' first words fell gently over the people like a kindly father instructing his family.[6]

This journey did not begin with you, my dear children. How often have you listened to our tale of deliverance as you gathered around clan fires in the evening? You are well prepared to tell your own children, and your children's children, the story. And tell it, you must, for we must never forget how Yahweh, Most High God, shattered the chains that held our people in bondage. What people has ever had such a God? A God who led them out of Egypt with a fearsome display of power. A God who brought them to his holy mountain and there in the fires of Sinai forged a new nation. Your parents were but newly-released slaves whose freedom would have destroyed them. But our God spoke to his people amidst fire and smoke from the blazing mountaintop. He invited them into an intimate covenant relationship. He gave them Torah to teach them how to live.

For twelve months, your parents lingered around that mountain—and while they built the tabernacle and its furnishings as a home for their God, his Torah began rebuilding them. It was a year of construction and reconstruction. A structure for the Lord, restructure for our people. At last, when the tabernacle was complete, the cloud of the Lord's presence entered it in a great display of glory. It was as if the fire and smoke of Sinai had moved into his portable sanctuary in readiness to travel.

We began our second year of freedom by celebrating Passover, remembering the night of our escape from Egyptian slavery. At that time Yahweh God spoke to our people again. "You have dwelled long enough around this mountain. Break camp now. Be on your way. Advance into the land of the Amorites. Enter the hill country. Enter every valley. Look! I have already given the land to you. It is yours. From the dry hill country of southern Canaan to the mountains of Lebanon in the north. From the coast of the Great Sea in the west to the river in the east. It is your inheritance. Long ago, I promised the Land of Canaan to your fathers—to Abraham, Isaac, and Jacob—and to all their descendants. Now go in and take possession of it."

As our people prepared to resume the journey, I saw they had become as numerous as the stars. We agreed to choose wise and experienced men to serve as military commanders and to help me judge between disputes. We appointed captains of thousands, captains of hundreds, captains of fifties and tens. Each warrior-judge added to a precise chain of command under their twelve tribal princes. Then, organized and ready, we set out.

For eleven days, the Lord led us as a shepherd leads his flock. Sheltered from the blistering sun, protected from scorpions, serpents, and wild beasts, he carried us through a terrifying desert to the very border of the Promised Land. But there his people hesitated. They said, "Let us send spies in ahead of us to see what we will face" Then, in spite of all the wonders the Lord had performed on their behalf, they rebelled. They listened to the report of giants that lived in the land, of cities with walls reaching up to the sky—and they refused to trust the Lord. The Shepherd's rebellious sheep would not go in.

The old stories always stirred Othniel. But this was more. As Moses told of Israel's failure to enter Canaan and the Wanderings of the next forty years, his voice resounded over the crowds so no one could miss a single detail, every word ringing against the rocks with the clarion clear authority of a war trumpet. Othniel knew the stories as he knew the backs of his own hands, but he heard them today as if for the first time. The fire of one miracle story after another flamed up in his heart—only to be doused again and again by buckets of shame. God's faithful provision; Israel's faithlessness in return. Othniel had never been so stirred. *When I come to the end of my days,* he prayed, *let me not be ashamed.*

Moses' next words jarred against Othniel's lofty ideals. This was concrete reality. No longer history. Moses was speaking of Israel's future, his future.

This is what will become of the fruitful Valley of Acacias. This is what will become of the rugged highlands of Bashan. The territories formerly held by Sihon and Og will belong to the tribes of Reuben, Gad, and half of the tribe of Manasseh. It will be their inheritance. In return, their warriors will cross the river with us. They will fight with the rest of the tribes until all have received their inheritance and found rest.

The children of Gilead, descendant of Makir of Manasseh, were instrumental in taking Sihon's valley. Their warriors fearlessly attacked the barred gates of high-walled cities and prevailed. Therefore, from this time forth, this broad and fertile valley will bear the name Gilead. The half-tribe of Manasseh will inherit the northern end of the valley along with the highlands of Bashan. The larger part of Gilead from its southern border with Moab to the territory of Manasseh will be divided between the tribes of Reuben and Gad. It will be their inheritance. Gilead shall belong to these three and their descendants forever.

"Yes."

"It is good!"

"The plan is fair. Let their warriors cross over with us as you have said."

Othniel snorted at the thought of the rumors that had rumbled through camp over the past few days. Today there was not a single word of dissent. Moses' wise leadership was affirmed once more.

The kingdoms of Canaan will not willingly return our inheritance to us. There will be war. But remember how God gave us all this land east of the river—from the Arnon Gorge northward to snow-capped Mount Herman. It was not your prowess in battle, my dear children, but the hand of the Lord that utterly destroyed the evil civilizations of these Amorites.

The warriors of Reuben, Gad and Manasseh are strong and numerous. They have already begun the rebuilding of the cities as a place for their wives and children. They will leave their loved ones east of the river, along with their flocks and herds, and lead the remaining tribes across the Jordan, trusting that God himself will watch over their families and keep them safe until they return.

Moses' voice took on a sterner tone.

Now open your ears. This is what Yahweh God says:

"Your territory ends with the Jabbok River which is the border with Ammon. You must occupy only the land that the Lord gives you. Do not harass the Ammonites nor provoke them to war, for I will NOT give you any of their land. The Land of Ammon belongs to the descendants of Lot, the nephew of Abraham. It is their inheritance. They are your cousins of the bloodline of Shem, the firstborn of Noah.

"Long ago, the fathers of giants were born to the line of Canaan, the son of Ham, the son of Noah. These giants—Emi, Hori, Zamzummi, and Anak—drove out the children of Shem and took their inheritance as their own. But that was not my doing," says the Lord. "The Zamzummites thought they dwelled secure in the land beyond the Jabbok, but I—even I, the Lord your God—removed them with a flick of my finger. I gave the land of the Zamzummites to Ammon, to be the inheritance of the children of Lot. In the same way, I drove the Emites out of Ar to make a place for the Moabites, for they too were the children of Lot. I did the same for Isaac's son, Esau, who fathered another nation in the line of Shem. I destroyed the Horites for Esau and gave him the region of Mount Seir as the inheritance of the Edomites.

Do not fear the vile and violent descendants of Canaan. Remember how I destroyed those giants—the Zamzummites, the Emites and the Horites. They were as strong and numerous and as tall as the Anakites that dwell in the land of Canaan today. They did as they pleased, laughing at any army that might oppose them, unafraid of any other nation because of their great size and strength. But when I sent storm-winds of judgment against such arrogance, they toppled like trees grown too tall for their roots. I cut them down and returned their territory to the children of Shem—just as I will utterly destroy the Anakites and the seven nations of Canaan for you.

"Know and understand that by my authority and for my purposes, nations arise and flourish . . . or decline and die," says the Lord your God. "For this reason, you must not covet the lands of your cousins: the Moabites, the Ammonites, and the Edomites. The land of Canaan is your inheritance."

The commanding tone Moses used to convey the stern warnings of Yahweh softened again to family intimacy with the next sentence. *"Open your eyes, my children, and see that you have nothing to fear."* The entire congregation seemed to exhale a collective sigh and Othniel felt the tension in his body relax.

You yourselves witnessed the destruction of the kings in this valley when they lifted their fists against the Lord. Can you doubt that he will do the same to all the kingdoms across the river who defy him? I say it again, you have nothing to fear. Do not rebel against the Lord and against Joshua when your faith is tested. I will not cross the river, but Joshua, son of Nun will. He will see that you inherit the land now held in the evil grasp of the children of Canaan. This is the Lord's command and promise to his servant Joshua. "Do not be afraid of them. I, the Lord your God, will fight for you—"

The Lord would fight for . . . Othniel's eyes turned naturally to the one standing almost hidden behind the great leader. *Joshua? Moses' camp aide? The assistant?* A chill shivered deep into Othniel's bones. Such a change now on the borders of Canaan? Joshua had served well as commander of the army—twice in fact—but always under the ultimate command of Moses. A dark cloud of grumbling rolled over the people. Who knew what they would face across the river? Giants. Walled cities. What else? Their parent's generation had panicked when they learned what the inhabitants of Canaan were like. They could not—or would not—bring themselves to trust

Yahweh's promise. Othniel keenly felt the emotions that fueled this wave of muttering, but he hunkered down, watching and listening from behind a shield of silence.

When the initial shock had been absorbed, Moses lifted his voice over the rumbling dissent.

Have you forgotten? Must I remind you again? I will not cross over into Canaan. I must bear the consequences of my disobedience. You know how I struck the rock when the Lord commanded me to speak to it. That angry outburst cost me dearly. I will never set foot in the Land of Promise. And, not I alone, but Aaron, as well. Emotion tightened his voice. *I have already laid my beloved brother to rest.*

I have been reminding you of this for two years and yet you have not heard. I myself hoped to change the Lord's mind when we reached this valley. I begged him to let me cross over with you into Canaan, but he did not change his mind. "That is enough," he said. "We will not speak of this anymore. But you will come with me to the top of Mount Pisgah. Look to the south and to the west, to the north and the east. You will not cross the Jordan, but you will see the whole land with your own eyes. Now commission Joshua. Encourage and strengthen him. He will lead my people across the river. By the sword of the Lord and of Joshua, my people will inherit all the land you see."

Finality. Chest-crushing finality. The announcement registered on Othniel like a heavy weight. Moses had poured out his life for them. Where was justice? Why should *their* faithlessness punish the one true man of faith? At the thought of losing Moses, women began to sob, men groaned in despair and grief, and the little children looked around in blank bewilderment, trying to comprehend what had just happened.

My dear, dear children, this is the beginning for you, not the end. Learn from my failure. Disobedience blocks the blessings of God, but in his mercy, he always responds with new plans. Good plans rising from the rubble of our unfaithfulness. O my children, if you learn from my mistake the importance of following God's commands exactly as he has expressed them, then my punishment will not be in vain.

Take hold of the blessings. Accept the changes with grateful hearts. The days of my leadership have ended, but the Lord guides you still.

Do not grieve. Rejoice! As my authority passes on to Joshua, you enter a new and exciting era for Israel. I have collected all the laws, decrees, and judgments of the Lord into a single scroll, the Book of the Covenant. Tomorrow, we will review the entire law in a solemn celebration. It is a gift that I will bequeath to the Levites before I leave you. It will be their responsibility to teach these words to you and to your children for generations to come. My dear children, never forget. Obedience is our part of the covenant with our holy God.

By this time, the sun had climbed high above the eastern hills. The striking halo surrounding Moses had dimmed and vanished with the westward movement of the sun, but the heavenly fire returned in the form of words. The people stood transfixed as Moses poured out all the passion of his ardent love for Yahweh and all his fatherly love for the chosen people in one final rush of shining speech.

The Lord brought you out of the smelting furnace of Egypt to be a treasure of pure gold on the earth. That is what you now are, O Israel. If you love the God of your fathers for what he has done for you, obey his law. Follow his commands so that you may live. So that you can go in and take possession of the land that he is giving you.

On the day the Lord spoke to you at Sinai, blazing fireballs shot from the mountain. Flames showered over you and thunders roared, but you saw no form of any kind. Therefore, do not become corrupt. Do not follow after the ways of the people of this land. You cannot reproduce the glory of Yahweh by making images of him. The creatures he called forth from the earth are far beneath their Creator. When you look up to the sky and see the sun, the moon, and the stars—the entire heavenly array—do not bow down to them. Do not worship them as do all the other nations under heaven. Watch yourselves carefully. You saw with your own eyes what happened here in the Valley of Acacias. Those who joined with that demon, the Baal of Peor, were destroyed, but all of you who held fast to the Lord your God remain alive today.

I will not cross the Jordan, but you will. You will cross over and take possession of this good land. Do not forget the covenant that the Lord your God has made with you. Do not ever make for yourselves an idol in the form of anything—for the Lord your God is a consuming fire. He is a jealous God, jealous to save you. Those idols are no gods. They are demons. Acknowledge and take to heart this day that Yahweh alone is God in heaven above and on the earth below. There is NO OTHER!

Moses finished with a deep sigh and bowed his head.

The crowds who had arrived garrulous and elated, stood now in a stunned stupor. Here and there, various individuals stood isolated and silently weeping. Othniel experienced the same grief, that sense of personal responsibility for provoking Moses' sin and causing his punishment. How could he return to the tent to resume the mundane activities of camp? He wandered aimlessly, not certain where to go. He avoided the clusters of lost-looking people who gathered in knots, parsing each word and phrase in the speech to be certain they had heard correctly. He avoided the groups grousing about the capability of Joshua to lead them. In the middle of all the confusion, one word rang in Othniel's head. *Obedience.* Obedience no matter the circumstances.

Story scenes flashed through his mind in rapid succession. Vivid images. The hubbub of breaking camp not much more than a year ago. The divisions forming blocks of perfect order under their banners. The sense of adventure as they left the stream behind again and headed down the road. But they had never really left it behind before. They had always discovered that same stream flowing near every new campsite. Every move in Othniel's entire life. This time, however, they followed the cloud into the barren desert of Zin. The billows of dust settled as they set up their tents, but there was no stream. He snorted a half-laugh. Today we call that place *Kadesh*—holy—a word evoking oneness with God, wholeness, life. The name now evoked the exact opposite.

There was little complaint, however, the day they set up camp. Water bags were full, and they were practically at the gates of the Land of Milk and Honey. Everyone sensed they were nearing the end of the forty-year road. Then Miriam died. For thirty days, the people honored her memory. But as they counted the days of mourning, the tight water bags grew soft. Thirsty children cried as parents rationed the dwindling supply. The flocks and herds bleated and bellowed their need—then fell quiet, conserving energy as they lay dying. The people wrung the last drops of water from flat goatskins, but still they lingered in that waterless land. Could they survive the thirty days of mourning?

They did. But when the thirty days ended, the cloud did not budge from its place over the tabernacle. A noxious mist of apprehension drifted over the camp, but Moses merely watched the cloud. When their leader showed no inclination to lead them to a better place, the storm broke. The first indistinct rumblings arose from the Egyptians and the mixed multitude on the margins of camp, but it was not long before clouds of fear and anger roiled and raged through all the tribes. A covenant with a God who would let his people die of thirst was worse than worthless. Clan chiefs and princes here and there attempted to rally the people in rebellion. A dozen factions arose around the various leaders. Moses and Aaron fled to the tabernacle again and again to plead with God.

Then, when Yahweh answered at last, Moses and Aaron called the people to gather before a rock. Othniel recalled the shock of recognition when he saw that colossal monolith. It was identical to the rock that had been present at every campsite of his entire life. The one forever gushing with streams of water—exactly as it had for four decades according to the elders. This rock in this arid spot was identical to the rock Moses had struck with his rod just after leaving Egypt. Identical, except that scorpions crawled on its parched surface and all the ground around it was dust.

Memory scenes continued flashing through Othniel's mind, one after another in rapid succession. He saw the restless, rebellious crowds assembled around the dry rock. He saw Aaron's face, gentle and kind. "Why have you grumbled to each other all these days? Why did you not ask the Lord your God for water?"

Aaron stepped up onto a shelf protruding from the rock. "Look. Moses will speak to this rock and streams of living water will pour out for you." He raised his hands and began to pray. "O God of our Fathers who led us out of Egypt, tenderly you have cared for—"

Angry shouts cut him off. "Enough of your holy blathering. We need water not words!"

"Our children are dying and all you can do is pray?"

"Can you produce water or not?"

One burly man shoved the elderly priest from his foothold. "Follow me—"

Moses cut him off as he seized Aaron's arm, stabilizing his brother to prevent a fall. "How dare you violate the Lord's anointed. Did you not learn the lesson of Koran, Dathan, and Abihu?" His glare drove the insurgent from his perch. "Would you die as they did in another gulping swallow of the earth? Would you bring another plague on Israel, another blaze of fire against the brothers who would follow you in such insurrection?"

Aaron had recovered from the scuffle and joined in the scathing wrath. "Do you not remember God's blessing on *my* rod? Must I show you again the leaves and blossoms and almonds bursting from wood previously dead? You dare question whether we can bring water from this rock for you? Let me get that very rod—stored as a remembrance in the holy of holies."

With eyes blazing, Moses leaped to the same rock shelf where his brother had stood moments before and bellowed at the faithless crowds. "Why are you so slow to believe? So quick to rebel?"

"Rebelling is the only sane thing to do. You led us out of Egypt to this terrible place to kill us all."

"Get us water now or get out of our way."

"Here! Here! Who will follow me back to the last oasis?"

"Forget that oasis. Let's be done with this incessant wandering. Follow me on into Canaan!"

"Canaan now! Water now! Canaan now!"

Rather than subduing the storm, Moses' fire had ignited a frightening, full on revolt. The memory, even today, quickened the beating in Othniel's chest. Even in the fog of his thirst that day, he feared Moses would not be able to stop the mutiny, that the nation of Israel would splinter before his very eyes. The next scenes slowed in Othniel's mind—deliberate, painful, and raw.

"Listen, you rebels," Moses thundered.

He lifted his rod high.

"Must we bring you water out of this rock?"

Moses cracked the rod fiercely against solid granite and the follow-through lifted it high in the other direction.

"Must I? Must Aaron?" Still raging with anger, he swung it fiercely at the rock from the other direction, and with the resounding crack of the second blow, water gushed forth.

The rebellion dissipated immediately as the people and their livestock sloshed into the stream and drank. Gleefully ignorant, people scooped up handfuls of water, flinging them into the air until all heads were wet with its rain. Water and laughter showered this miracle that saved the multitude. It was only later that Moses declared the cost—neither he nor Aaron would cross the Jordan because they had disobeyed the express command of the Lord.

"Ho there, Othniel."

The power of the memory evaporated as Eliab, Salmon, and Igal materialized out of the roiling crowds. "What do you think? Is Joshua up to the challenge?"

Othniel's muscles were coiled tight. His palms were damp and he could still feel the tingling, the hair up and down his arms standing on end as if he had just encountered a ferocious beast. He met his friends' eyes with quiet determination. "No matter what, I will obey. So help me God."

Apparently, his answer was so strange that none of the three attempted to engage him further. He snorted and began working his way through idle speculation and chatter. Above all else, he needed to escape. Just then, on the edge of the tangled crowd, he spotted his uncle Caleb making his way toward the river with Acsah at his side. This was a time to sit at the feet of wisdom rather than speculate with those who knew as little as he did. He followed them.

Acsah

Acsah leaned on her father's arm as he led them away from the assembly. His stare, straight ahead but not at anything lying before them, told her he was revisiting some event long past. She curled her arm tighter around his. Best not to interrupt. Her own questions and thoughts jumbled so wildly, one on top of another, that she couldn't voice a proper thought. Her father always brought back a nugget of wisdom or two from those memory trips and she treasured her collection of wisdom nuggets like a trove of gold. It would be worth the wait.

The crowds began to thin as they reached the western boundary of the meadow. But Caleb walked on into a thicket of acacias and on through its shaded depths until they could see the fresh green plain and hazy purple hills of Canaan alive in the sunlight on the far side of the river. He caught her eyes and grinned. "Look at what God has promised his people."

As he settled himself comfortably on the grass beneath a canopy of leaves, he mused, "Oh, the dark side of transitions."

Acsah leaned against the rough trunk of an acacia waiting expectantly for him to continue. *The dark side of transitions.* There certainly was a dark side to the transitions she had experienced recently. Her relationship with childhood friends was changing rapidly in mostly unpleasant ways. Abihail, the dearest friend of her childhood, was not only busy in her new role as Eliab's wife, but she had demonstrated a disturbing blindness to evil. Then Jonathan. She certainly had not seen that coming. She was as ready to marry and start a family as she was ready to cross over the Jordan and strike out for the unknown on her own. But yesterday brought the most disturbing change of all. Her normally wise father had shattered the sanctity of their tent with idol-worshiping Midianites. How would she ever adjust to seeing the daughters of seductive deceit lurking around her home day after day?

Her father's voice brought her back to the wisdom moment. "All this, yet we want to seize the new without relinquishing our hold on any of the old that brought us comfort on our journey. When we left Egypt, everyone was thrilled to leave the heavy toil and the whips of the taskmasters behind, but we also left behind the security of a constant water source. Markets, and gardens to eat from. Instead of taking on the challenge with God, we panicked. Now we are thrilled to leave the wilderness behind, but we want to hang on to the hand of our wilderness guide instead of trusting God."

Caleb closed his eyes and folded his hands as if he would take a nap. After a moment he added, "Joshua is a good man. Yahweh sees fit to take away our humble lawgiver and replace him with a humble warrior—a new kind of leader."

Acsah watched his lips curl into a smile at a long-forgotten memory. "Moses is a mountain of strength to the people now, but when we left Egypt, he didn't seem like much. A fugitive prince, a long-time desert shepherd, he came stammering back to civilization from the wilds of Midian, no longer fluent in the Egyptian language and unsure of himself before the people. What the people wanted then was a strong warrior. More what Joshua will become I suspect. Just wait. He will prove himself in time. He is the Lord's choice."

"Father, there is one unpleasant transition I believe we can avoid. Abihail has never been strong, and she is sure to have a tent full of young ones in the next few years. The Midianite girls—"

"There is a dark side to every transition," Caleb continued as if he had not heard Acsah's words or guessed her meaning, although she was quite sure he had. He laughed aloud. "Just wait until you hear the howls when the manna stops."

"The manna?" All thoughts of the slave girls vanished at the very idea. *Daily manna was as certain as the sunrise. Could it be that manna-fall would not be part of life in the land of milk and honey?*

Caleb didn't say any more. His chest rose and fell in a strong, steady rhythm. "Abba, are you asleep? I was beginning to tell you the plan I have for—"

The grass rustled softly behind her, and she glanced over her shoulder. *Othniel? Now? Even this precious time of talking with Abba ends in a dark side as I transition out of here.*

"Hello there, Cousin." Acsah smiled a greeting she did not feel. "You have come just in time to keep my father company while he rests. I was just considering how to leave him."

Caleb sat up and looked at her quizzically, "I wasn't asleep. I was enjoying our conversation."

"There are preparations to make for tomorrow," she said briskly, bending to kiss his forehead. "I will see you back at the tent later."

Caleb smiled broadly at his nephew. "Othniel, did you know that I bought my little Midianite girls back from Achor? Oh, of course, you know. They all went with your mother to hear Moses this morning." He flicked his eyes toward Acsah. "My daughter is not happy about having them."

Othniel's serious expression contrasted sharply with Caleb's jovial tone. "You were their savior," he responded thoughtfully. "They are devoted to you. I did not expect you to let them go."

Acsah turned back. "How was that, Abba? What does Othniel mean by *savior*?"

"Now she asks about the little ones." Caleb leaned against a tree trunk and closed his eyes again. For a moment she couldn't tell whether he was sleeping or remembering, but when he spoke again it was with his deep storytelling voice. "Phinehas' army had reached the last of the Midianite towns. We had pretty much rounded up all the women and children when I noticed, set apart from the houses, a large leather tent, dyed deep red and pitched on a stone foundation. More than a foundation really. The walls were nearly waist-high from the outside. Passing through the portal, I followed stone steps down into a dimly lit sanctuary, dug halfway into the earth."

Acsah glanced at Othniel, but his attention was fixed on her father. He knew the story, but obviously was eager to hear it again. She could not leave until she heard the end of this tale.

"I had stumbled upon a Midianite holy place where snakes were worshipped. There was an assortment of copper images of snakes displayed in niches around the stone walls. Behind a carved stone altar the hanging of purple and red striped linen had been embroidered with golden serpents gleaming in the light of six oil votives. The lights, three on each side of the altar, were held aloft on a set of copper lamp stands, fashioned with snakes twining up toward the branches as if slithering up a tree. I stepped closer wanting to investigate the inner sanctum, but then I spied three live adders coiled beside that altar. Fortunately for me, the reptiles were sluggish in the chill of this dark place.

"I seized one of the copper serpents from the wall and crushed the head of the closest adder. As I did, I was certain I heard a quick intake of breath from beyond the curtain. I suspected an enemy was hiding deeper within this tabernacle, but I felt it prudent to deal with the reptiles first. I did not hear another whisper of noise from the inner sanctum as I dispatched the last two serpents but my instincts told me that the greater danger lurked there.

"I drew my sword and cautiously pulled back the heavy curtain—and my heart dropped. There in the dim, reddish light behind the veil, a huge serpent loomed before me, reptilian hood flared. His head was raised so high that I looked directly into a pair of red eyes glittering with evil. Even as my heart pounded in my chest, I realized that this was only a cunningly-crafted image, a great copper serpent with a painted head and jeweled eyes. And there, cowering behind it, were three terrified little girls."

Othniel broke in. "I watched Caleb herd them to the gathering place for the captives. A father could not have been more tender."

Caleb snorted. "Well, the rest of you had to deal with snarling, snapping fox kits. These girls totally trusted me."

Acsah narrowed her eyes. "Abba. Do you think you are going to convince me that we need to keep these girls?

Caleb looked at her through slits between his eyelashes. "I have already decided," he said. "Those sisters lost their mother when they were very young, and their father was one of the soldiers slain the first night. The girls are orphans. Pretty resourceful little orphans at that. When they heard the shouts announcing our coming, Huldah decided that a quick death in the serpent temple—for herself and her younger sisters—would be superior to being captured or killed by a cruel enemy. Listen and learn from their story.

"When Huldah led her sisters into the tent, the priestess was gone. Huldah was about to stir the slumbering reptiles by the altar with her foot when she heard a voice clearly say to her. 'Wait behind the veil. You will find the safety and peace you long for.' She says all three of them felt what they described as a wild heartbeat of joy at that same moment even though Huldah was the only one who heard the words.

"Hodesh looked up at that very moment and said, 'We will be safe, won't we?' and little Hogluh stopped crying. Huldah told her sisters about the voice telling her to wait in the inner sanctum. The three girls clasped hands and bravely pushed through the curtain to wait as told. Their fear was gone—at least until I began smashing snakes and then cried out at my first view of the giant copper serpent.

"That startled them, but when they caught sight of me holding back the curtain, an Israelite warrior with sword in hand, the sisters ran toward me—not away. The littlest one threw her arms around my knees just as my own grandchildren do. The oldest one, Huldah, looked at me in wide-eyed sweetness and said, 'We know you have come to lead us to safety. A voice told us to wait here.'

"Now, what *voice* do you think she heard?"

Acsah exhaled a deep sigh of resignation. "How can I argue with that? So what did you do with your girls this morning?"

"I put them in the care of your aunt Sarah so you would not be distracted during Moses' speech. She will keep all three until you adjust to the dark side of this transition."

Othniel had been watching and listening silently. The hint of a smile curled the corners of his mouth when he finally spoke. "Mother is absolutely thrilled. She knows she needs the help." His voice was abnormally enthusiastic.

Acsah rolled her eyes. "I thought Aunt Sarah was doing well enough without help."

"You do not expect Othniel and Seraiah to be tied up with spinning and weaving and cooking when they should be preparing to defend the people of God, do you?"

"Seraiah is not old enough for war."

"He will be before long, and Sarah is happy to have the girl as a companion as well as helper."

"Huldah is very helpful already," Othniel added, "fetching water and wood for the fire. And she keeps a spindle busy constantly."

"So you gave away the one who actually knows how to work?" Acsah snapped at her father. This conversation was becoming increasingly irritating.

"But you said you could manage everything by yourself." Caleb's lips spread into a ridiculously wide smile. "By the time you are ready for help, they will be old enough to learn."

"They are yours, Abba," she said firmly. "You can teach them to mend wagons and harnesses." She turned and left the acacia grove, heading for the family tent. Her whole world was reeling and suddenly even the tent did not feel like home.

Moses

"I will not cross the Jordan, but you will."

While Moses was still speaking those words, Jonathan wheeled and left the assembly. Moses finished without allowing a ripple of personal pain to disturb the flow of his oration, but as the speech surged to its conclusion, he realized he was clutching at his chest to stave off the pain.

Yahweh is the only God in heaven above. He is the only God on the earth beneath. There is NO OTHER!"[7]

There was nothing more he could say. He remained on the stone podium watching his grandson threading through knots of people. The attention of the masses had turned to family and friends, and little groups began comparing reactions, their individual conversations sending a sound wave washing across the sea of people. He hoped they understood.

Moses' mind scanned back through his speech, trying to understand Jonathan's reaction. The entire congregation had been stunned by the announcement of Joshua as his successor. His grandson, no different than all the rest. It was when he mentioned his approaching death that Jonathan bolted . . . But there was something more. Before he even began to speak that morning, the boy's behavior struck him as odd. Not peculiar enough to be noticed by most in the crowd. He smiled and greeted friends as usual. But his circling held him back. Jonathan was always one to find the front of a crowd. Today, when Moses so desperately wanted to share his final thoughts, Jonathan seemed to shrink from the possibility of making eye contact with him.

The sting pierced him deeply, personally. More than either of his sons or his other grandchildren, this bright one reminded him of his beloved Zipporah. Not only did he inherit her beauty of face, but also her sense of fun. Her zest for life. And, like her, he was subject to bouts of despair. Like hers, his faith could soar above the clouds one moment, then crash to the depths the next. Sometimes in a single day. A single hour.

Although he was drained dry of spoken words, concern for his grandson and his people stirred the depths of his soul.

O Yahweh God, you saw how he left . . . left before I finished. How many more would have turned from my ramblings had they dared be so rude? There is so much I want to say, but I am an old man. I have been sequestered in the desert, far from civilization, for the past eighty years. How can I express the mind of God?

I don't have to remind you of that day at the burning bush. I tried to tell you to find a more fluent spokesman, but you would not hear it. This was my best, Lord—but I fear my best is not enough.

. . .

Sinai? Moses choked on a laugh at the thought God communicated to him. *No, I didn't hope to reproduce Sinai! I haven't forgotten the terror of the people at the sound of your voice.*

. . .

Well . . . yes . . . my heart does yearn for these children to remember my words here today, this renewal of their covenant, as we old ones remember Sinai. Perhaps, in a way, I did hope to reproduce that day at Mount Sinai for them. I hadn't thought of it that way. But is that not your desire as well?

. . .

Write down the words? Hmmm. Write. Yes . . . Another scroll.
Combine these orations with the detailed Book of the Law I just
compiled. Yes.

O Voice that set Mount Sinai afire,
    Unless the Fire of Yahweh speaks to the people—
unless it speaks to my dear Jonathan—
    all my mutterings are worthless noise.
Let Divinity set my human words ablaze.
    Infuse my imperfect speech with your perfection.
Make my final scroll your Sinai for all time.

It took but one brief conversation with the Almighty to transform despair to determination. Yahweh had just given him an assignment, the final challenge of his life. That task now merged the two deep passions of his heart. *Write the final scroll. Find the boy.*

Jonathan was out of sight now. Vanished into a thick stand of acacias. Most likely heading toward camp Levi. Moses left his rocky platform, picked his way down the trail, and edged into the sloshing billows of questions and speculations stirring the crowds. As he cut through the turbulence, intent on locating Jonathan, only a rare individual here and there attempted to stop him or request clarification. He marveled at how easily he could wave them off. People would rather discuss what he meant than simply ask him to clarify. He was glad to be unhindered in his quest, but it struck him as odd.

Moses stopped at his own tent only long enough to gather his writing materials and then headed toward the tent of his son Gershom. There he found the boy exactly as he hoped he might. Jonathan was resting near the doorway, face turned up toward the sun, eyes shut.

Such a fine face. The rounded lines of childhood were hardening into the chiseled planes of a man, leaving him looking a little less like his grandmother each day . . . and yet . . . an inrush of love and aching surged over Moses at what remained of her still. He approached silently, but as soon as his shadow fell across the boy's face, Jonathan tensed and his eyes flew open.

"I didn't mean to startle you, my son," he said lightly. "I was hoping to find you here."

Jonathan sat up, regarding him with an unusually dispassionate face.

"How would you like to be of service to your old grandfather?"

"Of course." An almost imperceptible negative shake of the head accompanied Jonathan's answer. "What can I do for you?"

Moses kneaded the fingers of his massive right hand with his left. "My hands begin to feel their age. I believe God has asked me to write down the words I spoke to the people today—and the words I will speak tomorrow. But I have been writing for so many days. Would you give my old hands a rest and be my scribe?"

"Yes. Yes, of course . . ." Jonathan's answer trailed off.

Moses turned and headed for the mountain without saying more. The boy was not nearly as willing as his ready words. Nonetheless, he had agreed to come. He heard one mumbling phrase behind him. "At least it will get me out of camp." After that, the only sound that followed him throughout the climb was the crunching of his grandson's lagging feet.

Moses stopped at the top of the trail to enjoy the cool breeze sweeping over the crest of the ridge. The sight of the tents of Israel, nestled among the dark acacia groves of a bright, emerald plain, was glorious. More glorious still, the serpentine line of the Jordan River, slipping silver through the lush basin it had carved for itself down the center of the Jordan Valley. The river itself was not wide, but it meandered where it chose through a broader depression, the *zor*. In twists and turns, abandoning an old channel here, cutting a new one there, the river created a lush home for itself in this valley-within-in-a-valley, bringing more rich soil deposits and abundant moisture to the already overgrown thicket. West of the *zor*, another plain mirrored Gilead. And beyond that plain, purple hills rose steeply upward and the blue outline of yet higher, more distant hills stretched westward as far as the eye could see. That was Canaan. The inheritance promised to Abraham, Isaac, and Jacob; the dream of every Israelite for the past forty years—only a river away.

Moses watched Jonathan brighten visibly as he drew in a long draft of the fresh, cool air. His own anxieties and cares melted away each time he climbed this mountain. His grandson was obviously finding the same relief from whatever troubled him.

"No wonder you come up here so often, Grandfather." Jonathan's irrepressible ebullience had returned. "My heart feels lighter than it has in days."

"The Heights of Inspiration, I call them." Moses smiled to himself. *So far, so good.* He made his way to his usual rocky seat.

"This is my final scroll—the fifth and perhaps the most important. It will begin with today's farewell address and include all I tell the people over the next few days, including the reading of all the laws God has given us. The people of Israel must understand the terms of our covenant and never forget. God is faithful. If His chosen people are faithful to their part, they will be the most blessed people who have ever dwelt on this earth."

As soon as Jonathan had chosen a flat-topped rock nearby and seated himself, Moses handed the bag of writing materials to him. He took a long, slow breath. *Lord, I am only your instrument, the pen in your hand. Take it from here.*

Then, infused with a surge of joyous energy, he launched into the opening lines. "Write this, Jonathan: *These are the final words of Moses, his farewell message to all Israel in the wilderness east of the Jordan . . .* "8

The ink-dipped quill flew rapidly across the parchment in Jonathan's meticulous script, line after line, hour after hour, with only brief pauses to shake out cramped fingers or to sharpen the quill point or to partake of a little food. At last when the sky began to flame red above the darkening landscape, Moses declared they were finished for the day. He watched Jonathan roll up the parchment and fasten it with a thin leather tie. This was not the same boy he found earlier pretending to sleep by Gershom's tent. He was smiling. No—more than smiling. He was grinning.

"And what is it about finishing our work that amuses you so?"

Jonathan's musical laugh preceded his answer. "How many people would stay to the end of your speech if it took as long to speak it as to write it?"

"And I could have said so much more."

Moses packed each item back into his shoulder bag as Jonathan handed them to him. He could feel the boy watching thoughtfully.

"I would be content to spend many, many days up here with you on this mountain, Grandfather."

"And I— " Moses' response was nearly drowned in a sudden wash of familial love. "Sadly, there cannot be many more days like this."

The shadow returned to Jonathan's eyes and he looked away.

"What is it, my son? What troubles you?" The face had become a mask of cold stone. "Surely not that I will be leaving you soon. That is the way of all mankind. The old die and the children take their places."

Their places. That was it. As Moses said the words, he suddenly understood. *Jonathan had hoped to take his place when he was gone.*

"You are so dear to me, Jonathan. Tell me what you are thinking."

Jonathan continued to stare out over the valley. The changing emotions that normally fluttered across his expressive face were as frozen as the voice that normally babbled in a continuous stream. Moses followed his gaze to the plains below and watched the evening pull a shadow blanket over the green-gold landscape. *Like a heavenly mother, tucking in her child for the night.* The thought filled him with peace.

"I am content with the judgment of the Lord," he said slowly. "How can a man of one-hundred-twenty years complain about facing the end of his earthly days? God has been more than good to me."

He paused to see how his grandson would respond.

The granite image of Jonathan did not move. Moses reached out and caressed the stone cheek lightly, and the touch awakened the image. Jonathan glanced at him with a questioning half smile.

Moses took a deep breath and asked bluntly, "So what do you think of the Lord choosing Joshua as my successor?"

That direct question and intense look loosed Jonathan's tongue at last. "Honestly, I don't understand it. When Uncle Aaron died, Eleazar took his place, and the Lord has already appointed Phinehas to take Eleazar's place when he is gone. Why did you not call my father to take your place? Why Joshua?"

Moses nodded. "Gershom and his brother are content to blend into life on the margins of Israel with their fellow Kenites. They hardly interact with the Levites, let alone any of the other tribes of Israel. He does not desire leadership. I think you know that too. This is about your desire, is it not?"

Jonathan blinked back the brightness of gathering tears. "I don't want to fraternize with the Kenites as Father does, and I don't want to be an ordinary Levite. I can't remember when I didn't picture Phinehas becoming high priest someday with *me* by his side as the leader of Israel. Like you and Uncle Aaron."

"God is the true leader of Israel, Jonathan. Never forget that. It is true that now the people look to me . . . and to the judges . . . to make decisions for them, but God's intent is that we become a kingdom of priests, a nation whose king is her God."

Moses paused for a moment, remembering his own call to leadership. "When I was a boy growing up, my Hebrew mother taught me that the time of Israel's sojourn in Egypt was nearly over and that God would need a leader to bring them out. I never forgot her teachings, even as my Egyptian mother organized the best education for me in Pharaoh's court. As I trained in the arts of warfare, justice, and literature, I dreamed of how it would happen. My expectations caused me to make foolish choices. I tried to force myself into that position of leadership. You know the story of my disgrace."

Jonathan nodded. "Grandmother's favorite story. Not a story of disgrace, but a crisis that brought a handsome prince out of the courts of Egypt into her arms."

Moses chuckled, "I can see by your expression that you treasure the story just as she did, instead of being properly horrified that your grandfather was a murderer."

"But Grandfather, the man was a cruel taskmaster, beating an Israelite."

"Murder nonetheless. God did not command me to do anything like that. I suspect that as you go into Canaan, he will have you do more watching than fighting. He has strange ways of winning battles if Egypt and our recent conflicts here are any indication. The point I want to make now, however, is that we must wait for God to call us to leadership. Perhaps, my impetuous act delayed the rescue of God's people by forty years. When we do what makes sense to us without consulting him, we usually deceive ourselves and go contrary to his will. God will use you some day for something great, something worthy of your talents. Wait for him to make the path clear to you."

"And will he make the choice of a wife clear to me?" There was more than a hint of bitterness in the words.

"Ah, so a woman is the cause of that melancholy I have observed of late." Moses paused, hoping Jonathan would reveal more of his heart. "Tell me about her," he urged gently.

"I thought I had found the perfect wife . . . wise and hardworking, strong in the Lord. She would be a perfect wife for a leader in Israel, and . . . not only that, but . . . I love her more than anything. I love to watch her. I love to hear her speak. I love to hear her laugh. No other girl is so beautiful and full of life."

"And . . ."

"Her father refused to make betrothal arrangements with my father. He left the choice up to the girl and she rejected me. Now I have not only lost a wife, but a friend. She avoids me like the plague."

"Just wait, my son. You are young. God will lead even in that, and I suspect when the awkwardness wears off, your friendship with . . . with . . . Do I know this girl?"

"I'd rather not say any more. The whole thing makes me feel like a bumbling ox."

"Your name means 'gift of Yahweh,' and that you are. Never forget it. Obey his every command and wait for him to lead. Someday, when you are a white-haired old man like me, you will find yourself looking back on a life far different than you ever could have imagined, and far better than you could have planned."

Stars were multiplying in the deepening purple of the sky. A paler blue lingering above the black outline of the western hills marked the place where the sun had slipped from view. Moses stood. "Will you come back with me . . . let's see, not tomorrow. Day after next? Perhaps we can finish this book in another session or two. Tomorrow, you Levites will help review the law with all the tribes. There will be no time for anything else."

Jonathan nodded, this time with no uncertainty. "It is an honor to be your scribe, and I will be looking forward to returning to your Heights of Inspiration."

CHAPTER THREE

CHEERS, TEARS, AND FEARS

Ahuzzath

Ahuzzath squinted into the darkness of the narrow street leading to the North Wall Inn. There was no moon, and lamp light in Jericho tonight was minimal. Most houses had shuttered their windows against the enemy across the river. "Fools," he muttered to himself. "If that rabble army should get past the gates and guards of the city, those flimsy window barriers won't be worth a rotten fig."

He had scoured the city for the king and was satisfied that the job was done. Every Midianite girl who had taken refuge in this city had been exterminated. Now, he could indulge himself with cheerier pleasures. By habit, he headed toward his favorite inn. No, more than by habit. It was his obsession.

Ahuzzath's body burned at the thought of the exquisite voice, the soft and sultry songs—and that fire fueled every sinew and muscle to hasten his pace. Others desired the sweet songbird of Jericho too. The whistles and shouts punctuating her performances made that clear, but a song was all anyone got these days. At least, as far as he knew. His face twitched with a fresh current of suspicion, and by the time he opened the heavy inn door, he was shaking with rage.

Pausing in the dimness of the antechamber, he took a deep breath and surveyed the room. It was still early. The low performance platform was empty. The singer herself was serving guests. He studied her face as she wove her way around the dining hall, her lips smiling but her eyes icy, detached.

No. Rahab did not give particular attention to any of the other men. The heat of his jealous fever plummeted as quickly as it had flared up, and a more pleasing sensation tingled through him as he watched the way she moved around this table, around that, delivering platters of food and flagons of liquor to the patrons packed in the large open room. It was a graceful dance and every step was bringing her closer to him.

Closer . . . and yet she had not looked toward the entry chamber.

Closer . . . still she had not noticed him. When she began refilling wine cups at a table not much more than an arm's length away, he lunged from the cover of shadows.

He was quick, but Rahab was quicker, dodging instinctively to the right and sloshing dark red wine on his sleeve. Alarm flashed in her eyes, but before he could blink, she donned a mask of practiced composure and held up the brass decanter. "Forgive me, Captain. My sidestep maneuver for evading charging bears doesn't work so well with this in my hand."

Ahuzzath ripped the vessel from her hands and tipped it up, sucking down a long draft of very fine wine. Finer yet were the eyes that watched him impassively as he lowered the empty decanter. He winked. "Mmm-mmm. We can't allow your father's assets to be wasted."

He could feel the little rivulets running down his beard and dripping onto the front of his robe as he passed the decanter back to her hands. Wiping his mouth with the wine-spattered sleeve, he tossed her as tender a gaze as he could muster. Surely he could help her dredge up some sweet memory of their special relationship. Surely the passion he felt for her would melt that icy stare.

"My sweet Rahab, you know that my every thought . . . my every longing . . . every moment . . . every hour . . . is for you and you alone." Hope fluttered inside him like a dove winging up to the sky as he whispered, "The Red Room? Tonight?"

"Ahuzzath, you know that is not possible." Her voice was barely audible. "I must begin singing in a few moments."

"Only a song? Again?" He dropped all traces of gentleness. "Well, sing then. But only for me. Any man who receives so much as a fond look from you is a dead man."

The flicker of fear in her eyes was delicious. The pleasure of the hunt. *You may run, my gazelle, but the beast will be satisfied.* He seized her arm as she turned away. "Arrange a seat for me in front of the platform, close to my little songbird."

"The inn is crowded tonight. Those seats are already taken."

"Your *father's* inn, yes? You *will* make room for your captain." He tipped her chin up to watch the power of his threats register in those incredibly bright eyes. "A word to King Nahari from me could imprison your father and shut this place down. Imagine what would happen. Jokshan, languishing in the dungeon beneath the palace, or maybe his head hanging from a spike on the wall. How do you think you and your mother would fare out on the streets while he was feeding the crows? Hmm?" He ran his knuckles down a velvety cheek. "You perhaps a little better than Keziah."

"I will do what I can to find you a seat."

Ahuzzath watched Rahab retrace her path across the room, weaving through the tables with the grace of a dancer as before, but the rush in her steps added a dramatic intensity that excited him all the more. A stop beside her mother. An urgent whisper. A glare from Keziah. A flurry of whispers with patrons just in front of the low platform, and then a beckoning for him to come. Just another of Rahab's songs for now. But, one way or another, this night or another. He would find a way to enjoy the intimate dance of the Red Room.

As he strode to the place vacated for him, Ahuzzath grinned at the two guests who had been moved.

"Our silver is as good as his," one said to the other.

The companion nodded. "Without the king's armor, he is no better than us."

Ahuzzath smirked as he settled into the softness of one of the cushions. *If that is so, why am I here and not you? The captain of the king's guard is never off duty, armor or no.* He leaned his back against a pillar and propped his feet up on the second cushion. Rahab had disappeared into the kitchen so he blew a kiss to Keziah and mouthed the words, "You did well."

Keziah shot back the look of deep-seated hatred that she had reserved for him for ten years now.

Ahuzzath felt a twinge of pity. The mother's hatred of him and his obsession with Rahab began on the same magical night, Asherah's night, ten cycles past. Keziah had once been the sizzling chanteuse of the inn as her daughter was now. It was not age that caused Keziah to lock her songs and haunting voice in some inner vault of silence and hang up her harp. She was still a fine looking woman, although, like himself, she had lived more than twoscore years of her life. No, her music ceased when his good fortune became her misfortune. He closed his eyes and slipped into his favorite memory.

He left the high worship festival at Asherah's temple that night agitated rather than content. Other men might leave sensing their lives realigned with the forces of sky and earth. They would return home confident that the coming year would bring prosperity to their fields or business interests. They could rouse their wives and father another child. Ahuzzath had no wife, no family, and as the new captain of the king's guard, his prosperity depended not so much on securing the favor of the gods as retaining the good will of the dangerously unpredictable King Nahari. In this unsettled state, he found his way to the North Wall Inn, expecting no more than a steadying drink and the soothing songs of the beautiful Keziah. But old Thahash the Crafty had crafted an unexpected delight.

As Keziah plucked her harp and sang the tales of the gods, the innkeeper brought her lovely little daughter out to dance for the packed room. In a fluttering tunic of fine linen shot through with silver threads, the curly-haired child shimmered in circles around her mother. The striking beauty of the delicate face and tiny perfect body was exceeded only by the exquisite grace of her every movement.

A spirit of wonder enthralled the crowd as the little one began interpreting Lord Baal's desire for his Lady Asherah. The liquor flowed and the dance intensified. The playful flirting and teasing morphed to unbounded passion as Asherah's song built to a climax. Patrons began beating empty barrels, pounding tables, stomping the floor in time to the beat until the whole room throbbed like one wildly beating heart. The goddess herself must have possessed the child, for the Flame of Asherah flashed through that room as never before.

Then out of the corners of eyes well trained for battle, Ahuzzath noticed the crafty uncle moving through the crowd. Immediately, he knew. Greedy old Thahash was selling access to the child. He abandoned his close-up view of the potent performance. Never mind the coda. Nothing else mattered but rushing to place his bid—a whole month's salary plus the gold medallion earned when he rescued the king from deadly peril at the battle of Scorpion Pass. What was gold or silver? He could go without food or drink when necessary, but in the same desperate way that a suffocating man needs air, he knew he must possess this little goddess or die.

Thahash grinned at his outlandish bid and nodded agreement. By the time Ahuzzath looked back to the performance platform, the room was suspended in a silent fermata. The child lay prostrate with the final notes of her mother's harp rippling over her body like moonlight on water. The very air of the room crackled with stifled desire. Some might say he had missed the finale, but for him it had just begun.

"I hope you brought a lot of sugar for me," the little one said in a flush of joy as he claimed his prize and led her up to the Red Room. Rahab was never again the same innocent child. And he was never the same man.

There were rumors that Thahash had to lock the child in the wine cellar for three days to get her to return to the platform. Whatever motivated her to dance again, she was always lovely, always tantalizing—but the Flame of Asherah never again blazed as bright in the child's performance as it had that first night. Some said that it was because a hired harp could not compare to Keziah's for the mother never touched her harp again. But still the tiny tot packed the inn, stirring the passions and expectations of her audience.

Thahash understood the value of his treasure and refused to squander it. Although she sang and danced nearly every night, a private dance in the Red Room with the exquisite little Rahab herself was reserved for the high festivals—rare and very expensive. Most nights, other women accompanied the men upstairs.

For six years, Ahuzzath squandered his wealth on that child. He spent every free evening at the inn—his life, his body, his very soul hovering on the knife-edge of wild hope and total despair. Twice in fits of lethal jealousy, he murdered men who competed and outbid him. One bled out in the crowded room with a knife in his back. The other convulsed over his cups. No one ever tracked the owner of the blade or discovered who slipped the apothecary's white powder into the beer, but no one tried to bid against him after the second mysterious death either. Whether at work or at rest, his mind replayed scenes of the little dancer. Every replay bringing back the throbbing desire in a continual loop until it became the definition of who he was and what he lived for.

When the old man died, the girl's father, Jokshan, took over the inn, and the change was as abrupt as it was unnatural. He placed a hedge of thorns around his daughter even though she would always be known as the little harlot of the North Wall Inn. Rahab sang now and played the harp as her mother had. She no longer danced, and no amount of silver or gold could buy another night with her in the Red Room.

As Rahab took her place a few feet away from Ahuzzath and began weaving the enchantment of her songs, his eyes devoured the fullness that filled out her dresses now. He had known the child. It was time to know the full-flowered woman. No, not just know her. *Own her*. He wiped his wet palms on his tunic and gulped down a long draft of sweet barley beer. This woman had long possessed his mind, his heart, his body, and his soul. It was time for him to possess *her*. But, how? Every offer to purchase her had been rebuffed. His sweetest, most seductive words never produced the rendezvous he burned for. His frustration stirred up a darkness inside him blacker than the moonless night in the streets outside.

As her sultry sweet voice moved over him and through him, his mind spun out plot after plot. All at once, the threads of his plotting began to form a web of entrapment. *The current threat of war . . . the insane responses of King Nahari.*

That fool. Fearing a possible siege, the king pulled much of the stored grain from the protected stone silos in the rocky bluffs and piled it in the city streets where it crawled with rats and mice. He had ordered every family to store water in their homes to breed blood-sucking mosquitoes even though the spring-fed fountain in the center of the market plaza had never run dry. Then, he ordered the flax crop to be cut early and brought in from the fields to cure on rooftops. With Nahari so clearly disturbed by the tribes that had settled across the river, it should not be difficult to find something about Rahab that smacked of treason.

All these people coming and going at the inn . . . I'll post a watch day and night. Find just the right pretext. Build a solid case against her . . . Then convince the king to place the treasonous wench in his hands. That would be the easy part. He had obviously pleased the king in his handling of those Midianite whores. What was one more girl to Nahari?

As Rahab finished her song, she looked up and their eyes met. Life-bright beauty mingled delightfully with melancholy sadness in those dark windows to her soul. Ahuzzath tried to imagine the thoughts behind that look. *She sang so passionately of love and now she is looking at me. Her father holds her captive, but she is a woman now, yearning for her man.* He chuckled to himself and blew her a kiss. Life would change for the two of them very, very soon.

Abihail

Knots of chatting friends and family gathered for the second day of Moses' farewell speeches. Above them, awash in morning light on the same outcropping he had used for his speech the day before, Moses conferenced with the princes and elders of Reuben, Gad, and Manasseh. The shock and grief regarding the previous morning's announcement had passed and expectation sizzled through the crowd again. Today Moses would review the law of the covenant. The thought brought Abihail a sense of comfort and belonging. Israel was at one with her God once more. Mount Peor, unfaithfulness, plague, war, and death were behind them. Soon they would leave this valley behind as well. Rumor had it that soon, very soon, they would be moving into their promised inheritance.

Eliab grinned and bounced on his toes like an over-eager child. "Can you feel the excitement in the air? Soon my little bride will have a home. A real house. No more tents. No more wandering." He squeezed her hand.

"It is almost impossible to imagine. A real house . . . gardens and pastures for our flocks and herds," Abihail replied. She giggled when she looked up at his face. He wore the very same smile she had fallen in love with when they were still children in the wilderness. "It *is* impossible to imagine a real house when I look at you. All I can see are little piles of sand, squared off and decorated with desert blossoms."

"The miniature Canaan you and Acsah built—that we boys stomped into the ground? I hope you also picture one little boy drying your tears and bringing you flowers as you rebuilt your shattered world."

"The little boy I have loved every day since."

The noisy press of people surrounding them supplied an odd sense of intimacy. Eliab nudged her chin up as if he would kiss her. Instead, he studied her face with such deep, heartfelt adoration that she wondered if any other girl had ever felt so loved.

"See if you can picture what I see. The child who once built sand houses, now grown to a woman reigning over a home furnished and draped in a manner suitable for royalty. I promise you, my darling, if I cannot find fine carved tables and chairs fit for my bride among the spoils of war, I will hire the finest artisans to make them. I don't know if our house will be large, but I will spare nothing to provide the best for the queen of my domain."

Abihail felt the protest of her negative headshake as her chin slid back and forth against the fingers that lingered on her throat. "I need not be queen of such a home. I am most content to serve you as my king no matter how humble our dwelling place."

"Oh, no," he corrected playfully, "I am your servant—not your king."

She dipped her chin and looked up at him coquettishly through her eyelashes. "But you already reign as king of my love."

Eliab laughed and pulled her close. "All right then," he whispered. "Co-rulers in love."

His warmth radiated into her with a most delicious blend of contented belonging and physical desire. She looked up with a coy smile and whispered, "Our bed will be the regal throne around which all else revolves."

Eliab laughed. "And from that throne, all the little citizens of our kingdom will spring forth. Our bed will be the one piece of furniture that cannot come from the spoils of war. I will make it for you myself, the first piece of furniture in our home. And the grandest." He held her back at arms length. "*Our* home, Abihail. Now can you picture more than just the little sand houses you and Acsah made?"

Jonathan

Jonathan watched the princes and elders of Reuben, Gad, and Manasseh making their way back down the trail. He couldn't help feeling just a little superior to the expectant multitude. These men were often a contentious lot, but this morning they wore agreeable smiles. Moses had succeeded in securing their agreement. Did anyone else in the crowd really understand the importance of that conference with his grandfather?

With no preliminaries, Moses announced. "The tribes of Reuben, Gad, and Manasseh will set aside three cities of refuge here, on this side of the Jordan. Bezer, in Reuben's territory on the wilderness plateau near Moab. Ramoth, in Gad's territory in the center of Gilead. And Golan, on the heights of Bashan in the region inherited by the eastern branch of Manasseh. If someone unintentionally kills his neighbor without malice aforethought, he may flee to one of these cities and thus save his life from the family avenger. When the remaining tribes are established in the land on the western side of the river, you must set up similar cities where a person can flee when the unthinkable happens."[9] Whispers hissed through the crowd like water spattered on fire. Israelites killing their neighbors? Family avengers? They had experienced no such violence through the forty wilderness years. Would they really need such places now? Within minutes, however, the eruption of questions morphed into nods of acceptance. Yes, accidents *might* happen as they built new lives in this strange new place: a hammer dropped from a rooftop, an oxcart overturned, the missed swing of an axe. Before there was a need, Moses had set up the provision. Spontaneous cheers began here and there, bursting into a joyful chant of "Canaan! Canaan!"

Jonathan caught his grandfather's eyes, almost laughing at Moses' startled expression. They exchanged amused smiles as the chant continued. The spirited reaction to the announcement surprised him as well, but why should it? The designation of these cities of refuge signaled the beginning. The breathtaking reality of new life in the Land of Promise.

Grandfather watched the brewing joy with a wistful smile. After a few moments, he raised his hand again for silence.

Hear, O Israel, the decrees and laws I declare in your hearing today. These are the terms of the covenant that Yahweh God made with your parents at Sinai. Most of you had not yet been born—or were too young to grasp the significance of that day. The Almighty God of all nations on earth chose us to be his holy people. He cut covenant with us, a covenant not merely for your parents, but for you and your children and your children's children forever.

Eliab and Abihail stood hand in hand just in front of Jonathan, and at the mention of children, Eliab hunched even closer to whisper in her ear. Just newlyweds sharing an intimate moment, but a sense of loss plunged into Jonathan's festering heart wound like a cold blade. Acsah stood not ten feet away, but it might as well have been a thousand. The entire time the crowd waited for Moses to begin, he had tried to catch her eyes, to at least share a smile. He was subtle, circulating from group to group, moving around her, joking and bantering with friends, but Acsah's turns were more subtle yet. She never broke off her conversation with her father once, but she managed to keep her back to him no matter where he was. It was obvious she had no intention of meeting his eyes, even accidentally. Suddenly, feeling out of place among the clans of Judah, Jonathan retreated to the cluster of Kenites, his father's relatives out on the edge of the crowd.

"Our family can stand proud today, eh son?" Gershom wore a broad smile. "My father has always been a great man, but never as magnificent as at this very moment."

Jonathan nodded bleakly. His father had no inkling of his torment. He soothed himself by repeating his grandfather's counsel. *God has a great calling for you, Jonathan. He has a plan for your life. The rejection of your love will not destroy you. It will change you.* A heartbeat of hope leaped in his chest. Even though Acsah rejected him, even though Joshua was named as Moses' successor, he was still Moses' grandson. No one could take that away from him. He turned his attention back to the oration.[10]

What God has ever overthrown the mightiest power of the world to free its slaves? What God has ever chosen a weak, disorderly people and made them a nation of righteousness? Search every legend, every story told around the campfires of the nations. Has any other people ever been so loved and cared for by their gods?

Never forget the words that Yahweh spoke out of the fire on the mountain. He tried to speak directly to your parents, but they were afraid. I stood between them and the thunder of the Eternal as I repeated his words.

Moses' form, backlit as yesterday, was even more glorious from this distance. When he spoke for Yahweh in a voice resounding from the surrounding hills, ardent and clear, no one doubted that he knew exactly what Yahweh would say to them.

I am Yahweh, your God. I rescued you from Egypt. I freed you from the cruel chains. I redeemed you from slavery to be my people.

"Because you are mine, never worship any god but me.

Because you are mine, never make idols in the form of anything I fixed in the sky or formed from the earth or placed in its waters. Never bow down to images of the creation for I am Yahweh, Creator God. I am jealous for your devotion. The worship of other gods will reduce your thinking to the level of beasts, and the consequences will not only fall on the parents who abandon me. It will bring weakness and pain to the children for three generations—even four. Oh, but my love will flow on and on to a thousand generations of those who choose to love me and keep my commandments.

Because you are mine, never speak the name of Yahweh your God carelessly. Do not take oaths in my name to twist justice or tarnish my glory. I will not overlook the flippant misuse of my holy name.

Because you are mine, keep my Sabbath holy exactly as I have commanded you. You have six days to labor. Six days for your own work. But the seventh day is mine. Do not do any work on my day. Neither you, nor your son or daughter. Neither your manservant or maidservant. The same goes for your ox, your donkey, and all of your other animals. Even foreigners staying within your gates must set aside their work on my day. Give your servants rest, just as the Lord has given rest to you. Remember the weariness of being slaves in Egypt. Remember how Yahweh your God brought you out of there with a mighty hand and gave you rest. The God who redeemed you, commands you to make his Sabbath a holy day of rest for all.

Because you are mine, honor your father and your mother. If you respect your parents, you will live long, prosperous lives in the inheritance the Lord your God is giving you.

Like surf whipped by the wind, battering the rocky cliffs with one wave after another, the powerful recitation grew to a thundering crescendo.

Because you are mine, never murder.
Because you are mine, never commit adultery.
Because you are mine, never steal.
Because you are mine, never lie about your neighbor.
Because you are mine, be content. Trust me to meet your needs. Never give in to desire for your neighbor's wife. Never allow yourself to long for his house or land, his manservant or maidservant, his ox or donkey, or anything that belongs to your neighbor.[11]

Moses paused to let the commands hang in the air. Then, in a voice as gentle as the one Jonathan remembered when his grandfather held him as a small child, he added:

Yahweh your God carved these commands in stone with his own finger. If you continue to walk in this path once you have crossed the Jordan, if you do not turn aside to the left or the right, you will live. You will thrive. You, and your children, and their children after them. All who honor and respect the Lord by observing his commands will live long prosperous lives.

Hear, O Israel, Yahweh your God is the one and only true God. Love him with all your hearts. Let your devotion saturate every thought. Let it motivate every expenditure of your strength. Let this law of love and goodness seep down to the very core of who you are. If you live by these commands and teach them to your children, you will flourish in that land flowing with milk and honey, just as Yahweh, the God of your fathers, promised you.

The power of the oration continued. It broke over the people like pounding surf, rushing at them first from one side and then from the other. Passionate pleas washed over them, calling to the highest and noblest motives for serving God without reservation. Then a recital of earthy rewards swept them back to the practical joys of life. Moses appealed to their gratitude for their deliverance from slavery. He appealed to their desire for material comfort, their hope of safety in time of war, and their longing for freedom from disease. Every godly impulse, every self-serving human motivation crashed in counterpoint, stirring the people with every possible incentive for serving the God who chose them to be his people. Love and admiration flooded Jonathan's heart, and the pain of his private grief was forgotten.

> *These commandments are not merely to be stored in the ark of the covenant. Store them in your hearts. Teach them to your children. Whether you are sitting around the table with your little ones or walking along the road, teach them my commands. Talk about them as you lie down at night and when you get up each morning. Let my commands protect the portals to your houses and guard your city gates. May every work of your hands and every thought you express shine with the light of my law.*

Jonathan shivered with a sudden awareness of his awesome calling as a Levite. God intended that his people enjoy more blessings than they could dream of. The culture of Canaan could be a deadly trap for Israel, but these laws would be a shield of protection from evil. It was his destiny to teach the people what covenant living looked like. He could not hold back his shout of joy. "We are your covenant people, blessed forever and ever. May our lives shine with the light of your law."

The people around Jonathan caught his excitement and repeated the refrain. "We are your covenant people, blessed forever and ever."

The small flame ignited within Jonathan by the flashing fire of Moses' words now blazed through the congregation. The story of Mount Sinai was marked by God's voice thundering out of visible fire. This day, here on the border of the Promised Land, those words sparked a living, breathing blaze of glory. The powerful chant echoed across the valley. "May our lives shine with the light of your law."

Moses paused. His face radiated with joy at their response. Jonathan was certain he would remember that expression for the rest of his life. It was his destiny to keep this truth in the minds of

God's chosen people and never let them forget. He shouted again, "We are your covenant people, blessed forever and ever. May our lives shine with the light of your law."

Moses repeated:

Yes, you are the covenant people. May your lives shine with the light of his law. In a few days, Yahweh your God will bring you into the land he swore to give your fathers—the land promised to Abraham, Isaac, and Jacob. This is what you will inherit. Large, flourishing cities you did not build. Houses furnished with good things you did not purchase or make. Wells you did not dig. Grain fields, vineyards, and olive groves you did not plant. When you have settled into your comfortable homes; when you sit back at the end of the day, satiated with an abundance of food and satisfied with everything your hearts desire, don't forget how you came to possess your inheritance. Remember the One who brought you out of Egypt, out of the land of slavery. It was not the gods of Canaan who gave you this good life. Do not worship any of them.

"The land of Canaan is good. Yahweh is good. We will worship only him."

When Yahweh your God brings you into Canaan, he will drive out the Hittites, the Girgashites, the Amorites, the Canaanites, the Perizzites, the Hivites, and the Jebusites—seven nations larger and stronger than you. They have filled the cup of iniquity to overflowing. Wipe the stench of their culture from the land with no mercy when your God delivers them into your hands.

"No mercy. Deliver them into our hands, O Lord."

Yahweh your God says, "I am your husband in covenant. Do not make treaties with the nations of Canaan. Do not allow your children to marry them. Do not give your daughters as brides for their sons. Do not take their daughters for your sons. They will entice your children to worship their demon gods and the flames of my anger will destroy your people along with those gods."

"No treaties. No marriage with Canaan. We are your people."

"Out of all the peoples on the face of the earth, I chose you to be my own. Do not be enticed by any other god. When you enter the land I am giving you, this is what you are to do. Hack down the sacred groves where Asherah and Baal are worshipped. Smash their phallic pillars. Tear apart the altars of their vile sacrifices, stone by stone. Cast every disgusting image into the fire. You are holy to me."

"We will be holy to Yahweh our God!"

If you are careful to keep this covenant with Yahweh, then he will keep his covenant of love with you. He will honor the pledge he made long ago with Abraham, Isaac, and Jacob. He will bless you in every way. Your people will increase in number and wealth and power. He will bless you with large families. He will bless your crops—your grain, new wine, and oil. He will multiply the calves of your herds and the lambs of your flocks. He will bless you in the land of your inheritance more than any people who have ever lived on earth. The Lord will keep you physically healthy and strong. He will not allow the deadly diseases you knew in Egypt to fall on you, but only on all who hate you. And you in turn will bless the earth.

"Bless us, O Lord our God as you have said," the people cried. Then, abruptly, as if the blessings were not enough to keep his people from forgetting their God, Moses thundered a warning.

There are giants as tall as cedars, the descendants of Anak, living among the nations of Canaan. Do not fear them. I will drive them out for you. But when that happens and everything in your life is thriving, do not think that your success is due to your own hard work or that the gods of Canaan have helped you. I testify against you today that such thinking will destroy you as it destroyed the nations I am driving out for you. Do not forget the Lord your God. Do even think of worshipping another god.

The tone was so suddenly stern, so formidable. But, why? Every heart, it seemed, was burning with devotion to Yahweh alone. Jonathan sensed consternation around him and knew the questions were those of his own heart. How could they forget their God? Were they not fully committed to the covenant? Could they forget the covenant promise they were making today? What would ever entice them to worship the gods of Canaan?

Moses surveyed the confused faces and responded in the form of a story, returning to the gentle, grandfatherly tone Jonathan knew so well. He told of his glorious meeting with Yahweh on the top of Mount Sinai. It was one of Jonathan's favorite stories—the people terrified beyond endurance by the rumbling of God's voice, Moses alone facing the fear, the thrill of danger. Moses alone climbing the mountain to encounter the flaming, thundering Presence and finding himself engulfed in an atmosphere of burning, invigorating love unlike anything he had ever known.

With his own finger, God seared the terms of his covenant into slabs of stone, two principles itemized as ten: be fully devoted to Yahweh alone, be devoted to kindness and love for everyone else. For forty days, Moses lingered with God. He absorbed every detail for building a sanctuary, the tabernacle, so God could dwell in the midst of his people. He absorbed every detail of how to order the camp and the worship services, how to train a nation to reflect the character of a God, perfect in justice and mercy.

While Moses was lost in the wonder and awe of this encounter, God suddenly ordered him to hurry back down to camp. The people had already violated the covenant. Tears welled in Grandfather's eyes as he continued telling the story, his voice falling over the convocation with the foreboding of a rumbling, impending thunderstorm. He described the fear of leaving the blazing fire of God's presence and starting down the mountainside clutching the covenant stones, but he could not believe the extent of the rebellion until he saw it for himself. Vows of fidelity broken almost before they began. Unspeakable unfaithfulness. Like a bridegroom turning from his bride to a whore—while still at the wedding feast. God's holy people wallowing in most unholy worship—drunken feasting, sensuous dancing, naked bodies copulating around the image of a gold calf.

He hurled the covenant tablets against the foot of the mountain in their sight. Sacred stones shattered just like their sacred vows. But the licentious worship did not stop. He marched into the midst of the celebration and toppled the calf idol. He confronted his brother in a fury. *How could you allow this?*

"We all thought you had died when you lingered so long," Aaron stammered. "Surely that inferno atop Mount Sinai incinerated you. Who could survive it?" The people begged for a symbol of their god less frightening than that seething mountain, he explained feebly. When the elders pressed him to make an image, he buckled a little. He proposed a test. "Bring me your gold," he told them, "and we will throw it into the fire." But somehow the rebels tricked him. They melted the gold down and poured it into a box of acacia wood. When they threw the box into the fire, the form of this calf emerged from the charred wood. Was that not a miracle? How could he stand up against such evidence?

Moses brushed aside all Aaron's feeble excuses. "You call that evidence?"

Moses smashed the idol with a hammer and heaved the pieces into the fire chunk by chunk. When the molten remnants cooled, he attacked the residue of their "miracle" with a hammer. "If this thing had any power to save you, could I do this?" he bellowed. He scattered the dust on the stream from which the people drank. Not a nugget of the symbol remained, but the majority of the people ran amok and no amount of threatening or pleading could get the drunken feasting, dancing, and adulterous coupling to stop.

Jonathan closed his eyes. He knew the next part of the story all too well. The terrible day when the Lord set the Levites apart as a tribe dedicated to His service. Many times he had heard his grandfather describe standing by the tent of meeting, his voice choking with grief, asking "Who is on the side of Yahweh?" While the chaos of the festival spiraled out of control, he drew a line in the sand with his rod and called out, "Whoever is for Yahweh, come to me." Few of the revelers stopped long enough to hear the words of judgment on their treason, but the entire tribe of Levi rallied to Moses and the Lord. All that day the bronze blades of Levite swords flashed back and forth through the camp in a bloody civil war that ended with nearly three thousand people dead.

The story of the golden-calf rebellion had never seemed so real before. Jonathan could still smell the blood and smoke of the rebellion fomented by Balaam's plot. He could still close his eyes and see blood-spattered Levite warriors, swords smeared with crimson gore. He would never forget the image of the cloud-covered, thundering dwelling place of God surrounded by death—gruesome carcasses of rebels hanging on a forest of crosses. Both stories were nearly unspeakable in horror, but both must be told and retold to prevent future generations from falling into the same trap. Yahweh God was life. Other gods brought death. Jonathan tingled from toe to scalp with a sense of who he was and why he lived on this earth. He would dedicate his life to teaching these things to the people.

Moses continued:

I threw myself down before the fury of Yahweh. The Lord had every right to be angry at such unfaithfulness in the face of his display of incomprehensible love. I could not stop praying—for only those prayers shielded you from destruction. I ate no bread and drank no water. I reasoned with the Lord in every imaginable way, pleading for you with tears.

Hardly a breath disturbed the air. Even today, more than forty years later, tears streamed down Moses' weathered cheeks as he recalled the words he prayed for the people. Jonathan looked around through the blurred vision of his own tears to see the roughened cheeks of grown men as wet as the smooth faces of their wives and children. He could not see a single face unmoved by the love this great man had for his people.

O Sovereign Yahweh,
Let not our failure mar your unfailing love.
  Overlook our ignorance and ingratitude.
Forgive our unfaithfulness
  and remember the faithfulness of your servants—
  Abraham, Isaac and Jacob.

Otherwise, the Egyptians will say,
"Yahweh was not able to take them into the promised Land of Canaan."
How then will they know that you are the King of kings?
   How will they know you are Lord of lords?
The nations will think that you hated us.
   That you brought us out in the desert to kill us.
They will not understand your tender kindness.
   That you chose us to be your people.
   That you redeemed us from slavery and
   led us out of Egypt in a great display of power—
   because you loved us.
How can you destroy us now?
The nations are watching.

For forty days and forty nights, I prayed thus for Israel. For forty days I fasted for you—and for my brother—just as I had the previous forty days on the mountain. How could I live if you did not? How could I live if Aaron did not?

After a dramatic pause Moses added softly:

My heart is still awed by the fact. Yahweh listened to me. He called me to come back up the mountain bringing new stones to renew the broken vows. He gave us a new covenant, not based on our promises, which are as unsubstantial as mist, but based on the enduring rock of his love and mercy.

Like Jonathan, most of the crowd were not yet born when this story happened. For the first time they realized how close their entire nation came to extinction just weeks after the exodus from Egypt. Had Moses not loved them so much, had God not been so prone to mercy, their story might have ended right there at the beginning while still at the base of Sinai. And more frightening still, how close had they come to repeating the failure of their parents right here in this valley?

And now, my people, what does Yahweh ask of you but to worship and serve him—to walk in the freedom and joy of covenant living. To obey the law he has given you for your own good. It is the law of Life. Yahweh is God above all gods. Lord above all lords. Awesome in deed. He is supreme in power and might. Towering above all earthly powers in justice. Magnificent in mercy and love. He does not ask a hard thing of you, only that you love him with all your heart. Only that you love the poor and the alien, that you care for the fatherless and the widows. O my people, serve the Lord with all that is within you. He is your God and has done great and wonderful things for you.

Moses finished with intimate tenderness and humbly bowed his head in conclusion.

Acsah

Acsah took a deep breath and rolled her shoulders to release the tension. She had been listening with breathless intensity and suddenly realized that she was utterly fatigued. As if he read her thoughts, Moses chuckled. He lifted his head, bright eyes peering out from under shaggy brows. "You have listened long enough to weary the strongest man, but there is so much more. Find a comfortable place to sit for the afternoon. Find a little shade, if you can, for the recitation of the law. While the priests and Levites assemble for that, refresh yourselves with a little food and water."

As people jostled tighter into family groups and settled comfortably on the ground, Acsah glimpsed Jonathan bounding up the trail like a gazelle. The last time she saw him, his face was a study of the darkest despair. She knew she was the cause of his misery and she could not bear to see him like that, but she could not change what had happened. Now his face radiated joy as he joined the cluster of priests and Levites around Moses and Eleazar. The gregarious, merry friend she knew so well was restored—and perhaps more than restored. *Good for you, Jonathan. That is the way I want to remember you . . . but I do not know how I want you to remember me.* She slid back among her nieces and nephews until she could no longer see Jonathan and hoped he would not be able to see her.

"I brought plenty of manna cakes," she said. "Who wants one?"

Seven-year-old Mushi looked up at her with round, doe-like eyes. "I'll have one. And I'll trade you a bunch of my raisins for one of those dried figs."

Jonathan

When the penetrating trumpet signal blasted against the rocks again, the people put away their food and resettled themselves for the reading of the covenant law.[12]

Moses held up a parchment scroll. "These are the commands of the Lord," he announced. Twisting his head like an owl, he turned back to view the priests and Levites. They were packed behind him, beside him, below him—an army of Levites spilling out into the trail and onto ledges up and down the mountain.

Since the days of Adam, mankind has had only the oral teachings of their fathers and the stories written in the stars to teach them of God's ways. But this is a new day. He brought our people out of Egypt to be a holy nation unlike any other in the history of the world. You will settle the Land of Canaan, and the laws of Yahweh will be the law of the land. For the past forty years, I have taught you God's commands bit by bit as occasion arose. Many are recorded in the Book of the Exodus and in the Book of the Levites along with the regulations for purification and sacrifice. Those scrolls I penned at Sinai. For the past month I have been writing the Book of the Wanderings, beginning when our tribes were numbered for warfare at Sinai until now. Those stories are also interspersed with law—law intensified by the stories, stories intensified by the law. This new scroll is the summation of all my previous scrolls.

"Eleazar, my son." Moses presented the document to the high priest in ceremonial solemnity, but his eyes glittered with the excitement of a child. "I place this book into your hands. It is for you to cherish and protect as you do the sanctuary and its furnishings." He looked around again. "It is for you, my faithful Levites, to copy and preserve."

Jonathan recognized that roll. Moses had shown it to him on the mountaintop. The speeches he was recording for Grandfather were to be attached to this code of laws written in Moses' own hand. The honor of his connection to this scroll thrilled through him. He glanced at his cousin Phinehas who merely nodded in solemn thoughtfulness. Was there anyone who had even an inkling of the importance of this moment to him?

Moses' next announcement recaptured his full attention.

Here in the valley of Gilead, before you cross over into Canaan, I charge all Levites with this solemn responsibility—to teach these words. When our people settle in the Promised Land, you will spread out among the twelve tribes to instruct them and continually remind them of every decree that the Lord has given. Read this entire law in the hearing of all the tribes at the end of every seven years, as well as in the Year of Jubilee. When Israel gathers before the Lord for the Feast of Tabernacles in those years, assemble all men, women, and children—even the aliens living in your towns. Everyone must hear the words of the law so that they may understand and obey every word. The children who have never heard, must listen and learn to fear Yahweh our God. This is how the covenant will endure in the land you are crossing the Jordan to possess.

The challenge burned through Jonathan like fire. His drab opinion of Levi, the non-tribe in Israel, was gloriously transformed. Why had he ever viewed being Levite as a sacrifice? His tribe was privileged above all the others. He was the guardian of the words carved in stone—as well as every word penned on the parchment scrolls. Even the parts he transcribed for his grandfather would be housed in the gilded ark, in the heart of the tabernacle, along with the tablets of stone. That was an honor above any he had ever dreamed of. But higher yet—this commission to see that the words also found a home in the hearts of the people.

"Will you accept this solemn duty?" Moses asked.

Jonathan joined his voice to twenty thousand Levite voices, thundering a solemn "Yes, we will" back to Moses.

Moses nodded to the Levites. "Station yourselves throughout the crowds. The time has come to read this Book of the Covenant together.[13]

These are the rules and regulations that you must be careful to observe when you arrive in the Promised Land:

Demolish the sacred shrines of the Canaanite gods in every place where they were worshipped.

Do not offer your sacrifices just anywhere. That is the practice of the people of this land, setting up the altars of their vile worship on every high hill and in the shade of every verdant grove of trees.

Worship only at the dwelling place of Yahweh your God. After you cross the river seek out the place of his choosing and establish his tabernacle there. Bring all your sacrifices to that one place. Bring your burnt offerings to cover your sins. Bring the purification offerings that render mere mortals acceptable in the presence of immortal perfection. Bring your tithes and offerings to accompany vows. Bring your fellowship offerings for family feasts, remembering the blessings of God. Celebrate and sacrifice only in his presence at the tabernacle.

Do not eat any of your offerings at home. All must be offered on the central altar of Yahweh at his sanctuary for he will be your guest at these feasts. If you desire meat at other times, you may butcher animals from your flocks and herds. These are not offerings to the Lord even though they are the animals used for sacrifice. You may eat them at home just as you would eat deer and gazelle, but you must never eat the blood. The blood is the life, and you shall not eat the life with the flesh.

The sun moved higher into the sky as Eleazar and Ithamar took turns reading. As they finished each passage, the Levites echoed that section of the law from their positions throughout the tribes and then the people repeated the words with them.

Do not eat anything abominable such as the camel, the rabbit, or the pig.

Eat nothing from the water unless it has fins and scales.

Do not eat birds of prey.

Do not eat anything you find dead . . .

When the Lord blesses the sweat of your brow, collect a tithe of all the increase of your fields and your flocks and herds. Every three years, store up your tithes on your farms and in your towns to supply the Levites as well as the needy. In the other years, bring your tithe to the tabernacle and share it with the priests and Levites. Share it with the widows and orphans, the aliens and those who have no land. Invite them to celebrate the goodness of the Lord with your families. If the distance is too great to easily bring all your increase, you may sell it, and when you come to the tabernacle, use that money to purchase whatever delicacies your heart desires. Rejoice with great joy in the presence of the Lord with your family and with the Levites and those who have nothing.

At the end of every seventh year, there is to be a canceling of all debts owed by your fellow Israelites. Do not refuse a loan because the year of debt cancellation is close at hand. You must lend the poor man what he needs without complaint and the Lord will prosper you. You must not charge interest on such a loan.

If you buy Hebrew men or women as slaves, you must free them at the beginning of the seventh year. Remember how you were once slaves and the Lord freed you . . .

You may come to the Lord's tabernacle as often as you wish to celebrate his goodness or to seek forgiveness for sin, but three times each year all men must come before me without fail, bringing their families as far as possible. Do not fail to remember these three Feasts. In the first month of each year, when the barley harvest is ripe, remember my Passover. Then count the days for seven weeks, beginning with the first sickle-slash of grain. On the fiftieth day, come before the Lord to celebrate the Feast of Weeks with your families. Remember to invite the Levites and the poor. In the seventh month, when the last crops are gathered in, come to the dwelling place of the Lord once more with thanksgiving. Build yourselves temporary shelters for the Feast of Tabernacles. Camp in the presence of your God for an entire joyful week. Rejoice in fellowship and feasting, remembering how the Lord brought you from the Wanderings to your inheritance in Canaan. The Feast of Tabernacles is the grandest festival of the year.

People covered their heads to shade themselves from the sun. They paused for food and drink. They paused to stand and stretch. With only those short breaks, they listened and recited the law through the heat of the afternoon.

Appoint judges and officers in every town. Choose men who will judge fairly and honestly, who will never twist justice to benefit a rich man, who will never accept bribes. If justice prevails, you will be prosperous in this land.

If you see an animal wandering away, an ox, a cow, a sheep, or a goat, do not pretend you did not see it. It may be inconvenient, but take it back to its owner.

Every house must have a guardrail around the edge of the flat rooftop. If someone should fall off, the house and its owner are guilty . . .

When matters come up that are too much for you—cases regarding a wrongful death, conflicting pleas for justice, or disputes over rights – take them to the tabernacle for the High Priest or the Judge of Israel to decide. His decision is without appeal and must be carried out.

When you have conquered the land, you may begin to think you want a king like all the other nations around you. Your king must be the man the Lord chooses. He must be an Israelite. He must not amass great wealth, hoarding silver and gold. He must not build up a harem. Many wives will turn him from the Lord. He must not gather horses and chariots and the latest inventions of war, thus putting his trust in his powerful army. Your king must trust in the Lord of Hosts. When he has been crowned, the first thing he must do is to personally copy the words of this Book of the Covenant. He must keep the scroll at his side at all times. He must study it, live it every day, and in humble reverence obey all these rules and regulations exactly as they are written.

When war comes and vast numbers of horses and chariots fill the horizon, don't be frightened. The Lord your God who brought you out of Egypt is with you.

As afternoon shadows crept into the valley, the people wrapped their head cloths close to hold in warmth. And still they listened and recited.

> *Do not neglect the priests and Levites. Remember that they have not inherited property like the other tribes. Support them with your tithes and offerings. Give them the shoulder, the cheeks, and the stomach of every herd animal brought for sacrifice. Bring the first fruits of your harvests to the Lord with thanksgiving. The first of your grain, your new wine, your olive oil, and the first fleece of shearing time are for the priests and Levites—give generously. The Lord is the inheritance of the tribe of Levi. They own no property for the Lord has chosen them to minister in his name. Do not forget the Levite when you come to celebrate before the Lord.*
>
> *When you enter the Land of Promise, do not be curious about any of the detestable customs of the nations now living there. Do not even think of sacrificing your son or daughter in the fire. Do not corrupt yourselves with divination, sorcery, fortunetelling, witchery, casting spells, holding séances, or channeling with the dead. It is because of such practices that Yahweh your God is driving these nations out before you.*
>
> *And when God sends you a prophet like myself, who has Yahweh's words in his mouth, listen to him. If a prophet does not speak the words of Yahweh, and what he says does not come to pass, do not listen to him. He is a false prophet.*
>
> *Be completely loyal to Yahweh your God. You are a holy people, his treasured possession.*

When the priests had completed the reading of the entire Book of the Covenant, Moses began to explain the ceremony of blessings and curses that would crown the first Feast of Weeks across the river.[14]

> *You have two choices before you today. Two paths. One leads to blessings and the other to curses. If you obey the commands of Yahweh your God, you will reap a life of blessings. If you disobey, if you break your covenant vows by following strange, new gods, you will fall under the curses. When you have crossed the Jordan into that land flowing with milk and honey—and you will enter it just*

as he promised—you must gather in the heart of the land. There you will dedicate a public monument to this covenant law.

In an awe-inspiring ceremony, you will recite the blessings and curses—six tribes proclaiming the blessings from Mount Gerizim, six tribes proclaiming the curses from mount Ebal. These mountains are on the other side of the Jordan River. When you have crossed, follow the road west, toward the setting sun. The road will lead you to a valley between these mountains. There you will find the great terebinth tree of Moreh where your forefathers, Abraham and Jacob, built large stone altars and worshiped the Lord your God as a testimony to the nations of Canaan. When you arrive there, set up large slabs of stone on Mount Ebal. Coat them with plaster. Write the exact words of this law on those stones as an announcement to Canaan that Yahweh's law of love now rules the land.

Build an altar to Yahweh your God there, an altar of uncarved stones. Do not use any iron tool to mark it in any way. Before you celebrate, offer burnt offerings on my altar to atone for the sins of your forefathers and the sins of the land. Then sacrifice your thanksgiving offerings. You should be there in time for the Feast of Weeks. Eat this sacred meal together as families, rejoicing in the presence of the Lord. Your God will be a guest at that meal.

Be certain that every word of this law is written clearly on the plastered stones you have set up so all travelers on that road may read it. Yahweh your God wants every inhabitant of Canaan to know and understand that he has ordained justice and righteousness for his land.

A roar of voices exploded from the crowd. There were cheers. They would be crossing the river soon. They were on the brink of a whole new way of life. There were questions. In an eruption of confusion, everyone began discussing this ceremony and how soon it would take place.

"We will rehearse the blessings and curses now," Moses' voice thundered from the mountainside—but the words were lost in the uproar.

"We will rehearse that ceremony now," he repeated, "for I will not live to see it on the other side of the river."

He turned first to Eleazar and Phinehas, but father and son were so earnestly engaged in dialogue that they did not notice. He turned to Ithamar who stood fingering his silver trumpet as he watched the crowds. Again Moses called out, "Listen, my people, we must rehearse that ceremony so you will know how to proceed when I am gone."

Jonathan could not believe the bedlam on this day of days. The few Levites around him who were still watching Moses did not seem to comprehend the need to regain order. Moses' fourth attempt to outshout the people hit Jonathan with a staggering sense of urgency. There was so little time left with his grandfather. Still he was shocked when he heard the bold blast of his own voice. "Be silent, Israel, and listen. You have now become the people of your God."[15]

Catching the eye of a Levite nearby, he pointed to Moses and repeated the call, louder and stronger. "Be silent, and listen."

The man followed his lead and two others joined voices in unison. "Be silent and listen." He continued the repetition until more and more Levite brothers repeated the call in ever-widening circles, spreading through all the tribes like rings in water at the toss of a stone. "Be silent, Israel. You have now become the people of your God. Listen now! Moses has more instructions for you. Be silent and listen!"

Jonathan had never been more serious, but when he saw Phinehas stop talking and look at Moses, he nearly laughed out loud. His cousin's eyes widened in surprise, obviously realizing for the first time that Moses was waiting to speak. He couldn't help grinning at the way his cousin glanced down at the unused instrument in his hands and then at him. The name Phinehas might mean *mouth of brass*, but today the Lord had used another mouth. Like a war trumpet marshaling troops, Jonathan could not stop the wind of God's Spirit that blew through him. He was only a humble instrument, but his heart soared with the freedom of such leadership.

Soon every whisper ceased.

Phinehas and Eleazar exchanged approving glances. "Thanks be to our God," Eleazar said, beaming full approval at this bold, new Jonathan.

Moses raised his great shaggy head toward heaven and held up both hands. "Yes!" he cried. And Jonathan's heart flamed with the joy of a most glorious day.

Shua

Shua cracked the door of the North Wall Inn open cautiously, breathing a prayer to the God of Israel for protection. She had stuffed a meager lunch and a bag of personal belongings into her water pot in case circumstances forced her to stay for a time on the far side of the river. She was as prepared as possible, but there were huge unknowns. Walking toward the city center with the other women should seem a perfectly natural thing. Going beyond the city gates and sloshing through the rising fords of the Jordan could prove challenging. When her eyes became accustomed to the bright sunlight, she noticed three men lurking in the shadows across the street wearing the uniform of King Nahari's elite guard. *So. The challenge begins on my own doorstep. The king must be suspicious of one of our guests—his insanity could make anyone suspect.*

She took a deep breath and threw the door wide. Waving to the guards as she positioned the water jug on her head, she called out cheerfully, "Come on in and break your fast when you are off duty. Free food. We'd like to thank the king for posting a night watch so close to the inn."

Unsmiling, they watched her as she pranced down the steps directly toward them. The youngest of the guards locked eyes with Shua, but he was only a pimply-faced boy who did not appear to have lived more than a single score of years. She would not show fear, certainly not to the likes of him.

She blew him a kiss and then called out to the cluster of neighborhood women gathering in the street with their water jugs. "Good morning, my friends. Well met. Actually, *doorstep* met, and *well* intentioned."

The women giggled over her silly pun and immediately engaged her in light-hearted repartee as she fell in step. *First challenge met.*

Gradually Shua became aware of a rhythmic slapping following the cloud of chattering and snickering morning gossip. Her heart lurched. Sandals. Not far behind. Heavy sandals. Definitely not the tread of another water-pot-bearing woman. At the end of the street, she glanced over her shoulder. *It could be worse. Only the young guard. Surely she could shake him with ridicule.*

She turned and faced him brazenly. "Are you following me, you handsome man? I'll return to the inn soon. Why don't you wait for me there?"

He scowled at her. His steps faltered momentarily, but he resumed his solid steps toward her without response.

"Be careful, Shua," one woman whispered. "He may be chasing down one of the king's enemies. Don't get mixed up in that."

"Enemy? Perhaps . . ." She flashed a flirty smile as the young guard came closer. "I prefer thinking I have an admirer." As the other women stepped to the side of the roadway to let him pass, Shua reached out an age-spotted hand to touch his blemished cheek.

He jerked his head back. "Stupid old woman!"

Shua's companions burst into giggles. The guard's face flushed crimson, and he shot threatening glances at all of them, making no comment as he stormed past and turned into a side street.

The cluster of women merged with other groups as they left the narrow side street and soon a large merry party swept through the market toward the central well. When the young guard did not reappear, Shua took a deep breath to steady her nerves. "Don't wait for me," she chirped as she broke from the group and dove into the stream of morning traffic flowing through the gates into the city. "I need to see a merchant down this way before I fill my jug."

Many of the vendors were still setting up as she fought her way against the slow, steady current. No one else seemed to be heading away from the city center. She glanced warily over her shoulder to see how much progress she was making. The river of people had totally submerged her group of women. She could barely see a few water pots bobbing along the surface far away—but there, only a few yards behind her was that pimply-faced guard, the only face in a river of people moving the same direction she was. She instinctively turned her head before he could meet her eye. When she dared take a second glance, he was gone.

Shua's mind raced. *I will never shake this wearisome shadow with a water pot on my head. Too far from the well and the other women.* She frantically surveyed the merchants displaying their wares around her. *Hahzel!* Her eyes settled on the imposing stall draped gaily with colorful bolts of cloth on the far side of the roadway. She had traded with him for years. Checking the traffic behind her and still not seeing the young guard, she plunged cross-current to the textile merchant. As soon as she reached the portly vender, she cried, "Quick, my friend! No time for a proper greeting. I must leave my water pot here while I deliver a bundle to a friend. I have no time to explain."

Hahzel's eyes narrowed even though he laughed. "What no new fabrics today? Only a favor?"

Shua winked at him as she seized her small bundle from the pot. "Could I see your wares and leave with empty hands? I will return shortly to choose my fabric, but you will have to send it to the inn. I have not yet been to the well, and I would not want to risk spoiling the cloth with water before even cutting it."

She did not wait for his response, but plunged back into the stream of hopeful buyers and sellers. Again, she was the only one attempting to swim laboriously upstream. She bumped and jostled and dodged through the flowing river of people until she found herself bobbing in a stagnant pool close to the tariff tables at the gate.

She froze. Ahuzzath himself, along with a platoon of his elite hooligans, was stopping every person who came into the city. Entire caravans dwindled to a single line trickling past that hated man—and no one was leaving the city. She glanced behind her. The young guard was leaning against a wall watching her. He smiled triumphantly.

Be careful, Shua cautioned herself. *He is not as green as he appears.*

She made her way back to Hahzel's stall. "No luck," she laughed. "Give me a length of this lovely purple fabric. Send it to the inn for me and Jokshan will pay you." She formed a sling with her cloak as she talked and fastened her small bundle within it. It was an awkward bulge, swinging at her side, but she balanced the water pot on her head as gracefully as possible and headed to the well. For the first time that morning, she was truly afraid.

Returning to the inn with the water a short time later, she paused at the top of the steps. Not turning or even thinking to remove the heavy jug from her head, she waited and listened with her hand on the door latch. She had not seen the young guard since leaving the city gate, but just as she expected, the familiar foot slaps were following. The eyes of the two remaining guards were on her. She could feel them, but she steeled herself against showing fear.

"Such a protective shadow," she cooed, peering over her shoulder as the young man rejoined his companions. "You hardly let me out of your sight even when I looked for a friend I was to meet down by the gate. Come on inside. We can get better acquainted while we share sweetmeats and almonds. I will serve you our finest red wine."

The older guards chortled.

"I'm following orders, you old fool."

"I haven't heard *that* excuse before." Shua batted her stubby gray eyelashes and water splashed lightly onto her head. Without a pause, she lowered the water pot to the doorstep and asked. "What is your name, handsome?"

"Whoohoo!" one of the older guards roared. "Captain Ahuzzath is obsessed with Rahab, and now it seems young Shinab fancies the grandmother."

"His name is Shinab, old woman. Shinab will be following you everywhere you go."

"Hee, Hee. He may follow you to bed tonight."

Shua threw back her head and forced a loud coarse laugh even as her hope died. She picked up the water pot and entered the safety of the inn with tears gathering in her eyes. *O God of Israel, I am trying to get to you. Help me."*

Abihail

Abihail was weary. She and Eliab stood in the crowds cheering and tearing, moved and motivated through Moses' speech all morning. They sat listening carefully to the recitation of the law through the afternoon. Now that the sun had dropped toward its place of nighttime rest behind the western hills, she was thoroughly depleted. But Moses was organizing a practice ceremony of the blessings and curses.

"The tribes of Simeon, Levi, Judah, Issachar, Joseph and Benjamin, move to my right," Moses commanded. "When you have crossed over the Jordan, you six will stand on Mount Gerizim to bless Israel. Reuben, Gad, Asher, Zebulon, Dan and Naphtali, move to my left. You will stand on Mount Ebal to pronounce the curses."

Abigail and Eliab were already positioned where they needed to be. She leaned against Eliab's strength as eddies of people swirled and boiled around them, seeking their proper places. The tribes had barely settled into a temperate simmer, when trumpets blared and a chorus of Levite elders surrounding Moses began a roaring chant.

Cursed is anyone who makes an idol—a thing detestable to Yahweh, the work of skilled hands—and sets it up in secret.[16]

The six tribes of the curses echoed the words from the southern side of the valley. Then at Moses' direction, all the people shouted "Amen."

Cursed is anyone who dishonors their father or mother.

The six tribes repeated the curse. And again, the rest responded "Amen."

Cursed is anyone who moves their neighbor's boundary stone.

Abihail buried her face against the warmth of Eliab's chest. "Why does he begin with the curses?" she whispered.

"Amen," the voices around them roared.

"Best to end with blessings," he answered, wrapping his arms around her.

Cursed is anyone who leads the blind astray on the road.

"Amen."

Eliab traced a soothing circle on her back. His next words were all but drowned in the thundering recitation.

"We are going to . . ."

Cursed is anyone who withholds justice from the foreigner, the fatherless or the widow.

". . . obey God's law.

"Amen."

When the people had responded to twelve curses, Moses held up his hands to halt the rehearsal.

Evening is nearly upon us and the complete recitation is for another time and place. You now understand the procedure. The blessings will follow in just the same way as the curses, only it will be these tribes on my right hand repeating the recitation of the Levites. Again, all will respond with an "Amen" to signal your intent to obey. Great consequences attend your obedience or defiance of these laws. O, my beloved children, my desire burns hot for you to live faithfully by these commands, even as fear chills these old bones that you will not.

The emotion tugged at Abihail's own heart and brought tears to her eyes. Then, with a mustering of intense passion, the dear old man began listing the specific blessings that would be theirs if they only followed the commands of the Lord. There would be blessings on their cities and on their fields. There would be blessings on their gathering baskets and their kneading troughs. There would be blessings on their flocks and herds. She snuggled comfortably into the closeness of her husband's embrace as Moses promised the blessing of fruitful families.

The Lord will defeat any enemies who rise up against you. They will come out against you from one direction, but scatter before you in seven. O, how Yahweh your God will bless you in this land he is giving you! He will fill your barns and give you success in everything you put your hand to. He will send rain on your land according to each season. He will establish you as his holy people if you but keep his commands and follow his ways, and all nations will respect you. He promises this with an oath because he wants the kingdoms of earth to see the blessings that fall on those who belong to Yahweh.[17]

Abihail felt her strength revived by the promises. She lifted her head enough to catch Eliab's eyes and smile at what these promised blessings meant for them. In a few days they would cross the river and begin to live their dream. With such blessings showered over them, how could they help but flourish in the land of milk and honey? *Yes, my love, you were right. It is best to end with the blessings.*

Then without warning, the sweet promises were swept away.

If you forget your covenant with Yahweh—
Your cities will be cursed.
Your fields will be cursed.
Your baskets and your kneading troughs will be cursed.
Your wombs will be barren.
Your crops will wither.
Your calves and lambs will be stillborn.
Whether you come in or go out, everything you do will be cursed.[18]

More and more specific the curses came, a verbal battering of body and soul.

> The LORD will send on you curses, confusion and rebuke in everything you put your hand to, until you are destroyed and come to sudden ruin because of the evil you have done in forsaking him. The LORD will plague you with diseases until he has destroyed you from the land you are entering to possess. The LORD will strike you with wasting disease, with fever and inflammation, with scorching heat and drought, with blight and mildew, which will plague you until you perish. The sky over your head will be bronze, the ground beneath you iron. The LORD will turn the rain of your country into dust and powder; it will come down from the skies until you are destroyed.[19]

Moses completely reversed the abundance recited just moments before, but the onslaught continued.

> The LORD will cause you to be defeated before your enemies. You will come at them from one direction but flee from them in seven, and you will become a thing of horror to all the kingdoms on earth. Your carcasses will be food for all the birds and the wild animals, and there will be no one to frighten them away . . . Day after day you will be oppressed and robbed, with no one to rescue you. You will be pledged to be married to a woman, but another will take her and rape her . . . Your sons and daughters will be given to another nation, and you will wear out your eyes watching for them day after day, powerless to lift a hand . . . All these curses will come upon you. They will pursue you and overtake you until you are destroyed, because you did not obey the LORD your God and observe the commands and decrees he gave you. They will be a sign and a wonder to you and your descendants forever. Because you did not serve the LORD your God joyfully and gladly in the time of prosperity, therefore in hunger and thirst, in nakedness and dire poverty, you will serve the enemies the LORD sends against you.[20]

If only she could run. Run far from this message. But the crowds packed tight all around her and the long listening had left her too weary to move.

101

Make sure there is no man or woman clan or tribe among you today whose heart turns away from Yahweh our God to go and worship the gods of those nations. Make sure there is no root among you that produces such bitter poison.[21]

There was a long pause. Abihail glanced up, hoping the assault was over, but Moses' eyes bored straight into her.

Don't think you can get away with walking in your own stubborn way while breaking your solemn covenant with the Holy One.

He spoke as one who could read her darkest secrets.

Such a person will bring unspeakable disasters down on the entire land and everyone in it.[22]

"He knows," she whispered to Eliab. "He knows all about us." But when she looked at Moses again, the judgment fire in his eyes had been replaced by the warmest fatherly love. He stretched out his right hand, palm open as if offering a gift.

Now what I am commanding you today is not too difficult for you. It is not beyond your reach. No. The word of this law is very near you. You have been memorizing these commands all your lives. They are already in your mouth and in your heart so you may obey the Lord.[23]

Abihail drew in a long, deep breath. She whispered the words aloud so he could not mistake her devotion. "I will try, Moses. I will try to keep the word in my heart and mouth."

See, I set before you life and prosperity—or death and destruction. It is your choice. I plead with you today to love Yahweh your God, to walk in the path he laid out for his people. If you obey his covenant law, you will live an abundant life, blessed every day by Yahweh your God. But, if you turn away from him and forget his commands, and if you are enticed to bow down to other gods and worship them, I swear to you this day—that you will perish.

Moses stretched both hands up toward heaven as his concluding words blasted over the valley and reverberated against the hills.

This day I call heaven and earth as witnesses that I have set before you life and death, blessings and curses. The Lord is your life, and he wants to give you many years in the land he swore to give to your fathers: Abraham, Isaac, and Jacob. O, choose life, so that you and your children may live.[24]

Moses squeezed his eyes closed at the conclusion of his speech as if in prayer. That he loved them was certain, but had any group of people ever before in the history of the world endured such a dark blast of words?

The sun had already set the clouds ablaze above the western hills. Abihail did not need to look up. She felt the glory of the skies, but she could also feel the approach of the dark shadow of the western hills. Darkness from Canaan would soon swallow the light. Why did that darkness seem more solid, more real, than the light? Why did the curses seem more certain than the blessings? She trembled at the thought of how easily she and Eliab had been deceived. *Truly, O Lord my God, I do not want it to happen again.*

Eliab

Choose life . . .

Eliab wrapped his arms tightly around Abihail as the echo of Moses' final words faded. He knew the shaking of her body was not due to the evening breeze. There was nothing he wanted more than to remove the black cloud that chilled her sunshine and joy. But, how? To him it was a matter of logic. Moses had laid two roads before them. Two sets of consequences. The choice was theirs—curses or blessings. What she heard or understood was beyond him, but all too clearly he knew it arose from his own failure. If there was one thing he learned from the evil conniving

103

of those seductive Midianite women, it was that there was a time to be friendly and a time to flee. He vowed he would never be entrapped like that again. But how many sacrifices would it take to remove the effects of one wrong act? Mercy was an amazing gift extended to disobedience. But, how much better if he had never strayed from the life of blessings.

He released Abihail from his embrace and tucked her hand into the crook of his arm. "Come, my love. This long day is over."

She clung to him as he led her through the dispersing crowds. No bantering words. No smiles. Numb.

"Moses warns us of the curses because he loves us so much," he said gently as they followed the crowds. "The recitation of curses is necessary. It will help our people choose life. It will ensure that we receive only the blessings."

Even when he led her inside the security of their tent, Abihail didn't seem to recognize where they were.

"Look around you, my love," he said with a light-hearted laugh. "We are already reaping blessings. We are blessed to have each other and this little tent. The rest of the blessings will be ours if we obey." When he took her hands and squeezed them gently, she gave him a feeble smile. "The curses never have to happen if we obey the law. Moses was just trying to make that point clear."

"No, Eliab. It was not Moses, but Yahweh himself making his point clear." Dark terror filled her eyes. "I stood before the judgment seat of God today, and I did not measure up. I felt the power of the curses crushing my soul—and it was no more than I deserved."

In a rush of passionate, protecting love, Eliab pulled her trembling body against himself and brushed his nose softly over her silky cheek. No tears. She was beyond tears. "God is good, my darling. You are good, not rebellious. Focus on the blessings. Imagine them. Our future. Our reality. An abundance of food. A house filled with beautiful and useful things . . ." He began kissing the smooth curve of her neck. "And many children."

Abihail pulled away. "Stop, Eliab. I need to talk to you about the gifts we got from the Midianites. Acsah said we should burn them."

"Acsah doesn't appreciate beauty like you do." He kissed the lovely arch of each of her eyebrows. "Moses said nothing about those gifts."

"Eliab, you are distracting me." Her dimples flashed ever so briefly. "The dark reality is that we have chosen to keep contaminated things in our tent. And I still love those things."

"Did you hear a single law today against keeping them? How are they different than the Midianite plunder that every single person in camp received?"

"But . . . when I am with Acsah, I feel . . . I don't know . . . *unclean* . . ."

Eliab lifted her chin gently and kissed her nose. "Then don't spend so much time with Acsah."

"Eliab, she has been my best friend my whole life."

"Don't get me wrong. She is my friend too . . . but now . . . she even makes me feel guilty."

Abihail's eyebrows lifted with surprise. "Guilty? About . . .?"

"That's just it. Everything. Since the plague, I feel as if she still views me as an adulterer and a Baal-worshipper."

Abihail's full beautiful smile lit her face for the first time in hours. She flailed her pointer finger at him. "You *should* feel guilty about that. You belong to me, not some temple goddess."

The words cut like a cold metal blade. "I can tell you truthfully that I will never get caught up in anything like that again. I offered my sin offering on the altar and the Lord accepted it. Please accept me now as a new man." He laid his finger on her lips. "Let's never mention it again."

Abihail backed away from him and fell to her knees on her pallet. She pulled a purple veil from a basket nearby and fingered it lovingly. "You don't understand." Her words were nearly inaudible.

He dropped down beside her, lifted her chin, and looked into her open, honest, and somber eyes. "I want to," he said.

"Acsah inspires me to be better, not simply feel guilty. She was so angry the day she found out about these gifts."

"Well, there you go. Spend less time with her and more with me. Think blessings." He pushed her softly back onto her pillow and swathed the lustrous fabric around her head. "Stunning in purple. Perfect for a blessed, fruitful mother in Israel." He brushed her hair back from her face and bent so close that his breath tickled her ear. "Think blessings," he whispered.

She closed her eyes and relaxed, letting his words and loving touch caress away her fears. "You are the only blessing I ever want or need," she sighed.

He slipped the silky purple veil off the pillow and tucked it back into the basket. "That is for the public eye. For me, simply you . . ." He loosened her robe and pressed his lips into the soft cleavage of her breasts. " . . . and the blessing of love."

She raked her fingers through his hair and pulled him close to encourage more kisses. "O Eliab, I don't need a Midianite veil to feel beautiful when I have your love."

"You have it. All my love." As his lips brushed the soft warmth of her skin, he willed her to believe there would never be anyone else for him—ever again. "And when I am not making love to the mother of my many, many children . . ." Her breath quickened as he caressed the abdomen that they both hoped would swell with new life soon. "She will be draped in ornaments of gold and soft, shimmering fabrics. This purple veil, but the first—"

"Stop." Abihail shook herself free of his spell. She pushed herself up on her elbows. "Don't speak so. Acsah said my greed blinded me to the evil purposes of those Midianite women. I know in my heart that she is right."

"I say she is wrong. You are not a greedy woman, Abihail. Surely God is not angry just because you received a few of the beautiful things you deserve." He cupped her face in his hands again and began covering it with kisses.

"You're trying to distract me again," she said, giggling at the soft tickling of his beard along her jawbone.

"Not distract—" he murmured as she settled back onto the pillow. "*End* this cursed conversation and get back to the blessings."

Abihail pressed her lips against his and pulled him into an embrace that boiled through him like fire.

CHAPTER FOUR

A TIME TO MOURN

Jonathan

It was the end. The farewell messages of love and warning had been spoken. The final words recorded on parchment. Jonathan plodded to the assembly, feet sheathed in lead. *O God, I've only begun to see how much I need him. Could you not give us just one more year?*

This ceremony would officially end the era of Moses and initiate the era of Joshua—and he was late. Throughout a long sleepless night, he was utterly consumed by an irrational fear that his grandfather would suddenly disappear like Enoch of old. More likely, Moses would bless his family as the patriarch Jacob had, then return to his tent or climb the mountain with Eleazar to draw his last breath and die. However it was going to happen, Jonathan did not want to miss a moment of his grandfather's final hours on earth. But when the trumpet summons jolted him out of a groggy slumber, he discovered it was already long past dawn.[25]

As he shouldered his way through the clot of Levites waiting within the tabernacle courtyard, every thought was grief-fogged, shapeless and gray. But one thing he knew with clarity, late or not, the back of the crowd would not do today. He was not just a Levite. Not just a scribe. He was Moses' grandson. His fellow tribesmen seemed to understand that and parted willingly as he pressed his way as close as he dared to the spot where Grandfather stood. Behind Moses' powerful frame, the flames licked the remnants of the morning sacrifice. The incense had been offered, the area of sacrifice restored to perfect order, and the priests were arranged on either side of the altar waiting; Eleazar and Phinehas on the right, Ithamar and his sons on the left. There was an aura of the eternal about the tabernacle, the priests—the entire system of worship—but none of it would exist if it were not for this man. For that matter, not one of the people in this crowd would be here if Moses had not led their parents out of Egypt.

Jonathan could see that Grandfather was feeling the pain of separation too. He cleared his throat and opened his mouth to speak. Then, as if words would not come, he closed it and simply let his eyes sweep over his people, gathering his children to himself one last time. Jonathan wanted to burn the image into his memory forever. The deep amber eyes filled with wisdom, love, and longing. The great white mane and beard. The craggy, sun-bronzed face and broad weathered forehead. This was not age but immutability. Moses was like the ancient hills surrounding this valley. He was more than a master to serve, more than a commander to obey, more than a grandfather to respect and love. For forty years, he had been the very voice of God to Israel. It was impossible to think of life without him. Joshua was a good man, but not an exceptional one. The thought of entering the Promised Land without Moses did not seem so promising.

Moses signaled for Joshua to come to his side at the courtyard entrance, and the rustling robes and scrabbling sandals gave way to a total gray silence as the silver-haired commander trudged reluctantly into place, almost crouching like a dog in trouble with his master. He too was reeling from the impending separation. Even after Moses placed a reassuring hand on his aide's shoulder, Joshua remained hunched with lowered eyes, a lean shadow beside his master's powerful frame. For the first time in his life, Jonathan felt a kinship with this man, and he was glad it was Joshua being consecrated today instead of himself.

Moses squeezed Joshua's shoulder encouragingly and raised his other hand toward heaven. In it he held a thick parchment scroll.

My son, I prayed that the Lord would appoint a shepherd for my people before I departed. He chose you, Joshua, a man filled with his Spirit. Take this copy of the Book of the Covenant. Keep it ever at your side. Read from it daily. Consult also with Eleazar the priest. He will pray for you, and he will advise you in the presence of Yahweh. He will consult the Urim and Thummim of the holy breastplate for you. You have served me faithfully for four decades. You well know that God's power, not mine, brought these people from Egypt to this place. You will lead them into their inheritance by that same power.

Joshua's shoulders trembled.

Moses pressed the scroll into his hands and leaned close to Joshua's ear. "He has called you for this role, and it will unfold exactly as He wills." He spoke the words in a low voice for Joshua alone. Jonathan wasn't certain if he actually heard or only read his grandfather's lips, but either way his heart knew the words. It was the same truth that lifted him out of his sinkhole of despair. The same truth that gave him hope after the ground under his feet disintegrated at Acsah's rejection. The powerful teaching was all the more dynamic coming from the lips of such a man as Moses. Grandfather not only believed it, he had lived it.

Joshua took the parchment and clasped it tight against his chest, nodding silently without an upward glance. Moses regarded his reluctant replacement silently for a moment, then trumpeted the commission so no one in that vast crowd could say they did not hear.

Receive now the full magisterial authority I received from God. You are the commander of this war camp of righteousness, Yahweh's army on earth. At your command, they will go out. And at your command, they will come in. You will lead the tribes of Israel across the river into the land the Lord promised to your forefathers. You will divide it among them as their inheritance. The forces of evil cannot prevent it.

Joshua raised his eyes, connecting with the eyes of his master.

Yahweh himself will go before you. Yahweh himself will stand beside you. He will never leave you. Only be strong and courageous.

While the blare of the announcement still rang in their ears, the cloud overshadowing the tabernacle fumed with heavenly fire. Joshua followed its pulsing billows heavenward, and its light transformed his face. "The heartbeat of Yahweh," he shouted, and for the first time that morning, he stood straight and strong.

The misty, leaden atmosphere that had plagued the day thus far evaporated. With a whooshing wind the cloud left its place and swirled around Moses and Joshua. It wrapped its ethereal arms around them in one blinding swirl of light and then roiled upward, stretching toward the sun, forming a flaming pillar directly over their heads—a heavenly monument permanently seared into memory. No one in that crowd could ever question the source of Joshua's authority.

But Yahweh was not finished. Divine words pealed over the valley repeating the commission with ear-splitting claps of thunder. *Be . . . Strong . . . And . . . Courageous.* Lightning flashed from the cloud with the crashing of each word.

At the booming sound, the crowd turned to stone. Jonathan wondered what the people across the river heard. Surely the message resounded from these hills all the way to the hills surrounding Jericho. Did they dismiss this as a manifestation of their own storm god Baal? Or did they wonder and tremble, hearing the undeniable message in that thunder as clearly as he heard it?

The roar of thunderbolts continued. "I promised with an oath that I would bring my people into Canaan. You, Joshua are the one I have chosen to do it. I myself will be with you. *Be . . . Strong . . . And . . . Courageous.*"

The clear words gave way to great rumblings, a sound like driving rain intermingled with thunder. The crowds remained transfixed. A few hunched in fear. Joshua fell prostrate on the ground. Moses alone lifted his face, listening attentively to the incessant thrumming. He alone seemed to comprehend a message in that roar. At last, the cloud had its say and drifted back to its place overshadowing the tabernacle. The silence that followed was so profound that even Moses dared not let human words distract from the encounter with Yahweh. He dismissed the people by a simple brushing of the air and no one spoke so much as a word as they returned to the tasks of the day.

Jonathan remained where he was, watching the people disband. He watched Moses lead Joshua to the laver and pour water over his head and hands. He watched Moses place his massive hands on Joshua's shoulders and then waited through a long, urgent dialogue. He did not wish to intrude, but he was determined to cling to Grandfather until the final hour.

With a sting of shame, he recalled his recent misgivings. *No. Call it what it was. Jealousy.* Now, as he watched the humble captain nodding in response to Grandfather's words, it was difficult to understand why he had ever harbored such resentment. It was enough for him to be a Levite, teacher of Grandfather's words and spokesman for Yahweh. He was born to teach those scrolls. Joshua was born to run the camp and lead the people into battle.

When the conversation finished, Joshua loped off, a more confident man than the one Jonathan observed as the ceremony began. Moses watched wistfully until his long-time assistant disappeared through the courtyard entrance. Only then did he acknowledge Jonathan with a wry smile. "Do not look so sad, my boy. I will not leave today. Come. Climb the mountain with me one last time."

One last time. In spite of the *I-will-not-leave-today* promise, a last trek up the mountain sounded ominously like the climb Moses' brother, Aaron, took last year—to his grave. Jonathan's misgivings increased as they trudged up the familiar trail. The path was enveloped in a damp gray mist. Then, halfway up the trail, Grandfather's lighthearted demeanor reverted to oppressive melancholy, and Jonathan's apprehension increased in proportion to the old man's sighs. When they reach the viewpoint at the top of the trail, Grandfather paused as usual. He drew in a deep breath, letting

111

it escape slowly and noisily through pursed lips. Without so much as a perfunctory glance to see if the valley below was visible in this fog, he scrabbled through his bag of writing materials. He retrieved a quill, then remained motionless for a very long time, fingering it with what seemed like dread, regarding it as a mortally-wounded warrior might gaze on his sword. As if he were conjuring up the courage to fall on it.

Jonathan broke the baleful silence. "What are you going to write, Grandfather?"

Moses didn't look at him. "I have to tell them."

Jonathan knew better than to ask what. He seated himself beside the large rock Grandfather always used and studied the rounded contours of its saddle-like top, buffed free of much of the normal gritty exterior of the surrounding rocks. How many days? How many hours of scroll writing did that represent? Jonathan wished there could be time for his smaller rock to acquire a similar polish.

"Yahweh spoke to me from the cloud this morning," Moses finally said.

"Yes. We saw."

"Humankind is allowed to see but one day at a time. Oh, Jonathan, that is best. It is a dreadful thing to have the Lord pull back the curtain to the future."

Misty clouds had shrouded this day from the beginning, even obscuring the view from the Heights of Inspiration. *Like the future* Jonathan mused. *But the cloud hovering over the heart of camp was something different. The voice might reveal terrifying things about the future, but the cloud was past, present, and future swirled into one visible symbol. Human leaders will die and be replaced by others, but the Eternal will remain.* The reality of that cloud was suddenly very comforting.

Moses handed the quill to Jonathan at last and dropped heavily onto his stone seat. "This is what the Lord God said: *You are going to rest with your ancestors, and these people will soon prostitute themselves to the foreign gods of the land they are entering. They will forsake me and break the covenant I made with them.*"[26] A tear traced a line from the corner of his eye to his beard. For the first time Jonathan could remember, Grandfather looked old.

"How blessed I am to have the comfort of your presence with me today, my boy. Would that I had gone to my grave believing that Israel's future would be a better one."

"What is to be done?"

"Only warn them. There is nothing more for me to do. My work is finished." He studied Jonathan's eyes for a long uncomfortable moment. "But the covenant . . . God's words . . ." Grandfather's voice trembled with emotion and he paused to gain control of it.

"May his voice echo long over this land like a lion's mighty roar. May it keep God's people faithful. And when they are not—when they forsake the Lord who led them out of Egypt with a mighty hand—may these words draw them back again."

Jonathan swallowed to ease the constriction in his throat. "Go to your rest in peace, Grandfather. I have dedicated my life to teaching the law and the covenant. The past week has changed me forever."

Moses pulled out a fresh strip of parchment. "We have work to do. Yahweh gave me a song. *Write it down,* he said, *and teach it to Israel.* After I am gone, Jonathan, attach it to my last scroll."

Jonathan took the parchment and prepared to write.

"*Have them sing it,* the Lord said. *Have them learn it, so that it may be a witness against them.*" Moses's amber eyes brightened, refocusing on some far-away vision. "Oh, that it is more—much more. May this song hold back the forces of evil for a long, long time."

The next day dawned miserably. The entire valley was overcast with a solid mantle of gray, erasing every outline of the surrounding mountain peaks. The chill drove through the people, body and soul, as they responded to the trumpet summons and gathered at the site of the farewell speeches. Moses waited for them on the rocky ledge of the grand orations, but no sunlight caused his form to glow today. He appeared thinner, as if the passion he had poured into the discourses of the past week had diminished his robust body and left it spent.

The people unconsciously leaned toward him, expecting to strain at the frail voice of a dying man, but Moses' final words blasted over them, as strong and clear as ever. "I am now one hundred and twenty years old and am no longer able to lead you.

Moreover, Yahweh Your God said to me, "You shall not cross the Jordan." But do not be dismayed, Oh my people. Yahweh himself will cross over ahead of you. Yahweh will destroy the nations before you, and you WILL take possession of their land. Joshua will lead you across the river, as the Lord said, and Yahweh will do to your enemies over there as he did to Sihon and Og. He WILL deliver them into your hand.

Be strong and courageous. Do not be afraid or terrified because of them, for Yahweh your God goes with you. He will never leave you nor forsake you. Only remember to do all that I commanded you.

Suddenly shattering the stately atmosphere, he burst forth in song.

Listen, you heavens, and I will speak;
Hear, you earth, the words of my mouth.
Let my teaching fall like rain
and my words descend like dew . . .[27]

He interrupted himself with a long musical laugh. "Listen now, my dear children, and learn a new song."

Bounding off the platform with the energy of a young man, he began descending the trail as he explained.

It is a song of the righteousness and mercy of our God. It is a song of the blessings and the curses—the faithfulness of Yahweh and the unfaithfulness of man. Fix these words in your hearts and minds. Sing them in your homes with your children, and sing when you work in the fields. Sing when you gather for the great feasts of the Lord, and sing when you commune with him in solitude. Let this song guard

*your hearts so that you never follow after the gods of this land. And
Yahweh will bless you above all peoples on the earth.*

When Moses reached the valley floor, he moved through the
crowds, gripping the shoulders of his princes and elders one by
one, lovingly brushing the many hands reaching out for one last
touch. For the next few hours, he walked among the tribes as he
sang out the song line by line. The elders of each clan echoed the
phrases, and the people repeated them yet again until the hills rang
with a reverse echo that grew louder and more emphatic with each
repeating.

When Moses was satisfied that the teaching of the song was
complete, he began to pass through the ordered ranks of Israel for
the last time. Making his way toward the mountain, he called down
a blessing on each tribe that he passed. Reuben . . . Simeon . . .
Judah . . . and then Levi. With a familial tenderness, Moses blessed
his own tribe. Each of his family members received a look of special
affection as he pronounced the Levite blessing, and Jonathan was
not ashamed of the tears coursing down his cheeks. Those tears
rose not from despair, but from an ocean of ardent determination.

> *[Levi] teaches your precepts to Jacob,*
> *And your law to Israel . . .*
> *Bless all his skills, LORD,*
> *And be pleased with the work of his hands.*[28]

Jonathan slipped his hand into the shoulder bag Moses had
bequeathed to him. He felt the cool parchment of that final scroll
under his fingers. *I will add your final words to this book, Grandfather,
as you asked. As a scribe and teacher in Israel, I will copy every word
you wrote. First for myself and then for others. May I be as faithful to
my task as you have been to yours.*

Another motivation, perhaps less noble, but no less passionate,
played in the shadowy recesses of his consciousness. *Perhaps thus
I will earn the respect and love of my beautiful Acsah.*

The remaining nine tribes, waiting for Moses' final blessing,
huddled close to the roots of Mount Nebo as if to draw strength

from the ancient rocks. When the last blessing had been spoken, Moses began ascending the trail, stopping a short way up the path to raise his hand in a silent benediction. Then, resolutely, and with great dignity, he resumed his final journey. The sun burst from the clouds, igniting the outline of the mighty man of God and casting a long, lonely shadow behind him.

The sight stung Jonathan's heart. No one should die alone. Aaron had gone off in the company of his son and his brother. He died in Moses' arms. Then, together Moses and Eleazar buried him on Mount Hor. He checked the urge to run after his grandfather, to minister to him one last time. Moses' own words echoed in his mind. "God commanded me to climb this mountain alone. He will show me the whole Land of Promise from the highest peak of Pisgah. Then the Lord himself will lay my body in the ground—in an unmarked grave. I could not bear the thought that my final resting place would ever become a shrine."

Jonathan swallowed hard and tried to picture Moses falling asleep in the arms of God.

The crowds remained weeping at the foot of the mountain long after the hovering clouds cloaked the last glimpse of Moses. A light rain fell, yet the people lingered until the time of the evening sacrifice. Joshua announced a period of thirty days of mourning, but it was not a necessary command. Crushed and desolate, no one had the heart to do more than what was absolutely necessary.

As the days wore on, the people honored Moses in various ways. Tuneful strains floated from tents where little groups rehearsed portions of Moses' final song. Others gathered out in the meadow with friends in spite of the drizzle, huddling close to the rocky foot of Mount Nebo where Moses' final words were spoken as if that might help them remember. As the rainfall continued evening after evening, family groups packed into tents to share stories as they would have around campfires and were startled to rediscover, through the recounting of these tales, how many amazing things Moses had done. Jonathan slipped from tent to tent and proudly read portions of his grandfather's powerful words to all who cared to listen.

Abihail and Eliab

For two weeks, warm spring rain fell on the valley as if the heavens wept with the people of Israel. Then, the weather cleared. Abihail was animated by that change—as well as by a shower of parting kisses. She tackled her morning chores with energy and laughter—energy because the power of cloudless sunlight was so quickly drying the soggy landscape; laughter because Eliab was hardly going far enough to merit such a farewell. He had already been to the meadow and back and had milked both cows and put them with their little flock of sheep out to pasture in the care of one of Caleb's grandsons. Now she could hear him rattling and clanking behind their tent, spreading tarps out to dry and checking their tools and stored supplies for water damage. She supposed that after being weather-bound indoors together for so long, a tent between them seemed like a mountain.

The two large crocks of fresh milk he set beside the tent door were begging her to transform them to cheese. Abandoning, for the time being, the countless tasks that had accumulated for her during the rains, she chose a sunny spot to set up her little cheese tent. The strong heat of this day would create curds very quickly so she left the flaps at the ends of the tent halfway open. She held her hand inside for a moment. The heat was building very quickly. She would have to check throughout the day to keep it from becoming too hot. She did not want to repeat the day she had killed the cheese and had to throw out a sour, watery mess.

A surly growl startled her. "Where is Eliab?"

She knew without looking up that this was Jamin. No one but Eliab's older brother would speak so rudely without so much as a proper *Shalom* of greeting. Abihail responded with practiced sweetness. "Shalom, Jamin. We are honored by your visit. Would you care for a cup of fresh warm milk? Eliab just brought this straight from the cows, much more than we need."

"I need Eliab," Jamin ordered demandingly. "Tell him Father wants him now. We're loading the wagons."

He had already begun walking away when Eliab appeared. "What is going on? Did I hear you say 'loading the wagons?'"

Jamin stopped but didn't turn around. "Have you seen the river? The fords are nearly past using. Father wants your help now. We're going across."

Eliab frowned. "Joshua hasn't given any orders to cross, so . . . why are *you* giving orders? You are not going alone are you?"

Jamin hurled a scowl over his shoulder with a throaty and threatening reply. "Don't think that being a married man makes you my equal. Father and I have decided. Any family member who wants to load anything onto the family wagons needs to help with Father's packing—today."

Eliab laughed nervously. "Well, I certainly can't carry all our belongings on my back, but . . . cross now? Alone?"

"The warriors of Reuben, Gad, and Manasseh are urging all men of war to follow them. They agreed to lead the army of Israel in fighting the Canaanites, but the river is rising daily. They don't want to wait until the dry season makes the fords accessible again."

"I thought they were rebuilding the homes and stables here for their families."

"They're finished. They will leave their families here just as they arranged with Moses. The rest of Israel needs to decide. Cross now with them, or wait months until the river subsides."

"And Joshua . . .?"

"Joshua hasn't said anything. He is no leader. He has always been Moses' shadow. With our real leader gone, he doesn't know what to do."

Jamin turned to fully face Eliab, delivering his final challenge with fists balled against his waist, elbows flaring like wings. "Father and I are committed to go fight with the army. Mara and Hattil want to go with us now and set up camp on the other side. If we don't load up and cross in the next few days, it will be too late. Are you with us or not?"

Abihail could tell that Eliab was as uncomfortable with this situation as she was. The family ties had been stretched almost to breaking since the night on Baal-Peor. *What harm could come of helping Achor pack? She and Eliab could still wait here, east of the river, and cross when Joshua directed.*

"You should go help your father, Eliab," she said quietly.

Eliab reluctantly followed his scowling brother, but the situation only became worse when the two of them reached the family wagon. Achor was lashing piles of tools and utensils into bundles. Those were mostly the familiar things Eliab had grown up with, but Mara and Hattil scuttled from tent to wagon bringing bag after bag that clinked like silver coin. Both women darted back and forth with anxious faces, looking this way and that—furtive and silly as a pair of squirrels who had come upon a trove of acorns guarded by a hawk. Foolhardy squirrels that found the treasure worth more than the risk. The women did not give Eliab so much as a nod, but Achor noticed his stare and responded with a broad smile.

"I was right, Jamin. I knew the boy would come to help his father." He seized a bag from Mara's hands before she could add it to the pile and shook it, his grin growing even wider at the metallic jingling. "I'll reward your labor well. Climb up and pile these at the front of the wagon. It is going to be a lot of weight."

Jamin only glowered as Eliab complied. His brother never seemed happy. His father, on the other hand, had never been more jubilant. "Midianite silver," he crooned, passing two of the bags up to Eliab.

Eliab added them to a row that nearly spanned the breadth of the wagon. He glanced down at the bags remaining on the ground. "I thought the Midianite plunder was divided equally." He forced a playful tone to mask his alarm. "How is it that my allotment is so small in comparison to yours?"

Jamin rolled his eyes. "That's why I didn't want him helping, Father."

"Shush, my son. He should know our little secret."

As Eliab reached down to retrieve another pair of bundles from Achor's uplifted hands, his father lowered his voice confidentially.

"We got our share and then some. Jamin was appointed to help carry our clan's portion to the Levites. He planned his route carefully so he went directly past our tent while Mara and I waited just inside the open door to relieve him of some of that burden. We posted Hattil outside the tent door spinning wool and keeping watch for nosy neighbors. She's a clever girl. Played her role well, feigning some need as often as necessary to detain her dear husband until the path was clear and he could hand the bags off to us. Look at all this silver. We haven't even crossed the river and just look at our wealth!"

"But it was for the tabernacle."

Achor's eyes glittered. "A waste. They would melt it down to make more bowls and platters for the priests. Enough already. Now it is Achor's turn."

"*And* Mara's," his mother said, dropping her next bag on Achor's foot.

"Oi!" Achor exaggerated the effort needed to extract his foot out from under the bag of silver. "And Mara's." He grabbed his wife and danced her around the piles of implements. "Hee- hee. We're on our way to being the richest Israelites in Canaan."

Suddenly, deadly serious, halting the dance, he let go of Mara and looked both ways for anyone who might stumble upon their work and overhear him. "We managed to get some of their sheep and goats too. That's why we must be among the first to cross. We have scrubbed and carefully clipped at the fur around the Levite mark, but you can still see it when you look closely. I don't want any nosy Levites noticing before time erases it completely."

Eliab added the two bags to the row and paused. Speechless. *What should he say?*

Achor laughed. "Don't look so horrified. We didn't actually *steal* anything since the Levites hadn't taken possession of it yet. They never even knew how much they had. It will be fine, Son. As soon as our things are loaded up, we will help with yours and Abihail's. I'll give you a goat for your effort. You don't have a lot of material goods yet, but Jamin and I will teach you to live smart."

Eliab looked numbly at the next two bundles his father held up to him. He wanted no part of deceitfully-gained wealth, but this was his father. Honoring your parents was as much a part of the commandments carved in stone as "Do not steal." His hands shook as he reached down and took the silver. *Abihail can't shake her guilty feelings just because we own legitimate Midianite gifts. How can I ever tell her about this?*

Salmon

The stars gleamed bright that night in a rain-washed sky. Noisy family campfires echoed across the valley for the first time in weeks, but Salmon stared into the leaping flames, disconnected from the singing, clapping, and banter around him. In the days following Moses' death, when constant rain had driven the people to the shelter of their tents, Salmon took comfort in the somber blanket of grief over the camp. The sudden change to fellowship and joy tonight jarred him to the core. He stood abruptly and left the circle of light.

Every day without Abba was a dark cave of despair. Could a home be more dismal and empty? No merry morning greetings. No teasing. No laughter. No eyes sparkling at shared jokes. His mother had to remind him to eat. She pushed steaming bowls of food in front of his face. "It won't help the family if you starve to death and we lose you too," she repeatedly reminded him. She would pinch his cheek and try to laugh as if it were a joke, but her red-rimmed eyes reminded him that these days were hard for her too. On top of his personal loss was a terrifying sense of insufficiency. The elders of Judah were coming to him in droves with the needs of the tribe. He didn't know how to replace his father in the home, let alone in the role of Judah's prince. A thousand questions came to mind that he wished he had asked his father. Before.

Always in the small sorrows of his childhood, Acsah had been there. Always wise. Always strong. Now, in the greatest loss of his life, she seemed to be avoiding him. Help came unexpectedly from Jonathan of all people, a subdued and meticulous Jonathan who had taken the time to copy all the words of Moses' final orations. Death had stolen from Jonathan too. But it seemed to give his life focus. While Salmon remained dismal and dazed by his loss, Jonathan dazzled with vitality and joy as he presented the scroll to him as a gift.

"Just in case God calls the new Prince of Judah to be our king," he said with his irrepressible laugh. "It is written in the law that any future king of Israel must read this book and live by it daily."

King? Hah! Salmon had more responsibility now than he wanted to deal with. But the scroll was proving to be a priceless gift for a boy who simply missed his father. Each day, as soon as he finished helping Abijah with the daily chores, he found a quiet place to study. Those hours immersed in the words of Moses were slowly reshaping him, giving him a larger horizon for viewing the events of his life. More and more often, a story came to mind when he didn't know what to do. Or a promise popped into his head when Ada or his mother needed to be reminded to trust in the goodness of God. Tonight, however, he needed someone to remind *him*.

He walked on, welcoming a growing silence. The rushing song of the river soothed him at the same time that it drowned the gleeful echoes of campfire fellowship. He glanced up. Star stories. Patterns of light and truth, sparkling with promise, clearer and brighter the farther he got from the dancing firelight. Promises as real as the stars—but both beyond his reach.

He stopped. *No! More than beyond reach. Vanished.* He stared at the dark, hulking hill that obliterated the night sky directly in front of him. It not only blacked out the stars, it expunged all his melancholy musings. This was the Simeonite high place of anarchy and death—the site of his father's murder.

The horror of that day slammed full-force against his chest. What malevolent force had led him *here*? He tightened his jaw and refused to crumple under its blow of despair. "It is just a hill now," he said aloud. "We cut down the polluted grove. We scraped all remnants of Baal worship from that foul high place." Looking higher, he could make out the outline of the summit, black against the starry sky. A bald dome now, but for one lone sapling.

"That is *me*," he whispered into the night, amazed at the bond he felt with that wisp of a tree. "Alone. You and I, scraggly one, alone on the heights, exposed to withering blasts of heat or storm. I grew up like you, a shoot protected by a forest of giants: Moses, Aaron, my Abba. Now? They're gone. Moses is gone. Aaron is gone. Prince Nashon of Judah, my father, axed at the root on the day of evil, along with so many others. All fallen like the lovely grove that once crowned this hill." A chill shivered through him at the thought of what Baal worship had wrought. "Be strong, little tree. I wish you well." Salmon intentionally turned away from the Simeonite hill and made his way to his father's grave.

The simple pile of river rock marking the burial site was more comforting than gloomy tonight. This was the first time he had come here alone. He flung himself down on the tangible connection to the joy and security of his childhood. A tear slid down his cheek onto the smooth, water-washed stones. "I love you, Abba." Suddenly he could not hold back a flood of deep, convulsive sobbing. *O God, I need him. Our family needs him. All Judah needs him. Help us. Israel needs a strong leader. A man like my father. I simply am not strong. The good people of Judah need a prince. What they have is a boy. O God, help me.*

His choking sobs gradually subsided, but the grief that flowed out in those tears left him drained. For a long time he lay there listening to the soothing rustle of leaves and the pulsing tweedle of crickets. The night wrapped around him with the warm comfort of a blanket, and he drew solace and strength from the solid stones that marked his father's grave. Reason argued that he should return to the bright fires of camp. To his mother and sister. To duty. But here he felt his father's strength. There he was just a boy mimicking a man.

He had no idea how long he had lingered in this somber place, soaking up quietness and peace, when unannounced footsteps crunched in the gravel close by.

Man or beast?

Salmon scrambled awkwardly off the cairn and stared into the darkness. At his movement, a good-natured, but hesitant voice called out. "Hello?" *The speaker was definitely human.*

"Is someone there?" the voice asked.

Definitely Israelite. The steps moved closer.

Salmon, irritated by the bold intrusion, brusquely questioned the dark shape emerging from the shadows. "Who asks?"

"I'm looking for Salmon, son of Nashon."

"I am—" All at once Salmon recognized the voice. "Joshua? Sir? Is that you?" He felt his face flush hot and was glad for the darkness. He hoped his irritation had not been overly noticeable in his tone.

"Forgive the intrusion. Your sister told me you had wandered off in this direction . . ." Joshua's voice trailed off as if in a question.

"No intrusion at all, sir. I just needed to get away from the idle chatter."

"I understand." Joshua stood silently for a few moments without saying anything, and then added in almost a whisper, "I have needed to get away recently as well. It is hard to lose the one you look up to most. Harder yet to try to fill the vacancy he left behind."

Salmon stared at the dark form of the old warrior in disbelief. "You? I thought it was my youth and inexperience."

Joshua chuckled and his teeth flashed white as they caught a bit of starlight. "Changes this great are difficult even for the old. Come. Walk with me over by the river. I need your help."

"My help?" Salmon felt his stomach flutter.

Joshua strode into the night without further explanation.

In a daze, Salmon followed him to the edge of the *zor*. The old captain had already seated himself on a large, overhanging boulder at the edge of the river basin by the time Salmon clambered down beside him.

"This is music that clears my head," Joshua shouted over the roar.

Salmon was astonished by the volume of water raging downstream. It had increased ten-fold, breaking the boundaries of its channel, submerging shrubbery and swirling around trees across the entire jungle of the zor. "I was told that the river has been rising over the past two weeks," he shouted back, "but I had no idea it was like this. No wonder people say the fords will soon be impassable."

Joshua sighed. "The visible too quickly eclipses the invisible."

Salmon leaned closer to the silver-haired warrior. He did not understand. Was Joshua commenting on the flood or something else?

Joshua looked at him as if he could read his mind. "What has happened to the passion Moses stirred up in his farewell speeches? The echo of his words grows weaker each day—and he has been gone but two weeks. Perhaps you have heard the faithless speculation whispered in dark corners?"

Salmon nodded imperceptibly, glad Joshua didn't ask him to disclose what he had heard.

"I hear them muttering. 'Why is Joshua continuing the thirty days of mourning on the eastern bank of the river? Let's cross while we can.' Seeds of mutiny—"

Joshua did not seem to be addressing Salmon anymore and his thoughts rambled. "The waters are rising. Of course I can see that. I didn't ask to be their leader. We have to wait. Wait for the Lord. "

Even though Salmon had been keeping to himself during this period of mourning, he had heard the rumors. The princes of Reuben, Gad, and Manasseh were threatening to lead their warriors across to the west before a crossing became impossible. They announced that if Israel did not go now, they would be absolved from their promise and simply would not go. They called for the rest of the warriors to follow them. The situation was close to mutiny as the eastern tribes declared they would launch the war for the inheritance of their brother tribes with or without Joshua. The old man could lead the families across after flood season.

Salmon cringed. *He should have been actively encouraging Judah to wait for the Lord. What would Abba have done? What would he have said?*

"I don't see how we will be able to cross until the spring floods subside again—unless we do cross immediately. But we must wait until the end of the thirty days of mourning. That is why I need you, Salmon. Judah is the leader of the tribes."

"But what can I do, boy that I am?" He shouted his response, but his voice sounded small over the rush of the Jordan.

"You are young, but no longer a boy. At your father's death, you became the Prince of Judah. I have seen your courage and quick wit. Most importantly, I have heard only good reports of your integrity and your passion to follow Yahweh's ways." He looked sideways at Salmon. "For this task, it is good you have no family of your own yet."

"But . . .? What?"

"Ah, yes, the task! I believe the people will respond well to a report of conditions on the other side. Only two spies, however." Joshua exhaled loudly and shook his head. "Twelve didn't work out so well last time. I want you to cross the river, spy out the western plain and the city of Jericho, and report back in a few days."

Salmon could feel the hair on the back of his neck stand up. Fear, excitement, and shock exploded through him all at one time. "But . . . how ?" The river all but drowned out his question.

Joshua continued as if Salmon had not attempted a response. "It will be dangerous. The news must have crossed the Jordan long ago that we cleaned out the viper's nests of Sihon and Og—and struck back at the treachery of Midian. I have seen Canaanite watchmen lurking by the fords. Without a doubt, they are on the lookout for any movement on our part."

He stopped and looked Salmon full in the face, his eyes steady, intense. "I plan to send spies right under their noses, downriver where the water is deep and the current is swift. Is this a challenge you are willing to take on?"

Salmon's heart galloped. He nodded and answered with a quavering, "Yes."

Joshua rose to his feet. "Very well. Meet me at my tent tomorrow morning immediately after the morning sacrifice. I will go over the plans with both of you."

Salmon felt his lips begin to form the question, "Who?" but Joshua was gone before he could ask.

Before the first twitters and trills from the songbirds in the Jordan jungle woke the dawn, Salmon was awake. For the first time since his father's death, he felt really alive. He rose, dressed, and completed his morning chores before the sky lost its crimson flush. Soon he was back in the tent for breakfast, grinning at his young sister and tousling her hair. "The porridge smells wonderful, Ada. Did you help make it?" It was all he could do to suppress the story as he ate.

Ada watched him with eyes narrowed to tiny slits. "What are you up to this morning?"

"Me? I just finished the regular chores."

"One would think you were about to propose marriage to someone."

"What?" Visions of a spindly young spy chased by Canaanite giants popped like a burst bubble.

"You. Marriage," she answered smugly.

"Marriage? What are you talking about?"

"Hmm, you can't sit still or keep from smiling. Let me think . . . who would it be? Hmm. Acsah?"

Salmon laughed loudly and patted Ada's hand. "I can assure you, my sweet sister, that I am not about to replace your wonderful cooking—or Mother's for that matter—with that of a wife."

Ada looked disappointed.

His mother studied his face. "Well, something has you riled up this morning. Aren't you going to tell us what?"

Salmon met his mother and sister's eager eyes uncertainly. "Well, I can't give you any details," he began cautiously. "Actually, I don't know a lot of details. It's just that Joshua wants to see me this morning."

Ada looked suspicious. "Why would he want to see *you*?"

"In the role of Prince of Judah. Quite an honor for one so young, eh?"

Abijah gasped. "Is he asking you to do something dangerous? We have not yet adjusted to the loss of your father. I cannot risk losing my son."

Salmon shrugged.

Ada studied his face for more clues, but Salmon's manner told her to drop the subject.

A tall, thin young man had arrived at Joshua's tent before him and was squatting just inside the entrance beside Joshua by the time Salmon arrived. He looked up with small bright eyes and a wide smile. "Shalom. I am Jathniel of Ephraim." The genial face was framed by a heavy beard and hair as wild and curly as sheep's wool. Thick, black eyebrows bounced up and down as he spoke.

"I am Sal—"

"I know, Salmon, son of Prince Nashon of Judah."

"My father is dead."

"I know." Jathniel seemed uncomfortable. His eyebrows twitched. "He was a good leader. My father respected him very much."

"Kind words," Salmon said as he squatted down beside Jathniel. "I'm glad to meet you."

Joshua cleared his throat. The boys watched him quietly as he folded back the rugs carpeting the floor and began tracing a map in the bare earth with the point of a dagger. "Yahweh has spoken to me twice about leading the people into Canaan. Each time he has commanded me to be strong and courageous. But this last time, he specifically warned me not to be terrified or discouraged." He looked at his spies gravely. "I suspect we cannot even imagine the difficulties we will encounter on the other side, but I want you to bring back some idea of what we will face." With a sigh, he continued, "I know our people. They respond to what they see and hear more readily than to the unseen. I must have a firm plan. Perhaps then I can allay the fears of our people ahead of time. Prepare them for what lies ahead so no one is terrified or discouraged."

Joshua gestured at his crudely sketched earth map. "Here is the ford . . . or what used to be the ford before the river rose so high. We are here in Gilead, and over here is the western plain."

Salmon and Jathniel nodded. The map was easy to understand.

"The west appears to echo the east. I believe we will find the plains there more than adequate as the first camp for all our people. Assess the amount of available pasturelands for our flocks and herds. I especially want you to note what crops are growing. We have no way of knowing whether or not the daily manna fall will continue on the other side."

Salmon and Jathniel looked at each other in surprise.

"Make a careful assessment of the fields, orchards, vineyards, and gardens. Then move on to the city. Jericho lies about five miles from the ford. About here." Joshua carved a small square on the map with the point of the dagger. "Confine your explorations to this one city and the surrounding valley. Jericho appears to be heavily fortified. You have no doubt seen its walls from here. The Lord revealed to me that this is the gateway protecting the western border of Canaan, and that they plan to attack us if we attempt to cross the river. However, we have no need to fear. Yahweh will deliver Jericho into our hands. He promised me that. Look for evidence to support the Lord's promise.

"Your reconnaissance of the city will be the most dangerous part of your task. Try to blend in with travelers coming from the south. We do not want them to guess that you have come from this side." Joshua pulled a clattering bundle from a dark corner. "I have gathered some Egyptian jewelry for you to sell in the marketplace. Declare yourselves to be first time merchants from Goshen in Egypt. You needn't mention that it was actually your parents who came from Egypt—and that forty years past."

Next, he brought out a bright bundle of dyed linen clothing. "Exchange your wool garments for these Egyptian outfits when you get ready to enter the city. Both of you could easily pass for Egyptians in my opinion, if you shave. Only be very careful what you say and to whom. Your speech will give you away."

Jathniel reached for the bundle. "When do you want us to leave?"

"Tonight. There will be no moon to brighten the river basin in the early watch following dusk, but it will rise about midnight providing minimal light for exploring in the later watches."

Jathniel's next question was tentative. "How do we get across?"

"That will be our task today; but first a word of caution. Don't forget for a moment that you are people of the covenant. Try to evaluate everything you do from what you know of God's commands and decrees. Do not be distracted or enticed by any of the material things you see—or by any beautiful women you meet in that city." He met their gaze solemnly. "Yahweh's decree: This city is to be a burnt offering to him. We will take no plunder whatsoever. No captives. He has made that very, very clear."

The two spies looked at each other and nodded.

"Make every effort to avoid viewing their Canaanite worship. It will haunt your mind for a long, long time if you do. Trust me. I know." The shadow of deep, repressed pain that darkened Joshua's eyes corroborated the truth of his statement. He blinked and the look disappeared. "Now follow me."

He led them down to the river and then south along its banks, stopping at a shrubby shelter by an old hollow log. "Stash the bundles of jewelry and clothing here until tonight. The river of Egypt was much wider than this, but it never ran so wild. Still, I believe you can cross on a raft similar to the ones that carried cargo up and down the Nile.

Now watch this. I've been doing some experimenting." Joshua stepped carefully down to the brink of the water. "Over the past few days, I have been lashing branches together and pushing them into the river, watching where the current takes them." Joshua scurried around examining the piles of uprooted brush deposited along the river margins by the flood. "I have found if I push them in here—just below this tree—the current carries them on across every time, reaching the far bank near that willow thicket. We are well below the ford here. Out of sight of any suspicious watchmen." He chose a large bough, thickly matted with dead leaves, and pushed it into the river. "Watch!" he shouted cheerily as he crashed through the brush along the river's edge.

The branch bobbed and swirled in eddies, but was moving faster than they could on the brushy bank. All too quickly, it rushed around a bend and out of sight. "Did you see how close to the far shore the current carried it? Just above the river bend? You will have a long pole to help you when you get close, but it will not be easy to fight the current to stop yourselves. As you pass close to those overhanging branches," he pointed enthusiastically, "whoever is not using the pole must grab them and hold on. Once you stop yourselves, you should be able to pull up to shore fairly easily. Climb up out of the thickets as soon as you can. You have heard the lions and hyenas down here at night, I'm sure. I think the floods have driven them off, but we can't be certain. Don't linger in the jungle. The Lord is not sending you to feed his wild beasts.

"Look for a secluded cave up in the hills to be your base. I trust there are as many caves riddling the hills over there as here. Spend your days out of sight and getting plenty of rest. You will need all your wits about you when you enter Jericho."

"But sir, if the Canaanites find the raft, they will come looking for us." Jathniel's eyebrows twitched as he asked, "Why don't we swim?"

Joshua stared at him for a moment. "Do you know how to swim?"

Jathniel turned red. "No, but I have heard it is not hard to learn."

"Even if you could learn quickly, just how would the two of you stay together? How could you hang on to your bundles? How would you stay afloat with a bag of gold and silver?"

Jathniel drew in his lips and tightened his mouth, the line growing flatter with each question. "We should kick off the raft after we land so it goes on down the river and doesn't give us away."

"Then how would we get back home?" Salmon asked

"Build another."

"Let's get started," Joshua responded. "We can fine tune our plan as we work."

Darkness settled, dense and foreboding in the river basin that night, and the rush and gurgle of the river drowned all other sounds as Salmon and Jathniel scrabbled through the brush toward the water's edge. It was nearly impossible to distinguish brushy thickets from open spaces. They hobbled with arms stretched out before them like blind men, remembering this rock, that stump, feeling their way to the spot where they had secured the raft, glad for the many trips they had made during a day of raft building and observing the currents with Joshua.

"The darkness is beautiful tonight," Salmon whispered, running his hands across the familiar roundness of a large boulder.

"Right. Blinds us, but also casts a veil over Canaanite eyes."

Salmon stopped and looked up. Hundreds of stars blinked and twinkled through the lacework of branches above the brushy, black-shadowed canyon of the river. Feeling like a tiny speck of humanity in the vast beauty of the night, waves of awe washed over him. How could it be that Joshua had chosen him for this adventure?

"Salmon, where are you?" Jathniel's whisper shattered the transcendent moment.

"Sorry. I just stopped to look at the stars and got caught up in the wonder of our assignment."

"Well, the wonder of the assignment entails getting across the river before the moon rises."

At the water's edge, the pair roped themselves together, and lashed their bundles to the frame of the raft. Jathniel climbed aboard while Salmon grasped the rope that tethered them to shore and then eased the raft off its gravelly shelf into knee-deep water. As the raft swung into the tug of the current, Salmon kicked and pulled to haul himself onto the bobbing, turning platform beside his companion. Leaden heaviness dragged down on his legs as he struggled up onto the raft from the water. Once aboard, he rested on solid buoyancy, a sensation of pure delight. "This is wonderful! We are actually floating on water."

"May I remind you this is lethally rushing water we're floating on? I'm a creature of land, not water."

"We could have been creatures of both if we hadn't grown up in the desert."

"Desert provides enough water for me if I have a spring to drink from. Free the rope now and let's be off."

Salmon's weight shifted to the left as he rose to his knees. The left edge of the raft dipped deep into the river. He shifted to the right, and the raft dipped to the other side. He tested the action playfully until the raft wobbled wildly back and forth.

"Enough of that." Jathniel took a deep breath. "Free the rope before I lose my nerve."

"As you wish, my brave fellow spy," Salmon laughed. He loosened the rope and eased them a little farther into the stream, leaving the long tether still looped around the tree. Just as he was about to release them completely, a thick log shot past, tapping a corner of the raft in a farewell salute and sending them into a spin.

"Let's go," Jathniel whispered in alarm.

The danger they were in suddenly immobilized Salmon. "All right. I'm going to cast off," he told himself. He loosened his fingers, and then hesitated.

"All right. Here we go." He willed his hands to open, but still found himself with a tight grip on the rope.

"Some spies we are," Jathniel groaned. "Between the two of us, there is quite possibly enough courage for one brave man." The raft wobbled again as he pushed Salmon to the side and yanked the line from his hands.

Salmon fell flat on the rough ribs of their floating platform trying to reel in the dripping tail of the rope as the raft sped into the surging stream. They bobbed, turned, and lurched with the torrent, rushing faster and faster downstream. Salmon grinned and let out an involuntary whoop at the wild sense of freedom, but the giddiness roused by riding the star-lit river ended within minutes as the black outline of the far shore rushed toward them.

"Be ready to grab. I've got the pole," Jathniel reminded him.

Salmon stared into the darkness. When they seemed about to collide with the dense black of the far bank, he stretched out his arms. But, instead of embracing the expected armload of vegetation, he found himself clutching only a few leaves. The branches continued rushing past just out of reach.

"Not close enough. I can't get a good grip," Salmon cried. "Can you touch bottom with your pole?"

"I am," Jathniel shouted back. "I can't hold us."

"Push harder!"

"Hurry and get those branches," Jathniel gasped as he brought their wild ride to a sudden lurching halt. A wave washed over the raft and gravel crunched as he dug in the pole, fighting to hold them in place. "Just hurry. The river is stronger than I," he cried as the raft spun away from the point of contact and strained to rejoin the flow of the river.

"It's so dark," Salmon huffed. "I can't tell what's here except by feel." With twigs snapping and clawing at his arms, Salmon groped among the flimsy green stems and brittle, dry brush for something substantial. At last, his arms closed around a cascade of strong, supple willow boughs. Then hand over hand, he began hauling the raft to shore, grabbing bigger and stronger branches ever closer to the heart of the tree. "Ah, sweet success," he cried, feeling and hearing the reassuring scrape of the raft bottom against the rocks at the same time. "We have arrived."

Soon both boys were splashing around the inundated willows. They pushed the raft up onto a ledge, then pulled it higher yet to a recess sheltered by an overhanging rock. Salmon tried to disguise the opening with a jumble of dead branches, but he had no idea how well camouflaged the spot would be once the sun rose. "Let's hope the raft is really hidden from anyone who has reason to be down here."

"Let's hope the river doesn't rise higher and wash the raft out of there. I wonder . . ." Jathniel's tone was half joking, half troubled. "Should we look for a more elevated hiding place?"

"I think we need to obey orders and get out of this river jungle as soon as possible."

Salmon and Jathniel spent the remainder of that night and the following two nights exploring the cultivated plain each way up and down the river. They secluded themselves by day, sleeping in a cave high in the hills all morning. Well rested by late afternoon, they peered down at Jericho from the cave mouth, watching until the last of the caravans lumbered out of the city and up the road toward the western hills. The gates were closed and barred each night.

For two days the young spies reveled in the glory of Canaan's spring. Trees of all sorts—fig, pomegranate, olive, almond and more—flaunted the living green of newly opened leaves and fragrant blossoms. In terrace after terrace, fat buds on the withered branches of carefully pruned grapevines were beginning to split and unfurl their verdure. Between these terraces and the river, lay a patchwork of color. Fallow fields of rich, dark earth nestled beside airy blue-green carpets of flax. Brilliant emerald wheat fields stretched off into the distance while, directly below the cave, the dancing seed heads of barley, drinking in the gold of the sun, were rapidly exchanging their green mantles for gilded ones. The barley would be ready for harvest by the time Israel entered the land. The bounty of the grain fields was beyond anything they could have imagined. Morning breezes blew across seemingly endless fields, whipping up miles of rippling waves on a sea of green and gold. They were eager to return with their good report. But first, they must scout out the city.

Joshua did not hesitate to quell the spirit of rebellion once his spies crossed the river. He met privately with the leaders of Reuben, Gad, and the half-tribe of Manasseh, reminding them that the moon had not turned once since they swore with an oath that their warriors would lead the whole nation into the Promised Land. Skillfully, he persuaded them to remember the promise they made to Moses and to wait for the leading of the Lord.

Then he called a solemn assembly of all the tribes. With the fearsome leaders of those three tribes standing in silent support behind him, Joshua paced back and forth like an alpha wolf reducing his pack to submission with low growls. "I hear your grumblings. You want to cross now. But I will not react to rebellion. Yahweh instructed us to wait."

Gradually his speech shifted to commanding barks. "I will move ONLY at the Word of the Lord. We WILL complete the thirty days of mourning. We WILL honor the memory of Moses. Then, ONLY THEN, will we cross. And we will cross as ONE UNITED PEOPLE."

Acsah watched in amazement. There was power in Joshua's short clipped phrases, and it elicited a dramatic change in the people around her. She had known Joshua all her life—an uncle, her father's brother in faith—but never had she seen Joshua like this. She glanced at her father. His lips curved ever so slightly in a smile, and he did not seem at all surprised.

"Trust the One who brought you out of Egypt," the deep baying voice commanded. "Did Pharaoh cower because *you* had become so powerful? Would Pharaoh's chariots have turned back at the sight of *your* warriors? Did *your* skill and might defeat them?

"No. No. No.

"Trust the One who split the Red Sea for you. Wait for the Word of the Lord. He will lead you across the Jordan at the right time. Wait for the Lord." Joshua stopped suddenly. His gaze swept over the crowds, reading their faces while the words hung in the air.

The air crackled with whispered admiration. "A true leader emerges from the shadow of Moses," a man behind Acsah declared.

"The Lord chose him. Who can doubt him?" a woman answered.

"Why would we follow mere warriors? We will wait for the Lord."

"Joshua will lead us across at the right time."

"Fickle folk," Caleb whispered. "The approval of God is what matters."

"Wait for the Lord, O Israel," Joshua repeated. "His plans ALONE will lead you into the inheritance of Jacob. His plans ALONE will bring you victory in battle. On our own, we are a pitiful band of desert wanderers, but when we match stride with God, we will march victorious. And the glory will be his ALONE."

The words rang across the valley and Acsah imagined them hammering against the walls of Jericho. Then suddenly lowering his voice as if he did not want to let his secret cross the river, Joshua announced, "This very morning, two of our young men stand on the soil of our inheritance. I sent them across the Jordan last night to spy out the land. They will assess the city of Jericho and return ere the thirty days of mourning are ended. The warriors of Reuben, Gad, and Manasseh agree to wait for their report."

As the leaders of the three eastern tribes nodded their silent assent, more whispers of wonder sizzled through the crowds.

"Like a lean and crafty wolf, Joshua silenced the jackals who threatened his authority."

"Well done, Uncle Joshua," Acsah breathed.

Caleb grinned from ear to ear. "I can hardly wait to hear the report Salmon and Jathniel of Ephraim bring back."

"Salmon? He sent Salmon?"

"I heard from Joshua last night. He asked me to handle any disputes or needs in Judah until our young prince returns."

"Salmon?" she repeated. "He is the last one I would have sent."

"I personally thought Joshua made an excellent choice."

The people settled into the remaining days of mourning, eagerly anticipating the return of their spies. They honored Moses with renewed study of his last words. They encouraged one another. They determined to follow Joshua into Canaan, no matter how formidable the enemy. Not another rebellious word was heard.

JERICHO

Salmon

The mouth of the cave framed a fading arch of stars curving over the moon-silvered valley. Back in the safety of camp, this soul-stirring time of silent beauty, anticipating the first flushed hues of dawn, was Salmon's favorite time of day. But not this morning. Not in this alien land.

He shivered as the cold night air permeated the thin linen of his Egyptian clothing and tightened the belt. *Don't know how that will help. What I want is a warm head covering and a wool coat.* He slipped his arms into the loose sleeves of the outer cloak and pulled the insubstantial linen close around him. The orange and yellow stripes were as gray in the dim light as his mood. Crossing the river, hiding in the cave, and exploring by moonlight was an adventure filled with just enough danger to heighten his senses. The thought of actually entering the maw of evil nearly left him paralyzed.

Jathniel moved up beside him and playfully wiggled the hairless bumps that had been his brows. "We certainly do not look like Israelites, but will the people of Jericho know that?"

Salmon laughed, not at Jathniel's words, but at the moonlight reflecting off his bald pate. Without the heavy brows, beard, and mop of thick black curls, Jathniel's head looked perfectly round, like a melon perched on a post. *Could this strange person slip into Jericho unnoticed?* Salmon had felt very Egyptian when they shaved their beards, heads, and arms yesterday, but now he thought perhaps they simply looked odd.

"Don't stare at me like that."

I'm not staring at you. I'm staring at a perfect stranger."

"Stranger?" Jathniel widened his eyes in an exaggerated return stare. "You look stranger than I do."

Salmon grinned and rubbed Jathniel's smooth scalp with his knuckles. "Let's not get separated. How would we recognize one another again?" He sucked in a long audible breath to give him courage. "All right. To Jericho." He hoisted the bundle of jewelry to his shoulder and led the way out of the cave, clanking lightly with every step across the moonlit slope. *So much for stealth.*

They traversed the slope northward, high above the vineyards and cultivated fields, keeping a careful eye on every mass of black shade cast by shrubs or rocks. Their muscles were tense, ready to leap and run should any shadow move. Their own shadows stretched diagonally down the slope from their feet. Jathniel's dark shape followed close behind his, both shadows hunchbacked as hyenas, skulking along the rim of the hills as they crept closer, ever closer to the shoulder of the western pass. At the crossroads, they crouched, watching. Nothing stirred above them on the broad trade route leading north and south. Nothing on the spur descending down to the city. They could easily have made a secret entrance . . . if the gates of Jericho hadn't been locked fast. Or if its walls hadn't been so incredibly high.

Jathniel pointed toward a field of flax stubble below them, about a furlong from the city. "Let's wait there as if we spent the night beside the road. When the first travelers appear, we can follow them in."

Although the flax stubble was prickly and their cloaks inadequate for the cool morning breeze, Salmon must have dozed for it seemed he had barely closed his eyes before first light crept over the eastern hills and long shadowy fingers reached across the valley to beckon the first rumbling caravan from the west. He watched a train of camels, donkeys, ox-drawn wagons and merchants crest the hill and begin the descent toward Jericho. The city gates opened.

Out of the corners of almost closed eyes, Salmon practiced the art of spying. When he could just make out the faces of the first figures at the head of the procession—two swarthy Egyptians swaying precariously in saddles perched high on the backs of camels—he sat up, stretching and yawning, and then shook his companion. "Time to get up. The gate is open at last."

"This has been a long, uncomfortable—" Jathniel grunted sleepily. Suddenly his eyes widened. Pretended or real, all traces of sleepiness vanished. Even without the bushy brows, he flagged a clear signal of fear.

When Salmon looked back toward the caravan, he could see nothing but dust and two sets of long camel legs ambling directly toward them. *Had they already been identified as Israelites?*

"The barley is nearly ready for harvest," a voice declared high above them as the camel drivers reined the beasts to a stop not four feet from them.

Salmon let the breath he had been holding escape slowly through pursed lips. It was the two lead merchants, but their interest was focused on the fields not on them.

"The grain near Jebus has barely begun to head."

"Indeed. This valley will have wheat by the time the rest of Canaan has barley."

Salmon stretched and yawned again, trying very hard to act as if it were a most normal occurrence to awaken fenced off from the road by eight camel legs. He untied the corner of his cloak and offered Jathniel a handful of the barley they had gathered on the first two nights of wading through the fields below the cave. As the caravan rolled on, they munched the raw kernels, watching the trundling parade. Salmon noted with satisfaction that their own shaved bodies matched those of most merchants in the caravan. Over the creaking and rumbling of wagons and the thudding hooves of oxen, he strained to hear the conversation of the two on their camels.

"And look at these orchards and vineyards. It will be a very good year for olive oil and wine as well."

"That will be for future trips, my friend, but I wonder if the processing of flax has begun. It is curious that it has been cut in many fields already, but there is none lying on the ground to cure."

"We must definitely inquire about that. Jericho's fine, pale linen fibers trade like gold."

"I wonder if finished flax is available now or if we must wait until we return."

"Let us arrange for the latter, if at all possible. Linen fetches a better price at home than in the north. If we exchange our cotton here for the Moabite pots the people of Damascus love and bring back the bronze swords in such high demand by King Nahari, we should turn a handsome profit at each trade. We will be rich men when we return to Egypt with our wagons full of Jericho flax."

"Excellent plan. Nahari can never get his hands on enough weapons."

"He that goeth not forth to battle, gains no plunder."

"Hah! That twisted, paranoid monarch rarely goes out to battle if he can hide behind his city walls."

Lucky for us, he hoards more and more swords anyway. We must spread the word that we will return in a few weeks with the finest Damascene bronze blades. He will hear of it."

"And, when he does, Nahari will ensure that his growers reserve top-grade flax fibers for us."

"Better yet, spun linen thread. We should leave pointed threats with the growers regarding the danger of disappointing their insane ruler. They *will* save the best for us."

His companion laughed heartily. "It wouldn't hurt to leave a hefty deposit as well. You know what they say about trapping more flies with honey than vinegar."

The taller of the two peered down at the spies. "Say there, we wish to contact the flax processors. Is this your field?"

"Oh, no," Jathniel answered quickly. "We have come to Jericho like you. From the land of Goshen. You know . . . in Egypt. We were with a large caravan. A few days ahead of you." His words gushed out, piling up in nervous spurts with a lift of his brows punctuating each phrase.

"We are merchants, as you can see," he said, jiggling their sack of jewelry until it rattled and clanked to prove his point. "But this is our first trek. We both got new sandals for the journey. No one warned us about that. My friend developed blisters the size of grapes. Had to stop for several days back in Jebus. We tried to sell our things there, but we had little luck." Jathniel patted Salmon's leg condescendingly. "My friend was ready to travel again yesterday . . . but even that journey took us too long at his altered pace. Bad luck again. We arrived at dusk. The city gates had already closed so we had to sleep out here in the field." His eyebrows remained lifted although he had finally finished.

"Goshen, eh? You have an unusual accent."

Salmon winced. *Had Jathniel totally forgotten Joshua's warning about speaking more than necessary?* Masking his fear, he scrambled to his feet and pointed enthusiastically toward Jericho. "The gates are open," he announced in his best imitation of the Egyptian's rolling tones. "It's time to see the sights of Jericho."

He pulled Jathniel to standing, glancing up at the Egyptians as he brushed off the twiggy bits of flax clinging to their cloaks. There were traces of amusement, not suspicion, crinkling the caravan master's eyes. Not certain if that was a good thing or not, he smiled at them. "Big day for us. Have to look presentable."

As he swung the clanking bundle of jewelry onto his shoulder, Jathniel gave the caravan a jaunty salute. Just as they began edging into the traffic-clogged road, a storm of grunting and squalling erupted around them. Long, hairy, trampling legs. Billows of dust. And high above their heads, gleeful laughter. Salmon and Jathniel scrambled for safety, but as quickly as it started, the squall ended with the lurching, loping, long-legged pace of the camels carrying their riders rapidly past lumbering wagons and heavily-laden donkeys. Before the dust settled, they were back at their place at the head of the caravan. "Wealth awaits us," the taller one exulted to his companion.

"Our speech is a fatal handicap," Salmon whispered discreetly. Without more discussion, they held back, falling into place at the rear of the caravan. They trudged upward in a continuous cloud of dust and brooding silence, feeling decidedly un-spy like as they began their ascent of the city mount. The walls loomed large and threatening above them. Salmon felt his breath come quicker and knew it was due less to the rising pitch of the road than to the yawning gate swallowing the caravan alive. As if in protest, the traffic bunched up and slowed to nearly a standstill.

The dust had not settled when a second camel train pressed up behind, and they were compacted in the middle of a clogged column of merchants and merchandise. They waited, inched forward, then waited some more. Salmon scanned the soaring rows of block that made up the wall. Like Heshbon, and the other fortified cities on the eastern side of the river, Jericho had a solid appearance from a distance, but nothing had prepared him for the reality of its walls up close. *What were they built to keep out? Giants? A sudden flood of panic brought back the story of the ten Israelite spies undone by the terrors of walled cities forty years before. Grasshoppers, they said. The giants and the huge cities made them feel as small as grasshoppers.* Always hearing the tale from the point of view of Caleb and Joshua, he had never been able to understand that lack of faith. He did now. *Think like Caleb and Joshua,* he told himself. *We have Yahweh. They have only these human-constructed walls.*

"This delay is to our benefit," he whispered to Jathniel. "Couldn't be a more inconspicuous way to examine this wall."

Jathniel leaned close, tipping his head toward the overpowering bulwark. "Awesome, but I can't see any way Israel could breech this."

"Nor I."

"God will have to *lift* his army over these walls."

Salmon craned his neck back to see where wall met sky—and connected with a pair of hard, cold eyes above the gate. His knees nearly buckled, and his attempt to build faith-based bravery toppled like a child's tower of blocks. Guards were posted at regular intervals on the wall above them. But this one, standing in the center of the bridge spanning the gateway, continued scrutinizing them carefully. His scowl made it clear that he and Jathniel did not blend in with the confusion of travelers as well as Joshua had expected. He must not let his terror show. Must not let his eyes dart away like a frightened bird. Should he nod? Salute?

God help us, he prayed. He chose a noncommittal nod and moved a few steps forward with the traffic. When he glanced upward again, the intimidating guard was studying other travelers and Salmon breathed more easily. He kept his voice as low as possible, consciously trying to look as if he were engaging in idle banter. He pointed out a wagonload of squealing young pigs and forced a chuckle. "Not only high, but so thick. I think we could pitch all the tents of Judah up there."

"With Ephraim beside her."

"That would be a strange encampment." Salmon chortled at the mental image that popped into his head.

"I have never seen such walls in all my life."

Salmon laughed again. "Of course, before last year, neither of us had ever seen any city walls up close." He glanced up at the guard. The cold eyes were fixed on them again, and they were almost directly below his post. *Could he hear their words?* "Quiet, Jath—"

"Look at the line halfway up," his friend interrupted in a volume that had grown carelessly loud. "The lower part of the wall leans in ever so slightly, and then the second part shoots straight up. I don't understand what holds it up."

"I don't understand the hold up either," Salmon responded quickly, glancing around to see who else might be listening. "But what do we know? We're just the sons of Egyptian merchants on our first excursion."

Jathniel blushed. "Yes. We *are* Egyptians, and this is all so new to us."

They were now able to move into the gate complex, and Salmon tried to dismiss the burning image of that guard's eyes. Looking through the inner set of gates, he could see that a second wall rose from the street level, encircling the city parallel to the outer one. That inner wall was three or four times a man's height, difficult in itself to scale. He could see now that the outer fortification plunged downward as far on the city mound as it soared upward. The outer rampart was made up of a wall built upon a wall, each as high as the inner one. The lower part was undoubtedly a retaining wall built to stabilize the earthworks making up the slope of the city mount. A freestanding wall had been built on top of it to match the inner wall with a space between large enough for usable rooms. It was obvious now what held it up, but not so obvious how any attacking army could conquer this city.

The sentries were assessing the wagon boxes just in front of them now, randomly inspecting a crate here, a pack there, while a burly captain with a grizzled beard grunted orders. Like the guard on the wall, he picked them out of the caravan with a sharp, direct look. As the traffic crept forward, the gaze of the captain returned to them again and again. *He guesses our identity. He knows we are Israelites.* Almost afraid to breathe, Salmon moved up for inspection, but the sentries took only a quick look in their bundle. The captain gave them one more visual sweep with his frighteningly cruel eyes. "Let them pass," he said.

Pass meant moving forward a few feet only to wait again, packed among the crowds between the two sets of gates, unable to move on. The growls of the captain sounded over the grunts of his guards, but none of it was directed at them, so Salmon returned to his analysis of the wall. A room for the sentries and their equipment occupied the space between those two walls. Perhaps any number of homes and shops had been built into that wall-space around the city. Salmon wondered if any such places had secret passageways leading to the outside. If not, an attacking army had very poor choices: breach *two* thick walls, scale a span that shot upward eight to ten times the height of a man or storm these fortified gates. There was no easy way to get over, under, or through such walls.

Just beyond the inner gate, the spies could see the merchants in front of them paying tariffs and accepting assigned places in the market to set up their wares. It wasn't hard to imitate the procedure, paying with some of the silver pieces from their bundle. But, an increasing sense of ineptitude—and doom—pressed down on

Salmon. He tried to shake it off as they made their way to the center of the marketplace at last, but he could not help glancing around and behind him, half expecting to see one of the guards following.

Instead, he saw vendors and shoppers buying and selling a wider variety of goods than he could ever have conceived of. It seemed no one found it unusual to see two young Egyptians unrolling their bundle and spreading out an impressive array of finely-crafted jewelry. One particularly beautiful young woman stopped a stone's throw from them, beside a spice merchant's stall on the other side of the walkway. She took the large water jar from her head and set it on the ground beside her. He expected her to come view their merchandise, but she held back only watching. A quiet echo of Joshua's warning about beautiful women stirred in Salmon's head as he turned his attention to the task at hand.

"So far, so good," he whispered under his breath. "The old captain at the gate really unnerved me."

There was no time for a response. "Good morning, Mother," Jathniel called brightly to a gray-haired woman who showed obvious interest in their wares. She reached for a finely-crafted armlet embossed with almond blossoms and leaves, her eyes gleaming as bright as the shining gold when she held it up. Salmon smiled to himself at the way Jathniel's brow responded in a ridiculously enthusiastic dance as he encouraged her. "You have excellent taste. That piece was created many years ago for an Egyptian princess. There is a mural in Pharaoh's palace depicting her wearing that very armlet. The princess died and her daughters were all too fat for this delicate piece. Eventually, it fell into my grandfather's hands. Try it on. I believe it will be a perfect fit for your arm."

It was a clever story, but . . . too many words. Salmon shot a warning glance at his partner as a large crowd gathered around. It didn't seem that Jathniel caught his meaning or else he forgot time and again, but he was good at sales. The glittering display vanished within two hours. "We should have done more listening and less talking," Salmon whispered as they folded the bundling cloth around the pile of coins and left their spot.

The young woman with the water jar had long since disappeared, but as they wandered through the crowded market, Salmon noticed her again at a leather worker's stall. He steered Jathniel in another direction, but soon he spied her again, looking through bolts of brightly colored fabric. She didn't seem to be interested in the two of them, but it seemed odd to him that she moved all around the market without buying anything.

"I think there might be someone spying on us," he whispered. "Not sure, but let's slip down this side street while she isn't looking."

Jathniel raised his brows slowly. "She?" He grinned. "You think Jericho uses its women as spies."

"We can't be too careful," Salmon shot back. "And you definitely need to be more careful about who you talk to and how much you say."

"I thought I was getting rather good at the Egyptian accent." Jathniel pointed to the wall soaring above the houses at the far end of the street. "Let's stroll down that way and take a closer look at the wall from inside the city."

"Don't point. Haven't you noticed all the guards roaming the streets. The green uniforms. . ."

"Guards, you say? The guys in green? So *that's* why they match the men at the gate . . . Do you think I'm a simpleton? I know a uniform when I see one."

Salmon fell silent as two green-cloaks sauntered toward them, their bronze helmets and breastplates gleaming formidably in the bright sunlight. Bronze swords swung in scabbards from their belts. As they passed, he noted the small round shields of bronze and leather slung over their shoulders. Even here in the center of such a well-fortified city, these guards were obviously prepared to attack or defend. "It's not the uniforms that concern me, but I don't care to hear the speech of their blades," Salmon finished when the guards were beyond earshot.

They were on a side street now heading away from the market, and the handful of shoppers around them began disappearing into one or another of the doorways lining the narrow cobbled roadway. The street ended abruptly with a heavy oak doorway built right into the huge expanse of masonry. A sign announcing, "North Wall Inn" above the door greeted the spies welcomingly.

Between them and the end of the street, a slim, but muscular figure in guardsman green leaned casually against a wall painted with a fresco of water pools and palm trees.

He was young and looked as if he were relaxing in a desert oasis instead of guarding something, but his eyes followed their movements closely. *Two strangers heading directly toward him on a nearly empty street. Supposedly traveling merchants, but why here where homes had replaced shops?* Salmon was still striving to concoct a rational purpose for being on this street as he saluted the guard. "You found a lovely oasis for resting on this warm afternoon," he said breezily.

The young man did not respond. The face was pimply, and he seemed boyish, awkwardly adolescent. The eyes didn't meet his but wandered shyly, almost aimlessly over the two of them—over their feet, over their clothing, but not their faces. Salmon's natural optimism took over.

"This is our first trip to Jericho. I think we made a wrong turn back there."

The guard didn't respond other than to lift the slow, sweeping inspection to their bald heads.

Salmon attempted to engage him again. "Are your streets always so well guarded?" *Ooh. Maybe that is not the best topic of conversation.* He shrugged nonchalantly and tried to cover his mistake. "We rarely see guards around the markets at home in Egypt."

"Why are you asking such questions?" The young man looked into his eyes at last.

Salmon laughed. "I was just wondering. Say, Jathniel, let's go back to the market center and find—"

"Obviously, the gate is not this direction," Jathniel interrupted, grabbing Salmon by the arm before he finished his sentence. He gave the guard a quick nod. "Excuse us. We must hurry if we expect to reach Jebus by nightfall."

"Halt." The guard stepped away from the wall with his hand on the hilt of his sword. "There are hostile people camped across the river. We have added more guards to watch for anything suspicious."

"Really! Do you know who those hostile people are or where they come from?"

"More important for me to know is who *you* are and where *you* come from. Those robes do not look like the ones we see Egyptians wearing anymore. My grandfather had an old worn-out one in that style."

"That's funny, actually." Jathniel danced into the conversation lightheartedly. His shaved eyebrows arched high making his eyes very open and very bright. "*Our* grandfather was the one who sent us on this trip. Before we left, he pulled these old robes out of a trunk and made us wear them. He said we had to dress to impress. Aren't grandfathers something?"

The guard stared at him without responding. Salmon's mind was scanning desperately in search of a clever way to extricate the two of them from this situation when heavy footsteps sounded behind them. "Why are you talking to these two vendors, Shinab?" It was the grizzle-bearded commander who had scrutinized them so menacingly at the gate.

"They were asking about the guards, sir. Odd questions from merchants."

A small crowd of shoppers seemed to appear from nowhere and collected around them. Salmon noticed the same young woman who had been watching them earlier with the interest of a spy. She did not have her water pot or a length of fabric or anything else from the market. *Why was she out here in the street again?*

"These two have finished their business," the young guard continued. "It is early enough to begin their homeward trek, but they headed away from the gate. They claim to be lost."

The older man stroked his beard slowly, studying them with hard, glittering eyes. "Are you boys trying to find your way back to the gate or are you spying on our city?"

"Right now we need to decide whether we can reach Jebus before nightfall or if we should stay the night," Jathniel answered quickly with a nod toward the sign at the end of the street. He yawned. "I'm suddenly really tired."

"A hearty meal and a good night's sleep at an inn sounds wonderful." Salmon didn't have to try to sound tired. His strength was draining out through his feet. "If you will excuse us, we've had a long trek and not much sleep. We sold all our grandfather's goods, and we really need a rest now."

"Not so fast." The captain prolonged his ominous head-to-toe scrutiny.

Don't squirm. Salmon warned himself. *Show exhaustion, not fear.*

"You are the very ones who looked suspicious to me when you entered with the first caravan of the morning. Where are you from?"

The circle of onlookers tightened. *The lion had not yet made his kill, but the jackals already smelled blood.*

Jathniel repeated their story once again. They were Egyptians sent by their grandfather to sell an old collection of jewelry.

"How do we know you are not spies from those marauders who just captured the plains of Moab?"

Salmon laughed nervously, "I saw the river from afar as we came over the pass. It is a muddy, raging torrent. Do you think we are birds that we could fly across it? Or fish that could swim?" He forced himself to keep smiling.

"Some people can swim. Most Egyptians, in fact."

"Well, not us. Besides, have you known of anyone swimming with such a heavy bundle of silver and gold ornaments as we carried through the gates this morning?" he chuckled. "That would be a sight to behold. Our grandfather really loaded us up."

Neither of the guards granted them even the hint of a smile.

Jathniel decided to take a different approach. "Say, we are thirsty as well as hungry and exhausted. Is this a good place to get a drink?" He winked at the guards. "We have done well with our sales. We will purchase refreshments for the two of you."

"I'll go with you," the older man grunted. "Shinab, I want you to inquire among the merchants who came in on the Egyptian road this morning. See if any of them know these two. Find out how long they traveled with that caravan."

The young man leered at Salmon and Jathniel. "Yes, my captain. I was waiting for you to give that order. I think the king's elite guard may trap us a couple of rats today. King Nahari will be pleased."

Salmon's heart sank. The *captain* of the king's elite guard? How were they going to get away from this man?

In his anxiety, Salmon had hardly noticed the woman. He didn't see her slip up beside the captain until he heard the lilt of a remarkably melodious voice. "Please . . . bring them to our place, Ahuzzath."

It was *her*, the spy. *How did he miss that seductive snake slithering in so close?*

"We have had so few guests this past week that Father has set me to tending the flax up on the roof." She pouted her brightly painted lips and wrinkled her nose in disgust. "It is ever so slow to break down even though I turn it faithfully several times each day."

An unnerving conviction that this was all an act slid through Salmon's mind. *What is her game? We have no more jewelry. She must be in league with the guards, but what can she give them now? They have already snagged their prey.*

"Just look at my hands, Ahuzzath." She held up her open palms. Salmon could see a number of fine, red cuts in the soft flesh.

"If I am reduced to such demeaning labor, how can I play my harp?" Her face was so brazenly close to the captain that she could have kissed him. "If you would only honor us as our guest this morning, my mother will surely insist that I sing and play instead of tend flax."

"I'm certain that Keziah does not consider me an honored guest."

The woman hesitated. "But don't you think I do, Ahuzzath. And . . . our place is practically empty. Not a bed was filled last night so Mother will be eager for any guest to linger in our hall. Um . . . did I tell you that my father is away on business this morning?"

Ahuzzath leered at the woman. The eyes were hungry, but the tightened jaw betrayed a battle within. Salmon watched the man's warrior sensibilities win. "I have a job to do right now."

The woman was also watching the captain's expression carefully. "Are you afraid these mysterious merchants will slip from your grasp?" she said teasingly. "Shinab is not the only guard posted on this street. I have seen two others just across from the inn. Oh! Of course you know that. It must have been you who put them there." She leaned close and murmured, "My captain thought to protect his little singer . . . Now your thoughtfulness reaps a second benefit. Your protecting guards . . . will allow you . . . to take a long overdue break with me this morning. Come. Relax a bit at the inn while you wait for Shinab's report. With the wise precautions you have already made, no captive could escape."

Ahuzzath's eyes narrowed with suspicion. "I don't need those guards. I can watch these men quite well myself."

"I don't doubt that. What I meant was your guards could do the watching while you . . ." She walked her fingers up his shaggy beard and caressed his cheek. "While . . . we . . . spend some time together like the old days."

Confusion flickered over the captain's face.

"Send Shinab on his way. Then at least come in and rest while you await his report. I'll sing a special song just for you."

"A song? Well, there are no rules against that." The captain visibly relaxed. "There is no reason I can't listen to my little songbird as long as it does not interfere with my work. Shinab, bring word to the North Wall Inn as soon as you learn anything." A silly grin spread over his face as he clutched clumsily at the fingers lingering on his face and pressed them to his lips. "I deserve a little diversion this morning."

Salmon was amazed at how mere words transformed this guard. The spy-woman smiled teasingly as she pulled her hand away from Ahuzzath's increasingly passionate kisses. She took the grizzled captain by the crook of his arm and led him toward the north wall. Salmon could not for the life of him fathom this woman's motives, but he was quite certain that her entangling wiles were weaving a deadly net.

"Watch for a chance to slip away with the crowds while she distracts him," Jathniel whispered.

"Look around. The crowds lost interest. They're all gone."

Suddenly Ahuzzath wheeled around. "Move you two. Walk in front."

"But we don't know where—"

"Just head straight through that door at the end of this street."

Jathniel shrugged nonchalantly as they complied, but fear froze his brow. "At least we have an opportunity to check out the wall up close and some of the rooms built into it," he mumbled morbidly.

Salmon stole another backward glance at the antics of the bewitchingly beautiful woman. The captain's attention may have been sidetracked by her, but he had the feeling *she* didn't miss anything. "God help us."

The seductive murmurings followed them all the way to the end of the street, but Salmon did not risk another look. He glanced helplessly at Jathniel when they reached the doorstep, loath to step freely into whatever prison lay within that wall. While he hesitated, the woman pressed past them. As she passed, she slid her hand along Salmon's arm. To others it might have looked as if she were lightly brushing him out of her path, but he felt something more. She raised her eyebrows to signal something. *Was she trying to get his attention or get him killed?* Whatever it was she was trying to communicate, he did not want to know.

She sashayed up the steps and, in one beautiful, fluid move, pulled the heavy door open, leaning against it to hold it with her body. When she gestured invitingly toward the interior, the captain bounded up the steps like an eager child. Jathniel followed the captain into the inn built into this astonishing wall, but Salmon froze. He glanced up. The wall towered high above the doorway. All that was within him willed for a way to be up and over it. He did not articulate a prayer, but surely Yahweh already knew their need and desire.

"I'm not going to hold this door all day," the woman said with a laugh. He felt her eyes on him again, intense, communicative, but he kept his averted, feeling foolishly naive. He didn't know what she was trying to tell him, but he was quite certain it had nothing to do with tunnels through buttressing embankments or escape routes over the top. He shuddered as he dragged his feet up the steps and crossed the threshold. He hoped she wouldn't notice his reluctance.

Apparently, she did and found it amusing. She laughed lightly and let the door swing heavily against his shoulder to nudge him completely in. "I was beginning to think you were not going to join the party."

The woman pressed past them through a dim antechamber into the lamp-lit room beyond. Ahuzzath followed like a pet dog.

"Getting away from that one might prove even more difficult than escaping the captain," Salmon whispered. Jathniel's frozen brows did not so much as twitch a response. The two of them remained glued to the door.

Ahuzzath wheeled around with a sudden growl. "Move, you two, and stop whispering about my woman."

Salmon looked at the captain in horror. *Had he heard?*

In two strides, Ahuzzath returned to face them, demented rage burning in his eyes, more bestial than anything Salmon had ever witnessed before. "I saw her touch you, you foreign slime ball, but if you ever return the touch—whether you are honest Egyptian merchants or desert rats—you will die."

"That will not be a problem, Captain," Jathniel answered instantly.

Ahuzzath pulled the door open and called to the guards standing in the shadows across the street. "Keep your eyes open, you two. These *Egyptians* do not leave this place without me, understand?"

"Understood, sir."

Ahuzzath shoved the spies roughly through the antechamber. It was a passageway that proceeded about eight feet—presumably through the first thick wall—then opened into a surprisingly long, bright room. Thick cushions in rich colors around scattered low tables covered much of the floor. There were no windows, but the light of oil lamps cast a warm golden glow throughout. A group of three patrons lounged on the far side of the room, eating and drinking quietly. A woman stood near them, leaning against a wall. Other than that, the dining hall was empty.

Ahuzzath removed his helmet and laid it atop his shield next to a stairway leading to a higher level. He backed to a stout pillar near the center of the room, keeping his eyes fixed on the spies as if daring his captives to bolt. "Over here," he commanded, unbuckling his belt and scabbard and dropping heavily onto a thick purple cushion. He positioned his weapon on the stone floor close to his right hand and then called to the woman across the room. "Keziah, bring me a drink. Make it your best. These two Egyptians are paying." His eyes glinted with cold, predatory evil as he beckoned to the young woman. "Now, sing for me, Rahab."

The spy-woman showed no emotion as she seated herself on a low platform a few feet from where Ahuzzath lounged, but when she picked up her harp—a beautifully crafted instrument, intricately carved with a lion's head and twining vines—when she began plucking its strings, Salmon felt the rush of a hundred emotions at once. He deliberately steeled his mind and body against the pull of the haunting melody she coaxed from the instrument. Then she began to sing and the sparkling notes resonated with his very life force like the clean, bright thrill of a rippling brook in a green meadow or the liquid praises of songbirds rejoicing in a new dawn. How could evil sound so good?

The notes filled the room, lulling all of them into a dreamlike spell. Salmon struggled to keep his mind alert as Rahab sang of spring, of roses and lilies, and love. He wanted nothing more than to drift on the current of her song wherever it led, but he squeezed his eyes shut as if that would help block the sound. *Help me, O my God. Don't let me succumb to this foreign woman's song.* He glanced at Jathniel, but his friend was intent on watching Ahuzzath. As the captain drained the last drops of his beer and called for more, Salmon took a cautious sip from the cup he had been given. The drink was bitter and burning. He coughed.

Jathniel caught his eyes and indicated a slight "no."

When Salmon looked back at Ahuzzath, the captain's eyes were half closed and he wondered wildly if they could make a quick dash for the door if the man fell asleep.

"Would you like to go up to the Red Room?" Rahab asked cautiously, stopping her strumming and reaching out to Ahuzzath with a graceful gesture.

The captain jolted to attention. "Are you trying to get me killed? I'm here doing a job."

"Forgive me, Ahuzzath. My mind was just muddled by having you here with me . . . practically alone." Her smile seemed contrived.

"Don't lie to me," Ahuzzath sniffed. "All you give me anymore are songs—the same as every other man."

"But you are not the same as every other man." Her smile did not match the pain in her eyes. "You know that very well."

Ahuzzath's eyes narrowed with suspicion. "When I try to buy time with you, your father refuses. When I try to win you with words of love, you put me off. What is different this morning?" His eyes were hard and threatening. "If I come back when I am off duty tonight, then what?"

"I will be here." She did not wait for a reply, but began to strum again, extruding a particularly melancholy, but sweet tune from her harp. "Relax now. Drift off in sleep and dream of tonight while I sing for you."

Ahuzzath sighed and leaned back against the pillar. "I hear longing in that song. You *have* been wanting me. I *knew* it. Just waiting for your father to be gone." He smacked his lips sleepily. "Tonight . . . at her request . . . her desire . . ."

He had nearly drifted off to sleep when he belched loudly and sat up with a start. "What—?"

Rahab's continued her sad-sweet song without missing a beat. Then Jathniel spoke up. "Actually, ma'am, the two of us are quite tired. We would be pleased to take you up on the offer of a room. We tried to sleep out in the fields last night, and believe me, it was not restful."

"The rats want to sleep?" Ahuzzath mumbled, rubbing his beard. "Or want my Rahab?"

The breath Rahab was taking in preparation for the next strain caught slightly in her throat and a fleeting glimmer of fear flared in her eyes. But the song flowed smoothly on.

Jathniel held his hand up in protest as a scarlet flush crept from his neck to his bare scalp. "Believe me, we just want to sleep." Jathniel's manner was so boyishly disarming that Ahuzzath could not suspect him of lying.

The captain regarded both young men with his searching eyes for a moment. "No . . . you green sticks are not competitors for my Rahab." He scratched his crotch and nodded at the woman. "Why not? Take them to a room—but not the Red Room. Hurry back, my little songbird. I'll be waiting right here." His eyes misted over and he yawned. "Aaaaaaah. Save the Red Room for me—for tonight."

Salmon caught a shadow of fear and revulsion cross Rahab's face as she laid down her harp and motioned for him and Jathniel to follow. She paused by the sleeping captain. "Yes, Ahuzzath. Dream of tonight."

His eyes popped open and he grabbed at her foot. "My little Rahab . . ." He slid his hand over her bare ankle and looked up with a simpering smile. "There has been no one else for me since I first knew you as a young thing."

"I will be back very soon to finish my song." Rahab's tone was cool and detached as she slipped from his grasp. "Come this way, you two."

The captain's face suddenly reddened with rage. He sat up straight and roared at her. "What are you up to, Rahab? I *will* have more than a song tonight."

Rahab turned back and stooped down in front of the captain, brushing her hand across his hairy knee. "More than a song, Ahuzzath. Calm down. Sleep now, and when you are off duty, the whole night will belong to you."

His eyes blazed hotly into hers and his voice dropped to an anger-choked mutter. "You better not be toying with me. Did you hear how I dealt with those disease-bearing harlots of Midian?"

The captain looked down at his huge hands and slowly crushed them together. His eyes glazed over and an evil smirk twisted his lips. "I strangled them, one by one. Squeezed each pretty little throat like this. A long, long, enjoyable night playing with them to raise their hopes and then dispatching them in obedience to my king's command." The vile grin spread as Ahuzzath withdrew into a private world of sordid pleasure.

Rahab's face was impassive as stone as she rose to her feet. "Follow me," she said to the spies. "I will show you to your room."

"Don't linger up there with those two," Ahuzzath growled.

Salmon couldn't move. He stared at the depraved captain in astonishment. The demented eyes caught his briefly. A warning. Then as if this was an ordinary social occasion, Ahuzzath picked up his cup and drained it. "Aaaaah. That was fine barley beer, Rahab. Tell your mother for me. So fine." Almost immediately, he slouched back against the pillar and his eyes returned to their former half-closed, sleepy state. He yawned noisily, "Aaaaah . . . sweet brew in my belly and even sweeter dreams . . . Mmm-mmm . . . of my lil' Rahab."

As the captain fell asleep, Rahab touched her finger to her lips and motioned for Salmon and Jathniel to follow. She prattled in a businesslike way as they headed toward the stairs. "If you stay just for the afternoon, it will be three shekels of silver. If overnight, four shekels. Women to sleep with are extra. Food or drink—"

Suddenly, Ahuzzath bolted upright again. "Wake me as soon as Shinab returns, you hear?"

Just as abruptly, he leaned his head back against the supporting pillar and closed his eyes. "Aaaaah . . ." His mouth stretched open in another wide yawn and a strand of saliva stretched from the upper lip to the lower one. "Take the rats upstairs, mmm? I'll just snooze a bit right here." He began to snore immediately.

Salmon looked at Jathniel. *Did they dare make a break for it now?* He flicked his eyes toward the door, trying hard to state his question without words.

Rahab gave him a sharp warning with her eyes, then jerked her head toward the stairs in an almost desperate signal to follow her. Salmon's temples pounded as she dashed up the stairs and Jathniel followed her. *There were guards watching the door. Ahuzzath dozed lightly in the dining hall. And this devious woman was leading them to an unknown place for an unknown purpose.* His palms and armpits were wet with perspiration, and he had the feeling they were trapped in a spider's web, increasingly entangled in its sticky threads—soon to be devoured by who knew which predator. Jathniel was already halfway up the stairs so he followed reluctantly. Above all else they must not become separated.

A long hallway with a line of identical doors transected the top of the stairs. Rahab opened the central door to reveal a room richly draped in heavy scarlet fabric. Light filtered into the room from a small, high window directly above a bed luxuriously pillowed and blanketed in red. "Quickly now. Inside!"

"The Red Room?" Salmon gulped. "The captain . . . We would prefer . . ."

Rahab ignored his hesitation and seeming almost frantic, pushed the two of them through the door. She closed and bolted it. "We have no time to lose," she whispered as the lock slid securely into place. "Follow me."

Before either of the spies could move, she flew across the room and clambered up a ladder attached to the wall. As soon as she reached the top, she pushed up on a small square door in the ceiling, exposing a bright block of sky.

"Don't just stand there gawking," she snapped. "Your lives are in grave danger. Mine too. Come up here."

Jathniel obediently responded to her outburst, but still Salmon hesitated. Perhaps they were about to exit the inn, but only the inn. That door would take them to the top of a very high, well-guarded wall. Not much chance of escaping Jericho that way.

"Come on, Salmon. We don't have a lot of choices here." Jathniel's tone had become as urgent as that of the woman he followed.

Salmon watched his friend disappear. He had a sensation of sinking rather than ascending as he forced himself to take the first step up the ladder. The late afternoon sun was blinding as Salmon emerged onto a flat rooftop covered with bundles of soggy plant material. The musty smell might have been unpleasant, but it was the smell of the earth, not city streets. A friendlier smell, a friendlier place than the inn below.

Rahab dropped the door carefully back into place behind him. Her eyes flashed when she rose to face them. "Could two spies be more inept?" she hissed. "I followed you around the market to help you, but you created this *mess*. What possessed you to engage one of the king's guard in conversation?"

Salmon looked at Jathniel. *What should they say?*

"Look, I know you are with the people across the river, the people of Israel. Your lives are in danger, and we haven't much time. You have to trust me."

Salmon's heart dropped and he had to tighten his jaw so it would not follow. He could not fathom this woman's true intentions, but here in the full sunlight, she looked much younger than he had first thought. The seductive expressions she had been tossing at the captain were gone, and now the heavy black kohl lining her eyes and the bright red lip color looked out of place. She was not much more than a child.

"You are no more Egyptian than I am," Rahab continued a little more calmly. A trace of amusement crinkled the corners of her eyes. "We entertain people from many countries here at the inn, and I have never met such ridiculously callow travelers. Have you never been in a city before?"

"What do you want from us?" Salmon finally managed to mumble.

"I know how your God leveled Egypt and led your people out. How he dried up the water of the Red Sea and destroyed Pharaoh's army. All my life, I have listened to the reports of caravan traders, telling how your God was keeping you alive in desert areas that normally swallow up anyone who goes there. I believe your God is the great God of heaven above and the earth below, and I believe he guided me to you." Her eyes shone as she continued. "Most importantly, the people of Jericho are well aware of what you just did to Sihon and Og—and Midian. When the people of this city heard of it, their hearts melted. Courage fled."

Salmon stared at her, hardly believing the words he was hearing.

"My grandmother raised me with the belief that you would someday come to take over this entire land, and I have prayed to your God that he would deliver me—and my entire family—from this place by his mighty hand as he delivered you from Egypt." Her eyes darted from Salmon's to Jathniel's and back rapidly. "Here is my proposal. I will help you escape if you promise to save us."

Salmon hesitated. He felt genuine compassion for this girl, but Joshua had repeatedly reminded them the entire city and all its inhabitants were destined for destruction. He specifically warned them not to be enticed by the women. While he was struggling to frame an honest reply, Jathniel spoke up. "Our lives are in your hands. What do you want us to do?" His survival instincts had obviously taken over.

"Lie down over here and I will cover you with flax."

She continued whispering as she worked. "Ahuzzath is quite suspicious of you, but he will be slower to suspect deceit from me. I am sure of it. He has known me . . . well . . . most of my life." Rahab's words became more and more muffled as she laid the thick bundles of flax over them, blocking out light and fresh air.

"We have had so much rain that none of the fibers are ready for processing. I'm going to thicken this layer and leave decoy piles about the same size curing all around the rooftop." Swishing and scraping sounds followed her movements. When the rustling of the straw ceased, she bent so close they could hear her breathe as she issued her last command. "Don't move. I'm going to stick my pitchfork between you in this pile."

Salmon felt the crunching pressure between himself and Jathniel. "I must hurry back down to finish my . . . lullaby," she whispered. The door creaked open and softly thumped closed again. He heard two or three light scraping footsteps on the ladder, and then they were left in oppressive silence.

Time passed, and the moisture in the flax created a dreadful stench and a sticky itching as the fierce afternoon sun beat down on the rooftop. Salmon ignored the discomfort, trying to work out an escape plan as he forced himself to remain absolutely motionless. Whether moments or hours later, he couldn't tell, but a barrage of angry words woke him with a start. The entire inn below rumbled with the heavy stomping of feet, the voices of men and women in battle, sounds of splintering wood, shattering pottery, and slamming doors punctuated by shrieking protests and cries of pain. He pictured the heavy, bronze-clad war sandals of the guards. There were far more feet down there than just Ahuzzath and his scrawny assistant.

Not long after the commotion died down, the rooftop door creaked open and a raspy voice mumbled, "Flax curing up here just as she said . . ." The voice was unquestionably that of the grizzled old commander. The door creaked again, and Salmon imagined he heard it lightly touch closed. He was sorry for the disturbance and destruction below in the inn, but it seemed that Rahab's plan was working. The innkeeper's daughter had outfoxed the fox.

He remained unmoving in the ensuing silence, but when he heard the inn door slam and footsteps in the street, tension released his coiled muscles like a hand setting a bowstring free. He nearly flew from the steaming vegetation like an arrow, but caution warned him to wait. He calmed his beating heart with slow, measured breaths, allowing only mental applause for Rahab's craftiness. He would wait for her at least until well past dark.

With a sudden loud crack, the door slammed back against its hinges and the gravelly voice grumbled. "The quiet didn't bring any rats out of hiding. Now I have to search through this stinking mess."

That old fox has been watching and listening. Waiting to trap us.

Salmon held his breath as heavy boots scraped against the rungs of the ladder and then shuffled through the flax straight for their hiding place.

He knows. The man-sized mounds covering us are a dead give away.

The shuffling stopped just a step away. The straw at his side rustled. He felt the pull on the pitchfork. With a soft, shushing crunch a few feet beyond him, Ahuzzath jabbed the pitchfork back into the flax. More jabs, more crunching followed the muttering voice as the captain worked his way slowly across the rooftop. "That little vixen let those rats sneak away." Jab, jab, crunch. "The king's dungeon would be a waste though. I will take great pleasure in punishing her carelessness myself."

Jab, crunch.

"Ha! This flax gives me an idea. Just the place to teach her a lesson." The captain's voice thickened as he jabbed more and more vigorously, the crunching of the pitchfork moving farther away with each thrust.

"A little prodding with her own pitchfork." Jab, jab, crunch. "I'll get more than information from the little harlot tonight. More than a song. Oooh, she'll give what she promised."

There was a moment of silence, no footsteps or jabs. "Clearly, they are not up here. I should have known. Rahab doesn't have to be told I would have to kill her if she helped them." The heavy tool clattered on the stone floor and the heavy footsteps scraped on the rungs of the ladder again.

Ahuzzath's coarse laugh sent an icy shiver down Salmon's spine. "Ha-ha! Oh yes! The perfect place for interrogation. Ha-ha, hee-hee! She'll give me answers, even if a bit unwillingly—then she'll give me what she promised down in the Red Room. Hee-hee, ha-ha!" The door banged sharply closed, dampening the evil glee as it muffled the steps descending the ladder. "This time, it will be *me* singing the song. Hee-hee . . ."

Rage shot through Salmon. Moses' command flashed through his mind, "Do not pity them. Make no treaty with them." They *had* made a treaty of sorts but not with the likes of him. Surely a good woman like Rahab should be saved. As Salmon thought about the captain's revolting plan, he realized it meant Rahab was alive and that she had not been thrown into the king's dungeon. *Yet.*

There was no assurance that this would end well for her—or for two inexperienced spies. The muffled silence, this unnerving time of waiting seemed to stretch on for hours—maybe days, or even weeks. Part of him yearned to push away enough flax to get a deep, fresh breath of air, but the rest of him was frozen with fear. He was too agitated to sleep and too anxious to devise an effective escape plan. There was no question that Rahab would die if they were discovered. It was only right to rescue her from this place. But would they escape Jericho? And if they did, could they return to rescue her before it was too late?

When the stifling heat began to decrease, Salmon guessed that the great shadow of the western hills had crept over the city. Panic gripped his throat again. The city gates were never left open after dark. *Does Rahab know of another point of exit from the city?* Suddenly, he was filled with fresh doubts. *Can we trust her? She seems sincere, but so many were deceived by the women of Midian. God, show us the truth.*

At last, the squeaking hinges turned again. The footsteps padding across the straw were soft and light. "The pitchfork," Rahab gasped. "Noooo!" As she flew to their flax pile, both men bolted up out of their bed of straw.

Rahab stopped and stared at them. "Are you—?"

"All right." Jathniel and Salmon finished her question, answering in duet.

"I feared he had killed you," she said in a teary voice. She turned her face away and began fluffing the straw to obliterate evidence of their hiding place.

"Thanks be. He did not find us," Salmon whispered.

Jathniel almost giggled in giddiness. "It worked," was all he could say.

When Rahab finished putting the straw—as well as her emotions—in order, she stood up facing the two spies again. The sky was jeweled with stars already and the muffled sounds from the city seemed far away. It was a beautiful night, but the moonlight reflecting across Rahab's face revealed dark bruising on her cheek and a swollen left eye. A cut at the corner of her mouth was still oozing blood, but no one had ever seemed more beautiful to Salmon. She was the bravest woman he had ever met. "Rahab—"

She turned and headed for the trap door. "Follow me."

Salmon and Jathniel instantly obeyed. Salmon had no doubts now that she meant only to help them and was capable of doing so.

As soon as they slipped down the ladder to the unlit room below, Rahab moved a bedside table directly below the window. After pulling back the heavy draperies with a red cord, she retrieved a coil of rope from under the covers of the bed. "My grandmother says this will nearly reach the ground. She purchased it in the market a few days ago with the idea of escaping the city herself."

Salmon watched with a growing sense of wonder as Rahab lashed the rope around a heavy oak beam. Her grandmother shared stories of faith in Yahweh. Her grandmother had been devising a plan to escape from Jericho. He had no idea how he would explain the situation to Joshua, but they must honor their promise to save this family in exchange for their lives. "You risked your life to save us," he said boldly to her back as she worked. "If you and your family do not betray us, we will treat you kindly and faithfully when Yahweh gives us the land."

Rahab did not stop to look down at him. "Agreed."

"Our bag of silver is still in the common room. Take it. Use it for yourself and your family. Whatever you need in the days ahead."

"Food costs are rising here in the city, and the past few months have been lean ones for the inn. My father will be grateful." She turned to face him and attempted to stretch her swollen lips in a smile, but her face contorted in a wince of pain. "I'm grateful too. It just hurts to show it."

The light-hearted attempt at humor brought tears to Salmon's eyes. She took that battering for him and for Jathniel. "May my God protect you and your family from further harm," he said earnestly. "Do not let Ahuzzath into your house tonight. He has fiendish plans to harm you. I heard his mutterings while he was searching the rooftop where we hid."

"Do not be concerned about me. Ahuzzath will be occupied looking for you tonight and the next. The king has ordered his elite guard to search the city. Then, of course, they will broaden the search to the surrounding countryside. There will be no stopping for anything else—unless they find you. I pray in the name of your God, they will not. Now you must go."

"How will we get to the river without getting caught?" Jathniel blinked nervously. His eyebrows arched high above small, black eyes.

Rahab offered a look of steadying confidence. "Go to the hills. Your pursuers will not expect you to go that way. Hide yourselves in one of the many caves there until the guards give up the search and return to the city."

Jathniel's eyebrows lowered a notch, but he still seemed apprehensive. "We have a cave already. How will we know when they have given up the search?"

"I know the king. He will not give them more than a few days to search for you. If they fail, judgment will be swift. Wait three days. It should be safe then. Just watch the city for signs that the search has ended."

Jathniel's eyebrows knit together tightly, giving him an odd, stern look. He pointed to the cord holding back the draperies. "We need to identify your house when Israel takes the city. The oath we swore to you will not be binding unless your window is marked with this scarlet cord when we enter the land."

Rahab nodded.

"And you must be sure that your father and mother, your brothers, and all your family are in this house. If anyone goes outside your house into the street, his blood will be on his own head. We will not be responsible."

"Yes, now go with God." She gestured toward the rope.

"As for anyone who is in the house with you, his blood will be on our head if a hand is laid on him."

"Exactly as you say," she replied. "Now go!"

"But if you tell what we are doing, we will be released from the oath you made us swear."

Rahab pushed him toward the window impatiently. "Do you think I am a fool? My life is in danger too."

Jathniel mounted the small table below the window and clambered out with his feet kicking awkwardly at the window frame and draperies until he disappeared and the rope grew taut against the sill. As soon as it slackened again, Rahab motioned Salmon toward the window. "I have a bundle of food and two skins of water for you. Enough for three days. I will let them down once you are safely on the ground. Then I will release this rope as well. Please take it. You may find it useful, and it would not do for Ahuzzath's hooligans to find it here or on the ground below this window. He would probably hang me with it."

"I have no doubt of that," Salmon whispered. The blackness of Ahuzzath's soul made her courage shine. Odd as it seemed, he felt a deep connection with this Canaanite. "We will return soon to rescue you. May Yahweh be with you and keep you safe." He took her hand and squeezed it to emphasize his promise and his prayer.

"Your much speaking will be the death of us all," she hissed, breaking free of his grip. "Go. Hurry." Her nudge toward the window was not gentle.

Salmon obeyed, scrambling hastily over the windowsill. The rope burned his palms as it slid through his grip and he wondered how hard he would land. Too late it occurred to him that he should have gripped tighter and slithered slower. He hit the ground with enough force to bring twinges of pain to both ankles and knees—but he was outside Jericho.

Jathniel helped him untie each water skin and the food bundle as Rahab let them down one by one. As soon as the rope dropped in a loose pile on the ground, the heavy red draperies closed across the high window above them. In an almost imperceptible movement, the end of a scarlet cord slipped over the sill, a faint symbol of hope dangling pathetically small against the pale blocks of Jericho's massive walls.

CHAPTER SIX

DUNGEONS AND CAVES

Salmon

Salmon and Jathniel stole quickly and quietly through the shadows of the palm grove. Low fog crept up from the river and swirled around their feet like a friendly cat, fog that might hide them if they made for the river. Against all reason, they headed west toward the ridge, away from Jericho—but also away from home.

"Going this direction feels so wrong," Salmon whispered.

Jathniel did not answer. Maybe he did not hear, but the palm fronds overhead swished in agreement and an owl screeched urgently. *Flee, fool! Flee, fool!* They reached the edge of the grove and paused to study the valley. From here, their cover would give way to open fields and vineyards. Every impulse within Salmon was summed up in that owl's call. *Flee, fool.* Run for the raft, the river, and the ride to safety.

Jathniel leaned close. "It is all so different looking away from the city instead of toward it. I'm not at all certain where our cave is." He seemed so calm, so committed to Rahab's directive.

Salmon studied the brooding threat of the dark ridge. The conviction that packs of guards lurked like wolves somewhere in those shadows gnawed at the edges of his courage. Jathniel expressed those fears in simple words. "We certainly don't want to get caught stumbling around looking for it."

"No, we don't," Salmon answered, "but look." He pointed east away from the ridge. "The hills are exposed by the moonlight, but see how the river basin is completely shrouded in fog. Logic says to cross the Jordan tonight under cover of its night vapors."

"That is just the logic the guards will employ as they search for us. Follow Rahab's advice. Seeking our old cave seems quite logical to me right now. Besides, I will need the three days in the cave as she suggested for recovery."

"For . . .?"

"For healing. I twisted my ankle when I hit the ground below the window, and then there's this." Jathniel pulled up his robe enough to reveal a dark line of puncture wounds running diagonally across his thigh. "I cannot limp far or fast tonight."

All Salmon's forebodings vanished at the sight of the ugly wound. "What happened?"

"The first jab of Ahuzzath's pitchfork was on target, but the Lord sealed my lips against an outcry of pain."

"But how? How did you manage to walk this far?"

"Fear supplies surprising strength."

"Enough to get up that hill to the cave?"

"I'll be fine if we aren't chased," Jathniel waved his hand dismissively. "The important thing is *finding* the cave before someone sees us."

Salmon scanned the western horizon with a different urgency now, and its outline no longer evoked danger but refuge. He pointed to a silhouette mounding blacker than the dark sky on the top of the ridge. "See that oak? I believe it is the one just above our cave. It's the only one that large along the rim."

"You, my friend, are one amazing spy. We can cut diagonally through the barley fields until we reach the vineyard terrace directly below it. We'll have good cover from there on up."

Now that Salmon's anxiety had lifted, the cave did not seem so far away. The cut stubble where they waited for the caravan was just across the road.

"Flax field, here I come." Jathniel suddenly bolted from his side and hobble-sprinted across the road toward the wide-open fields.

We are committed now. Salmon broke from the protective shadows and ran after his friend. He caught up just as they reached the plowed field—just as Jathniel faltered on the furrows of uneven ground. Salmon lunged at him before he could fall and seized an arm to steady him. "If you can't give me any warning, at least give me that heavy water bag." He pulled Jathniel's goatskin from him and slung it over his own shoulder alongside his.

"Thanks. Looks like I need more than fear to keep me on my feet." The inner edges of the bare spots that should have been Jathniel's eyebrows scrunched up as he offered a pained, apologetic smile.

"Lean on me. This field is too exposed a place for the slow stumbling of an injured man."

With the bags of water and provisions bouncing and slapping together awkwardly on one side and his friend limping on the other, they raced in awkward tandem. The misty vapor following their feet across the open fields hovered close to the ground, covering the flax stubble with pale, feathery whiteness. Salmon found his fear fading in the mysterious dream-like quality of their flight. He marked the direction to the oak on the ridge, noting where the field ended and the terraced vineyards began, and then concentrated on steering his friend's unsteady gait along the most level paths. Skillfully dodging mounds where the crops protruded above the billowing blanket of fog, occasionally surprised by sinking into depressions where knee-high billows of mist had settled, Salmon zigzagged across the field. All at once, the fog rose in his face. They were totally enveloped in a featureless world of moonlit gray. All the stars above them were eclipsed.

"That was sudden," Salmon groaned. "Every guide gone. I don't even know which way we need to head. I was focused on the ground right in front of our feet."

"Have no fear. I kept my eyes on the goal while yours were so intent on our path. We were angling toward the northern end of the vineyard terraces. If we maintain this same bearing, we will reach the vineyards well to the north of the cave."

"Then what? Hide until we can see?"

"You don't *see*, do you?" Jathniel laughed at his own joke. "Remember the rock outcropping jutting down from the cave entrance? The vine rows will keep our path straight until we meet those rocks and follow them up to the cave. We can't miss it."

"The way everything else has gone wrong today, we will."

"No way. That rocky track was the last thing I saw before the world vanished. It forms a direct line from just below our oak down into the lowest terrace. We will find those rocks, and they will lead us home."

"Home?" Salmon sniffed indignantly.

"It will feel like home to me tonight."

Salmon found that it helped to close his eyes rather than be confused by the billowing gray, better blind than stumbling, muddled by a world that whirled and roiled until he couldn't tell if he was standing straight or precariously close to toppling over. He kept a firm, supporting hand on Jathniel, while trying to maintain a straight trajectory. All he wanted was to go home, the real home in camp, and here he was heading the opposite way in a mental as well as physical fog. He remembered the horror on his mother's face when she learned of this mission. What would happen to her and Ada if he never escaped this nightmare? "Surely, our spy mission is cursed," he groaned aloud.

"I was just thinking how blessed we are. We escaped the hands of Ahuzzath. Rahab provided us with food. And now Yahweh conceals our flight to the cave." There was a tremor in his voice. "I wonder if this could be *The* Cloud."

Salmon snorted. "I hardly think *The* Cloud would leave all Israel to follow two spies, but . . . you are right. Focus on the blessings. As long as we don't lose our way . . . or bump into our pursuers in our blindness, we are bless—"

"Listen. Voices!" Jathniel's whispered chastisement was almost inaudible. "Our muttering *will* curse this whole endeavor."

Salmon stomach twisted at his carelessness. *Our enemies may be blind tonight, but not deaf.* The obscuring cloak had caused him to feel somewhat safer. Now Rahab's battered face rose before him. She had saved their lives, but her life depended on two inept spies getting safely back to Joshua. *Her life—* His throat tightened at the strange thought, an Israelite boy so concerned over the safety of a Canaanite stranger.

As soon as they scrambled up the stone wall to the lowest of the vineyard terraces, Jathniel pulled from Salmon's grip and dropped to the ground. He stifled a moan and gripped his leg. "I cannot go on."

Salmon studied the vague branching shapes, barely visible in the surrounding mist. "Crawl over there," he whispered. "The vines have leafed out enough to hide you even if the fog clears. I'll be back straightaway."

Hunching down to the level of the vines despite the cover of fog, Salmon sped swiftly alongside the neatly-trellised row until a large rock barrier barred his path. Jathniel had been right about that. They couldn't miss the rocks. Now if only it would be as easy to find the opening of their hideout.

He clambered over and around the rock extrusion, but as he left the highest of the three terraces, the grade of the hill increased sharply and became more uneven, forcing him to detour around boulders, pits, and thickets of brambles. The direct line of the stony outcropping was soon completely lost. By the time Salmon reached the crest of the ridge, the mist had thinned, allowing a murky vision of objects at least a stone's throw away. He still could not see the landmark oak and he had missed their cave.

Dread filled his stomach with lead. It was all on him. Jathniel's life. His family's welfare. Rahab's salvation. Her family. He picked his way down the ridge until he hit the rocks once more, this time determined to search every craggy gap and not leave the formation. He crisscrossed the rocks again, scratching through brambles, stumbling over the rough terrain in the murky darkness, fighting a panicky desperation when he heard that same owl's call. *Flee, fool! Flee, fool!*

Maybe it wasn't an owl. Maybe it was a guard lurking and laughing at him from behind the one of the dark masses of shrub or rock, signaling a partner who was ready to snag him as he passed. The snap of every twig seemed explosive. Every stone rattling away from his feet seemed to thunder into the silent vapors below, and yet the cave mouth continued to elude him. Dread grew to despair. He stopped. He could see the dark leaves of the vineyards spread out not far below him. In his blindness and panic, he had missed it again.

Flee, fool. Flee fool.

That bird, if it was a bird, was more than annoying.

Flee, fool. Or was it *Flee here?*

Salmon looked up just as the owl rose on silent wings from their landmark oak. The familiar tree shape, backlit by the misty glow of a quarter moon, was magically cheering. Just that quickly, despair took flight, leaving him rooted in hope as solid as that ponderous tree. Scrambling back up the ground he had just covered, it wasn't long before he found the small, black opening just as they had left it—far too well disguised with brush.

Dropping the water bags, rope, and food parcel inside, he returned to help Jathniel. Very shortly, both men settled inside their cold, dark haven—chilled and hungry, but safe and out of the drippy fog.

As Salmon pulled the tangle of brush back over the entrance, he heard the shouts and calls of Ahuzzath's guard again. Not faintly, not far off by the river, but louder, closer. Jathniel had collapsed immediately on the hard floor. He lay unmoving while Salmon retrieved the soft pile of their old clothing. Good. It did not appear to have been disturbed. He crept back to Jathniel and silently pressed one of the folded woolen garments into his hands, it hardly mattered whose was whose. Jathniel was shaking from shock and cold.

All the time that Salmon was helping his friend slip out of the soggy Egyptian garments and into dry ones, all the time that he was pulling the familiar wool tunic and cloak around himself, the sounds of searching guards echoed across the ridge, answering calls far down in the fields below. There were two groups beating toward each other, determined to flush out the escaped spies. Salmon felt vulnerable and small, but so grateful to be huddled safely in this spare shelter. Never had simple head coverings felt as good as this, tied warmly over baldness on a damp, chilly night. Never had those rough woolen clothes provided such comfort.

When both men had changed their garments, Salmon ripped strips of linen cloth from his Egyptian robe as bandages for Jathniel's wounds. It was too dark for hand signals and too risky for even minimal words, so there was no communication but touch as Salmon pressed a few morsels from Rahab's provisions into Jathniel's hands. They ate together in silence. Then, Salmon carried his injured friend deeper into the black depths, and they huddled together for warmth in a sleeping nook untouched by even the faintest ray of starlight.

Rahab

Rahab concentrated on her chin, holding it high, defying the fingers of fear gripping her throat as Ahuzzath led her down the empty, moonlit street to the palace. She knew of many who never returned after being escorted to the king. As she thought of it, she could not recall anyone she knew personally who *had* returned from there: whether petitioners gone voluntarily, girls taken for Nahari's pleasure, or suspects taken for questioning.

Her emotions had swung wildly in the hours since helping the spies escape—from the first breathless fear of immediate detection to anger at the property-destroying search of her father's inn. Hours later, she was much more relieved than fearful when Ahuzzath returned for further questioning. The fact that he was still searching meant that the spies had not been apprehended. That thought gave her a strange sensation of power as she endured a second battering interrogation. Then Shinab burst through the door with the report that the second, very thorough sweep of the city had been fruitless.

Did the captain want him to add those brigades to the platoons already searching the valley?

Ahuzzath exploded with demonic rage. Rahab knew this volatile and hateful man well, but this was far beyond anything she had ever witnessed in him before. His eyes flamed with wrath. He threatened to slaughter her entire family. He lashed out against the incompetence of the entire king's guard and Shinab in particular. Still muttering threats about petitioning the king to shut down the inn forever, he left with his scrawny underling in tow. Strangely, his threats had no sting at that moment. It was obvious that Ahuzzath's courage was unraveling at the thought of returning to King Nahari with no spies and no good leads. She found that revelation deeply satisfying.

The pleasure was short-lived, however, for Ahuzzath returned to her door not more than an hour later with the chilling summons. The king himself wished to question the last person who had seen the two Israelites. The muttered threats against her father and the inn haunted her now that they approached the king's massive dwelling. She had endangered her family in the attempt to save those spies. Her own life was disposable rubbish, but she must devise a scheme to protect the ones she loved. She had to. But . . . her mind was blank as she followed the captain up the stairway.

At the top of the steps, they entered a portico well-guarded by a score of men in cone-shaped helmets. The pair standing on either side of dark, olive-wood doors, snapped to attention, pounding the shank end of their spears on the pavement three times in rapid succession. The guard on the left whispered hurriedly, "Take care, captain. The king's mood is deteriorating."

As soon as a triplet of pounding echoes answered from within, the doormen simultaneously flung the doors wide and Rahab found herself staring down the aisle of a long, torch-lit room to a throne elevated on a stone dais at the far end. The monarch sat darkly on his imposing throne. Waiting. *Oh, may his ire fall on me. Not my parents and grandmother—better yet on his captain.*

"Permission to approach the king," the first door guard called out gruffly.

King Nahari did not so much as shift his eyes at his doorman's request, but when he raised his fingers in an almost imperceptible signal of assent, the response was dramatic. "Go!" one guard barked. Both doormen worked in tandem to sweep the pair into the cedar-beamed room with the long shafts of their spears. Immediately, the doors slammed behind them.

While Rahab was still fighting to regain solid footing, Ahuzzath shoved her forward again. She could feel the tip of his sword pressed sharply into the small of her back as a new set of guards fell into place beside her. Still the king remained motionless, watching without the slightest reaction to the scuffle in his courtroom. She stared at King Nahari. She had never seen him this close before. Sprawled carelessly on the cushioned seat of his intricately-carved cedar throne, long legs stretched out in front of him, head resting against the high, ivory-inlaid back, her king appeared less god-like than in his public appearances.

He watched the entering party with half-closed eyes, but he was not as relaxed as he appeared. Rahab felt the intensity of those eyes on her—like a lazy, beast-king watching his prey being driven into reach by his pack. Ignoring the sharp jabs prodding her back, she met Nahari's eyes with boldness. Although war sandals tramped noisily all around her and Ahuzzath marched with the stance of a victor behind his captive, her calmness increased with each step through that aisle of posted soldiers toward the king. She would do her best to make Nahari understand that his own captain was the one who let the spies slip away.

All at once, the escorting guards stomped a noisy rhythmic halt. "Kneel here," one grunted, enforcing his command with a swift knee-buckling blow to the backs of her legs. Her knees collapsed and slammed against the pavement, but she doggedly masked any response and clenched her jaw to suppress the cry of pain—even when Ahuzzath staggered, his blade grazing across her back as he nearly fell over her. She smiled smugly to herself. The action of Nahari's guards had caught the captain by surprise as well, providing a clear demonstration of the doddering fool he really was. As soon as he regained his footing, Ahuzzath sheathed his sword and bowed deeply. He finished his obeisance with a smart military salute, but no posing could restore the dignity lost in that ungainly entrance.

King Nahari shuffled his feet and pushed himself back on his throne, stretching up tall and proud. His prominent black eyes, hooded with well-defined lids, bulged wide open now, and Rahab could not look away. "You have delivered her promptly, Ahuzzath. A little rough on such a fine citizen, perhaps." His eyes wandered over her bruised face. "Rahab, daughter of Jokshan, the keeper of the North Wall Inn. Correct?"

Rahab nodded silently, and the king continued with hardly a pause. "Your popularity with the common people of the city is well known. Perhaps I will call for you to entertain me here in the palace some night." He paused and studied her face for a reaction. "Would you like that?"

"It would be an honor, my lord." She returned his gaze with steady eyes, allowing neither her fear nor her revulsion to show.

"I knew that would please you." He cleared his throat. "But that pleasure will be for another night. We understand you have had visitors from across the river. They are of great interest to us and we should like to . . . uh . . . question them."

"I have just learned, your majesty, of Ahuzzath's suspicions regarding the two guests in question. It was not until *after* they disappeared that I was told they might be Israelite spies." She turned to look over her shoulder at the captain. "When your captain brought them to the inn, he called them *Egyptians*."

The king gave a dismissing flick of his fingers. "But where did they go?"

"That I do not know, my lord."

Ahuzzath started to speak, but the king held up his hand. "But you knew my captain was watching them."

"Yes. But I did not know why. My task is to make sure the guests at my father's inn receive what they need."

"And just what did these men need?" The king leered at her.

Rahab did not flinch. "They stated they had spent the night on the caravan road. And indeed, they appeared very tired. Your captain granted their request to go to a room to rest. I complied and did my job."

"Did you sleep with them?"

"No, my lord."

King Nahari's eyes shifted below fearsome, overhanging brows. He fixed his captain with a cold glare. "Ahuzzath, you did not set a guard outside their room?"

"I had guards posted on the street just outside the inn, and I waited in the common room downstairs. They could not have escaped without help."

"I see," the king mumbled to himself, stroking his beard and silently studying Ahuzzath's face. "But they did."

There was a long unnerving pause. "Well, you are not the one under interrogation here, are you?" He asked the question almost absently then jerked his head sharply toward Rahab. "They simply walked away from the inn with no one seeing them? Where were you?" His voice was shrill and high.

Rahab maintained her outward composure. "Ahuzzath solicited my promise to sing for him after the guests were settled so I hurried back—only to find him sound asleep. I decided to go up to the roof to turn the flax crop that is curing there." Rahab held her hands out, palms up, to display the signs of her work. She forced a laugh. "I have many jobs in my father's business. You can see that some of them are less genteel than singing and harping."

The king did not laugh. "Or assisting my enemies?"

Rahab resumed her narrative calmly. "The guests must have escaped during the time that I was up on the roof. When I finished tending the flax and returned to the dining hall, Ahuzzath was still asleep. I began to sing for him anyway— to enhance his dreams as I had promised." One side of her lips curled in a twisted smile. She could feel the other side trapped in the mass of bruising on her cheek and jaw.

"It seems my captain may be overly fond of the singer-harlot of the North Wall Inn. Mmm?" The king leaned forward with his elbows resting on the arms of his chair. He laced his fingers together with his index fingers forming an obelisk. He lowered his chin until the points of his fingers brushed his lips and stared, not really at Rahab, but through her.

Rahab could not read the emotion in the dark eyes beneath those scowling brows and she did not want to know it. She dropped her gaze to the stone floor and waited. After a few moments of chilling silence, the king continued his questioning in a low, controlled voice. "When did you first notice your guests were gone?"

"As I told you, your majesty, I began singing for Ahuzzath as soon as I returned from the roof. Just as I was finishing the first song, Shinab burst into the inn. Not one merchant from Egypt knew these men, he reported. No one in that first caravan had seen the suspects before they appeared here near the city gates this morning. The masters who chartered the caravan encountered the two strangers sleeping in the fields near the city and questioned them about the flax crop. They confirmed Shinab's suspicions that the accent was not Egyptian. As far as I can recall, that was the report. And that was the first I had heard any question regarding their Egyptian identity."

"And the captain?"

"Ahuzzath was instantly awake. He flew up the stairs in a rage to arrest both the men." Rahab lifted her eyes to meet the king's gaze again and finished softly, "But they had vanished."

"And that is all you know?"

"Yes."

With cool self-possession, King Nahari signaled the guard at his right hand. "Take this woman to the dungeon. My instincts tell me there is more to her story."

Ahuzzath bowed low. "Your majesty, may I suggest that you turn her over to me? I am also of the opinion that she knows more than she is telling." He straightened his back and shot a demented glance in Rahab's direction. "I know this woman well, and I have already devised a plan for extracting the truth from her."

Terror clutched Rahab's entire body. The palace prison was the wrong place to be when Israel's army attacked. Safety lay in the room marked by the scarlet cord, but Rahab would rather die in the king's dungeon than be given over to Ahuzzath.

The king slouched back in his throne again, resting his head against the ornamented back and stared at the beams above their heads. He did not answer. Rahab looked up at the beams as well, but her silent pleading went far beyond the ceiling of the throne room.

Yahweh, God of Israel, not now. Please. I am not an Israelite. I have no right to ask for anything from you, but I have heard you are merciful and good. If I must perish in the king's dungeon, so be it. But, if I have gained any favor in your eyes by helping those spies, grant me two requests: don't let the king hand me over to Ahuzzath. Not now when deliverance is so near. And, whatever happens to me, save my family.

The king spoke at last. He leaned forward and locked eyes with Ahuzzath. "No. I will keep her here."

"But, sire, have I not—"

"Silence. You say you are certain those men are no longer in the city."

"Certain, my lord. We have searched every quarter twice."

King Nahari sneered. "As certain as you were that the men were upstairs while you slept—lulled by barley beer and your harlot-lover's songs?"

Ahuzzath's face paled.

"Flax curing on the roof of the very place where they disappeared. How well did your men search there?"

"I searched it myself, my lord. One of the first places I looked."

The king whispered quietly to the guard on his right. Rahab braced herself to be led off in chains, but instead the man hurried from the room.

Nahari looked sternly at his captain again. "Assign twenty of your men to scour the city again tonight. Choose soldiers with the brains to think like vermin. Have them start with the inn. Send them back to the roof and move every straw of that stinking flax crop. Search the wine barrels, even large storage pots. Men do not simply disappear. They hide, and the inn is still the most likely place. Don't dare prove that two desert rats are more shrewd than my elite guard.

"I will see to it myself, my lord."

"No! You failed me there already." Nahari leaped to his feet like a snarling leopard. "You will feel the full force of my wrath, Ahuzzath, if those spies continue to outwit us. Take the remainder of my elite and search the Jordan valley. The city gates will be closed and barred behind you. Whether the spies are within or without, I *will* have them found before they cross back over the Jordan. My captain cannot fail me twice."

Ahuzzath clenched his hands to stop the trembling and steadied his voice. "I sent a score of guards to the river as soon as we learned that the spies were missing. They have spread out along it and will intercept any attempt to cross. Another team is searching field and terrace from the river to the ridge as we speak." He leaned forward toward the king and held out his hand in a gesture of openness and sincerity. "I have served you faithfully for many years. Trust me in this. Further search and more troops out there tonight would be a waste of effort. A dense fog has so cloaked the valley that the spies could hide standing in the middle of a plowed field." Ahuzzath attempted a weak smile. "We would capture nothing but drenched clothing and dripping beards."

The king did not return the smile.

Rahab closed her eyes and directed her energy to the saving of the spies. Her life was insignificant. If those Israelites were captured, it would mean the death of everyone she loved from Grandmother Shua and her parents to her rambunctious nieces and nephews. *O God-Above-All-Others, you redeemed your people from Egypt and led them through the Red Sea in order to bring them back to this land. This is a small thing for you. Conceal your spies until they reach the safety of a cave and shelter them there with your mighty hand.*

Ahuzzath wiped the sweat off his forehead with the back of his hand. "The guards I have posted along the river are more than adequate to watch tonight. No one could cross without being apprehended. I would stake my life on that. Tomorrow when the vapors lift, I will take the entire division and comb every rock and bit of straw in this valley until we flush out those desert rats."

He dropped to his knees on the bottom step of the king's dais. "Tonight, we must break *her*. Don't you see? She mocks me with her lies. She defies you with her silence." With each whimpering phrase of his final appeal, he crawled up the steps of the stone dais until his entire hunched bulk nearly touched his master's toes. "My skills would be most useful with this treasonous harlot. My lord, give her over to me for the night."

The king's lip curled in disgust and he drew his foot back as if preparing to kick at the groveling captain. "The music of this harlot caressed you to sleep this morning. That will be your last comfortable snore—ever —if you return to the city without those spies."

Ahuzzath's eyes rolled almost pleadingly down toward Rahab as if asking for her help, then back toward the king. "Broken, your majesty. Broken. I can. I have to. This proud beauty . . . must be broken." He seemed to be sinking into lunacy. He took hold of Nahari's sandaled foot and sobbed. "I can break her. I know I can."

"Get up." The king shook his foot free of Ahuzzath's grasp and dropped heavily into his lavishly cushioned seat. "You will search tonight. You have three days to find those spies."

A triad of staccato raps from the back of the room punctuated his decree. It was immediately answered by a second set and the heavy chamber doors crashed open. Attention snapped to the back of the room. Momentarily forgotten, Ahuzzath slithered back down the steps and staggered to his feet, swaying with anger and confusion while attention was drawn to the king's right-hand bodyguard returning with a spindly, pimple-faced guard close behind.

Rahab recognized the young man as Shinab, one of the contingent patrolling her street, but the arrogant pup was not so full of himself here in this room. His eyes darted warily from man to man as he passed through the corridor of guards. Suddenly, his face paled, betraying the moment he allowed himself to look at the king himself. His blemishes seemed to multiply, constellations of purple stars on a fear-blanched face. When he reached Ahuzzath's side, he stopped and bowed obsequiously low before the glowering monarch. Standing upright again while his escort stomped to his post, Shinab saluted his captain with a solid blow of his fist against his chest.

King Nahari lowered his chin, black eyes fixed on the pair in a glare smoking with danger. Rahab thought of bulls she had seen pawing up dust before they charged. That was Nahari at this moment. Ahuzzath had always been such a powerful figure in her life. Now the vicious dog and his simpering whelp faced a raging bull. Perhaps there *was* some justice in Jericho, even from a king known to be as hard and cruel as his city.

The interruption had given the grizzly captain time to regain his composure. He returned his underling's salute and donned an unreadable expression. Shinab blinked rapidly several times, then dropped his gaze, uncertain of what to do next. As the awkward silence stretched into minutes, he began twisting his arms behind his back, clasping and unclasping his hands. Rahab held her breath as the king continued to study the pair, working his jaw slowly. Nahari held the dogs at bay, but he was a dangerous savior.

In a transformation as sudden as it was unexpected, the fierce stare relaxed. King Nahari leaned forward on his throne and smiled benevolently at the young man squirming before him. "Shinab, you have done well. I understand you were first to suspect the two spies"

"Yes." Shinab did not look up.

The king continued, his voice low and gentle, "and I was told you were the one who made the inquiries proving the false identity of these spies. I need men like you."

Shinab said nothing, but his shoulders relaxed.

"Now hear this. I have given Ahuzzath and the entire guard three days to find those Israelites. My captain will direct the search from the river to the hills, up and down the valley. Go with him. If at the end of three days he has not apprehended those spies, you will be my new captain."

A gasp of horror ripped the silence beside Shinab. By the time Rahab could turn her eyes to Ahuzzath, there were no more sounds, but his mouth was twitching.

Nahari took full advantage of a long, chilling moment while everyone waited for his next words. "Ahuzzath," he said at last, flashing an overly-sweet smile at his captain. "I have grown fond of you over the years. I would be grieved to see your head hanging beside my gate, but carelessness has consequences."

The king's pleasant smile morphed into a twisted grin. "Shinab, I expect you to make Ahuzzath's beheading your first act as captain, if it comes to that."

The skin underlying the dark reds and purples of Shinab's blemishes blanched even whiter. With a look of pure horror, he saluted the king. "We will find the spies, your majesty."

King Nahari turned to the bodyguard on his left. "Go with Ahuzzath and be certain the entire guard understands my decree before they leave the city. Should the captain attempt to walk back through my gates without those spies, the lot of them will die." He turned solemnly to his captain. "Ahuzzath, until now you have done well for me. I truly desire that you may undo the damage you caused. May the gods go with you and bring you success."

Salmon

Salmon and Jathniel slept fitfully, frequently waking to the barks of soldiers who moved like packs of wild dogs, now toward the river, now up in the hills. At times, they heard faint baying cries far down the valley; at other times, the yapping was as close as the vineyards and barley fields directly below their hideaway. Ahuzzath's leering grin and glinting eyes drifted through Salmon's dreams followed by phalanxes of soldiers brandishing swords, driving them through vineyards, sweeping them out of the barley fields, and finally trapping them at the river's edge. Each time the enemy closed in, Salmon awoke, cold, sweat-drenched and stiff on the cave floor—feeling far, far away from the safety of camp and the comfort of family and friends.

At last, gray morning light diffused into the cave, but still the cries of the pursuers continued. When a stone rattled down the hill past the entrance, Jathniel seized Salmon's arm. His eyes bulged with terror. He did not need words.

Quickly and silently, Salmon scooped up their bags of provisions, signaling Jathniel to get the coil of rope and Egyptian clothing. He took one last glance around. No sign of their stay was detectable on the stony cave floor.

Two black mouths yawned from the shadowed folds and recesses at the back of the cave. Two choices. The one on the left was smaller and wetter with long stone teeth piercing the aperture from above and short stubby ones rising up to meet them from the ground. *The less inviting, the better for our purposes.* As Salmon ducked between the teeth, wet droplets dribbled onto his neck. The hungry chamber salivating over a long-awaited taste of warm flesh.

Within a few paces, the long gullet tightened, its ceiling dropping to waist height. Not a glimmer of gray light touched the passageway ahead, but Salmon slumped to his knees and continued scrambling as fast as possible away from their pursuers. The lowering ceiling and tightening walls produced the sensation—the increasingly unpleasant sensation—of passing into the cave's digestive chambers. But only when his head collided with a rocky fold hanging into their path and the damp, pebble-strewn clay floor dropped to a lower level, did he even consider stopping. Even then, his natural inclination was to go as far as he could.

"What do you think?" he whispered over his shoulder. "This passage gets tighter and tighter. We'll have to crawl down to another, deeper level if we want to try moving forward. I can feel the passage floor less than an arm's length down."

"Well I hardly favor going back."

"Might be hard to retreat if we get stuck. We could just wait here until it seems safer."

"And when would that be?"

"Rahab suggested three days."

"And how do we know when three days are up? It's impossible to determine the passage of time when we can't tell day from night."

"So . . . stay here or move forward as long as we can?"

"Just our luck to take the route that dead ends."

"Not a dead end. The wafts of cool air in my face tell me this is merely a tight corridor to somewhere."

"Well, we're reduced to rats then. Let's take the rat run, because I'm not too keen on just sitting here for hours and hours."

"Nor I," Salmon agreed. "But once we start slithering down this tight throat, there will most likely be no turning around. If our way is blocked, we'll have to wriggle back feet first. Time and energy we might have spent quietly resting here."

"It's not as if we have something better to do."

Leaving all but the rope and one small packet of parched barley-corn behind, Salmon inched into the utter darkness of the nether channel with Jathniel just behind. Creeping like salamanders, they followed the descent of the shrunken passageway. At last, the constriction eased and they were able to move forward and down, ledge by ledge, with greater ease. Suddenly, the walls receded beyond Salmon's fingertips, the ceiling vaulted upward, and the floor fell abruptly beneath his hands. "What now?" he whispered.

Jathniel crawled up beside him. "I think we just reached the center of the earth and it's empty."

"Maybe, maybe not." Salmon tentatively dangled one leg into the darkness, feeling for footing. "There's a fairly flat place large enough to stand on just a few feet down."

He eased himself carefully out of their conduit and splashed into a puddle. A lightly pattering rain fell on his head and cool air circulated freely all around. "Listen." The sound of the drips resonated in a cavernous void he could sense, although he could not see even his own hands before his face. "This chamber is huge," he called, enjoying the hollow resonant sound of his voice.

Huge, huge, huge . . . The cave echoed back a sneering, menacing announcement in the black void.

The constriction of the passageway had been discomfiting, but this emptiness suddenly stirred up sheer terror. Salmon pressed back against the wall, small and helplessly blind. Every muscle was instantly frozen by the immensity of this unknown. In a few moments, the shock resolved and reason took control of panic. *Am I standing on a broad floor at the bottom of the entire chamber or merely on a ledge that drops down to a rocky grave hundreds of feet below? That should not be difficult to ascertain.*

He inched his toe forward in little taps, feeling for an edge. He found nothing but more flat, sandy floor. He stretched out a little farther with only his fingertips connecting him to the solid rock behind him. More sandy floor. His sense of adventure came waddling back from the edge of fear.

"Good solid floor here," he announced boldly. "Come on, Jathniel."

Jathniel, Jathniel, Jathniel . . . The echo rang ominously.

Jathniel's words sounded, soft as a breath, along with the echo of his name. "Whispers would be prudent. The mouth we crawled through felt anything but friendly. I suspect it would happily report our presence to Ahuzzath."

"You are right," Salmon whispered. "So, come on down. We can't exactly lip read or give hand signals here in the dark."

Jathniel mastered his fear, clambered out of their passageway, and pressed close. "I didn't like the tight part, but the size of this abyss is even less agreeable."

"But its size could very well save our lives."

"Save our lives? *Live* three days in this abyss?"

Salmon nodded in the darkness. "I don't wish to spend any more time than we have to in this black gullet. Just locate a hiding place."

"A hiding place?" The quiet echo rang with incredulity. It was not the room repeating Salmon's whisper, but Jathniel.

"Just a little nook that could conceal us even if our pursuers brought torches down here. Come on. Let's explore."

"Explore?" Jathniel echoed again. "How will we find our way back?"

Salmon could picture Jathniel's brows arched high. "Exploring doesn't mean stumbling around blindly. We'll be systematic. We need a sensible plan."

"A sensible plan." His tone had gone from incredulity to sarcasm.

"Here's one: We feel our way along the wall until we find the proper nook, then we mark the path to it with our rope."

"With our rope. All right. And if we come to the end of our rope?"

"On the other hand, maybe we should use the rope to lash ourselves together in case the floor drops out from under us."

"In case the floor drops out from under us?"

Salmon laughed. "Ho, listen to that. A whispering echo that sounds remarkably like you."

"Very funny."

"Good words are worth repeating."

"I don't think suggesting the floor might drop out from under us qualifies as *good words*."

"We must be prepared. How could I bear to lose you down some deep pit."

"Lose *me* down a deep pit?" This time Jathniel laughed. "Oh no! If it comes to that, it would be *me* saving *you* from the pit because you will be leading the way." He paused a moment. "I see one problem. Even if we follow the wall, how will we locate *this* spot again to find the right passageway out of this place? There may be scores of others leading who knows where."

"Let's leave our cloaks here by this rock to mark our way back to the world. We can't miss them when we feel our way back along the wall."

"I would not trust blind men feeling their way along a wall to find cloaks in the dark. I suggest we pace off our steps as we move from here and count our way back. "

"Hmmm. How do we get an accurate count when we're likely to retrace our steps over and around and back again as we explore? Obstacles of all kinds in a cave."

"I thought of that. We'll tie together with the rope, leaving all the length between us. I'll hold the slack in a coil easing it out for you as you explore. You can work at keeping us out of pits and dead ends. If you happen to drop into a hole, I'll keep you from hitting bottom."

"And when I have determined a good path and come to the end of the rope, you will count the steps as you follow it to where I am."

The words tumbled out faster and faster as the ideas developed. "I think it will work. By the time we have chosen our hiding place, we will have an exact count of our steps. Unless you get mixed up or forget."

"I don't forget things when my life depends on them. Trust me to have a perfect count back to this rock and our cloaks."

"With a perfect count to the exit passage, we can't miss it." Salmon whooped his joy—and the room echoed back its celebration-damping hope. *Miss it, miss it, miss it.*

"Sorry," he whispered.

And so the exploration began. Salmon groped his way around limestone pillars, deep vertical folds, and jumbles of boulders until he was certain he had found the best path forward. Jathniel counted the steps, recoiling the rope until they were together again. For hours they hugged the walls, cutting their hands on razor sharp outcroppings and rough cascades of dripstone. They bumped their heads passing through small stalactite-festooned grottos and knocked their knees against stalagmites and pillars. At last, they found a small dry hollow behind a huge diagonally-flowing limestone curtain that seemed perfect. Burrowing down like badgers, they crammed themselves in to try it out.

"This is just right. The formation catches all the water and leaves us dry," Jathniel whispered.

"And we would be all but invisible here even if the soldiers lit the whole room with torchlight."

Jathniel didn't respond for a moment. When he did, his voice was troubled. "This darkness is getting to me. I would be most grateful for the faint light of that dismal cave entrance"

"Me too."

"You follow me this time," Jathniel insisted and clambered out of their burrow. "I'm the counter. One, two, three, four . . . and I know just how long a stride to take. Five, six, seven, eight . . .""

The route back to their cloaks did not take long, and it seemed like no time until they found their way out of that long ascending passageway. They burst into the gray light of the entry room with the joy of moths leaving the confines of their cocoons. And like moths to flame, they crept toward the light.

"Just look at the tints of pink and rust rippling in these rocks." Jathniel caressed the limestone frame of the entrance. "Beautiful!" His bare brow danced up and down with each word.

"I think it's the deprivation of sight for so long. Even your fuzzy round head looks beautiful to me right now."

"I'm going to look—" Jathniel's sentence ended in a soft gasp.

Salmon saw it too. The camouflaging brush they had used to conceal the entrance had been shoved aside and the imprints of a pair of war sandal marked the sandy threshold.

"Looks like they didn't find anyone home. Best not replace the brush and give them reason to reconsider."

Jathniel grinned. "Best not replace the brush so I can watch the sunset." He flopped down on his belly and slithered half a body length out of the entrance.

"I would join you watching the sunset if only our cave faced west."

"Ha! There's a blush over the eastern ridge. That's enough for me tonight."

Salmon flopped down beside his friend and together they watched the dusk glow fade and the stars appear. When they heard soldiers far off, they retreated to the interior of their cave, huddling in silence near the escape route to their hideaway. When, after a long time, they had heard nothing but crickets, night birds, and a gentle rustling breeze, they crept back to the starlit entrance with a few morsels of food. Salmon sent up a silent blessing for Rahab as well as to God for these provisions. The two of them ate in silence, then retrieved the bundles of Egyptian clothing to pillow their heads. They lay side by side for a long time, listening, planning, thinking, but never feeling quite safe enough to risk a conversation.

The next day dawned uneventfully. The king's men had moved beyond the immediate surrounds of Jericho, and only occasional faint calls drifted back to remind them the search was not over. In the afternoon, Jathniel wriggled on his belly past the opening of the cave and created a blind for himself using a little of the brushy debris pushed aside from their entrance. It was not long before both men were peering through the lacework of twigs and branches from that vantage point. Across the river they could make out vague hints of the camp, but they spent most of the afternoon watching Jericho and the road leading to it.

The gates were closed and there was absolutely no traffic on the road so there was not much to see, but after nearly two full days of darkness, the golden sunlight filtering through their tangled camouflage warmed them inside and out. The sound of a caravan late in the morning aroused them from a drowsy stupor. They watched as the lines of merchants with their wagons and beasts of burden plodded down from the mountain pass to Jericho. But the gates did not open to receive them and they went on their way, tiny dark specks slowly crawling back the way they had come, undoubtedly passing on the word: "Don't waste your time on Jericho." Apparently the word was out, for few travelers darkened the road.

At the close of the third day, the calls and barks of the soldiers ceased completely. Just at sunset, a small dark line crawled back to the city like ants. Jericho's gates swung open for the first time in three days. She swallowed her troops, slammed her maw closed again and no more soldiers came out as replacements. "Their failure, our success," Salmon announced.

Jathniel's eyebrows gamboled in their habitual display of joy, and he whooped softly, "Whoo-ee! Tonight, we go home."

"Hush," Salmon warned.

"You spoke first."

Salmon grinned. "But I thought better of it. Let's proceed as if they are still out there. Just in case." From somewhere up on the ridge above them, an owl hooted mournfully, *Flee, fool! Flee, fool!*

Rahab

The walls of Rahab's cell cracked and groaned. The stone floor beneath her thin straw pallet shook violently, jolting her from a wondrous dreamworld of light. She tried to pull the scene back as one would a warm cover on a chilly night, but already the vision was fading. She had been leading her family through a sunlit meadow—Grandmother Shua, her mother and father, her brothers with their wives and little ones—all wading through swaying stands of anemones and lilies in a parade of celebration. She knew the spies were with them, ushering them all into a new life, although she could not see them. But the dream slipped away. She couldn't hold on any more than she could have grasped the last sunbeam to prevent the falling of night.

As the pavement rolled and heaved again, Rahab curled herself into a tight ball. She did not fear the tremors of the earth. Such were common in the Jordan valley. But this one had jolted her into a looming nightmare. If total darkness was *day* here in the king's dungeon, *night* had just fallen. A nameless malevolent force, darker than darkness, pressed around her. It was indistinct when she first awoke, but had distilled into a presence. The dark thing pressed so close that she could not breathe. In desperation, she cried aloud, "Who *are* you?"

There was no answer. Suddenly, a huge form appeared, glowing with cold, red light, a living form of Baal, more terrifying than any image. His eyes blazed like burning coals in a hate-filled face. His muscled chest and shoulders were bare above a scaly, black garment that covered his loins, and a red cord hung from his waist. Not just any red cord— *her* red cord, the one from the window. Vulture-like talons clicked together as he grasped the cord in his fingertips and swung its tasseled end in front of her face. His eyes burned into hers and without a spoken word, his thoughts filled her mind. *This was your hope, your sign. Now you have nothing. Worship me, or you will die in this dismal hole and all your family will be lost.*

"Yahweh, God of Israel," she cried out, "I choose *you*."

The creature's malignant grin twisted into an angry grimace and he seized her shoulder savagely. "Do not speak that name."

Rahab winced. His grip was icy, but the pain that shot through her body from his touch burned like fire. She clenched her teeth and raised her chin defiantly. "You cannot control me with fear."

Unspoken words blasted her like a desert sandstorm. *I control all Canaan. You have no hope but me.*

Words so brief, so believable. Rahab crumpled. Over and over, the dark thoughts pounded with fury against her faith shield. She grabbed her head with both hands, willing the demonic voice out of her. "Yahweh, you are a good God," she cried out in despair. "If you cannot deliver me, let me die here, but remember my family. O save them. Replace the red cord, the sign of our deliverance."

The red light flared blindingly, then with a hiss like a fire extinguished, the apparition vanished. Rahab's body shook uncontrollably, but the oppression lifted and a peaceful confidence settled over her again.

She took a deep breath to calm herself as she kneaded the cold ache in her shoulder and stared into the blackness of her cell. "Yahweh, your name is awesome. You are a shield of light in darkness."

Salmon

Salmon took a final survey of the cave. Food rations consumed; water bags all but empty. He rolled the Egyptian garments into a tight ball and flung them into the dark recesses of the cave. "Good riddance."

Jathniel was coiling the rope in neat loops from elbow to hand. He glanced at Salmon and inhaled with deep satisfaction as he finished. "It's time," he said and wiggled his brow.

Salmon grinned. "Home sounds unbelievably good."

Jathniel nodded. He tipped up his flaccid water bag and drained it. "Thank you, Rahab," he said, wiping his mouth with the back of his hand, "but we are done with Jericho." With an exaggerated motion, he drew the goatskin back, preparing for a long toss. "Bring back nothing, but a story of deliv—"

"Stop!" In a fit of desperation, Salmon leaped at his friend and stayed his arm.

Jathniel held his hands up defensively. "I'm not disrespecting Rahab. Just getting rid of excess baggage."

Salmon didn't try to explain it. It hardly made sense to lug empty water bags back to camp, but he had a nagging feeling they must. From a dark place in his mind, the thought rose that the anxiety of the past few days had shattered his sanity. But the purpose of his life had never seemed clearer. His senses were more alert, his focus sharper, his devotion to God more intense. He left Jathniel scratching his head and strode to the entrance. "Just bring it," he said.

"Wait for me."

Jathniel was still pulling the strap of his empty water bag over his shoulder along with the coil of rope when he caught up. Jathniel was a good friend. Loyal even if it might seem his fellow spy was going mad. With empty goatskins flopping against their sides, they began scrambling down the hill toward home. Overhead, the gleaming pathway of the River of Milk led the eye across a dazzling display of heavenly diamonds, but the pathless hillside was dark and ominous. The farther Salmon crept down the hillside, the stronger grew the feeling that certain peril lay ahead. The muscles and sinews of his body tensed, ready to flee or face attack as needed. No moonlight defined the features of the landscape, only minimal shadows cast by the cold light of stars. Every black, crouching mound of rock or shrub, every menacing rustle of leaves—even Jathniel's scuffling footsteps behind him—whispered of danger.

Within minutes, they reached the scant cover of the vineyard rows. The fresh scent of spring growth and rich, earthy soil was a welcome change from the musty smell of the cave, but Salmon's nose seemed to sniff unknown peril even in this, and the troubling premonitions only increased as they clambered down, terrace by terrace. By the time they crouched in the final row of the lowest terrace, the weight of his fear throbbed in his head. His stomach lurched, begging to vomit the last bites of food and water provided by Rahab's kindness.

Scanning the stars only increased the sense of panic. The Scorpion was rising above the eastern ridge. If they headed toward it, they would reach the river near the raft. That was the plan, to slip across the fields with their eyes fixed on the stars until they reached the tree cover beyond the cultivated fields. But the message of the Scorpion tonight was that he was watching his turf. His heart red as blood. His stinging tail poised to strike.

Salmon deliberately turned his eyes from sky to earth, assessing the barley field they needed to cross. Pale, level, and unbroken for at least a mile, the sea of waving grain stretched out before them. He tried to rebuild his courage by imagining the two of them slithering through the tall barley, hidden like snakes, but the mere thought of venturing into it knotted his stomach and brought back that wave of nausea.

He glanced toward the city. Pinpoints of torchlight flickered here and there through gaps in the thick stands of palms. In the dark of night and at this distance, he could not see guards on the walls, but he knew they were there. "If only we had the mist that fell the night we fled Jericho," he whispered. He kept his voice as soft as the leaves rustling in the night breeze. Like the leaves, it trembled.

Jathniel cocked his head to one side and studied his face. "Courage, friend. Considering what we've managed to survive in Jericho, we can do this. Let's go."

Salmon clutched his arm. "We cannot. We must not."

"I'm afraid too, but we must follow the plan."

"Too open."

"Come on. Just like we planned. Stealthy as serpents."

"We're not serpents. Just timid, frail mice—or worse, scuttling cockroaches—an abomination to the people of Jericho. We'll be spotted and crushed under their feet if we cross that field."

"It's the only way home."

"We will never reach the raft."

"I'll go first. Follow me."

"No." Salmon tightened his grip on Jathniel's arm.

"Hey! Get a grip on yourself, not on me."

Salmon's head throbbed as bits and pieces of a dream came back to him. The Fords. Float. No Raft. How could he convince Jathniel of a new plan born of a dream? Best just say it. "We will head for the cover of Jericho's palm groves and cross at the fords."

"Salmon, you *have* lost your mind." Jathniel thumped the empty water bag. He assumed a fatherly tone. "Stick with the plan we made when you were thinking clearly. The thought of crossing this field terrifies me too, but we *have* to get to the raft. Tell you what, let's head farther south and cross the fields as far from the city as possible.

"Our lives are in danger as we argue." Salmon touched his finger to his lips and leaped up. Without giving his friend a say in his decision, he took off in a crouching run between the vine rows toward Jericho.

Jathniel chased after him, whipping him around forcefully as soon as he caught up. He seized Salmon's face between his hands, mouthing his words emphatically so Salmon could not miss the message although the words were nearly inaudible. "The fords are *not* fordable. The raft."

Salmon felt calmer than he had all evening. He bent close to Jathniel's ear and whispered. "I'm positive I know the only safe way home."

"Follow the plan."

"Trust me. I had a recurring dream every night we slept in that cave. While we hesitated back there, I realized that Yahweh had spoken to us through it."

"Then why did you not mention this recurring dream before?"

"Fear must have chased it from my mind when I was awake and we were listening to Ahuzzath's pack on the hunt for us. But I remember it clearly now, and I'm certain the dream was telling us what to do."

"*I'm* certain. The plan."

"Do what you want. I will follow the dream." Salmon pulled from Jathniel's grip and turned resolutely toward the place of danger and death.

Jathniel exhaled noisily. The foolishness of arguing in clipped
whispers in the middle of enemy territory must have convinced
him, even if heavenly intervention in the form of a dream did not.
"Lead on," he muttered, "together to our deaths."

As he hunch-walked between the vine rows, using a slower
pace now with Jathniel close behind, Salmon almost grinned at
the melancholy loyalty. *Yes. Together to our deaths.*

When they reached the end of the vineyards, they scrambled
down through a belt of rocky rubble stretching from the rim of
the hill to the flax field where they first intercepted the caravan.
They crouched there beside the field, thankful for the moonless
night. It would be just a short sprint across the open stubble, then
the road, then through the shadowy palm groves surrounding the
city to the river.

Jathniel took a deep breath and raised his eyebrows. The panic
in his eyes was replaced by resolve. "Let's do it quickly. Before I
change my mind."

As one, they leaped up and sped across the flax field and road
like cats in the darkness, pausing for breath only when they reached
the hovering fringes of the palms. Salmon pressed his hand on his
chest, jubilant at their success, but trying to suppress any loud gasps.
Jathniel sucked in the needed air through his nose, then signaled
his joy with a wiggle of his naked brow. Salmon almost laughed.
Shaving had turned his friend into a comic caricature of himself.

After a short rest, they turned eastward, creeping through the
palm grove toward the river, toward home. Salmon shrank back
from the treeless exposure of the city mount, that slope of stony
rubble leading upward to the base of the massive walls of Jericho.
His focus was so consumed with maintaining a solid canopy of
foliage above him that he caught his toe under a fallen palm frond
at the same time that he stepped on it with the other foot. The snaps
and crackles of his stumbling in the dry debris were not loud, but
alert ears high on the bridge above the gate heard.

"Who's out there?"

Salmon froze.

First one torch and then a second waved back and forth as guards searched the shifting shadows of the palm grove below. The spies instinctively moved to keep the narrow shelter of palm trunks between themselves and eyes on the wall.

"You're nothing but a girl!" a second voice grunted gruffly. "You have *me* jumping every time the wind flutters the trees."

"That was more than wind. Maybe just a fox, but something's moving through the trees."

Salmon could not see the guards, but portions of the gate leaped with light then darkened. He did not risk another step as the light retreated. Even a deep breath seemed risky as the light moved back and forth over the palm grove farther and farther toward the east. Glancing up through the foliage, he met the huge unblinking eyes of an owl. He stared back a wordless challenge. *Whether you are friend or foe, do not let me hear the words "Flee, fool" again tonight.*

He returned his attention to the pale blocks of the city wall—advancing and retreating, section-by-section in the moving torchlight. As the searching illumination passed across a small dark shape, empty eyes suddenly appeared. Bloated features scowled and yawned and stretched in mocking expressions as the shadows shifted with the light. Even from this distance, there was no mistaking the wild, blood-matted bush of grizzled hair and beard. Ahuzzath.

"I told you, there's nothing out there." The voice from above filtered through the trees, breezy and unconcerned in contrast to the horror that shuddered through Salmon. He could not keep his eyes off the hideous, decapitated head as the guards continued their search.

"Better too wary than wind up like captain here," the first guard grumbled.

"You think they'd honor a couple of buzzards like us by hanging us up there with the important ones?"

"Shinab would if he thought we missed an opportunity to snag them spies."

Salmon's throat constricted at the thought that the two of them would most definitely join the unfortunate captain should they be caught.

The torchlight slowly retraced the sections of the gate, then illuminated the wall again, section by section, returning to the guard station just above Salmon. As the scuffling of feet and gruff repartee settled in its starting point, the owl spread her wings and flew to another tree.

"See that. You just heard that old owl shaking a bunch of dates to the ground."

"Well, it could have been a skulking spy."

"Not likely, right here by the city."

"Well, they are out there somewhere. I wouldn't want to be us if we missed them."

The second guard sniggered. "Even if they are out there, we're up here. Who could accuse *us* of missing something?"

"Captain Shinab would if he saw so much as a footprint that wasn't there this morning. He might not spike our heads up there honorably by the old captain's, but I don't doubt that he would remove them from our shoulders."

"Well, it wouldn't make sense for them spies to be lurking around the city."

"Sense has nothing to do with it. Let's patrol. If those spies made that noise, I want to catch them, not stand here yammering. I would be quite sorry to part with this noggin o' mine if we missed them."

"Nothing out there but the trees tonight—"

Flee, fool! Flee, fool! the owl hooted.

"And an owl."

Retreating footsteps stomped and muffled the reply. Salmon smiled grimly. *Trees and an owl and two fools that really need to flee.* But no matter how much he wanted to run for the river, he could not move at all. As the guard's voices grew increasingly distant and indistinct, he felt Jathniel slip close to his side. The thought of moving his feet, risking the snap of another twig, cemented him in place. Jathniel brushed his arm, but he could not even force his head to turn enough to look at his friend.

Flee, fool.

The haunting call did not seem frightening or annoying this time. *I surely am a fool if I am too afraid to flee from the wicked city of Jericho. Maybe God is speaking to us through her as he spoke to Balaam through his donkey.*

"Flee, fool," he hooted softly in his closest approximation of the owl's call. He gave Jathniel a pointed look, and then, before he lost his nerve, he slipped to the next tree. He could sense more than hear Jathniel following close behind him as he made his way through the trees paying very close attention to where he placed each foot. As they got farther from the gates, they broke into a run on their toes, silent and swift as deer, leaving the looming walls of the city behind, faster and faster through the last of the palm grove, down the rocky shoulder of the river basin and into the thickets of the Jordan jungle.

Blood pounded in Salmon's ears. His chest felt as if it would explode, but he drove himself on and on, not stopping, not slowing, not looking back until they reached very edge of the roaring river. When he collapsed at last on the ground, Jathniel flopped down beside him, and the two lay side by side, drawing in simultaneous gulps of air and a sweet, sweet sense of relief. Jericho was behind them. Any danger they might face in crossing the river would be tame in comparison to all the perils they had already faced. When their gasping finally slowed, Salmon grinned. "I think I held my breath the whole time we ran."

"Me too. As if that would help," Jathniel snorted. "Any guard who was listening closely would have been able to hear the drumming of my heart."

Salmon paused, listening to the surging flood of the Jordan. "I love the thundering sound of this river. For the first time in three days, we don't have to worry about Ahuzzath or his men overhearing us."

Jathniel laughed. "That bloated head won't be hearing anything—ever again."

"That should be funny or at least gratifying . . . but it is too awful. A week ago I could not have conceived of such horrors."

"Nor I. The Jathniel who returns is not the same boy who rode this river a mere week ago."

"Jathniel, the man," Salmon said thoughtfully. Then he grinned. "Definitely not the same. Jathniel, the boy, had way more hair."

"Don't think Salmon the Hairless looks any prettier than I do." Jathniel tackled Salmon and rubbed his knuckles on the sprouting fuzz of his head. "At least we won't have to worry about getting snared by our hair in this jungle." He scrambled to his feet and waved his hand toward the thicket of willows and oleander. "To the raft!"

"We're not crossing with the raft," Salmon answered calmly.

"We're not what?"

"We're crossing right here. We won't use the raft."

"Um. These *Egyptians* don't know how to swim. Remember?"

"Watch." Salmon untied the mouth of his goatskin and shook the last drops of water on the ground.

"Wha . . .?" Jathniel watched Salmon begin blowing into the opening, wide-eyed with astonishment.

Salmon puffed and blew and huffed and wheezed. Each time he took a breath, he glanced up at Jathniel's growing incredulity, finding it amusing that his fellow spy could not frame a word, let alone a coherent sentence. When the goatskin was rounded and tight with his breath, he twisted the opening, lashed it securely closed, and held it up proudly. "Better than a raft."

"You *have* gone mad, my friend."

"I told you I had a dream our first night out of Jericho. The dream recurred on several nights, maybe every night. I wish I had remembered in the mornings. We could have discussed it. It was a light, happy vision of us bobbing across the river holding onto Rahab's water bags. It seemed strange because even in my dream I knew they should sink. But they didn't. When we were hiding in the vineyards earlier, the words came to me clearly, *Beware the raft. Your breath will carry you safely across.*" He held up the bag again and grinned. "All of a sudden I could see us inflating these and I knew they would carry us home."

Jathniel's eyes narrowed with suspicion. "And all the time we were discussing our plan, you never thought this dream was relevant?"

"I'm no Joseph. I completely forgot about the dream when I was awake. But each time I dreamed it, I remembered I had seen it before, which made it seem more and more important."

"How do we know your mind isn't just playing tricks on you? I say forget the dream and let's go find the raft."

"As we stared across that barley field, I couldn't shake the certainty that we were in terrible danger. That's when God warned me about the raft and the dream came back in dazzling clarity."

Jathniel shook his empty goatskin in Salmon's face. "I have humored you all evening by carrying this ridiculous thing, but it is dazzlingly clear to me now that you *are* mad."

"I rather thought so too back in the cave. I couldn't explain myself. But when the dream came back to me, I realized why I reacted so when you were going to dispose of that thing. It wasn't fear. I just knew we needed it. I wanted to discuss it with you back on the terraces, but it was too much information for our hand signals and I didn't want to risk having some last, lingering guard hear us."

"Your dream is crazy. First we run toward the city. Now you want us to cross without a raft. Look at that wild water. We can't swim. We don't even know if these bags would really hold us up. And you would jump in anyway?"

"My best argument is your face back at the vineyards. Your eyes told me you knew crawling to the raft through a mile of open barley fields was just wrong. I knew it too, and the dream confirmed it."

"My gut revolted again when we ran toward Jericho. Queasier yet when the guards were searching for the source of the noise in the palm grove. My inners are even more unhappy now—but unfortunately, we are here, we have these, and you seem fixed on drowning us. Excuse me if I vomit." He took a deep breath and began to blow into his water bag.

Salmon picked up the coil of rope, wrapped one end around his waist, and knotted it. "Rahab may save us again by this rope. If one of us gets in trouble, the other can help him." He looped the other end of the coil around Jathniel and tied it securely. He watched Jathniel finish, then slipped the strap of his water bag diagonally across his shoulder, under his arm, and around his back.

"And now, the test." Salmon wrapped his arms around the fat, goat-shaped air bladder and grasped the leg stubs with both hands. "Tethered together, for better or for worse," he called and plunged into the icy water.

He floated delightfully. "Woo-hoo. Let's go home."

THE CROSSING

Salmon

Relaxing into the safety of the rope that connected him to Jathniel and the shore, Salmon let the water lift him. It pulled him into the light current along the margin of the river. His feet flew out in front of him, and he moved his legs around, enjoying the wondrous sensation of freedom. He remembered his own words in the marketplace—about not being birds that could fly or fish that could swim. Was this pleasure more like swimming or flying?

"Hurry, Jathniel. This is more fun than the raft."

Jathniel responded to the challenge with a solemn lift of his brows. He had already finished tying off the mouth of the goatskin. Now he was methodically laying knot over knot. "At this moment, I am more concerned about safety than fun," he said as he secured the strap around himself and took hold of the inflated hide. "And I'm not sure I trust this bulbous thing."

Salmon grinned as Jathniel squeezed his eyes closed and prepared to leap into the water. "Hey, quite the display of bravery."

Jathniel didn't answer or look. He splashed into the water. "Ahhh! You didn't tell me it was cold!" He instinctively took a step backward onto the half-submerged rocks at the water's edge, then scrambled to regain solid footing. The rest happened quickly—his feet giving way, his hand sliding off the leg stub, the goatskin balloon rolling, his head disappearing under a wash of muddy water. But with only a little thrashing and splashing, he popped back up, bug-eyed and gasping.

Salmon laughed. "It will be safe *and* fun if you just hold on."

The rushing current challenged his flippancy, sucking him into the center of the river, and whipping Jathniel along behind him. With no control over their direction, they gripped their floats. At first they swirled toward the east and home, then swished back again toward the western riverbank. Salmon recognized the patterns of the current that carried them. They had spent hours with Joshua, testing it, tracking a remarkably consistent path in the rushing flood. The river washed them now toward the spot where they had landed with the raft. From there it would snake right, then left. The streaming pull of that S-curve would propel them homeward. The new plan, altered according to the dream, was merging beautifully with the original. Unlike the first crossing, no fear of the unknown dampened the novelty of this ride.

"Woo-hoo!" Salmon cried. He caught Jathniel's eyes and grinned. "Our dream floats work perfectly."

"You'll get my final applause when we're safely home."

"Raft landing just ahead. Want to stop and get it?"

"Very funny."

"No complaining then. Wild and free, it is!"

In the next instant, a voice croaked from shore, "What? In the water?"

Salmon's joy dissolved as a tall form in the uniform of the king's guard burst out of the shadowed shrubbery. There was no mistaking the pale, pimpled face of Shinab—and the wickedly cold river was delivering them right to his feet.

"Help. How do we turn ourselves?" Jathniel gave voice to the panic they both felt.

As the current swept Salmon within a few yards of the place where Shinab stood, bow in hand, their eyes met. "Thought you would escape?" The familiar reedy voice was grim and determined as he reached over his shoulder in a smooth, quick motion to retrieve an arrow. "Think again."

Why had he ever thought Shinab looked less cruel than the other guards? The eyes taking deadly aim at his head were as cold and unfeeling as a snake. Salmon tried to rotate his body, but the watery highway continued carrying them directly toward the point where they first landed. *Oh, make his arrow miss its mark. Make the current pull us away. Deliver us from this hostile shore.*

As the arrow hissed past Salmon's ear, the barrage of prayers dissolved into a desperate cry, "O God, help!" A second shot thudded behind him just as they washed past. The third arrow splashed into the water inches from Salmon's head. Then they swooshed around the bend in the river, safely out of range.

"That was close," Salmon gasped.

"Beyond close," Jathniel whimpered. "The second arrow is here in my goatskin." His voice was small and desperate. "I think I'm sinking."

Before Salmon could think to draw him closer with their rope, Jathniel's anguished face disappeared beneath the water.

Salmon memorized the spot—a foamy, boiling cauldron surrounded by three boulders close to the western shore. He jerked his body around. He thrashed and fought against the current, keeping his eyes fixed on the point of submersion. The water whipped wildly around him with every kick. Despite an exhausting effort to get back, the river continued to pull him away. Just when he felt he could battle his watery foe no longer, the river signaled its superior power.

A frothing wave washed over his head. It blinded him. It filled his nose and mouth. In desperation, he seized the limp rope and pulled with both hands, but as soon as he let go of the stubby handles, his float rolled backwards, submerging him again. While he fought desperately for the surface, the river fought to rip the strap from his shoulders.

He couldn't do it. He let the surging flood carry him where it would. It took all his strength to cling to the slippery wet fur covering the water bag. Rahab's rope still lashed him to Jathniel, but he could neither swim against the current nor take up the slack to draw his friend to him. The sense of helplessness nearly made him vomit.

All at once, the rope pulled tight and Jathniel appeared again, this time churning in the wild water downstream. Salmon suddenly realized that while he was struggling back, intent on rescue, his friend had passed by him below the surface. The Jordan gave Salmon one good look at his friend—coughing and sputtering, flailing wildly with his arms—then sucked him under again. Salmon did not try to memorize the spot this time. It was obvious that a body moved as fast under water as on top of it, and it was the river that decided where they would go.

"River Jordan," Salmon screamed in outrage, "you are as cold and heartless as Jericho."

In answer to the accusation, the river washed Salmon so violently toward the eastern bank that it was all he could do to hold on. Then, just as swiftly as it had swept the two spies into danger, the current dropped him in quiet waters. Feeling the crunch of sand and stone under his feet, Salmon scrambled wildly for a foothold and found a submerged tree stump. Praying that it was not too late, he wedged himself against it, digging in his heels for stability, straining at the rope. Little by little, hand over hand, he pulled. He struggled frantically to maintain his grip on the slippery wetness of his friend's lifeline as if his own life depended on it. When he had gathered in several loose coils, he looped the slack around the stump and pulled some more. Three more loops and then a white face appeared no more than a body length away. Jathniel was no longer struggling, but he coughed and seemed to take a breath before he went under again. Salmon redoubled his efforts, power surging through every muscle as he pulled with all his strength.

Then with a plunging rush, the world was swallowed by murky darkness. Salmon's elbows hit the gravely riverbed and his feet kicked at the water above his head. In the midst of his life-or-death scrambling back to his feet, Salmon's head bumped the goatskin bobbing freely above him on the surface. He rejected that place of life and breath. He would not go there without his friend.

His feet found the stump again. Pressing against it with both feet now and hauling hard, he kept the pressure on the rope. His body was screaming for air, but with the next grasp of his hand—a tangle of clothing and arms and legs. He shoved Jathniel's head above the water first, found his footing, and exploded out of the water. As he broke the surface and drank in a deep gulp of wonderful, sweet air, he coughed and laughed, and laughed and coughed, lightheaded and giddy. *No Shinab, we most definitely are not fish. But we are home.*

Dragging his sputtering friend with him, he crawled to the shallows. As he rested there panting, listening to Jathniel coughing and retching, the chill of the Jordan seeped into his bones.

"I'm a believer in your dreams now," Jathniel mumbled after a while. His eyebrows flickered weakly.

Salmon's mind laughed, but his giddiness had fled. An audible response was too much effort. He was bruised, thoroughly exhausted, and beginning to shake from the cold.

Jathniel struggled to his feet. "Enough of this. Let's go see Joshua."

Salmon couldn't muster enough energy to answer.

Jathniel reached down and grabbed his hand. "Remember Joshua's warning? Remember the lions in the river basin?"

"Too wet. Too cold."

"You are probably right. Only a mighty hungry lion would leave a warm, dry lair to get cold and wet snacking on the two of us."

"I mean . . . *I* am too wet . . . too cold . . . to care."

"Well, *I* care." Jathniel pulled him up out of the water. "I don't care to live with nightmares of you devoured by lions—or stiff and dead of Jordan chills for that matter."

Salmon smiled a response in his mind and wondered at his friend's newfound vitality.

Battered and aching, leaning on each other for support, definitely too tired to watch for the burning eyes of wild beasts, they stumbled over rocks and fought their way through brush. Warmed by the exertion of climbing the steep slope of the river basin and even more energized by the sight of the beautiful tents of Jacob, they crossed the meadow with quickened pace and made straight for Joshua's tent.

Joshua

"Joshua."

"Who's there?" Joshua blinked in sleepy confusion at the staggering shadows rustling at his doorway. His hand instinctively felt for his sword. *Friend or foe?*

"It's Jathniel and Salmon, Commander . . . sir."

"My spies? At last." Joshua sat up, instantly awake. "Where have—?

"Yahweh saved us!"

"Jathniel? What? Where? Your parents' concern has been growing by the day."

Jathniel didn't stop talking over Joshua's stammering questions. "We couldn't use the raft. Salmon dreamed up goatskin floats."

"Salmon? Abijah has come to me every day since you left. What detained you?"

"Jericho, sir, but all of Canaan is melting in terror because of our people."

Joshua stared at the boys in the darkness wondering if this was merely a dream. "I didn't know what to tell your families . . . except to trust God."

The spies report piled up in an incoherent heap as both young men spoke at once. "Evil city . . . Rahab . . . king terrified . . . inn . . . suspicious captain . . . piles of flax . . . a believer in Yahweh. . . escaped by rope . . . a red cord . . . three days in a cave . . . guards searching day and night . . . nearly drowned. "

"Whoa. Slow down a moment." Joshua threw back his blanket and set his feet solidly on the floor. "I expected you days ago, but there is ample time for a coherent story."

"The story we can tell with confidence, sir, is that Yahweh delivered us," Salmon declared. "Jericho's walls are formidable—but our God is stronger.

Joshua chuckled. "The light of your faith brightens the inner hallways of my heart, but this tent needs light as well. Sit down. Sit down."

Joshua methodically lit a small oil lamp and set it on a high stand, assessing the battered faces and wet clothing illuminated now by its warm glow. But no sooner had he turned back to his spies then Jathniel began speaking again.

"We understand now why the ten spies with you and Caleb panicked over high walls. We—"

"Hold the report. We need to tend to you first."

Joshua brought out dry tunics and layers of soft sheepskin blankets and then began daubing the cuts on their faces and hands and arms and legs with oil. He mixed up an herb poultice and plastered it over the smoldering redness of the puncture wound on Jathniel's thigh. When he was satisfied he had done all he could, he settled back on his bed to listen.

"All right, *now* we're ready for that report. But, one at a time. Salmon, you begin."

His boys were warm and comfortable, most likely more than they had been for days, but they were far from ready to sleep. Joshua yawned more than once while they chattered until dawn, detailing all they had seen in the land beyond the river and everything that happened to them in Jericho.

At first light, Joshua sent a message to Eleazar to summon all the people for a convocation at the tabernacle following the sacrifice. Then, as the silver trumpets began to blare, he sent the spies to their tents to sleep while he went to address the people.

Joshua found particular satisfaction this morning at the sight of the ram smoldering on the altar and the fragrance of the incense wafting heavenward along with the people's prayers. As the priests tidied up following the ritual, Joshua's gaze followed the rising tendrils of smoke connecting the bronze altar to heaven itself. So tenuous, this visible manifestation of the people's devotion to their God, yet so much depended on the connection. Yahweh was faithful. If only he could perform this new leadership role faithfully. If only these people would remain faithful.

O, changeless God of Israel, so much is about to change for us. We offered this ram in accordance with your law. May it cover our sin and guilt. With our eyes on your holiness and glory, make us holy through and through. Faithful to the covenant. A people worthy of your Name.

He dropped his gaze and scanned the sea of faces. His old friend Caleb stood front and center, the beautiful Acsah at his right hand, his sons and their families in loose clusters all around. One old man in a sea of youth. The sole remnant of those who left Egypt with him on that night of triumph and terror so long ago. All the rest, the entire crowd, were the offspring of the exodus generation.

A flood of love welled up so suddenly within him that he could hardly breathe. All these strong young men and women, lively boys and girls—they were the children and grandchildren he never had. *Is this how Moses felt? This mixture of fatherly pride and protectiveness. Proud to lead a people with such a high calling. Fearful of the choices that could topple them in a moment.* He gulped back his emotions. The people were waiting. He cleared his throat in preparation for the most important announcement of his life.

"In three days the period of mourning for Moses, the man of God, will end. He is no longer here to guide us, but his words remain. God's words. They will guide us now. If you are careful to do everything written in the Book of the Covenant, blessings will fall on you like Canaan's early and latter rains. Faithfulness will yield rich harvests, not in the field alone, but in your families and in everything you put your hand to."

There was mild applause.

"Listen my people, this is a day to celebrate. Our spies have returned. They encountered dangers. Even faced death. But they have returned safely, gratefully proclaiming God's miracles of protection. Above all, they cannot stop raving about the bounty awaiting us on the other side of the river."

Joshua briefly outlined what he had learned about the valley and city across the Jordan and the fear that had fallen on the inhabitants of the land. The surging power of the message rushed through him and his words came faster and faster, rolling over the people like surf against the shore, building to one grand, final wave. "It is time to cross the river."

The words hung in the air for an instant, hovering in a curl of restrained power, then crashed into a deafening roar of shouts and cheers like a breaker crashing against the shore. Its thunder all but drowned Joshua's final words. "You have three days to prepare your belongings and your hearts. On the third day—we WILL cross the Jordan."

As the people rejoiced and hugged one another, it struck Joshua as odd that no one asked how such a crossing would happen during this season of flooding. He himself did not know, but God was leading as he had led Moses. God spoke the word, and they would follow. That was all he needed to know.

When the excitement died down, Joshua's demeanor became somber. "The time when all our tribes dwelt together in one place has come to an end. You remember the agreement Moses made with Reuben . . ." Joshua paused after he called out the name, waiting for the prince of that tribe to come to his side.

"Gad . . ." He paused again.

"And half the tribe of Manasseh." When the three princes stood boldly at his right hand, Joshua stated his purpose. "Today, these tribes will confirm their assent to that agreement."[31] The three princes nodded. Then Joshua addressed the trio directly. "God has granted rest to you and your families here, in this land east of the Jordan. While the rest of the tribes pack their belongings to cross over into Canaan, you must finish settling your wives and children in the homes you have prepared for them in Gilead and Bashan. They will remain east of the river along with your flocks and herds and all your possessions, but your fighting men must cross over ahead of the remaining tribes. Yahweh himself will watch over your families until you return. Your troops will go ahead of your brothers until they find rest as you have. When they have taken possession of their inheritance in Canaan, you may return to your families and the inheritance Moses allotted to you here, east of the Jordan toward the sunrise."

The multitudes populating those three tribes shouted out in joy, but thousands of faces among the other nine paled at the thought of the rending of the Twelve. When the noise subsided, Ira of Manasseh stepped forward and saluted Joshua with a pounding of his fist on his chest. "All your commands, we will obey, and wherever you send us, we will go." All three warrior chiefs saluted together and then Ira stepped back into place.

Heled of Reuben stepped out and responded next. "Just as we listened to every command of Moses, so we will listen to you." He laid his hand on Joshua's shoulder in blessing. "Only may Yahweh your God guide you as he did Moses."

Joshua dropped his head humbly as the trio saluted their assent to this blessing.

Finally, Abiel of Gad stepped forward to pledge his support. He raised his hand to heaven in the sign of an extreme oath. "Whoever rebels against your word in battle and does not heed your orders—whatever you may command—will be put to death." None who looked at him, standing tall and proud, doubted that his threat was real.

In perfect military precision, the three representatives saluted one last time as they called out in unison, "Lead on. Be strong and courageous."

Joshua acknowledged their allegiance with a return salute. "Call forth your warriors to be blessed by God."

Dual trumpets blared. Armed men emerged from the chaotic masses of Reuben, of Gad, and of Manasseh, morphing into ordered units, ten abreast, rows of ten, solid blocks of fighters, marching in a large loop around the tabernacle. The tangled throng immediately fell back so a broad passageway allowed the troops to pass in review before Joshua and the priests.

The circuit followed the white linen fence of the tabernacle courtyard, returning again to the entrance where Eleazar blessed each group of one hundred before they dispersed. Cheers swelled from the throngs of onlookers as the impressive legions continued coming: ten, twenty, thirty . . . forty thousand of the mightiest men in Israel. Forty thousand warriors demonstrating their intention to lead the rest of the tribes to their inheritance beyond the river.

Acsah

Acsah gazed at the march of the troops with awe. The day following the end of the plague, when Eleazar recited the number of warriors from each tribe, she had not really pictured what a formidable army Israel had. "So many," she whispered. "Amazing."

"Definitely amazing," Aunt Sarah answered, "There are no other words for it." She did not add her usual qualifying negative.

Othniel grinned in amusement at the uncharacteristic animation in his mother's voice. "Amazing," he agreed.

"Even more amazing than this impressive array," Caleb observed, "is that these very men threatened Joshua's leadership only days ago. Today they threaten anyone who does not follow him."

The last division passed before Judah, their strong backs receding into the hosts of Israel like a wave pulling back to sea, exerting a strong tidal tug at the heart. "It is not a small thing," Acsah noted, "for these men to leave their families east of the river to go with us to fight for our land."

"Brave and loyal," Caleb responded. "But never again our encampment of twelve."

Othniel gave a barely perceptible nod of agreement, but his mother surprised everyone by brushing aside the melancholy reflections. "Whether twelve tribes or nine, Israel really is going to cross the river—in three days." She hugged Huldah close. "That land of milk and honey over there will be our new home, sweet

215

child, just as this valley now belongs to the tribes of Reuben, Gad, and half of Manasseh."

It was odd that Sarah could be so cheerful. Acsah simply could not. "You look forward to something all your life," she mused, "and never does it enter your head what you will lose by gaining it."

Caleb cleared his throat noisily.

Acsah glanced at him. She had the feeling he wanted to say something important, but she had no idea what it could be. "Well," she said. "I do not have time to stand around and think glum thoughts. There is too much to do."

"Acsah." Her father's voice was gentle but commanding. When she looked full in his face, however, the crinkle around his eyes indicated humor. He placed his hands on the shoulders of the two younger Midianites. "Perhaps a few extra hands will be useful?"

Acsah had not spoken to the little ones since the day her father tried to bring them home. As far as she was concerned, they could stay with their oldest sister helping Aunt Sarah forever. They seemed happy enough, the three of them together, as they arrived at this assembly, but as soon as they saw Caleb, they ran to him with giggles and hugs. Their adoration of her father was something she could relate to.

Hogluh looked up at Acsah with wide, innocent eyes. "We know how to wash clothes in the river. We have helped our sister wash for Mistress Sarah."

Hodesh chimed in proudly, "Give us all the soiled clothing and we will bring it back—clean, sunshine fresh and dry—all folded for packing."

Acsah rolled her eyes and sighed, but she could feel a smile playing at the corners of her mouth. "Abba is right as always."

Othniel snorted back a laugh.

The joke was on her. Any attempt to save her pride would be futile. "Extra hands *will* be a blessing today. Hodesh and Hogluh, I would be most grateful for your help. Follow me."

Salmon

Salmon slept into the afternoon swathed in the comfort of his own bed in the tent of his childhood. This was not fitful dozing, drifting in and out of dreams edged with fear. This was solid sleep. When he finally awoke, he blinked at the familiar surroundings and did not remember any dream at all. The terror of the city, the discomfort of the cave, even the haunting beauty of Rahab of Jericho seemed dimly remote and unreal. Only goodness, safety, and joy surrounded him. He would have enjoyed lingering in his bed, but the sun beating down on the tent was stifling, and the thought of cool, fresh air stirred him to action.

He leaped out of bed and winced at the protest made by his body. "Alright arms, legs, back—I hear you. The crossing was quite real and happened only hours ago." He rolled his shoulders, stretched his arms, and arched his back to limber up the stiffness. Then, for the first time, he noticed all the rustling, thumping, and chattering outside. The sound of his mother's and sister's voices was like music. He couldn't quit smiling as he began to don his clothing. The drift of their words was impossible to comprehend, but the excitement and energy was contagious. He had surprised them by slipping home and going to bed while they were at morning tabernacle services. This unusual flurry of activity must mean that his family was outdoing themselves in preparation for a grand welcome-home feast.

He had nearly finished dressing when a third female voice added to the hubbub. Melodic, with a timbre of strength and authority—and oh so familiar. That voice was more welcome at the moment than any other joy of his homecoming; fresh air of another kind.

"He's a lazy bones. Still sound asleep," his sister was saying. "I'll go wake him up for you."

"Ada! He must have been up all night just getting home. Come back this evening, Acsah."

"No, no, no," he called out. "Don't leave, Acsah. I'm awake now."

Although he hadn't finished tying his cloak, he threw a head covering over his baldness and poked his head out the doorway. "Shalom—"

"Wait!" With the terrifying beauty of a warrior goddess, Acsah held up her hand to block his greeting. Her eyes were frighteningly piercing, her finely chiseled features set with grim determination. Then as if she were a statue carved of ice, she melted into a stream of laughter. "What happened to your beard and your eyebrows?"

"You want a really good laugh? You might as well see the whole picture." Salmon snapped his head cloth off in one swift movement and rubbed his fingers across the stubbly baldness. "We were supposed to look like Egyptians."

"How am I supposed to respect the prince of Judah? You look five years younger without your beard and just plain weird without eyebrows or head hair."

"Truth be told, I woke up feeling twenty years older, stiff and bruised by the river crossing last night. But now that I see you, I do feel like a boy again. As for weird, you will have to agree I have always been a little bit weird. So let's start this greeting over. Shalom, my friend."

The amusement that had softened Acsah's lean, sculptured features vanished again. Her eyebrows pulled into vertical furrows. "I don't deserve your greeting. Not until I redress the rudeness of our last meeting. I was upset and in a hurry to take something to Eleazar, but I had no right to take it out on you. I was wrong."

Salmon laughed. "What? I remember nothing. You were forgiven before the offense, if there was an offense at all." He dove into the refreshing green of her eyes like a desert traveler plunging into the cool shade of an oasis on a hot day. "Oh Acsah, you have no idea how good it is to be home."

218

Acsah

Acsah stepped back. An image of Jonathan flashed through her head. No. Salmon's eyes stirred only the fleeting memories of their shared childhood. The same honest smile pulled at one side of his mouth. She relaxed. The man is still the boy. Still my childhood friend.

Jonathan was an aberration.

Salmon looked around and sighed. "After all I have been through in the past week, it is incredibly good to be home."

"You repeat yourself." She shook her head and laughed. "But, I am thinking the grieving Salmon is much himself again. I didn't know how to relate to that morbid fellow."

"You are absolutely right. Before I crossed the river, this tent, this neighborhood—the whole camp even—seemed only a depressing void. Everywhere I turned there were only reminders of my father's absence. I had to fight for footing every day as if I were standing on the edge of a deep, dark sinkhole. Standing here in the sunshine on this gorgeous day, it is almost hard to recall that feeling. One week over there, deprived of home, cleared my vision. I can see how blessed I am. Judah is not a heavy burden. It is my fulcrum of comfort and strength." His lopsided smile pulled into a full grin. "And you, my friend, supply a huge portion of its regenerative powers."

Acsah felt a stab of guilt as she remembered why she had come. Salmon was so very dear and so kind, and yet she had snapped at him just because she was having a bad day. She did not deserve such unconditional kindness and friendship. "My behavior was particularly inexcusable," she mumbled, "when you had just lost your father."

Salmon brushed the air and opened his mouth to interrupt, but she could not let his compassion prevent her confession. "When Joshua announced that spies had been sent across the river. When I discovered that you were one of them." She paused, searching for the right words. "When I thought of the danger you faced, that you could die over there, I was so fearful. What if in your final moments, you would remember only—"

"Oh, I *do* remember! Othniel and I were discussing the request of Reuben, Gad, and Manasseh to stay here east of the river when you came marching up the tent row toward us, obviously on some mission of great import. 'No time for friends . . .' you said—a bit more brusquely than usual. Where *were* you going?"

"That is irrelevant. The whole thing haunted me while you were gone. I could not bear the thought that my last words to you might be ones spoken so hastily and cruelly in your time of grief. You did nothing to deserve that."

Salmon chuckled at her distress. "I deserve far more scoldings than I have ever received. But I have returned safe and sound, as you see. Our friendship goes on." He reached out and pressed his thumb on the furrow between her eyebrows with a gentle turn. "It is time to lose that frown. So, how did you know we were back?"

Her brow instantly relaxed. Apparently, Salmon had no idea Joshua had announced the crossing in three days. There was no way she was going to reveal it quickly. "Oh, of course. How could you know the news of your return is all over camp today?"

Ada rushed past just then with an armload of tools. "Joshua gave an official report at a general assembly." She piped her comment into the conversation without even stopping.

"Thanks for letting us have an uninterrupted conversation, Ada," Acsah called after her.

Salmon stared after his sister in wonder. "Where is she off to with all that?"

"You would know if you hadn't missed the assembly today."

"Today? A general assembly already? I just woke up."

She laughed. "Yes, Prince Salmon—who ought to know what is going on in camp. *Today* is more than half over. You slept through trumpet blasts, cheers and applause, martial fanfare . . ."

"Slept through . . . what?"

"You missed the blessing ceremony of the army's new vanguard. Forty thousand very impressive warriors from the tribes of Reuben, Gad, and Manasseh."

Salmon stared at her as the tidings registered. "Joshua managed to regain their respect and obedience while I was gone? Astounding. So . . . is that *all* I missed? Your eyes tell me there is more."

"More?" She tossed out a teasing smile. "Well, you did miss a rather important announcement."

"Important?"

"Announcement," she repeated.

"I don't suppose you will tell me what it was."

"It was an important announcement."

His grin widened. "I'm guessing you can hardly hold back the news."

"I suppose an announcement is meant to be announced." She took one deep breath and then the good news exploded from her. "We will be crossing in three days. Look around. Every campsite is a frenzy of cleansing and packing."

"That is wonderful news. It also explains all the disorder, the scurrying and scrambling." He gestured toward the right. "Also explains the empty spot down the tent row. I guess Igor's family are quick packers. You can miss a lot by sleeping through a morning."

Abijah emerged from the storage tent with a large basket of dried figs. "There is manna porridge in a bowl over there for you. Sorry, you have to eat it cold on your first day back—What happened to your hair?"

"I'll tell you all about it later. Do you need help, Mother?"

"Not until you have yourself straightened up and belt tied. You can help strike the tent as soon as we have the last of the bedding packed up." She stacked the basket beside a growing pile near the tent door, covered it with a cloth, and disappeared.

Salmon finished knotting his belt. "Only three days, eh? I need to set myself to making a good-sized raft for all our stuff straight away. Is that what Joshua told the men to do, construct rafts?"

"Rafts? Joshua said nothing regarding the method of crossing. Father is repairing our wagon, not making a raft. We were told to pack our tents, get food supplies ready, and move down to the river."

"But, the flood?"

221

She laughed. "I don't know about rafts, but I'm quite certain, we're not going to slosh through water over our heads in some ritual of purification. Joshua commanded us to purify ourselves, and our things, *before* we cross. Eleazar has provided a huge heap of purification ash down by the river. I gathered extra hyssop branches if your family needs them."

Abijah was stacking more baskets nearby. She looked up. "Thank you, Acsah. But Ada and I completed the purification rituals early this morning while my returned spy slept."

Salmon watched his mother rush back inside the storage tent. He looked thoughtful for a moment, noting the growing piles of foodstuffs and utensils. "Our belongings have doubled since we moved into this valley. I wonder how we *will* get everyone and all our livestock and all our household implements across." Suddenly he gave her an intense look. "Purify, pack up, prep food, *and* move to the river— And how is it *you* have time to stop in the middle of such a busy day to visit your friend?"

Acsah felt a flush of embarrassment burn a fiery path up her neck to her cheeks. "Much as I hate to admit it, I have my father's Midianite girls to thank. Young as they are, Hogluh and Hodesh helped me wash all our clothing and rugs in the river this morning. While our things are drying, the girls are packing our food stores, making them portable. They are not evil like their mothers. I was so wrong to treat them as I did."

Salmon raised his eyebrows and looked at her curiously. "Is this truly Acsah standing before me? Admitting being wrong? Pretty powerful purification ritual, I'd say."

"It was the hardest part of all this preparation for the crossing. I've never been one for heart-searching, and now I know why. One look within almost undid me. Unkind, independent, quickly angered and—worst of all, abominably proud." The relief and healing that came from verbalizing those thoughts to Salmon surprised her. "I know the blood of the daily ram covers my individual sins, but when Eleazar explained the importance of the bull of purification this morning, I realized I needed more. I needed purification from my unholy core."

Salmon tugged at his ears in an expression of disbelief.

"I am serious. If we are not pure through and through, how can a holy God dwell in our camp?"

"Acsah, you don't know unholy until you see a place like Jericho."

"My goal is not to be better than Jericho. It is to be at one with God and at one with everyone else. I spoke to Othniel and Abihail following the assembly. I made things right with Hogluh and Hodesh as we worked together. As soon as you forgive me, I can resume packing in peace."

Salmon

Salmon gazed at Acsah in awe. She was proud at times, overly proud perhaps, but also remarkably teachable. This is what the forty years of wilderness wanderings were all about, creating a teachable people who would live by the covenant and want to be one with a holy God. Behind her, on the far side of the river, he could see the hills of Canaan rising against the sky. Israel would face tremendous challenges when they ran head on into the evil lurking there, but Acsah had the strength to match the challenges of those polluted hills.

"You, Acsah, my friend, should be the prince of Judah—well, the princess. I would not fear anything the future might hold for our tribe if you were in charge. Expect to always be my most important advisor."

A crescendo of giggles and girlish prattle shattered the thought. "There he is. Right over there." Ada's piping voice floated above the chatter of her friends. "Salmon," she called. "Salmon, my friends want to hear about Jericho."

Salmon held up both hands defensively as four little girls stampeded in his direction, then surrounded him like young lambs butting at their mothers at feeding time.

223

"Ada, I just got up. I haven't even had time to eat."

Acsah quickly grabbed the bowl his mother had reserved for him. "Here is your breakfast, Salmon."

He pushed through the little flock and dropped his chin with a plea only for Acsah's ear as he took the porridge. "Save me. I am not ready to answer a thousand questions."

Acsah stepped in front of him protectively. "Sorry, girls. We are leaving as soon as your brother finishes eating. My father is waiting to hear the full report."

A chorus of groans erupted from the girls, but they remained in their places carefully observing every move of the returned spy. Maybe they waited in high expectation of astounding tales of Jericho—or maybe it was just the novelty of his baldness. Whichever it was, he did not enjoy the sudden fame. "You and your friends will have to wait," he said firmly, waving them off as he gulped down the last bite of porridge. "I don't know who made this, but it was wonderful even cold."

Ada's shoulders sagged as he began walking away.

He came back and wrapped her up in a brotherly hug. "Don't worry, Ada. I promise I will tell you all about Jericho soon."

"Let's go, Salmon," Acsah interjected with an unwavering tone.

"After I talk to Caleb, alright?"

An impish smile spread over his sister's face and she began whispering to her friends, but Acsah did not seem to notice. She chattered amiably as they walked away. "When my father took a load of utensils and tools out to the wagon, he told me he would stay to prepare tethers for the animals and repair the harnesses. A timely blessing for a returned spy in need of escape, don't you think?"

"Timely unless my sister and her friends follow us there," he whispered. *Why on earth were a ruse and spy-like whispers necessary when he was home? Spying techniques should be behind him.*

Acsah wheeled to face the little group that was indeed trailing after them. "This is no time to be idle," she said commandingly. "Go help your families prepare parched grain and pack up the dried grapes and figs."

"But Acsah!" they groaned in chorus. "We want to hear Salmon's story."

"Go. All of you. Your stomachs will be quite grateful for something to eat in Canaan. We don't know if there will be manna on the other side."

"Odd thought," Salmon remarked over the groans of the children. "Joshua asked Jathniel and me to assess the foods growing across the river and raised that same question of manna-fall in Canaan."

"It *is* odd," she said, "Abba mentioned it following one of Moses' speeches too. Only he and Joshua are left to remember that it did not fall in Egypt, only in the barren desert and only for our people."

"Did Joshua mention that at the assembly this morning?"

"No. He simply told us to pack up all the stores of food we got from the towns and farms of this valley." With a supercilious lift of one eyebrow, she added. "We can't pack manna, as you well know."

Salmon laughed. "No bags of worms cross with us." He tried to imagine life without manna. "What do people *eat* day in and day out if they don't have manna? What *does* your father expect?"

"He doesn't know what to expect. Manna, or the immediate need to plant and harvest. Miracle peace, or years of war. He is more eager to hear your story than your sister and her friends, if that is possible. I am dying to hear it too."

"I thought you were leading me away from those thousand questions."

She laughed. "I promise not to ask any if you just let me listen in."

Acsah

Acsah fell into a comfortable silence, wading through knee-high drifts of bright purple anemones and fragrant blue spires. It was a different world once they left the noisy bustle of the tents of Judah behind. Bees buzzed over the flowers in a frenzy of activity. The sun warmed their backs. Gradually, she became aware of soft humming, a melody in baritone floating lightly on the air and harmonizing exquisitely with the insect orchestra—a perfect pastoral symphony punctuated by the intermittent chorus of sheep and the *basso profundo* of the cattle. She glanced sideways at Salmon, but his eyes were focused on some distant place and one corner of his mouth curved upward with his ever-charming smile.

"What an engaging melody. Spring itself captured in a song."

"What?" A flush rose from his neck to his scalp. "Song?" He laughed uncomfortably. "I heard it in Jericho. It constantly returns to my head."

Acsah looked at him with curiosity. "The look on your face right now is exactly like the little boy I knew years ago whenever he was in trouble."

"Trouble? I don't know about that. I just pray it is not a sin to retain this melody. We were not to bring *anything* back."

"I hardly think you should feel guilty about such a lovely song."

Salmon's little boy look tugged the little girl out of Acsah's past. "Race you to the wagon," she shouted without warning. Giving in to the sudden urge to run like the wind, she broke into a full sprint.

When she looked back, Salmon was lagging far behind. With a smirk, she sped across the meadow even faster, plunging into the jumble of flocks and herds and wagons gathered by the men of Judah. She smirked again as a quick backward glance revealed the stern looks Salmon received from those men. He had slowed to a walk, following the mooing, braying, and bleating trail she left behind, apologizing to the men he passed, clucking soothingly as he moved through the livestock—but the frightened animals continued kicking up dust and rolling frightened eyes while their owners glowered in *his* direction, not hers.

Acsah sauntered over to the wagon where Caleb worked over a well-worn harness and kissed her father's leathery cheek. "Salmon is right behind me," she said innocently.

"I believe I hear him coming." Caleb grinned. "Can you hold these straps together like this? I thought I was finished and then this line broke."

Acsah watched her father's timeworn hands deftly drive the awl through the harness bands and begin threading a leather thong through the holes to lash the broken ends together. "I brought Salmon out here because I thought you would be eager to hear more details than Joshua gave us this morning."

Caleb looked up as Salmon approached, shielding his eyes against the bright afternoon sun with the hand that held his awl. "Shalom," he said. "Shalom, shalom." A wry twinkle brightened his eyes.

"Thank you. I need double peace. For me and the disturbance I leave in my wake."

Acsah vaulted up onto the wagon, swinging her legs back and forth. "What took you so long, Salmon?"

"I got tangled up in a whirlwind and had to repair its damage."

Caleb snorted a single laugh. "I am quite familiar with that very whirlwind. My dear Salmon, it is shalom you bring, not shalom you need to receive."

Acsah smiled down at both of them. "True enough. All my life."

For the next hour, Salmon related all he had seen in the valley across the river and what he had learned in the city of Jericho. Acsah listened aghast as Salmon told how Ahuzzath took them into custody and how a harlot saved them. She was completely engaged in the story when a forced cough startled her.

"We . . . um . . . we do not want to interrupt you."

Acsah turned toward the sound, but her mind was still trapped in the fearsome darkness of Jericho and its surrounding caves. She noticed her father had all but forgotten to finish repairing the harness in his hands. Eliab and Abihail had slipped up behind him and stood waiting to be acknowledged, Eliab fidgeting with the gleaming obsidian cascade of Abihail's hair. He was clearly tense.

"I have lingered here far too long when there is so much to do back in camp," Acsah said, quite certain they had come seeking her father's sage advice, not hers. She gave Abigail a sisterly wink and pushed herself from her perch on the wagon, landing beside Salmon with a commanding look.

"I'll go with you," he said in instant response, leaping to his feet. "I promised to help my mother strike the tent."

"No, please stay," Eliab responded. "Both of you. We value all your opinions."

Abihail glanced apologetically at the awl in Caleb's hands. "But we don't want to keep you from your work."

Caleb laid the tool down in the grass by the unfinished harness. "Sit, my child, sit. Whatever I was doing can wait. And, certainly, Acsah and Salmon can linger a bit longer if they can be of help. There are yet two more days to complete these tasks."

Acsah sat down and patted the grass beside her. "Come. Tell us what has happened. The distress on your faces is out of place on such a joyful day."

"We have determined to follow Yahweh wholeheartedly," Abihail answered cautiously.

Caleb's eyes crinkled with pleasure at her words. "Nothing is more important than that. It is not just our obligation, but our primary delight."

Acsah looked at her friend hopefully. *She's going to rid herself of the pollution of those Midianite gifts.*

Abihail made no attempt to speak. She settled down on the grass, looking expectantly at the young husband slumping into place beside her.

Eliab inhaled deeply and then exhaled with a long, slow breath. He did not look anyone in the eyes.

"There is no other way to begin than by simply coughing up the first few words, my son."

"This morning—" Eliab coughed and then smiled sheepishly.

Caleb chortled and nodded in his encouraging fatherly way. "Now cough up another."

"This morning . . . when . . . Joshua . . ." Eliab labored at his speech. He glanced once more at Abihail, and she added her own encouraging nod. "When Joshua called on us to purify ourselves as well as our belongings . . ." At last the words began to flow in hesitant bursts. "I knew I had to go to Abihail . . . with something that has been troubling me for some time. Concerns so dark, I withheld them even from her." His eyes swept over their faces with a look of utter wretchedness.

I hope it is about the Midianite scarf and necklace, Acsah thought.

"Concerns about my family," he mumbled and dropped his head into his hands. "As soon as I told her, Abihail suggested that we come to you."

When Abihail laid her hand on his, Eliab smiled weakly at her. "My love for this beautiful girl inspires me to live a true and righteous life."

"Tell him what happened, Eliab."

Eliab looked down at his hands again. "I would rather not share every detail, but it all started when the weather first cleared after that long spell of rain." He hesitated. "Jamin and my father asked for my help. They planned to cross the river back then . . . before you and Jathniel even left to spy out Jericho, Salmon. There was a large group making plans to go, along with the warriors of Reuben, Gad, and Manasseh."

Caleb closed his eyes. "And Joshua aborted that plan when he sent the spies and then convinced those three tribes to stick with Moses' plan. I'm sorry to hear your father joined that rebellion."

Eliab nodded. "I wish that were all. My parents and my brother bragged to me about what they consider smart choices. I see them as frightening choices, as outrageous greed. I haven't had much contact with any of my family recently, but then Jamin told me this morning that Abihail and I must return the tent my father gave us and that we cannot use the family wagon for the crossing unless I support them in their avarice. I suspect he wants to entangle me in their sin, so I will not disclose what I know. My dilemma now is how to obey the commandment to honor my parents while separating myself from pure greed."

"Your first duty is to be true to Yahweh. If your parents do not obey his commands, you must never follow them in that disobedience."

"So I said." Abihail's smile dimpled her cheeks. "Tell Achor and Jamin that we will find our own way to transport our things across the river."

"Are you prepared for the possibility that this might sever relations with your family permanently?" Caleb asked, arching one wild white brow.

Eliab's answer was almost inaudible. "Their choices have severed us already."

"We are your family. Judah is your family," Salmon answered, clapping one hand solidly on his friend's shoulder.

"And I love you all for your support." Eliab took a deep breath. "Caleb, can you show me how to construct a litter? That would be enough for us. We don't have many belongings yet."

"Better yet, add your things to our wagon. Acsah and I will not fill it."

"I do not mind making a litter."

"But there is no need," Caleb broke in. "Please join us."

Acsah felt a ball of lead weighing down her stomach as Abihail's usual sweet smile brightened her face. "Are you certain?" she was asking, looking from Caleb to Acsah.

No, my friend. We do not have room for certain things. Tell her what we will not carry with us, Abba.

Caleb laughed instead. "Of course. You have tagged along with us since you were knee high. Acsah would want you to enter Canaan right beside her."

A fierce determination flashed up from within and Acsah shot to her feet. "There are a few things we do not have room for. Our wagon is purified and dedicated to Yahweh. Nothing tainted with evil will go in it."

"I have already made that decision," Abihail replied with great seriousness. "You were right all along about the Midianite gifts. The law says nothing about such things, but my heart tells me that they affect my devotion to God. I am ready for that burning ceremony. Can we do it at your family's campfire tonight?"

The following day, Acsah worked side by side with Abihail, folding blankets and rugs and bundling personal items to pack in the wagon. The long slanted rays of afternoon sunlight streamed down the hills and across the valley, warm and strengthening, a beautiful symbol of the happiness flowing through her. Everything was right again between herself and her dearest friend—and they would enter Canaan together, a fulfillment of their childhood dreams.

Straightening up and stretching her back, Acsah paused to take in the scene of wonderful chaos and confusion around them. Goatskin tarps, rolled around tent poles and lashed with coils of rope, replaced the ordered rows of tents. A symphony of jubilant shouts reverberated against the hills as families finished packing tents, baskets of food, cooking utensils, and assorted bundles into wagons, litters, or backpacks and headed toward the river.

"This is just as I imagined it, Abihail, you and I packing up together. At last, we are going to enter the Land of Promise."

Abihail seemed to force her smile of response. "It is hard to really grasp what is happening."

Acsah studied her intently. "You aren't sorry you decided to burn those Midianite things last night, are you?"

"What? Never! I feel so clean. So relieved. Why would you ask that?"

"Just wondering about the dark shadow lurking on the edge of your smile."

"For myself, I am completely happy. But my husband— Eliab looked so dejected when he returned from telling Achor and Mara that we would be traveling with you. He expected anger, but never dreamed his own parents could be so spiteful."

"Keep reminding him. He did the right thing."

Abihail wiped a tear from the corner of her eye. "But to be told by your own mother that you are more loathsome in her sight than a rat or a pig, that you are no longer worthy to be called *son*."

Acsah thought of her own attachment to her father. "I can't imagine what it would be like to make that decision. He has shown great courage." She began folding another fleece rug, gazing blankly toward the heart of camp, preoccupied with Eliab's situation. All of a sudden she saw the void, the emptiness where the tabernacle had stood. The Levites had reduced the holy tent to rows of bundles and covered pieces of furniture. That was normal for a move. But Yahweh's cloud always remained over the tabernacle site until it was time to journey on. When it slowly drifted forward, Israel followed. Today, not only was Moses gone, but—

"Look, Abi!" she exclaimed in a panic. "The cloud has vanished."

Abihail stared. "How will Joshua know where to go?" she whispered.

A quaver of doubt tingled through Acsah. Following the death of Moses, the cloud had been a reassurance that God would continue to guide them. How *would* Joshua know where to go? *Stop.* She warned herself. *God is not about to abandon his people at the gates of Canaan.*

"Joshua doesn't know where to go," she answered slowly. "But he doesn't need to. My father spoke with him last night. He will wait for the word of the Lord. He does not even know how God intends to take everyone across that flood, but he was clearly told to make preparations."

Abihail giggled as she finished tying up a bundle of mats and flat cushions. "God's preparations for this move included packing up his cloud. I can't wait to see when and where he will unpack it again."

Phinehas

At daybreak on the third morning, Phinehas stood beside his uncle Ithamar, silver trumpets in hand. The camp of Israel was perched now along the rim of the eastern plains, the tribal divisions in blocks side by side rather than in their assigned places around the tabernacle. His camping spot with the priests and their families was at the center front of all the tribes. Before him, the rocky deposits forming the eastern flank of the *zor* rolled downward to the muddy, surging waters. The roar of the Jordan mingled in his mind with the promise they would cross today, kindling a fire within him unlike anything he had experienced before. He didn't know how, but they were leaving the nightmare of the Valley of Acacias behind. They were moving on to sweet Canaan.

With eyes on his uncle for perfect synchrony, he drew in the breath necessary for the three short blasts that would awaken the tribes. He could not explain why the two of them turned to face the river as they sounded a signal for tribes packed five furlongs deep beside and behind them. They had not discussed it. Both men simply turned that direction as if they were giving notice to the river that the people of Yahweh were there. *That is exactly what we are doing*, he decided. He lifted his voice like a prophet above the rush of the waters, "Be forewarned, O mighty Jordan. You will suffer defeat today."

Ithamar grinned and shook his head. "Let's go find your father and see what is next."

To the north, to the south, even behind them toward the rising sun, the temporary camp exploded in a rush of activity at their signal. People began striking their small shelters, rolling up the tarps, and packing them away for the crossing. Phinehas and his uncle returned to the simple altar of river stones where Eleazar, assisted by Ithamar's eldest son, had just slit the throat of the lamb for the burnt offering. The sight of any blood still brought back images of Cozbi, the corpses of rebels hanging on crosses, and the carnage of the Midianite war. Phinehas took a deep breath and looked away.

The Levite men were beginning to gather beyond the altar, finding their places beside the collection of shrouded furniture and bundles—the sanctuary in transit. Phinehas directed his attention to them and beyond. The remainder of the tribe of Levi, carefully maintaining the proscribed safety space between themselves and the sanctuary, stretched back across the plain in an orderly block, packed and ready for travel. An impressive sight, considering his kinsmen were fewer in number than any of the tribes.

Eleazar quickly set the daily ablaze. There could be no usual sanctuary routine on this unusual day. As the smoke of the morning ram rose over the river, the four priests left their places, trekking through the tribes with Eleazar waving the incense-filled censer and the four chanting the familiar blessing that Moses had always pronounced before every move.

> May Yahweh bless you and protect you;
>   may Yahweh make His face shine on you
>   and be gracious to you;
> may Yahweh look with favor on you
> and give you peace.[32]

As they blessed the first division—Judah, Issachar, and Zebulon—Phinehas sensed the people of Yahweh absorbing the blessing bestowed by his holy name. Judah's division normally marched first under a banner emblazoned with the lion of Judah, but the formation of the temporary camp was unfamiliar. No one seemed to know how the tribes would proceed. More importantly no one had any idea how it was possible to cross this raging river. And yet the tribes of Judah's division waited with a mood of expectation.

Not so the division that normally marched as rearguard under the bold blue eagle banner of Dan. When the priests intoned the blessing again—*may Yahweh look with favor on you and give you peace*—Phinehas cringed at the muttering.

"Give us peace, they say. This is the worst possible time to leave this valley."

"How will we proceed without Moses or the cloud?"

"I just want to know what we are supposed to do next. Where is Joshua? What is the plan?"

It wasn't that Phinehas couldn't understand the questions. No one enjoys waiting long on a long-awaited day. And yet, how many times had Moses instructed them to *wait on the Lord*? He snorted. This group was not even willing to wait half a morning for instructions from Joshua.

He trailed behind the other priests, wading morosely through the swamp of muttered doubts. "We should follow the river north to find a place with small tributaries close to the northern mountains. That would make sense this early in the spring."

The suggestion was immediately countered with a dissenting opinion. "Too far. We should head south to see if there is a shallow delta where this river empties into the sea. There must be quiet shallows where we could ford safely."

"Fine, you head south, and I'll go north," the first man snapped.

A woman spoke up. "Don't go thinking that either of your families are willing to head into unknown territory. If we want to cross north or south, we need to send spies ahead of us as we did to Jericho."

"The point is we need a leader," a third man opined. "Where is Joshua?"

Truth be told, the uncertainty about the day's proceedings and the lack of familiar organization were beginning to wear on Phinehas's patience as well. *Almighty Yahweh, give your people peace.*

It was still early morning when they finished blessing the last of the divisions. No one had seen or heard from Joshua so far as he knew. There was nothing to be done but take a little nourishment and wait. Any peace bestowed by the blessing evaporated as the morning sun continued to climb high and hot over the eastern hills and their leader did not appear. As it approached its zenith, even the air over his Levitical kinsmen buzzed with whispers of apprehension and questions of frustration.

"How are we to cross today? So far Joshua has done nothing."

"Can he split the river as Moses did the Red Sea?"

"Where is he anyway?"

"Perhaps he is hunting for the cloud." The comment stirred up a cloud of derisive laughter.

As if in answer, Joshua marched triumphantly out of a hidden retreat in the acacia trees. "Do not be distressed that the cloud returned to the Lord," he called out as he passed through the people. "It led us through the desert where its shade and moisture preserved our lives, but Yahweh is bringing us at last to a land of clouds and rain. As the Ark of the Covenant leads us physically into unknown places, the words contained within it will guide our lives when we face things we have never faced before. The cloud has served its purpose. From this day forward, we will be guided by the covenant and all the words of the Lord."

Some faces were puzzled, others anxious, still others cynical. *Moses and the cloud had given very clear guidance. The Ark of the Covenant could only go where it was carried, and it was always borne protectively at the heart of the procession.*

Joshua blasted a war signal on a ram's horn. It was a strange cue. Why not the silver trumpets of the priests? A ram could be strong. Ram's used their horns to defend the flock, yet battle between a ram and a really ferocious beast like a lion or bear inevitably left the ram bleeding and dying. It was a strange cue, but the prearranged one the clans of Levi waited for.

The designated men of the Gershonite and Merarite clans had already left the ranks of their families and clans behind and gathered in preparation. At the sound of the horn, they lifted the frames and drapings of the tabernacle and formed orderly columns. The men of Kohath moved forward. Each band shouldered the carrying poles of its assigned pieces of the sanctuary furnishings and joined their brothers, ready to march in neat regiments. The rest of the tribes watched uncertainly, some standing at attention beside meager piles on litters, others slumping down to rest on the ground beside their bulky shoulder packs, still others leaning against wagons that groaned under heavy loads.

"Only once before in the history of Israel did the Ark lead the way," Joshua called out jubilantly. "That was when your fathers left Mount Sinai for the Land of Promise. Today will be our second attempt to enter Canaan, and God again has changed the order of things, signaling that we have come full circle. The forty-year interruption of our journey is behind us. Now listen carefully. The sons of Kohath will not carry the Ark as God commanded in the past."

Phinehas felt a strange flush of anxiety mixed with pleasure at this new responsibility. The four priests—his father, Uncle Ithamar, and their two eldest sons—had been told to wait on the margin of the *zor*. Smoothly and ceremoniously, the Levites transferred the Ark from their shoulders to the four priests. Phinehas felt a tingling sensation as the pole settled on his shoulder, perhaps simply because this was new and God was clearly planning to do a new thing for his people—or perhaps he was experiencing a divine infusion of strength so he would not stumble in the task. He chose to believe the latter. The joy of being asked to carry the Ark of the Covenant mingled with another joy. He was standing on the meadow of deceit and bloodshed for the last time. Once they crossed the river, he hoped he would never be asked to return.

"When you see the priests with the Ark approach the river, move from your positions and follow," Joshua shouted. "The vanguard of forty-thousand warriors from Reuben, Gad, and Manasseh will cross north of the ark. At the same time, the division of Judah will cross south of the ark, falling into place behind the vanguard on the other side. Those who march under the banner of Ephraim will follow the vanguard across the river next, falling into their normal position behind Judah, once they reach the other side. Keep a distance of at least a thousand yards between yourselves and the Ark at all times. Do not crowd near it. It must be visible to all.

"The Gershonites and Merarites will cross next bearing the holy tent, the Kohathites following with its furnishings. The half tribe of Manasseh is all that remains of the division of Reuben. They will follow the Levites and the tabernacle in the battle formation we have used for forty years. Those marching under the banner of Dan will take their usual place as rearguard."

Joshua drew his sword and waved it toward the river basin, challenging the deafening roar of the waters. "Do not be dismayed at this flood. Yahweh has promised we will pass safely through it. Watch and see what your God will do."

As the Ark led the way down the rocky slope to the river's edge, nine and a half of the tribes left the beauty of Gilead behind, descending slowly into the rugged river basin with their children, their flocks and herds, and all their possessions. The warriors of Reuben, Gad, and Manasseh reached the water's edge first since they did not need to manage livestock or wagons. They stood at attention in their formations, occasionally turning to glimpse the land and loved ones they were leaving behind. Over the past month they had settled their wives and children in towns scattered across the plains of Gilead from the border of Moab northward to the heights of Bashan. All the women and children from those tribes who were able to had returned to watch the crossing. They stood now on the meadow, watching wistfully as the long lines of their brothers and sisters dropped down into the river basin and stopped at the edge of the rushing water. The trepidation and hushed expectancy was palpable.

Again Joshua disappeared. Again the people waited. Occasionally, a small child would escape, darting into the spray and splash of the water's edge chasing frogs or dragonflies. Anxious, wild-eyed parents dashed after them, snatching the little ones lest they tumble into the raging torrent. A new set of questions about Joshua's leadership erupted. Moses had always led Israel himself. Joshua had just turned that duty over to the priests, and now he had disappeared. Again.

"Moses would have split the water and taken us across by now. Where *is* Joshua?"

"I think he went off to pray."

"Well, he should have done *that* long before today."

"He did—and he does. He goes off to pray before dawn every day."

A raspy, impatient voice called out. "Well, then he has prayed enough already today. It is time to act. Are we to wait all day?"

"I keep hoping the cloud will reappear."

"Joshua doesn't need the cloud. He reads the scrolls every day. Yahweh speaks to him through them just as he spoke to Moses."

"That's right. My family and I will wait."

"Well, we can't wait down here long. There is no pasture for the flocks and herds. Listen to them."

The animals had been restless the whole of the morning, but suddenly an eruption of bellowing and bleating overran the idle questions and speculations. The ground shook violently. A distant rumble mingled with the cries of the animals and frightened shrieks of many of the people. Strong warriors staggered like drunks, while parents scrambled for solid footing, securing their children and their belongings as a swollen wave thundered down the already flooded river, splashing against its banks, hungrily gobbling bites of brush, rocks, and chunks of earth.

In the midst of the chaos, Joshua appeared on the slope behind the people. His face shone with triumph. He blew the ram's horn long and hard once more, then called out: "The time has come . . ." Like Moses, his words blasted forcefully clear above the tumult. "The time has come for the priests who carry the Ark of Yahweh—the Lord of all the earth—to step boldly into the Jordan."

Now? Just as this rushing swell is passing through?

Joshua's teeth flashed white in a triumphant grin. "We must never forget this day. Each tribe has a chosen representative to gather a river stone from the Jordan, one for each tribe. Twelve memorial stones to build a *gilgal* of remembrance. Today Yahweh will bring you through the Jordan into your inheritance—on dry land. Open your eyes. Watch and see how the Lord your God works wonders."

Phinehas watched the silver-haired warrior bound down the slope with the agility and verve of a young man. Joshua's energy coursed through him and seemed to electrify the entire nation.

"This is what the Lord your God says. Today you will know he is the living God." Joshua's words rolled over the people as calming as oil on boiling water as he assumed the position of commander at the front of the vanguard. "Today, you will know he is with you and that he will certainly drive the Canaanites, Hittites, Hivites, Perizzites, Girgashites, Amorites, and Jebusites out of the land before you. Behold the Ark of the Covenant descending into the Jordan ahead of you. Follow it."

Expecting the waters to divide as in the Red Sea story of their fathers, the people watched breathlessly. The priests steadied the poles on their shoulders and carefully picked their way into the shallows. Eleazar and Ithamar did not hesitate as the water sloshed into their sandals. Although the large, surging wave had subsided, the torrent did not split and congeal as at the Red Sea. Step by step, the four priests carried the ark deeper into the Jordan. The water spilled over their feet and around their ankles. It rose to their knees.

The people stared, wide-eyed in disbelief at what they saw. Were they supposed to follow the ark into foaming water clearly over their heads? Obedience should not look like this. They watched the progress of the Ark. Soon their priests would be neck-deep and then what? They remembered the reports of the difficulties Jathniel and Salmon experienced. God had obviously delivered the two spies, but this situation was beyond comprehension. They longed for Moses and the rod that drove back the waters so the people could cross on dry land. But Joshua was not Moses. He carried a sword. Not a rod of power.

By the time the priests reached the center of the channel and planted themselves there in defiance of the swollen river, the people realized the flood had not risen much above their knees. In fact, it was swirling around their ankles again, rapidly continuing to decrease. No new water poured down from the north as what remained of the river flowed southward, guzzled by some downstream abyss. The people began to cheer as the deafening roar of the flood faded to soft gurgling. Within minutes, the priest's sandals reappeared and the last dribbles of water, trickling here and there between river rocks, drained every remaining puddle, leaving the rocks and sand as dry as a desert wadi in summer.

Joshua sounded the ram's horn once more and the shouting ceased. In profound silence, the people stared at the foursome shouldering the sacred chest in the middle of the dry riverbed. Shekinah light blazed above the courageous war-priests who marched into the wrath of the storm god. The brilliant gleaming bathed the Ark in radiance brighter than sunlight. This blocking of the Jordan was no freak act of nature. Just as in the plagues of Egypt, this was a contest of the gods. And victory over a river was no contest for Yahweh.

Phinehas glanced down at the dry sand under his feet. He wanted to shout, but the awe of the miracle stole his voice.

Acsah

The hush over the multitudes of Israel exuded wordless praise. This was a procession unlike any these children of Israel had experienced before. There was only the soft scuffling of sandals as the tribe of Judah moved into the dry riverbed, a breathless quiet broken only by an occasional whisper here and there between child and parent clarifying what had taken place. Acsah exchanged a quick glance with her father. *Now I know, Abba. I really know what it was like to witness the plagues, the crossing of the Red Sea, and the fire of the Lord on Sinai. I, too, have seen the finger of God.* The crinkles of joy around Caleb's eyes told her he knew just what she was feeling and rejoiced in it as much as she did.

Salmon was just ahead of Acsah, leading the tribe of Judah for the first time. His father, the dignified, smiling prince she had loved her whole life was gone. Her throat tightened with a tender, aching regret that Nashon had not lived to see this day, that he could not lead the tribe on the last leg of the journey, just as he led them out of Egypt as a young man.

I am proud of you, Salmon. You truly have laced up your sandals and stepped into the days the Lord has given you. The child, Acsah, would have scampered through the riverbed right by your side, following your father at the front of the line with you. But this is your own bittersweet moment, one to share with your mother and sister as the new Prince of Judah.

This would be her own moment to share with her father, it seemed. In spite of a lifetime of plans, Abihail was not beside her either. She and Eliab insisted on guiding the family wagon with the sheep and cows tethered behind, allowing Acsah the freedom of crossing with Caleb. Looking back, Acsah could see her now diving into the wooly clouds of sheep and coming up with a tiny, vigorously bleating lamb. Exchanging a big smile with Eliab, she lifted the newborn onto her shoulder. The sheep around her jostled until what must have been the mother fell in step, nuzzling Abihail's side and baaing in comforting sheep talk to her baby. She could tell by the twinkle in Caleb's eyes that he had noticed the sweet scene also. She grinned at him. She was so blessed to be his daughter.

He returned the smile, then startled her with a whispered command. "Go on ahead. I want to put some thought into the proper stone to represent Judah."

Her quiet cousin, Othniel, was walking on the other side of her, but for once he did not seem to notice when she looked at him. *Was she always to remember this momentous day of the crossing walking beside this strange, quiet cousin? He was young and strong. Why couldn't he collect Judah's stone so she could treasure this occasion with her father?*

Oblivious to her, Othniel glanced over his shoulder when Caleb first dropped back and then again as Caleb began wandering among the river rocks. At the third glance, he left her without a word, dropping back to join his uncle. Aunt Sarah closed up the space left by her eldest son. She was walking arm in arm with Huldah, who had become more a companion to her than a servant girl. The smile she flashed at Acsah seemed more contented than any she could remember. Just in front of Acsah, the younger Midianite girls, Hogluh and Hodesh, had joined hands in a threesome with Salmon's sister, Ada. Their chain broke apart when a boulder obstructed their path—and then reformed once the obstacle was past. It seemed to Acsah a metaphor for her own friendships now. They would all link up again, she knew, but a sweet-sad longing rose for the childhood days when she, Abihail, and Salmon had made play of every march much like these little girls. Underneath the joy of the miracle today, lurked the leaden awareness that the generation of their parents was gone. It made her feel old.

I defy that deadly notion, she told herself.

She skipped ahead, linking one hand with Ada, and the other with Hogluh, who held hands with her sister. "Straight ahead," she whispered with a grin as she scrambled over a boulder that lay directly in their path. "Don't let anything break us apart." She was not old as long as she could still play the straight-ahead game as she often had with Abihail and Salmon in the growing up years of the wilderness wanderings.

Othniel

Othniel's heart pumped with awe and wonder. Old stories, fresh marvels were flung madly together in this riverbed. No longer merely the faith-building tales of his father. Today he was walking through his own miracle, and the sound of dry sand beneath his sandals was all the sweeter when they crunched in tandem with two of the people he loved and admired most. Then Caleb dropped back and began meandering among the boulders close to the eastern shore. Othniel continued walking for a moment beside his beautiful cousin. It was a thrill perfect for this thrilling day, but it wasn't right. A memorial stone grand enough for the tribe of Judah would be large. Surely the old man would need his help. Without even a silent farewell salute, he left Acsah and followed duty.

Caleb was rolling a water-rounded, oddly-elongated rock up on end when he noticed Othniel's watchful gaze. "Perfect," he declared. "The perfect stone. It stands firm, and it reminds me of a goatskin stretched tight with water. A reminder of God's perfect provision."

As Othniel helped lift that stone onto Caleb's shoulder, the feel and weight confirmed his initial suspicions. "I know this stone," he said quietly.

Caleb only grunted and rolled his shoulder so the weight fell more comfortably into the hollow between his neck and shoulder joints.

"It's heavier than it looks," Othniel warned. "Let me—"

But the old man lurched away, picking his path carefully through the river rock strewn across the gravelly riverbed. There wasn't the slightest bow in his tent-pole-straight back in spite of the ponderous weight.

Othniel shrugged and followed Caleb while happy images of the recent celebration feast flooded his mind. Igal whirling and tossing that very stone into a bed of red lilies. Asriel gasping as he carried it back to the group. The boisterous challenge. The rush of strength fueling his own attempt to heave it—followed by the surprise of losing the stone to the river. How his group of friends would laugh when he told them their stone finally came to rest at the very place the tribe of Judah would cross! How awesome that it would be carried into Canaan on the shoulders of Israel's oldest warrior! On that day of thanksgiving months earlier, no one could have guessed the terrors and triumphs Israel would witness. But now, this particular stone would always stand as a reminder.

From their vantage point high on the meadow above the Jordan, the spectators from the tribes of Reuben, Gad, and Manasseh watched their fellow Israelites cross the Jordan along an expanse that ran miles in both directions from the Ark. It was long past noon by the time the last of the nine and a half tribes climbed up to the high ground of the western plains, every foot standing at last on the Promised Land. Only then did the Ark of the Covenant, with the glorious Shekinah blazing above it, leave the riverbed. As the priests scaled the slope rising from the sandy riverbed to the western half of the valley, the air filled with the sound of rushing wind, the sound of a storm passing through trees. The families of the eastern tribes looked around at the acacias and oaks behind them and on the ridge across the Jordan. They scrutinized the willows and oleanders of the river basin. Hardly a leaf fluttered anywhere, but the rushing grew to a deafening, rock-grinding roar. All at once, a foaming, frothing wall of muddy water churned down from the north, driving boulders and uprooted trees before it.

Within minutes, the gushing flood of the Jordan reclaimed its channel. With their own eyes, the wives and children of Reuben, Gad, and the half-tribe of Manasseh saw the miracle. A flood separated them from their warriors and from the rest of Israel, but they had the promise of Yahweh's protection. They turned away, departing for the cities and towns allotted to them. It was their permanent inheritance. They were home.

GILGAL

Rahab

Rahab stared into the darkness. *Had it been four days, five . . . six? How do you separate endless black into segments of day and night?* She tried to tell herself it didn't matter, but she couldn't stop analyzing all that had happened since Ahuzzath brought her before the king. Three days had passed for certain. King Nahari summoned her for interrogation two times after that first night. She assumed they were on successive days, although she experienced time here as endless stretches of dozing and wakefulness in an utterly black world.

"Has the dungeon aided your memory?" the king asked at the beginning of the third and final questioning. "Any details at all that might help us apprehend our adversaries?"

His tone was the type used to inquire if someone slept well, but as soon as she assured him that she recalled nothing more, his cool detachment altered. He leaped from his throne with a black leather scourge, its brass barbs clattering together as he circled her, lashing it in the air. His black eyes bulged, his face was beet-red with fury, and the cords of his neck pulled taut as he bellowed out question after question in a rapid barrage, punctuating each with a stinging snap of his whip.

She quit trying to answer. The king didn't want answers. He wanted the spies. Or he wanted someone to pay. When Nahari's wrath was spent, Rahab hobbled back to her cell prodded by the tip of Shinab's spear. Her back, arms, and thighs stung from the hundreds of wounds inflicted by the flagellation, but her integrity was intact. Just as her tattered clothing was glued to her skin with drying blood, she was permanently glued to the God of Israel by the blood of her torment. This imprisonment was unexpected, unjustified, but it had turned vague hope into unwavering faith that the God of Israel had a plan—and that he would triumph.

King Nahari never called her back after that, but he did not release her either. Only three times since that last interrogation had her cell door opened, allowing her a squinting peek at any light at all. Those three baths of welcome gray light were just that countable—and not recent. There was the time the jailer brought food, a bowl of watery gruel set just inside her door as one might feed a dog. And there was the filthy boy, reeking of human waste, who came twice to exchange her overflowing slop bucket with an empty one. They must have assumed that a prisoner out of food and water would no longer fill the bucket, for he never came back again. How long since the last glimpse of light? She had no idea. Perhaps days.

The ladle in the large pottery jar by the door no longer brought up water. She lifted the heavy pot one more time, tipping it toward her parched mouth, hoping for a last dribble. But there was none. *King Nahari never intends for me to leave this cell alive. And he does not intend to support a long imprisonment.* As soon as the thought crystalized, she knew it was true. Oddly, she was not afraid. She had played her part in the plan of Yahweh of Israel. He would see her through to the end whatever it might be.

All at once, the dungeon floor heaved and fractured beneath her, hurling her to the stone pavement. As the violent shaking continued, she crawled to the back wall of her cell for safety. Her scrambling hands and knees felt a deep fissure running through the center of her floor. The half of the cell toward the west was higher, uplifted by the breadth of two thumbs. In a city known for its tremors, this shudder was far deeper than any she had experienced before. She pressed against the cold stones of the back wall, half expecting the palace above her cell to cave in on her at any moment.

The scenario of her dark underworld breaking open to the sky—just as King Nahari tumbled into her cell along with the solid blocks of his throne room—jolted a melody from deep within her. It was a new song, indistinct at first, then as the rumbling and rolling subsided, its beauty welled up, a song of light filling every part of her. King Nahari could lock her in darkness. He could separate her from her family. He could separate her from her harp. But no one could remove the music from her soul. Baal himself could not keep the God of Israel out of her cell. Her fingers twitched and began moving as if plucking the strings of her harp as she sang:

> Yea, though I dwell in Baal's dungeon,
>   the dominion of darkness can't bind me.
> Sing, oh my soul, of your glorious God—
>   Even here his radiance finds me.
>
> Though mountains quake,
>   and cities shake,
> My feet find a solid foundation.
>   How can I fear
>   for Yahweh is here—
> My light, my strength, my salvation.

Rahab was still singing when the solid oak door of her cell rattled and the lock bar grated along its track. She squinted into a flood of wan light from the corridor. After so many days of darkness, even that light hurt her eyes, and at first she could not comprehend the images she saw.

"Don't just sit there, you blinking fool. Come greet your visitor."

As soon as she heard the nasal voice, Rahab pictured the pinched, white face that went with it. Nahari's rat-faced young guard. The spritely silhouette hesitating in the doorway just in front of him . . . *Could it be? But how? Why?*

"Rahab?"

Rahab leaped up with a shriek at the beloved timbre of an old woman's voice. "Grandmother! Oh Grandmother!"

"Get in there, you bothersome hag," Shinab snarled, flinging Shua to the floor like a discarded rag.

Rahab leaped to prevent the fall, but her momentum hurled her against the young guard. Shinab fumbled with his spear as if he were under attack, but Rahab was already pulling back in revulsion and anger. "You are despicable. How can you treat one of our honored aged ones so poorly?"

Shinab jabbed at her with the point of his spear as if containing a dangerous beast. "Don't think either of you will ever leave this cell." His tone was chillingly unruffled. Then in one swift movement, he heaved the door closed and slammed the lock bar in place. Darkness closed around Rahab once more. Darker yet were Shinab's next muffled words, barely audible over the echo of his retreating footsteps. "Israelite traitors, the whole lot of you. The North Wall Inn will not be in business long."

Rahab groped the darkness for Shua, finding her still crumpled on the floor. She clutched the old woman in a warm, protective embrace. "It is so comforting to feel your warmth in this cold place—but—oh Grandmother, you shouldn't be here! Why were you arrested?"

Shua clucked softly and stroked Rahab's hair. "Not arrested. I wore Shinab down."

"Wore him down?"

"I tried to reason with him. 'If you won't release her, at least let me visit,' I told him more times than I can count. He knows very well that other motives led Ahuzzath to drag you off to the king. I begged, I nagged, and I bartered—any fear I had of that weasel faded as my anger grew. Shinab has no evidence linking us to treason, yet day after day, he refused to let me see you. I followed him around from sunup to sundown. Sometimes I pleaded with him, sometimes I taunted him for his inexperience and poor judgment, and sometimes . . ." Shua giggled like a young girl. "Sometimes, I flirted with him in front of his men."

"Grandmother, you were flirting with death."

"Shinab is still young enough to be influenced by the opinions of his peers. The older guards are all quite fond of you. I get a little respect as Rahab's grandmother—more than their respect for Shinab. I think the whole garrison found the repartee amusing."

"But he is the captain's favorite. You might have entertained the common guards with your antics, but Ahuzzath—"

"Oh, my dear girl. You do not yet know. Shinab is the new captain of King Nahari's guard. Ahuzzath's head has been three days rotting on the wall beside the city gate, carrion for the birds."

Rahab choked on a sob of . . . *what was it? Relief? Freedom?*

"Not tears? Surely this is not unwelcome news," Shua exclaimed. "He will never touch you, never harass you again."

"No. For certain, I don't grieve that foul man." Rahab's voice still shook with emotion. "But his fate has repercussions for all of us—the spies, you, me, and our whole family."

"That hateful man has nothing to do with us."

"But don't you see. Now we know for certain." Tears were streaming down Rahab's cheeks now. "The king threatened Ahuzzath if he did not find the spies. I was there. I heard him. His death means they escaped back across the river. And if they escaped, they will return to save us."

"In that case, good riddance. Hello deliverance." Shua rustled with her cloak.

"Deliverance at least for the rest of the family. We may starve here in this dungeon.

"That is why I brought this round of flat bread. I guessed they have not been feeding you properly."

Rahab could smell the homey goodness of the fresh-baked barley bread as soon as Shua began untying the corner of her cloak. When Shua pushed it into her hands, Rahab just held it close to her face inhaling deeply. The reek of human waste in this cell had been unbearable when Shinab first brought her here, but her nose was dead to it now. She slowly breathed in the fragrance of the bread again. "More than the comforting aroma of home, this is the aroma of Paradise to me."

"I didn't go to all this trouble so you could stand around sniffing when it's food you need."

"We should ration it," Rahab said. "Come dinnertime, you will want some too. Why on earth did you not bring more?"

"That would make sense if we planned to settle in down here. I certainly don't plan to." Grandmother's voice did not brook argument. "Eat."

Rahab let her teeth sink into the edge of the round loaf, savoring the moist freshness in small nibbles like a mouse. She felt like a mouse—small, powerless—but surviving even when larger predators like Ahuzzath were eradicated. The hollow of her stomach twisted as she continued chewing the first bite, but she was reluctant to let the savory morsel slide down her throat.

She could hear her grandmother's feet shuffling through the pile of straw she used for a bed and then scuffling on the bare stone floor. She could hear her hands brushing lightly along the stone walls. Strange how sounds were amplified in the absence of light. She wondered vaguely what Shua was doing, but right now, her mouth had a more important task than talking.

"I suspect that Shinab intends for us to starve in retaliation for the spies' escape," Shua muttered as she scrabbled around the perimeter of the room. "I haven't let him forget you are down here. I've been pestering him to let me visit you from the day the guards returned from their manhunt. That squeaky little rodent. He should be locked up in a cell and forgotten." She was fumbling with the door now. "Moreover, your family has not forgotten you for a single day. We have been constantly asking the God of Israel to deliver you."

"How many days, Grandmother?" Rahab mumbled. Her mouth was stuffed with a bite too precious to swallow.

"Days? Since that old Ahuzzath snatched you away? Six, this evening. Finish that bread now. Don't be using up all your strength talking?"

"I think *you* are doing most of the talking, Grandmother. I only asked one question." Then, as images of her encounter with that hideous Baal creature flashed into her mind, Rahab gasped, "Oh! I almost forgot. Is the red cord still in the window?"

"Of course. Who would take it down?"

Rahab quickly related the story of her demonic visitation. "I don't know whether it was a dream or real . . ."

"I would believe either. Such a frightful, stinking hole for you to be in all alone."

"Actually, I have not felt alone. Not since I saw that apparition of Baal. A spirit of peace hovers over my cell unlike anything I have ever known." She sighed with a bit of exasperation. "And I'm definitely not alone now that you are foolishly trapped here with me. If I weren't so glad to see you, I would be quite angry."

"Well, we won't be here for long."

"No," Rahab responded sadly, "Not long. Our options aren't good, are they? Perish from lack of food, be crushed by the next earthquake, or slain by the hand of the conquering Israelites when they take the city because we are not in the rooms protected by the red cord."

"I was thinking of escape."

"There is no way. This dungeon is as solid as the city walls."

"Exactly. That was a fearsome earthquake just now. Ran cracks through the streets and up those formerly solid walls. I was out in the street not far from here berating Shinab as usual when it happened."

Rahab could not believe what she was hearing. "No wonder he arrested you."

Shua's fingers whispered in the darkness as she rummaged around the iron-banded door. "Let's see . . ." She rattled the lock. "You are getting ahead of the story. I told you he never did arrest me. The ground began to shake, swaying back and forth, rolling up and down. The pavement beneath our feet shuddered and heaved. Fractures broke open in the street and shot up the walls. We could hear the entire city grinding, shifting, and cracking. Shinab was totally unnerved by it all and began shrieking like a crazy man."

Shua found a good handhold on the door, gripped it firmly, and rattled it vigorously as she imitated Shinab's high, reedy voice—"I cannot think with a fly buzzing around my head all day." When I reminded him of how he could get rid of me, he seized my arm and wasted no time marching me down here."

"And you actually thought you could help me escape?"

"Huhh!" Shua grunted. "I brought our old log-splitting wedge with me. Tied it in my cloak, padded by the bread so it wouldn't clunk suspiciously. Huhh!" she grunted again as she jiggled the door vigorously a second time. "A better inspiration struck as Shinab brought me down here. Each door was a struggle to open and the guards at each one begged to leave their posts before the palace collapsed on top of them. That jolting obviously unhinged the young captain as much as it unhinged every gateway in the king's palace. He cursed every portal we passed through." She cackled like a mother hen. "I trust it has torqued this one enough for my purposes." As she rocked the door back and forth, back and forth, the lock bar on the outside clattered in its track. She shook it all the harder, until it fell open and the comfort of light invaded the cell again.

Rahab jumped, startled, blinking into the light, half expecting to see Shinab standing there, but Shua just laughed. "You better be believing, Rahab. That earthquake was Yahweh's answer to our prayers. You vowed by the name of Israel's God to stay in the inn marked by the red cord, and that is where he wants you to be." She darted into the corridor. "The guards are long gone. Let's go home."

Acsah

Each division remained in place on the western bank—watching until the remaining tribes had crossed. They gazed at the priests solemnly bearing the Ark up out of the riverbed. They gaped in awe as the flood of the Jordan reclaimed its home. Then they broke out in a riotous cheer. Although they were on alien soil, fear had no place in a day filled with such wonders. Still linked in a happy chain with Ada and her little Midianites, Acsah joined the happy procession following the Ark, everyone singing and dancing as they made their way along a broad, sandy road within sight of Jericho. As the parade advanced into the shade of a palm grove, even the animals frolicked and frisked exuberantly, capering past luxuriant springs and pools.

But when the Ark passed through a portal at the end of the thick tunnel of trees, the entire entourage slowed nearly to stopping as each little group paused to view their first campsite, their first home in the Land of Promise. When it was her turn, Acsah brought her string of young dancers to a halt and peered out of the shadows at a broad expanse of lush green grasses, even more lovely than the Valley of Acacias across the river.

"Look children, our new home."

Hodesh laughed and twirled her younger sister. "Life with Father Caleb just gets better and better."

"See over there," Ada pointed out informatively. "The Levites are already beginning to set up the posts that hold up the walls of the sanctuary courtyard. As soon as it is complete, each tribe will know exactly where to line up their rows of tents."

"And even without that perimeter, do we know which side of the meadow we will be on?"

"The eastern side," the three youngsters cried in glee. "Let's go."

Following the girls into the meadow, Acsah noticed the warriors of Reuben and Gad setting up a long line of bivouac tents close to the palm grove on the southern border of the meadow. A shiver ran down her back. A permutation of the normal arrangement. They were setting up these small tents on the side of camp normally assigned to their division, but the large family tents were missing. As vanguard of a war camp in enemy territory, their tents created a solid defense line stretching from the river to the hills, a protective wall between Israel and Jericho. The warriors of the half-tribe of Manasseh, also part of the vanguard, were in the process of stretching out a second line on the west, forming a buffer at the base of the ridge perpendicular to Reuben and Gad.

Salmon paused and turned back. "What do you think, Ada?" he called. A full grin replaced his jaunty half smile as he waited for Acsah and the girls to catch up. "Can you believe it? We are standing on the land promised to Abraham, Isaac, and Jacob." His tone was the big brother one he used when talking to Ada, but his eyes never left Acsah's. This was what they had dreamed of since they were toddlers.

Just in case Hoglah and Hodesh had not been told, Ada turned to them with great seriousness and explained, "This is the inheritance God assigned to the descendants of Shem when he gave the nations their boundaries following the Flood."

Salmon's face was glowing as he pointed out the new formation laid out by the vanguard. "The traditional places of Reuben, Gad, and Manasseh just happen to position them perfectly to protect the rest of us."

Acsah strained to return his smile. "Isn't that just the way of our God?"

"Preplanned to prevent a sneak attack from enemies in Jericho," he confirmed. His mother shuddered visibly at the words *attack* and *enemies*, but Salmon pulled her into a comforting hug. "Trust God, Mother. Think how he brought us here."

Ada wiggled free of Acsah's hand. "Let's go. Where do we set up?"

Salmon gave Acsah a nod of farewell. "This way. Follow me, Ada. Come, Mother."

"Can we go with Ada if we promise to watch for our wagon? There is nothing to do until it gets here." Hodesh and Hogluh plied their request with sweetly-pleading faces, but skipped away before Acsah could even nod her assent.

She watched them running to catch up with Salmon. *A family well on the way toward healing.* The picture was perfect: A glorious blossom-studded grassland. Her friend Salmon, now the Prince of Judah, leading the tribe into the Promised Land. Abijah, representing the remnant of the generation that left Egypt as children, now finding their place of rest in Canaan after forty years of rigorous training. Beside them, an ox cart of more belongings than they ever needed in their simple wilderness life—and completing the scene, a new set of children, running and leaping in joyful abandon, gathering fistfuls of flowers.

This was the Canaan Acsah had dreamed of since childhood. And hadn't they made a grand entrance? Just ahead of her, a riotous patch of flowers in tabernacle colors of red, purple, blue—even accented with gold and white—nodded their heads encouraging her to pluck them. Free of any of the obligations of adulthood, Acsah gave in to their allure. Once Abihail and Eliab came with the wagon and the campsite was in order, the children could help fashion garlands. It would be a small way to thank the God who deigned to dwell among them.

Soon she had more than enough flowers to festoon their tent site in holy colors. Cradling her overflowing armful of color and a heart full of joy, she started to stand upright, but when she saw two figures break away from the hive of activity in the Levite sector, she sank back to her knees in dismay. It was Phinehas and Jonathan—and they were heading straight for her. There was no place to hide here in the open meadow.

Embarrassment and anger crept up from her stomach at the memory of that night when the returned warriors shared their stories of the Midianite war. Jonathan thought to impress her with his valor and charm, and she naively laughed at his animated rendition of the battle, never guessing his intentions until he thrust them in her face the next morning. Images of the necklace and marriage proposal began looping wildly through her mind. In a determined effort to compose herself, she began gathering more stems of deep blue lupine. She was not going to let Jonathan spoil this day of miracles for her. Maintaining intense concentration, she chose a perfect red anemone to balance the added blue. She refused to look up until two shadows stretched long on either side of her like the jaws of a trap.

"Acsah."

The voice of her priest-friend greeted her first.

"Oh, Phinehas—what a surprise." She flashed what she hoped was an appropriate smile of acknowledgment. "Shalom."

"The Lord's blessings on you and your family." Phinehas pronounced his words with dignity.

The boy she had known in the wilderness had changed markedly since the day Cozbi and Zimri strutted boldly into the grieving camp. His priestly bearing was a reminder of that awful day—but in him the terror had been transformed into nobility. "Phinehas, priest of Israel," she responded, standing and greeting him properly with a graceful bow. "May Yahweh's blessings be on you and your family as well."

"Acsah . . ." was all that Jonathan managed to say. She looked at him now and her discomfort evaporated at the sight of his hesitant, anxious eyes. He lifted his eyebrows nervously.

She flashed a reassuring, compassionate smile. "And shalom to you my friend."

Jonathan was uncharacteristically at a loss for words. "Acsah," he repeated.

She laughed. "It is obvious you still remember my name."

She turned back to Phinehas. "Is this not the best day of our lives? How wonderful to stumble upon two good friends of my childhood on such a day."

He laughed congenially. "We didn't just happen to stumble upon you. Jonathan has been edgy as a cat, watching for you. He pressed me to leave our work and come with him to greet you." He nudged his cousin with his elbow. "Now it seems he has nothing to say."

Acsah left the comment hanging in the air and merely smiled.

"It is good to see you." Jonathan stammered nervously. "I did not want to miss seeing you today of all days." Suddenly the ice dam of frozen speech broke. "I can't believe we just crossed the Jordan. Of course, you know that. I mean, the flood. So, what do you think? We watched the waters drying up . . . just like the Red Sea. Of course, we weren't born yet when the Red Sea parted. We didn't *see* it, but we've all heard the story. Do I really need to explain that? Why are you out here in the meadow alone? Of course, this is where Judah will set up camp . . . but where is Caleb?" He slapped his hand to his forehead. "I am making no sense."

Phinehas rolled his eyes. "No, Jonathan. You are not making sense. You are babbling."

Jonathan took a deep breath and pulled himself up to a more poised stance. "It *is* good to see you, Acsah. Our paths have not crossed for days."

"Weeks actually."

"I have been here all along," he said, "hoping to see you, of course." A handsome smile flashed from the short curly beard, revealing a perfect row of white teeth. His confidence had returned. He took a step closer.

She deliberately stepped back. "I have been in Judah. You in Levi."

As if connected to Acsah by invisible cords, Jonathan moved forward as she retreated. His eyes searched hers, traveling over her lips, her chin, her cheeks, and back to her eyes as if memorizing every detail of her face.

Acsah stiffened at the familiarity of his gaze and turned to Phinehas. "What a day! It is difficult to absorb what God has just done."

"Absolutely true. Joshua told us we would see wonders and so we have."

"Who would have guessed we would witness a miracle on a par with the splitting of the Red Sea?" She risked a mischievous glance at Jonathan. "Actually, my friend, I understand why today has rendered you both speechless and babbling."

Jonathan's eyes twinkled, but he replied with a priestly dignity rivaling his cousin's. "But we can only expect more wonders in the weeks and months ahead. I have been reminding my cousin of the many promises written in my grandfather's scrolls. God will be with us in a mighty way as we stake out our rightful place here in Canaan."

Acsah raised one eyebrow. "Is this my erstwhile fun-loving friend?"

Phinehas laughed. "He is becoming quite the scholar, Acsah. You would be quite surprised at how diligently he attends to his Levitical studies every day. He has been instructing anyone and everyone who will listen."

"Really?" Acsah's eyes twinkled with new appreciation. "Now I know who to turn to should a question arise concerning the law."

Jonathan beamed.

With a formal bow, Phinehas said, "It is good to see you, Acsah, but we are needed in camp Levi."

Jonathan's smile faded. "So soon? Ithamar is still directing the setting up of the courtyard."

Acsah looked straight into his eyes and answered with a seriously business-like voice. "At the moment, I have no questions about the law. Only a need to be alone to think. That is why I was out here ahead of my family, gathering flowers to make our new tent site festive." She lifted her armload of flowers to emphasize her point, and then stooped down to pluck more before Jonathan had time to respond.

Othniel

Othniel meandered across the dry riverbed at his uncle's side while the old man labored under the heavy weight of Judah's memorial stone. The miracle energized him in a way that would be hard to put into words. It was as if the power that dried up the flood infused him with greater dedication as a warrior for the Lord. He pictured it flowing into his body, strengthening him to the point where he could toss that very stone clear across the river if need be. *Doubly strong.* He snorted at the improbable thought. *Right now doubly useless.*

Twice he came as close as he dared to insisting his uncle let him carry the rock, at least for a short distance, but Caleb ignored his words. It was not until they climbed up out of the riverbed and

Caleb stumbled and nearly fell at a sandy depression in the road that Othniel adroitly captured the weight. After that, they passed it back and forth several times as they trudged through the delightful forest of palms and oleanders surrounding Jericho.

Caleb paused at last where the shaded canopy opened to sunlight. The road skirted around open grassland all bustling with activity. "We couldn't have hoped for a more perfect site for our first camp in Canaan."

"Mmm," Othniel grunted. It was impossible to carry on a conversation while straining under such a load.

"Put down the stone," Caleb commanded. "I never tire of watching this."

Othniel obediently lowered the stone to the ground and stood kneading a knot from his shoulder.

In the center of the wide expanse, the gilded wooden frame of the tabernacle gleamed gold within the silver posts of the courtyard. A troupe of Levites made quick work of hanging the linen panels to complete the courtyard walls. Still others were unpacking the various rolls and bundles of the sanctuary walls. Leaving the mandated space all around the perimeter, Levite families found their places in relation to the courtyard wall and began the process of transforming the new sites into homes.

Othniel knew he dared not look away from the tabernacle site for a moment if he wanted to see anything. He had witnessed the raising of the tabernacle many times, and yet these quick flashes of gold-plated frame and the intense colors of the inner curtains were precious—the only fleeting glimpses that common eyes ever had of the beautiful interior of the Lord's dwelling place.

He held his breath as one group of Levites hung the gold-plated boards that formed the walls while another group revealed a brief flashing vision of an angel guard embroidered in gold on royal colors. It was the curtain that divided the holy from the most holy place. No sooner had another group of Levites overspread the structure with the brilliant blue, scarlet, and purple sheeting that made up the ceiling of the holy sanctuary, than another group unrolled the great tarps of its triple coverings, almost instantly smothering the dazzling beauty beneath a tarp of dark goat's hair, which was then covered with a second of ram's wool, dyed red and the final waterproof layer of Egyptian sea cow hides. In minutes, the holy beauty vanished.

As the Gershonites spread the coverings, the Kohathites arrived with the furnishings. Immediately, the places for the bronze laver and altar were paced off in the courtyard and marked. Once the altar of sacrifice was set, another group of Levites began stabilizing its hollow base with *adam*, earth, a reminder of the first man and the first sin that made all this blood and death necessary. By the time the laver was in place and filled with water, the priests had finished carrying each shrouded piece of the golden furnishings into the holy place. Only there, hidden within the holy sanctuary, would they be uncovered. By the time all was perfectly arranged, the priests arrived with the Ark of the Covenant.

As they carried it into the inner sanctum, the holy of holies, Caleb stretched his hands toward heaven, face raised, eyes closed, and held the position for a moment. "Come, to your people, Yahweh God of Israel. All is in readiness."

Othniel silently repeated the prayer in his heart.

"We must never let the fact that he actually does dwell with Israel become a common thing, Othniel. It is an awesome privilege. No other nation has been so blessed."

When Othniel stooped to retrieve the stone, Caleb stopped him. "We might as well leave it here until Joshua tells us where and how the monument is to be set up."

By the time Caleb and Othniel arrived at their campsites, the families had already unloaded the wagons. Othniel joined his mother and brother in finishing the unpacking and organizing, racing the shadows that rapidly pulled this glorious day to a close. The tent cities of Judah, Issachar, and Zebulon filled the eastern quadrant of camp as quickly as mushrooms after a rain. The blood-red banner of Judah was set in place, the lion frolicking playfully in the breeze high above the standards of Issachar and Zebulon. Othniel found himself glancing at it frequently. The occasional flapping of a strong gust gave the appearance of a beast in smooth feline motion, bounding forth in conquest.

All Israel was blessed, of course, but he was quite proud to be among the three tribes of the eastern quadrant. The fathers of these tribes were men of integrity, the three sons of Leah who had never brought dishonor on their family as the older brothers had. Judah—the name meant *praise*—proved worthy to be ruler above all Israel's sons. *I want to be like Judah,* he told himself, *a praise to the God of Israel.*

Caleb

Caleb had just finished setting up the family tent when Joshua appeared. He saluted his old friend with the respect due a high commander. "Today your leadership in Israel is secured."

"Praise God," Joshua responded immediately. Then, dropping his voice confidentially, he leaned close. "I did not see how the tribes would ever come to respect me after forty years of following Moses. Leave it to our God to cut a path through the waters again."

Caleb's eyes glittered. "We are finally here. The camp of Israel in the Promised Land at last—and with a finer entrance than any of us could have imagined."

Joshua looked up and down the tent rows. "The eastern quarter looks the same as always—as does the north. The Joseph tribes on the western quadrant are a little slimmer with half the families of Manasseh remaining in Gilead. You will be impressed when you see the formidable defense line the warriors of Eastern Manasseh have thrown against the base of the ridge. But just wait until you see the south. The large family tents of only one tribe remain under the banner of Reuben, only the families of Simeon. A stout triple wall of Reuben and Gad's military shelters barricade our closest side from Jericho. Quite impressive. They have already posted guards at every corner of camp. These men are serious about protecting the camp—also serious about taking possession of the inheritance here and getting back home."

"Tomorrow I shall go see them for myself. It is rather reassuring to know they stand guard."

"But we must not forget the spies' report. I believe the fear of the Lord will hold back any attack for a while. The Lord assured me we will have time to settle in and celebrate Passover before any more of the gory business of war."

"Passover, eh? Doesn't that mean circumcising the lot of these young men first?

Joshua turned and disappeared in the direction of the tabernacle as the question was being asked.

Rahab

A loud shout barked the announcement that curfew was being enforced immediately. Rahab crouched back into the shadows of the exterior portal of the dungeon beside her grandmother. *Odd, this reaction to an earthquake. Even a strong one.* The sun marked early afternoon. Usually a sleepy time of day, but here on the street in front of her chaos reigned. People scurried in every direction. Soldiers charged here and there, herding the crowds with threats, prodding the people with the butts of their long spears.

Shua pulled her shawl over her head and close around her face and indicated the open street with a jerking nod of her head. "The command is: Return to your homes. Well, that is the only way home."

Rahab disguised herself with her shawl as well and together they plunged into the tumult. Carefully avoiding encounters with soldiers, they worked their way toward the north wall, staying in the thick of the roiling masses. As they got closer to home, however, there were fewer and fewer people remaining on the street and Rahab began feeling exposed and vulnerable.

Vacant and shuttered windows watched with dead eyes from every side of her street. Each portal or gap between buildings loomed as a potential hiding place for Shinab's guards. By the time the inn was in view, only old Zuph ran ahead of them. And then even that old woman darted into her doorway. She peeked back from a narrow opening before she slammed the door, her face a mask of bewilderment and fright as if Shua and Rahab were suddenly enemies rather than long-time neighbors. How many times had she accompanied Shua to the market or the well? But today, not a wave of the hand or even a hint of recognition before she vanished. The inn signified safety, but it no longer signified home. Rahab and her family were aliens in Jericho.

"Run for it, Rahab." Shua flicked her eyes toward the top of the wall. "No crowd to hide in now."

Rahab did not need to look up to know that a cadre of guards patrolled the parapet above them. *Would Nahari's curfew enforcement allow people time to return to their homes or would those guards shoot a few stragglers as a warning that the king was serious.* Expecting a rain of arrows at any moment, she burst into a sprint as Shua made a dash for the inn door. The throbbing pulse of her own blood in her ears drowned every other sound as she flew up the steps and burst into the inn, still a pace behind her surprisingly spry Grandmother.

Jokshan stood waiting inside the entrance. Waiting, but obviously not expecting *them.* "Where—?" he stammered in astonishment. "How—?"

"Father, what is happening?"

"Jokshan, why has Nahari called for a curfew?" Shua's words mingled with Rahab's.

The innkeeper stared at them blankly for a moment. "They are here," he finally replied.

"Who? The guards?" Rahab's heart dropped. "Shinab? Here, at the inn?"

"Not guards . . . not Shinab. I need to sit down."

"*Who* is here, Jokshan?" Grandmother demanded.

"No one . . . *here*, at the inn . . ."

"No one? Father, you are not making sense. No customers?"

"You know there are no travelers."

"Well then, *who* is here, Father?" Rahab felt the pitch of her voice approaching hysteria. She tried to slow down, to ask her questions slowly and deliberately. "Not Ahuzzath. Who then? Our regulars?"

"No, no, no, my dear. Definitely not that old captain rotting on the wall. And none of the regulars either. Word has gotten around that we have no wine and no sweet singer." He patted Rahab's hand absently. "Not a single patron has crossed the threshold for two days. But *they* are here. In Canaan. North a bit, settling on the plain close to the river."

As he spoke, Keziah peeked cautiously from the kitchen. When she saw Rahab, she shrieked. She ran and threw her arms about her daughter. "Oh, my heart! Rahab. My dearest Rahab. From fear for my life . . . to this joy." She sucked in deep breaths between convulsive sobs. Suddenly, she looked at Shua and Jokshan with a puzzled frown. "Where were you? All of you, that you are safe? I was certain that you all perished in falling rubble. The inn . . . everything . . . rumbled and shook so."

Jokshan embraced his wife, his daughter, and his mother-in-law, patting first one, then the other.

After a moment, Keziah became visibly calmer. "I have been hiding down in the wine cellar, certain the whole city was destroyed. Oh Mother, I knew you went out following Shinab again. A dark voice in my head kept telling me you were buried in the rubble of the streets, and that you, my darling daughter, had been crushed beneath the king's palace. Oh, Jokshan, I knew *you* were up on the roof. What hope for you with such a violent earthquake? I did not want to face life on my own," she began sobbing again, "but I was too afraid to kill myself."

"Hush, hush, my dear. I would have come to you, but I had no idea where you had gone."

Just then, Rahab's brothers and their families burst through the inn door. With tears and hugs, each one reassured the others that the entire family had survived the shaking. Anxieties dissolved into gratitude as each member shared a unique version of the earthquake saga. When the hubbub subsided, Jokshan patted the air with his hands. "Be calm and sit now, my dear family. I was about to relate the astonishing thing I witnessed from the roof."

The family pulled a circle of thick dining hall cushions close together, slumping into family comfort, finding a need for the reality of touch. With each one clasping hands or leaning on the knee, arm, or shoulder of another, they drew strength from the connection of an unbroken circle as Jokshan began his tale. His voice was quieter and more humble than anyone could remember.

"I was on the roof, bundling the cured flax. Suddenly, the first jolt of the earthquake threw me to my knees. When the stones under my feet ceased swaying and rolling, I scrambled to my feet again and found myself facing the river. A strange smudge darkened the pale stony embankment for miles along the eastern margin of the river basin. I was still trying to work out what it was when I beheld another curious sight. The silver reflection of the Jordan began slipping toward the Sea of Salt like a serpent crawling to its lair. I could still make out the sheen of the water far upriver, but somewhere—must have been up in the vicinity of Zerethan—the river stopped. The rest slithered away from that point like a silver snake, leaving behind only a dry trail. Then, here at the fords, a bright light appeared above the river basin. Too bright to stare at. It reminded me of the times that you boys would come up to the top of the wall to catch the sun in a polished bronze mirror and flash that blinding light at me while I was on the road approaching Jericho. Averting my eyes from the light, I watched the dark mass on the eastern bank flow westward across the Jordan. Only then did it dawn on me that the camp of Israel had vanished from the eastern plains and *they* were that smudge moving across the Jordan."

He sat bolt upright and made a solemn pronouncement as one would swear in a court of law. "I am a witness. In the middle of flood season, Israel crossed on dry land, just like the stories of the Red Sea. They have come to claim their land. *They* are here in Canaan now."

There was a heavy thud beside Rahab. Amid a flurry of gasps and cries, the family discovered Shua, slumped on the floor in a dead faint. The startled family dove toward her to help, but Shua sat up on her own, rubbing a knot on her head, waving everyone back. "Stop your goggling," she snapped. "I am perfectly fine. Just shocked off my cushion. That's all."

Jokshan's serious demeanor splintered. "You were asking why King Nahari imposed the curfew?" He held his sides to control the shaking of deep, liberating laughter.

Othniel

As the sun slid down the sky and touched the western hills, dual trumpets wailed. In minutes, the bustle of camp ceased and the tribes obeyed the long, low call summoning them to the first solemn assembly in Canaan. The representatives of the twelve tribes had already been instructed to bring their monument stones to a rounded grassy knoll east of camp toward the river and prepare a site for each stone. Now all the people gathered, arranging themselves around the designated hill—a mammoth wheel of humanity surrounding a hub of twelve stone-bearers.

"Today, we witnessed the defeat of Baal." Joshua's voice rang confidently over the surrounding countryside. "The spring rains, attributed to that storm god, filled the Jordan to overflowing so no one could pass through. But, when faced with the Ark of the Covenant of Yahweh, the river stopped its flow. To commemorate this momentous day, we brought these twelve stones from that empty riverbed. Here we build a *gilgal* of remembrance. Return to this monument when you face difficult times. Touch these stones, and continue to believe that our God will prevail over any difficulty you encounter."

The old commander gave an imperceptible nod to the twelve, and one by one, the stones thudded into place in a circle around the man who led Israel into Canaan. It was an awesome, holy moment, but as Caleb set Judah's stone in its place, a chuckle Othniel could not control escaped. Sarah flashed a warning glare at him as if he were still eight years old.

"Respect!" she whispered sharply.

"Not lack of respect. Believe me, Mother." *No, I do not disrespect this holy place. I will tell the story of the miracle crossing for the rest of my life. I will bring my children here and retell the story as their small hands touch these stones. I will teach them what God did—but they will also learn the whole story of Judah's stone.* Othniel said no more, certain that anyone who knew the story would be equally amused.

His younger brother, Seraiah, wrinkled his brow quizzically. "What is so funny?"

Under her breath, Sarah muttered words he could not understand.

Othniel knew he had to explain. "Remember the day of celebration across the river . . ."

"Hush. Joshua is going to speak again."

Othniel shrugged. *Maybe it didn't really matter to anyone else. Who besides the friends that were part of the contest would really care to hear the story of Judah's stone?*

This spot will ever be known as Gilgal, the circle, because the gilgal of Israel is complete today. God has brought the children of Abraham back to this land just as He promised. This was the inheritance promised to our fathers centuries ago, but in his patience and mercy, Yahweh held us back to give the people of Canaan the opportunity to demonstrate the motives that rule them. Now the land overflows with every evil. The inhabitants are in full rebellion against the goodness of God. The pain and suffering must end. The time of Canaan's dominion is over. The mouth of the Lord has spoken.

In the future, when your descendants ask you, "What does this Gilgal mean?" tell them the story:

Yahweh our God brought our fathers to the border of the Promised Land, but they refused to go in, they refused to believe he could give them the inheritance he promised. Forty years later, the Wanderings over at last, Yahweh, in his mercy, led the children full circle. He dried up the floods of the Jordan for us, just as he dried up the Red Sea for our fathers. These rocks testify to all the nations on earth that the hand of Yahweh is powerful. The Gilgal is an assurance to our children and our children's children that he is able to do what he has promised. We look at this land with the eyes of man and see only cities and the nations that rule them: the Canaanites, the Hittites, Hivites, Perizzites, Girgashites, Amorites, and Jebusites, but the fight is not between these kingdoms and us. The fight is between our God and the invisible powers of evil that have held this land captive far too long.

The Land of Promise is a land of mountains and valleys that drinks rain from heaven. It is not like the land of Egypt from which your fathers came, where we planted our seed and irrigated it by foot pump with water from the river. Here you must have the blessing of rain. Do not be deceived by the Baals of this place. Their worship will not lead to fertility, but to death. Yahweh your God cares for this land. His eyes are continually on it from the beginning of the year to its end. Worship him alone, and celebrate his appointed feasts. Do not seek prosperity through the evil practices of these people.

The sinking sun suddenly ignited a bank of fiery clouds ringing the sky above camp, a celestial gilgal. The reflected light struck Joshua's face and silver hair with the colors of fire as he finished speaking, a perfect flaming image to end a long, amazing day. The people cheered. This monument, built on a tiny toehold of their inheritance, announced the end of the Wanderings. More solid to them than the stories and songs that memorialized the crossing of the Red Sea, these river stones would stand throughout the generations as concrete evidence that God was with them.

BLOOD SACRIFICES

Swift riders rode out of Jericho. They pressed hard into the night, galloping toward Ai and Bethel, toward the cities crowning the central ridges of Canaan, riding hard to the north, to the south, and on to the cities along the shore of the Great Sea. The message was dismal:

> *Israel has defeated the raging Jordan. They swarmed across the river like locusts from the desert and rest now on our own shore. We must implore the aid of our gods. We must unite to defeat them before they consume our prosperous nations as they did the kingdoms of Sihon and Og.*

Kings and commoners alike trembled as they imagined what the devourers would do next. How could such an army be stopped?

Caleb

Caleb watched the glow of first light creep across the tent ceiling above him. His head ached from lack of sleep, but there would be no more today. It was the dawn of the first day in Canaan. Abib, the month of beginnings. The first month according to the reckoning that began at the Exodus. In this particular month of Abib, Israel was beginning a second time—and oh, what a beginning! The passage from Egyptian slavery took place by way of the Red Sea, forty-one years ago. The passage from the Wanderings by way of the Jordan River—yesterday.

A wavering, wailing bleat knifed through Caleb's skull again. High pitched, insistent, and . . . loud. Just on the other side of the tent wall. He pressed his fingers against his temples to ease the throbbing pain as he staggered to his feet. This noisy creature did not know it had been chosen for the Passover meal, only that it was separated from the flock—and the little fellow was not happy.

Last evening, as soon as he had seen to the pitching of the family tent, Caleb searched his growing flock for the perfect little yearling and brought it back to the tent as prescribed by the law. They had three days to observe it, ensuring it had no defect. This young ram was not about to endure the isolation quietly. Obviously, his lungs were not defective.

Sometime during the night, Acsah had gone out to sleep beside the wretched little beast. Even after that, sleep was sketchy at best. Once their ram settled into sleep snuggled against his daughter, Caleb could hear the more distant bleating of thousands upon thousands of paschal lambs staked out beside tents across the camp, a shrilly-incessant, sleep-disturbing racket. Now this one had begun again.

Caleb threw on his cloak against the morning chill and made his way to the stake behind the tent where the lamb was tethered. He had not heard his daughter leave, but the manna basket was gone and the lamb obviously missed her. "Poor little one, are you so lonely here with us?" Caleb crooned. He crouched beside the wooly beast, scratching the bony head all around the stubby horns. When he offered a handful of barley kernels, the yearling pushed itself up to knobby, calloused knees and nibbled hungrily, regarding him with dark, trusting eyes as it chewed. Caleb felt a stab of guilt.

"If our hearts were not so prone to evil, I don't believe we would be required to spill your innocent blood."

Passover, he mused. *The original Passover was a meal of terror consumed more than forty years ago. The memory of that night, the doorway of their home slathered in blood, the long time of waiting for the angel of death to pass over, still sent chills down his spine. A year later, Israel commemorated their new status as a free people with Passover as a national festival. The excitement of that first celebration, as they looked forward to new homes in the Promised Land, was short lived. Within a few weeks, Israel rebelled. The training days of the Wanderings commenced, and all Yahweh's required feasts were suspended. But here at Gilgal, cycles were beginning anew.*

The ram bumped his horns against Caleb's empty hand. "More? It is only right to share this grain with you." As he scooped more parched grain from the basket, the ram responded with encouraging nudges against his back. "Passover does not just look back to the deliverance from slavery. It also looks forward to God's provision in the future. Yahweh is Lord of the barley harvest."

Caleb kept up an amiable stream of chatter as he held out a second generous handful. "This grain is from the other side of the river. No harvests here until two days after Passover. Did you know about that? Eleazar will launch the harvest season each year by cutting the first handful of barley and waving it in thanks before the Lord.

"Where will we cut our Canaan barley this time? I don't rightly know since we have neither tilled nor sown any crops in this land ourselves. All I know is Yahweh commanded. He will provide."

When the lamb finished the grain, he sank to the ground, laid his wooly head on Caleb's knee, and closed his eyes. "So . . . now that you have kept me awake all night and roused me from my bed at dawn, you trustingly fall asleep on my lap?"

Caleb dug his fingers into the thick wool coat. This truly was a fine animal. Solid, well-muscled, perfectly adequate for the family feast. More importantly, the best of his flock for the Lord. "Just as the Lord provided a ram for Father Abraham to sacrifice in place of his son, the Lord provided you to help us remember the blood of all the rams that saved the firstborn Children of Israel when the death angel passed over Egypt."

"Sounds like a teaching moment, Abba." Acsah set the basket of fresh-gleaned manna on the ground nearby. "Either you feel this poor lamb needs to understand his significance, or you have taken to instructing yourself aloud when no one is around." Her laugh dwindled to a long sigh and settled into an expression of pain as she pulled out the cook pot and utensils for morning manna.

Caleb understood. He contemplated the little face sleeping so sweetly on his knee. It was one thing to slaughter a lamb and eat it. It was another to live with it first. "I'll get some wood and start the fire," he said, slipping his knee carefully out from under the slumbering lamb.

"Are we really required to do this to ensure he has no defects?" Acsah muttered aloud. "Or is it to ensure that our hearts are broken when he becomes our Passover feast?" She did not look up from her work and her tone indicated that she did not expect a reply.

Caleb did not supply one.

"All right then." She glanced at the sleeping mound of wool with a look of quiet determination. "We will fill the last days of your little life with more pleasure than you would have had in a whole lifetime as a ram in the field."

Caleb caught her eyes briefly and lifted his brows in support. This was hard enough for him, but she had grown up on manna, not meat. Death had never been necessary to ensure a supply of food. Yet, his heart told him she would ignore the conflict of her compassion. She would obey the commands of God. Obedience came easily for her, if not always happily.

As he gathered an armload of wood, he thought about each of his sons and their families. He wished he could be as certain they would keep the covenant law. Moses prophesied that Israel would forget the God who delivered them. A shudder ran through him at the thought of his own children neglecting this celebration after he was gone. Strong and vigorous as he was, he was overwhelmed with the urgency of a man on his deathbed.

How many more times would he celebrate with them? Perhaps this Passover would be his last. He must make them understand. The renewal of the annual feasts was another gilgal. This cycle of harvest celebrations must become as solidly part of the identity of Israel as the circle of stones crowning the rise down near the Jordan.

On the night of this feast, he vowed to himself, as he dropped the wood beside the fire pit, *I will ask every member of my family to swear that he or she will not let a year pass without celebrating Passover.* Surely the smells and tastes of the roasted lamb and the bitter herbs would fix the story of rescue from slavery in their minds. Surely Passover would keep his children faithful to the Lord.

King Nahari

King Nahari paced the floor in front of his throne, too agitated to sit. As soon as the simpering faces of his priests peeked through the doorway, even before their presence could be announced, the king raged at them. "Where is Asherah? Where is Baal in all this?"

He took a single stride toward his cowering minions and then stopped, throwing his fists on his hips, arms akimbo and cape flaring. He had been told this pose was as intimidating to a man as facing a cornered bear. This rat pack needed intimidation.

"You rob my treasury year after year," he snarled. "You say it will induce Baal to flood the Jordan, to send his raging waters that Jericho might celebrate the grain harvest without fear. You rob my citizens and assure us we have secured the favor of our warrior goddess. I repeat. Where is Asherah's protection today? Where is Baal's favor now?"

The priests sputtered, "Do not lose heart. This battle is of the gods. Who is like Asherah, first in war, in love, and bounty? It is she who miraculously raised these walls around our city and she is our protector. Who is like Baal? He will arise on wings of thunder to drive the invaders from our land."

The toothless high priest stepped forward confidently. "There are no stronger fortifications in all the earth. It is impossible for any army to breach our walls. Surely Baal held back his flood to lure Israel into crossing. It is his intention to trap them here between the hills and the raging torrent. Offer the required sacrifices, then send your army out under the banner of Asherah. We will exterminate them forever."

The subordinate priests nodded in agreement. "But first the sacrifices."

"Our victory will be costly, but it is certain."

The king eyed his priests suspiciously. "And at what price to me?"

"Blood sacrifices to Asherah and Baal."

King Nahari scowled at the fawning cluster of clerics. "We have sacrificed hundreds of bulls over the past months and yet the Israelites claim victory after victory. They defeated Sihon and we sacrificed a hundred bulls. They defeated Og and we sacrificed another hundred bulls. They defeated the Midianites and we sacrificed more. Now they have defeated the floods of the Jordan. How many bulls does Baal require before he defends his territory from this strange God? How many bulls are needed to induce Asherah to help us? She did not come to the aid of either King Sihon or King Og. Did they not worship her as devoutly as we do?"

"For this," the priests nodded in agreement, "not bulls. We must give the goddess of love and war, the fruit of love. Our children."

The high priest lifted both hands above his head and intoned solemnly. "Return strength to the one who bestows it. Offer all the firstborn children who are two years and younger to her glorious radiance. Asherah will summon the help of her lover Baal, the Storm God, ruler over Canaan. This sign of our high devotion will awaken our gods, and they *will* smite our enemies."

Nahari slumped down on his throne. He pictured the toddlers and infants in the women's quarters with his wives and concubines. They were the products of his strength and he was proud to have so many. Two years and younger. That would wipe out a third of his offspring. He suspected the priests were only guessing how to win the favor of the gods. He despised the whole lot of them—yet he was afraid not to accommodate them.

He closed his eyes and sighed. "So be it. My guards will collect the firstborn of commoners throughout the city tonight. Jericho's king will lead her people. We will begin the sacrifices at dawn with the royal fruit."

Joshua

Joshua paced back and forth in front of the tabernacle courtyard. Every sense was alive as never before. A new day. A new land. As the silver trumpets blared the summons, his entire body tingled with anticipation. Not for the bloody ritual, of course, but for what it signified. He recalled the day of his own circumcision in the safety of remote Mount Sinai. Blood, yes. Pain, yes. But, also, a profound sense of rebirth. All his manly strength dedicated to Yahweh. That kind of mass ritual should only have happened once, each newborn male from that day forward circumcised at birth, but circumcision had been suspended along with Passover and the cycle of annual feasts.

As the clan chiefs and princes of each tribe marshaled their brigades, Joshua was gratified to see the caskets of flint knives. Following the construction of the monument the previous evening, he asked them to come prepared this morning. Every tribe complied. No one challenged his authority. His smile was grim. At least there was unity of opinion that this ceremony be as painless as possible. No bronze blade could come close to the razor-edged sharpness of chipped flint.

He studied the young warriors gathered in response to the trumpet summons. God could use these boys in a mighty way if only they would rise to the challenge of holiness. Still pacing like a wolf, he raised his chin high and began.

Here at Gilgal, the nation of Israel is beginning again. The Lord God led your fathers out of Egypt with a mighty hand.

He split the Red Sea so they could pass through.

He drowned all Pharaoh's army in its depths.

He led them to Mount Sinai where he appeared to them in fire and smoke to give them the law, the terms of his covenant.

After those wonders, your fathers were circumcised as a mark of their loyalty to him. Then, when they had built the tabernacle so their God could dwell and travel in their midst, Yahweh led his people to the borders of the Promised Land.

But when your fathers saw the evil of this place,

when they saw the walled cities,

when they saw the towering Anakite giants,

their faith vanished like smoke.

They refused to follow the Lord into their inheritance.

Forty years have passed and now the almighty hand of Yahweh has brought his people full circle here at Gilgal. You, the children, will claim the inheritance in Canaan that he promised your fathers.

In the final days of Moses, east of the river, you received the scrolls of the law—just as your fathers received the commandment stones at Mount Sinai.

Yesterday, at the Jordan, our God demonstrated his mighty power when he stopped the raging flood for you—just as he split the Red Sea for your fathers.

Today, it is time for all wilderness-born warriors to declare their loyalty to the covenant by submitting to the circle-cut of circumcision—just as your fathers did at Sinai. Gilgal represents a new beginning for our people. The Lord God declares that all reproach has been rolled away at last. Will you now seal your commitment to him with your own blood?

"We will." The roar of men's voices thundered over the camp and echoed incoherently against the walls of Jericho as they pledged their loyalty. "Blessed be the God of our fathers. We will worship him alone. We will follow wherever he leads. We will obey all his commands. We submit to the mark of circumcision."

Joshua nodded with satisfaction.

This requirement will be ongoing. In the days ahead, we will move into our inheritance. But the land of Canaan is befouled with the vile orgies of pagan worship. As your tribes separate from one another and spread out in this land, encountering these evil practices, your circumcised bodies will remind you that your life-force is dedicated to the one true God. The land of Canaan is polluted with the blood of children sacrificed to idols. The male children of each new generation of Israelites must be circumcised on the eighth day as a reminder that they too are dedicated to Yahweh, the one true God. Your children are never to be sacrificed to the hideous . . . gods . . . of—"

Joshua choked as a barrage of images from his days of spying battered his speech. He paused to clear his head. More than forty years later, those horrors still haunted him. "Your children are *never* to be sacrificed to the hideous gods of Canaan." He shouted the command with all the authority he could muster, and then paused again to survey the beautiful sea of faces before him.

Yahweh God, give me words to help them understand.

Heaven-sent calmness lifted him over those disturbing memories like a smooth ocean swell and he continued gently as a father with his child.

It is not enough for your bodies alone to be circumcised. The covenant must also be in your hearts. Who was it that rebelled and grumbled against God and perished in the wilderness? Was it not your fathers—my brothers who were circumcised along with me at Mount Sinai? Who was it that died because of the adulterous worship of Baal and Asherah on Mount Peor? Was it not the last of those who submitted to the knife after passing through the Red Sea? Their bodies bore the seal of the covenant, but their lives were marked by gross unfaithfulness.

Listen! Hear the echo of Moses' last words. The LORD your God will circumcise your hearts and the hearts of your descendants, so that you may love him with all your heart and with all your soul, and live.[35]

With one voice, the sea of men and boys answered, "We will love the Lord our God with all our hearts, and with all our minds, and with all our souls. We dedicate ourselves completely to him."

Joy rose up within Joshua from the depths of his being, and he raised his hands in benediction. "May the One who is faithful to all *his* promises keep you faithful to yours."

Acsah

The alteration to an abnormal world of women on this, the second day in Canaan, amused Acsah. Except for a few men like her father who had been circumcised forty-one years before at Mount Sinai, the only indication of male presence was the occasional deep-voiced groan from the privacy of tents where the warriors of Israel lay healing. While Caleb took balm and encouragement to the men of Judah, Acsah marshaled the assistance of Hogluh and Hodesh. All morning, they carried water and carried wood. They tended the flocks and herds of Sarah, Abihail, and any other neighbor who seemed overburdened by the work their husbands and sons normally did. A world run by women, she decided, was a very efficient place.

After a quick midday meal, Acsah settled beside her father to transform a basket of wool into yarn for weaving. As the white fluff flew through her spindle, Acsah's imagination spun a wild scenario. She saw the armies of Jericho attacking the tents of groaning. She pictured newly-circumcised men hobbling about in their attempt to defend the camp. She watched them trying to hold the weight of their robes away from their bodies as they wielded their weapons . . . if they could move at all.

When a loud moan rent the air from the family tent of her youngest brother, Jezliah, two tent spaces away, Acsah dissolved into laughter at the images marching through her head.

"What do you find so amusing, Acsah?"

She looked up and met a piercing look from her father's steely gray eyes. "Surely you do not find mirth in the pain of the men of Judah." No smile crinkles softened his face.

"No, Abba." She flashed a mischievous smile at him and returned her focus to her spindle. "I was just thinking of the ignorance of the Canaanites—them not knowing the condition of our men."

"Ah." Caleb resumed sharpening a well-worn scythe. "It is no joke. The Canaanite armies surely would stream from their cities to attack if they had any idea. Humph. No joke at all."

"I know, Abba." She watched her father hammering nicks out of the bronze blade and wondered about the previous owner. Did that Amorite warrior in Sihon's army, bent on destroying Israel, have a daughter who loved him as much as she loved her father? "War is never a joke," she said in all sincerity.

"The sons of Jacob do not return to this land with the neutrality of an innocent people. Remember the story of Shechem? The slaughter of the entire Canaanite town by Jacob's sons, Levi and Simeon? Deceit and treachery when the men of that city were indisposed as ours are today. The rape of their sister, Dinah, was a terrible thing, but their revenge was even more repugnant. I'm certain the inhabitants of Canaan would find it quite fitting to massacre every one of his descendants to settle the score."

Acsah worked in sober silence for a while, then smothered another laugh. "Would you like to know the strange vision I had of such an attack?"

Caleb didn't answer.

"I pictured you arming me and all my female friends. Can you imagine yourself as captain, leading *women* out to defend the healing warriors of Israel." She glanced at her father to see his reaction.

Caleb shook his head in wonder. He understood her well, but not completely—this daughter of his old age. She listened with respect to his attempt to bring deeper meaning to yesterday's mass ritual. "The day of dedication was a grisly day. One to be taken seriously," he said. "Joshua had to reprimand some of the young men yesterday. They were joking irreverently about the bloody mound, growing by the hour as a result of the thousands of circumcisions.

They declared the name of this place would forever be *Gibeath Haaraloth*, Foreskin Mountain. *Hmmph.* Joshua reminded them the Lord himself gave us the name *Gilgal*. We must focus on what God has done for us, not our own misery."

"Gilgal is a much better name," Acsah agreed. "Much shorter. And meaning *circle*, it rolls off the tongue much more easily."

Caleb studied her face to see if she was serious or mocking.

"Gibeath Haaraloth," she repeated with great seriousness. "Who would want to memorialize the gore when we have the glory of the Gilgal?" She made every attempt to suppress any smiles.

"Exactly." When at last her father seemed satisfied with her attitude, he continued. "Gilgal is to be remembered forever as a place of new beginnings. The nations of Canaan mocked the God of Israel when we did not take the land forty years ago. They boasted that the power of their gods turned Egypt's former slaves back into the wilderness. Israel was disgraced. But here at the Jordan, God's grace displaces our disgrace. At Gilgal, our warriors chose to receive the mark of God's holy people and follow him, no matter what lies ahead. They *rolled away* the last remnants of the reproach of Egypt. "

Acsah had reached the bottom of the wool basket. She rose to her feet and kissed her father's leathery cheek. "Your wisdom always helps me see more clearly, Abba."

"This is not my wisdom, Acsah. The Lord named this place." Caleb fell silent as he concentrated on his work.

Acsah glanced at the sky above Caleb's head. Clear blue. Only a few small clouds grazing the western horizon. There would be no rain today. She could wash Caleb's bloody tunic and the piles of towels, stiff and brown with the dried blood of yesterday's circumcisions. "Hogluh! Hodesh!" she called, "Come with me. We have some washing to do at the river. We must build a shallow pool along the side where the mud can settle out before we wash. If we hurry, we will have time to play while the sun dries our things."

Hogluh's high-pitched voice asked excitedly, "Will there be frogs and dragonflies on this side of the river?"

"I hope so." Hodesh chimed in. "I try and try to see how the frogs eat them. It happens so quickly. There is a dragonfly . . . then it is gone. Just old Master Frog looking so smug with legs and wings poking out of his mouth."

"I love the water so much, Acsah. We have never lived by a river before."

Acsah scooped up an armload of deeply-stained towels and rolled them in her father's stiff, sullied tunic. She shook her head in wonder over the amount of blood. *How many male members could one man cut in one day?* "We have a lot of work ahead of us," she reminded the girls. "No splashing until we finish spreading the clean things high and dry where you won't soak them again."

Hogluh caught her sister's eyes with a grin. "But . . . there might be accidents . . ."

"Bring the other basket of soiled clothing, you two." She had to laugh at the mischievous little faces. She just might surprise the girls with a cold-water accident of her own.

As they headed down the path to the river, she heard Caleb's faint murmur, "I love your laughter, my little anklet, my Acsah."

Acsah woke up on the morning of Passover with her arms wrapped around the yearling. Her heart twisted. How could she watch as this innocent ram was slaughtered? She knew him so well. She knew that the bright green, new growth of sweet bay laurel was his favorite food. She loved the way he circled her, nearly tripping her when she brought him a bouquet of those sweet leaves. She loved the way he bumped her legs with his head after he had devoured the leaves as if that would produce more. She loved the way he dipped his head as she scratched around his horns, and she loved the way he called for her when chores took her out of sight. As she left with the manna basket, his cries nearly broke her heart. Would he remain so stubbornly vocal about being left alone if he knew how the family would betray him today? Her nieces and nephews always responded to his cries while she was out gathering, and as expected, by the time she returned to make the morning porridge, he was surrounded by a flock of happy children.

The preparations for Passover would keep her busy today. That was good. She did not want time to contemplate his fate. After breakfast, Hodesh and Hogluh helped her mill barley flour for the unleavened bread while her young nieces and nephews doted on the lamb, offering parched grain, grasses, leaves—even flowers and raisins. The happy chatter of the children and the ram's eager bleats and baas punctuated the scraping and grinding noises of stone on stone. *Was she the only one whose heart grieved over the impending feast?*

After lunch, when chores were laid aside for a midday rest and the yearling slept contentedly surrounded by half a dozen children, Acsah slipped away to the meadow. Her sisters-in-law would bake the barley flatbread. Her father and brothers would slaughter the lamb and roast it. She assigned herself the task of collecting the bitter herbs. She would collect them far away from Judah. So far that she could not hear her lamb's last pitiful cry. She would return just before sunset, in time to add the greens to the feast.

She had watched the daily sacrifices all her life, but never had the shedding of innocent blood been so personal or painful. She could hear her father's oft-repeated words. *"If our imperfect hearts grieve over suffering, how much more the perfect heart of God?"* Right now that didn't help. If that were true, why would God *ask* them to slaughter perfect, blameless lambs, ask them to live with the lamb for days, and then ask them to *eat* it in celebration?

She took a few deliberate steps into the open meadow pondering these things, but she did not want to think. She wanted to run. She lifted her arms like a zany, off-balance bird with her herb basket rocking wildly in one hand and ran. She flew past the flocks and herds. She soared down the long, gentle slope of the meadow toward the rounded hill of the Gilgal feeling like an eagle in flight. Perhaps the carefree days of childhood were gone, but in the simple act of running, she recaptured a bit of its fading freedom.

So many changes had occurred since her people first entered the Jordan valley, and most were changes she would never have chosen. Her flying feet declared her intention to outrun them as she had her pursuers in long-ago, childish games of tag. As the land leveled out, Acsah raced even faster, allowing her momentum to carry her up the slope into the embrace of that circle of solid, unchanging stones. She fell panting against one of the pillars of the Gilgal.

EPILOGUE

Othniel

Startled and flustered by a thud, a clatter, and noisy panting on the far side of the Gilgal, Othniel leaned out and around Judah's stone to see who had interrupted his solitude.

"Oh!" Acsah seemed as flustered as he was to find someone here. Then she giggled. "Did you come here to be alone?"

"Yes." *What does she think? I'm here looking for a crowd?*

"Me too." Acsah's laughter, rippling like a brook in early spring, washed away his annoyance.

He shook his hair back over his shoulders, lifting his face to the sky. This afternoon, it was an unblemished dome of brilliant sapphire blue. Not a cloud in sight. The sun was warm, but not too hot. He leaned his head back against the stone and closed his eyes.

"Well, we can't both be alone here," Acsah said. He could tell by the rustling and scuffling that she was scrambling back to her feet. "I arrived last. I will leave you to your serene seclusion."

Othniel did not open his eyes. "I wouldn't mind if you stayed."

There was no sound from Acsah. The sunshine, warm on his face, had cast a drowsy spell over the valley. There was no lowing from the ruminating livestock in the distant meadow. The early morning twittering of songbirds in the Jordan jungle had long since quieted. The air was so still that not even the grasses or leaves rustled. Only a few insects droned over the fragrant lupine and anemones scattered around the Gilgal.

He had almost forgotten about his cousin until he heard her footsteps moving across the grass toward him and her clothing rustling as she settled into a resting place at the stone adjacent to him.

"I can't remember a time when quiet was more pleasant," she said.

"Mmm."

"Now here I am spoiling your quiet." She laughed.

Othniel did not answer.

After a few moments, she said. "Abba will slaughter our Passover lamb this afternoon. I have grown so attached to the little fellow that I could not stay by to watch or hear. How do you deal with this shedding of innocent blood?"

"Our family didn't need its own lamb."

"Of course. Since there are only three of you, Abba invited you to join us."

"Mmm."

"Sorry. You came here to be alone. I won't talk anymore."

"I don't mind."

"No, really. I'll be quiet. I have a lot of frustrations to think through."

"Think out loud if you want. I'm a better listener than talker."

Acsah

As Acsah began pouring out her heart-wrenching grief over living with an animal that was going to be eaten in celebration, she found her cousin was indeed a good listener. His mumbles implied listening and understanding, but not judgment. She soon found herself venting her frustration about the many changes that were turning her life upside down.

"When you men went off for military drills in the wilderness, it was nothing. It was just a game. There were no wars or rumors of war. But, here in Canaan—it is different. Father expects there *will* be war and separation. You will go off for weeks or months fighting battles while we women and children are left behind. You will witness the wonders of God shining forth gloriously. But that is not what I will witness. I will know only grindstone and loom, cook fire, livestock, and garden. You will live miracles. I will live mundane monotony." Acsah stopped and laughed at herself. "Not a very noble attitude, is it?"

Othniel stared into the distance for so long that Acsah wondered if he had even listened. At last he said, "I can understand how you might feel left behind. It reminds me of the contribution Hur made to the battle with the Amalekites long ago. As Joshua tells the story, Hur felt left behind when he was asked to accompany Moses and Aaron up the mountain to pray, knowing he would only observe the fighting from afar. As it turned out, though, he was one of only three who truly saw the battle that day. Joshua and the warriors on the battlefield only knew that sometimes they were winning and sometimes they were losing, although they constantly fought as hard as they could. From the hilltop where Moses prayed and held up his staff, Hur could see that defeat quickly followed the lowering of Moses' hands—and success came as he raised them again. Victory that day came not because the warriors fought so well, nor because Moses prayed so powerfully, but because Aaron and Hur stayed beside Moses to support him in his prayers and hold up his hands. Never feel that staying behind in prayer support is unimportant."[36]

Acsah looked at Othniel in wonder. "You sound like my father. Wise, I mean. You are so very right, and that makes me feel like a petty, peevish child."

"Who of us would not feel exactly the same way as you under these circumstances unless God provided a different view point? That is why the stories are important. Always remember the stories."

Othniel

Acsah was quiet for a long time. Othniel found his curiosity building until he had to open his eyes. He rolled his head toward his cousin for a quick peek and found her studying his face. He sat up a little straighter and started to shake his hair back over his shoulders, but somehow that felt silly. When he looked at her again, their eyes locked, and to his surprise, it was comfortable.

"I love the stories too," she said.

Uncle Caleb was the one person Othniel had been able to confide in since his father died. But here today, he detected the same thoughtfulness in Caleb's bright, ebullient daughter. Here was someone with whom he could share the deepest secrets of his heart.

"Let me show you something," he said. He rose to his knees, twisting so he was facing the pillar of Judah. Reverently, he placed both hands on the stone he and Caleb had carried from the riverbed. "What do you see?"

"I see the stone of Judah. What on earth do you see?" A smile teased the corners of her mouth. "Is there a mystery I am missing?"

Othniel averted his eyes, studying the odd shape of the pillar. Not much of a mystery. Not really much of a story either. Just a stone, shaped like an elongated goatskin stretched tight with water. Plain and common, like himself. But something within him burned to tell her about it. "I haven't even told your father the story of the rock he chose from the riverbed." Keeping his eyes fixed on the stone, he told the story of the contest on the day of celebration. When he finished telling how this particular stone was lost to the river, he paused, staring into the distant haze. There was more to say, but the story was finished. What words could express the secret longings of his heart?

"My father will laugh . . ." Acsah giggled, but when Othniel caught her eyes, her laughter froze. Her face grew serious. She understood there was more and waited respectfully.

Othniel searched to find the right words. "As I walked away from that contest," he said at last, "my heart flamed with the desire to be a hero like your father. For the first time in my life, I felt like it was possible. Nothing has ever thrilled me more than hearing stories like that of Joshua and Caleb—as well as all the old heroes of Israel. But I always expected to fight alongside the next generation of heroes when we fought for this land. There, on that day of celebration, for the first time, I was struck with the thought that someday, somehow, somewhere *I* might be the hero."

Acsah nodded. "You will be. I truly believe it. A hero like my father." She looked at him so admiringly that he had to look away.

"I don't expect to be a Joshua or Caleb, certainly not a Moses or Abraham. Stories of the things they have done for God fill whole evenings by the campfire."

Acsah's eyes sparkled at the mention of those names.

"In the end, I just want to know my life mattered." He could not seem to muster normal volume. He knew his words were almost inaudible and wondered if she heard him.

"It will," she said simply after a thoughtful pause.

Othniel ran his hand over the smooth surface of the memorial stone. "That I once threw this, and that in God's providence it came to this monument is all the fame I need. At the end of my days, I simply desire for my name to be recorded among those who lived for God, settling this land for him." He grinned. "I don't expect a long story. I would be quite content with one brief sentence—"

Acsah leaped to her feet to complete his thought, her eyes glittering as she raised her hands toward the clouds in a prophetic gesture. Mirth rippled like a melody through her voice as she announced, "One sentence—Othniel, hero of Israel: a dedicated life that brought righteousness, goodness, and peace to the Land of Canaan."

He blushed at her enthusiasm, but he could not take his eyes off her. Half child, wide-eyed with wonder; half the perfection of womanhood—wise, nurturing, and, oh, so beautiful. He had watched her from afar, but never up close like this. The newness was startling. Yet when he looked into the forest depths of her green eyes, he felt as if he had finally returned home after a long, meandering walk through a desert. A powerful urge to ask Caleb for Acsah's hand in marriage surged through him. At the same time, common sense told him a celestial being like Acsah should never be earthbound by such a common creature as himself. This was simply a wonderful moment to enjoy for what it was. Othniel had tilted his face up to watch her antics. Now the muscles and nerves in his neck twitched, the natural pull of habit to break contact, to flip his long golden mane back over his shoulders and withdraw into himself. This time he fought it, and their roles were suddenly reversed.

Acsah shyly averted her eyes as she repeated her oracle. "I am certain of it. Your name will be summarized forever and always by one bold sentence. *Othniel, hero of Israel.* That is all." When she finished, she bowed with a graceful flourish that would have honored the world's most glorious sovereign.

Othniel stood and faced her boldly. His thick, golden mane fell onto his face as he acknowledged her bow with a courtly nod of his head. This time he didn't shake it back. He didn't break contact with the glittering green eyes. "I would be most honored by such a sentence as that," he said. At the very core of his being, he wanted her words to prove true. He settled back on the ground, letting his head roll back against the stone. The Gilgal grounded him even as his heart soared.

"And so begins another gilgal in our journey," he said.

Acsah didn't reply, but her flashing smile and the emerald beauty of her piercing eyes confirmed his certainty that the new gilgal would be every bit as exciting as the last one.

ENDNOTES

Chapter 1:

¹ Psalm 90:1–2 (NIV).
² Psalm 90:7–8 (NIV).
³ Psalm 90:12, 14 (NIV).
⁴ Exodus 15:21 (NIV).
⁵ Chapters 2–4 are intended to give the author's impression of what it might have been like to be in the crowds listening to the final words of Moses over several days, as recorded in the book of Deuteronomy. The author has quoted in part and added background based on other scriptures to aid understanding—well aware of this warning from Moses himself: "Do not add to what I command you and do not subtract from it, but keep the commands of the LORD your God that I give you" (Deut. 4:2 NIV). The author urges you to read the book of Deuteronomy in its entirety.

Chapter 2:

Moses' First Farewell Speech
⁶ The author has summarized, amplified, and paraphrased the first of Moses' farewell speeches as recorded in Deuteronomy 1–4:40.

⁷ Deuteronomy 4:39, author paraphrase.
⁸ Deuteronomy 1:1, author paraphrase.

Chapter 3:

⁹ The announcement Moses made regarding the cities of refuge is found in Deuteronomy 4:41–48. More detail is given in Numbers 35.

Moses' Second Farewell Speech
¹⁰ Deuteronomy 5-11, the second speech summarized, amplified, and paraphrased by the author.
¹¹ Deuteronomy 5:7-21, The Ten Commandments, author paraphrase.

Review of the Law
¹² Deuteronomy 31:9–13, 24–29 hint at a ceremony in which Moses presented the Book of the Law to the Levites, presumably the laws listed in fourteen chapters embedded between Moses' second farewell speech and the third speech.
¹³ From Deuteronomy 12–26. The author has paraphrased a sampling of the laws detailed in these fourteen chapters.

Moses' Third Speech and the Ceremony of Blessings and Curses
¹⁴ Deuteronomy 27:1–8, author paraphrase.
¹⁵ Deuteronomy 27:9 (NIV).
¹⁶ Deuteronomy 27:15–19 (NIV).
¹⁷ Deuteronomy 28:3–14, author synopsis and paraphrase.
¹⁸ Deuteronomy 28:15–19, author paraphrase.
¹⁹ Deuteronomy 28:20–24 (NIV).
²⁰ Deuteronomy 28:25–26, 29b, 30, 32, 45–48 (NIV).
²¹ Deuteronomy 29:18 (NIV).
²² Author's paraphrase of Deuteronomy 29:19.
²³ Author's paraphrase of Deuteronomy 30:11 and 14.
²⁴ Author's synopsis and paraphrase of Deuteronomy 30:11–20.

Chapter 4:

²⁵ The commissioning of Joshua is described in Deuteronomy 31:1–8, 15. During that ceremony, God warned Moses of Israel's

future unfaithfulness and gave him the words of a song as "a witness against them" (verses 16–23).

[26] Deuteronomy 31:16 (NIV).

[27] Deuteronomy 32:1–2 (NIV), a small part of the Song of Moses.

[28] Deuteronomy 33:10–11 (NIV). The words to Levi as Moses blessed the tribes.

Chapters 5–6:

[29] Joshua 2, the story of Rahab and the spies.

Chapter 7:

[30] Joshua 3, the story of breaking camp and crossing the Jordan.

[31] Joshua 1:12–18. The original agreement of the Transjordan tribes with Moses is found in Numbers 32.

[32] Numbers 6:24–26 (Holman Christian Standard Bible), the Aaronic Blessing.

Chapter 8:

[33] Joshua 4, the story of the Gilgal.

Chapter 9:

[34] Joshua 5, the restoration of circumcision and the Feast of Passover.

[35] Deuteronomy 30:6.

Epilogue:

[36] Exodus 17:8–15, the story of Hur at the battle with Amalek.

BIBLICAL BACKGROUNDS
OF THE
PRIMARY CHARACTERS

Othniel—Hebrew meaning: lion of God.
- Read his story in Judges 1:9-15, and 3:7-11.

Acsah (also spelled Achsah or Aksah)—Hebrew meaning: anklet.
- Her story is found in Joshua 15:13-19 and repeated word for word in Judges 1:9-15.

Abihail—Hebrew meaning: father of strength or *source* of strength. A fictional character—the daughter-in-law of the real biblical character, Achor or Achan.
- You can read about the family she married into in Joshua 7.

Salmon—Hebrew meaning: garment, something that wraps around or covers. It is also possible that the name derives from *shalom* meaning peace or wholeness as in the name Solomon.
His name appears only in genealogies (sometimes as Salma).
- 1 Chronicles 2:11 lists him as the elder, or prince, of the tribe of Judah during the time of Joshua.
- Ruth 4:18-22 lists him among the princes or chiefs of Judah in the genealogy of King David.

- Matthew 1:5 includes his name in the ancestry of Jesus and gives us a hint of his love story.

Jonathan—Hebrew meaning: gift of Yahweh.
- His story from Judges 17 and 18 will not be told until the last book of the series.

Phinehas—Hebrew meaning: mouth of brass. The serious, highly-principled grandson of Aaron and future High Priest of Israel shows up a number of times in this period of history. Each time in a rather war-like role for a high priest.
- We first meet Phinehas in Numbers 25:6-13 as the young priest who takes charge rather violently when no one else dared to. This righteous act of courage is commended in Psalm 106:28-31.
- Shortly afterward, he is rewarded for his violent valor with a military commission as commander of the entire Israelite army in the Midianite War (Numbers 31:6-8).
- About seven years later, he is sent to investigate a possible breach of the covenant by the Transjordan tribes (Joshua 22:9-34), handling the problem with wisdom and restraint.
- Around twenty-five years later, when Phinehas is the anointed high priest, his name comes up again as the military and spiritual advisor of Israel (Judges 20:27-28).
- In the last horrifying story from the book of Judges (chapters 19-21), the people come to Phinehas four times at the tabernacle to seek guidance and "weep before the Lord."

Rahab—Hebrew meaning: wide or large. The name implies fierceness, insolence, and pride. In the book of Job, Rahab is the name of a sea monster. In Isaiah and Psalms, it is used as a metaphor for Egypt, a monster in the eyes of God's people. All those ancient implications are largely forgotten today, upstaged by the story of Rahab's incredible faith. Even her name is a story of redemption.
- The well-known story of the clever Harlot of Jericho is found in Joshua 2.

- She is one of three foreign women named in the genealogy of Jesus the Messiah (Matthew 1:5).
- James 2:25 uses Rahab's story as an example of faith demonstrated by actions.
- Rahab has the honor of being listed—along with Sarah the wife of Abraham—as one of only two women found in Faith's Hall of Fame (Hebrews 11:31).

THE
STONES OF GILGAL
NOVELS

Step into an ancient world and brace yourself for a plunge into the chilling conflict between a good God and the evil forces that hold his creation hostage. The thrills and travails experienced by the main characters of the *Stones of Gilgal* novels bring life and light to the riveting era of Joshua—an epoch long obscured by the mists of time, truth darkened by the sinister lies and insinuations of the dark side.

As prophets, priests, and kings jostle for power and cultures collide, your heart will be touched by the sorrows and chilled by the fears of one brave Canaanite girl and six young Israelites who discover that claiming their long-lost inheritance and carving out a new life in the Land of Promise, entails more than crossing the Jordan River. The names of these seven have all but disappeared, pebbles cast long ago into the pool of history, but the ripples of their lives extend to eternity. *The Stones of Gilgal* saga pulls these seven out of the murky water of ancient Scripture for a second look.

- Book One, *Balaam's Curse,* explores one of many Old Testament tales of terror. The seductive plotting, the bloody civil war, the total annihilation of five Midianite kingdoms, and the impaling of a princess are, indeed, cringe-worthy biblical episodes, but they are part of the war story of the universe, balanced by glimpses of a love greater than the darkness.

- Book Two, *A River to Cross,* is a fresh telling of the crossing of the Jordan, plunging you into the raging torrent of the river and the perils of life in the city of Jericho. The powers of darkness are strong, but no contest at all for Yahweh. In an astonishing display of glory, the God of Israel announces to all Canaan that a new day is coming.

Coming Soon:

- Book Three, *Trouble in the Ruins,* explores several signature tales of triumph and terror from the book of Joshua: the toppling of the walls of Jericho and the stories of Achan and Ai.

- Book Four, *Pursuit of Zedek,* explores the question: Was *every* nation of Canaan unredeemably evil? Contrast the Confederation of Gibeon with the ruthless kingdoms of Adonai-Zekek and his cohorts. Experience a day of battle so stupendous and of such import that it brought the sun to a halt while Joshua finished his mission.

- Book Five, Othniel's love story and his emergence as a young hero, defeating the remnant of Anakite giants.

- Book Six, Othniel saves the young nation of Israel from oppression as the first of its hero-judges. This last book in the series will unveil the final destiny of each character, shaped through small choices over a lifetime.

The Stones of Gilgal novels take you through some of the goriest tales of Scripture along the path toward some of its most glorious miracles. If those years seem confusing and chaotic for Bible readers, imagine how difficult it must have been to live them. At the crossing of the Jordan, Yahweh told the people to build a *gilgal*, Hebrew for *circle*. In the midst of the miracle, each of the twelve tribes chose one stone from the dry riverbed for that circle. The ensuing years were fraught with more peril than anyone could have imagined, but the Stones of Gilgal remained through it all as a solid reminder that their God was powerful and real.

EXCERPT FROM
THE STONES OF GILGAL
BOOK THREE

TROUBLE IN THE RUINS

L ed by a vanguard of swordsmen sentries, Israel's immolation brigade swarmed over the broken walls into Jericho. Their orders were to burn the entire city to the ground, the command as clear as it was drastic. Nothing was to be salvaged but precious metals for the tabernacle. No plunder. No captives.

Energized by the staggering demonstration of Yahweh's power they had just witnessed, Achor and his eldest son Jamin charged down the mountain of tumbled blocks into the uproar as part of the platoon from Judah, adding the smoke of their torches to the miasma of rising dust. As they skirted a jumbled pile of crushed masonry blocking entrance to the street, a colorful flash of purple registered on the edge of Achor's field of vision. At the same time, he heard a weak voice pleading, "Help me."

"Stop, Jamin." Achor turned aside and peered into a cove formed by two fallen pillars. "What have we here?" He could just make out five twisted bodies, sprawled within the darkness of the shelter. The central figure was dressed in the brilliant purple that had first snared Achor's attention. As he thrust his torch back into the shadows for a better look, he could see that the richly-garbed man clutched a crown.

"It must be the king," he whispered in awe.

His son's eyes widened. "Look at that fabulous robe!"

In the flickering torchlight, a multitude of jeweled eyes winked and blinked from the wide leather belt cinching the king's waist. At the neck and from mid-thigh down, the rich purple cloth was embellished with alternating rows of gold and scarlet embroidery. Achor had never dreamed that such an exquisite garment existed. "The sight of such a thing leaves me nearly speechless," he gasped as wonder and reverence for such beauty flooded over him. "May Yahweh allow me to find another as fine as this in one of the cities where we *can* take plunder."

Jamin did not respond directly to his father's words. "One of these Canaanites called out. Someone is still alive here. Our job is to eliminate all survivors and their belongings."

Achor kicked at the body of a young, pimply-faced guard close to his feet. "Up now," he commanded. But the man did not move. Handing his torch to Jamin and stepping over the dead soldier, he ducked his head low to enter the shelter in the rubble. The three bodies swathed in priestly garments were as unresponsive as the guard, but when Achor's toe nudged the fallen monarch, the corpse wheezed.

"This must be the one we heard moaning," Jamin noted, grabbing for his sword.

Before Achor could react, prominent hooded eyes snapped open, staring at him.

"He's alive," Achor croaked, stumbling and falling backward over the dead guard. "The king is alive!"

"For the moment," Jamin replied flatly.

Achor lifted his head and shoulders and found himself looking directly into forbiddingly cold, black eyes. "Help me," the injured king repeated, the words more a whispered command this time than a plea of desperation.

Achor stared at him in horror.

When there was no answer from either Israelite, he struggled to a sitting position, wincing with the pain of his effort. As short, rapid breaths began to restore the king's strength, Achor felt increasingly uncomfortable under the scrutiny of his disdainful authority. All too aware that he, the conqueror, was still sprawled over a crumpled dead body looking up at his defeated foe, he pushed himself to his knees, eye level with the king. "Let's set this cove aflame and catch up with the platoon."

"Wait," the man commanded. "I am King Nahari of Jericho." He held up the crown, shrewdly trapping Achor's eyes as he toyed with the bejeweled symbol of his power. "This spot was the antechamber of my palace, but all is worthless to me now. Take this crown and help me escape."

Jamin crouched down and pushed the torches into the dim shelter. Although the piece in the king's hands glittered in the light of the fire, Jamin barely glanced at it before knocking it to the pavement with the butt of his torch. "What need have we of a crown?" he said coldly. "We are but simple Israelites."

King Nahari's eyes swam momentarily with desperation. Then he looked down at his robe. "This . . . this garment was a gift to me from the king of Babylonia when I took his youngest daughter as my wife." His fingers fumbled at the turquoise and amethyst studded girdle around his waist. He unfastened it and tossed it toward Achor.

As the king began pulling the magnificent purple garment over his shoulders and head, Achor's mouth went dry. He picked up the wide belt, gripped by the urge to seize the thing and run. Instead, he squeezed his eyes closed and steeled himself against the thought. "You and your city are beyond help. Everything will burn."

Nahari ignored the words. A wave of his hand drew attention to his thin undergarment. "You can see that under the royal trappings I too am but a simple man in a tunic." He turned one of the inside-out purple sleeves right again, panting with the effort as he continued. "I heard your words of admiration when your eyes first fell on this choice garment. I perceive you are a rare man, as I am myself. One who appreciates fine things." He met Achor's eyes boldly. "Take it. There is no finer garment in all Canaan. It is said to bestow mystical powers of authority on its wearer. You would be a fool to let it burn." He hissed those last words with contempt.

"*You* are a fool if you think we would help you just to gain such a thing," Achor snapped. "An Israelite would never dare to wear clothing from Jericho."

The king seemed to sense a crack in Achor's resolve despite the emphatic words. He turned to Jamin with a confidential tone. "I have a secret treasury back here: wedges of gold, bags of silver. My robe for the elder. Silver and gold for you. Take as much as you can carry," he coaxed. "Only help me. Surely my gods will reward your kindness."

"Such an act would be treason against our God and our people," Achor answered, firmly repulsing the power of the temptation. He turned his back on the king and started toward the opening. "Ignite this den of temptation, my son."

"Wait, Father." The young man thrust both torches firmly into a crevice and fixed the king with a hard look. "Give me the robe. You may wear my outer cloak as a disguise and walk with us until we get outside the city. Then you will be on your own."

"Agreed," the king promised, his voice rising with hope. "I will flee across the desert to Babylonia. I swear I will never stir up revenge against your people, nor join with anyone who dares attack Israel."

Jamin held the robe and girdle out to Achor. "Conceal this beneath your cloak, Father. We will keep it hidden until Israel has taken other cities and is permitted to carry off the plunder from them. Who could ever know that it came from Jericho?"

Achor stood motionless. "Yahweh will know."

"The question is . . ." Jamin sneered, "will he care? We can sacrifice something of equal value to him later." He dangled the robe in front of his father. "This garment suits you. Clothing acquired in another city will burn as brightly in sacrifice to Yahweh. This or another, what is a robe to God?"

Jamin pressed the royal robe into his father's hands and then leaned over the king in a threatening pose. "Where is your silver and gold? Show me. I will not give you my cloak as disguise until I see it."

"My steward stocked it close at hand . . . this very morning. Too late—" the king choked on his words. "We thought to escape the city at nightfall."

Achor felt a twinge of pity for the man. "We will help you make that escape. Where is this trove?"

The king climbed over the bodies of the three priests. "These charlatans deceived me. Burn them. Burn their filthy bodies." He kicked at the priestly corpses angrily as he crawled farther back into the cove until Achor could see only the white undergarment covering Nahari's back parts and the soles of his sandals. The king's voice echoed back from the depths of darkness as he scrabbled in the ruins. "Oh, that I could have torn them to pieces with my own hands while they lived. I could have fled. But they urged me to sacrifice more and more of the treasures of Jericho. To what end? Your people could not be stopped."

Tossing more complaints than clattering rock, Nahari worked at clearing the rubble. "Long before its walls fell, Jericho had been plundered by its own priests. Looted by its own irrational goddess. They depleted my treasury. Emptied my stables. Forced me to watch as they slaughtered Jericho's infants. Even my own flesh and blood . . . Can one of you help me here?"

Jamin ducked past his father and assisted the ranting monarch, pulling a large chunk of broken masonry from the front of a splintered door.

"We sacrificed Jericho's fairest virgins on Asherah's altar. To what end? While my priests clamored for more and more, my gods remained silent . . . Here." The king pushed two heavy bags toward Jamin. "Two hundred shekels of silver."

Jamin picked them up and heaved them toward Achor's feet as the king continued rooting around in the blackness of his storage vault. "Take this wedge of pure gold. Can you carry more? I fear not. I have not the strength to carry but a few silver coins. I will flee to Babylonia a pauper. But *my* fate is preferable to that of my subjects who could not escape Yahweh's hand and my own conniving priests." He turned toward Achor with the gold.

As Achor took the heavy wedge from the king, his eyes brightened. "It must weigh fifty shekels," he murmured with a quiver of delight.

He lifted his eyes just in time to see Jamin bring a massive chunk of masonry down on the king's head. As the stone crashed into the rubble, King Nahari slumped to the ground, never knowing he had been deceived yet again.

Jamin rolled his eyes at the look of horror on his father's face. "With that crimped hair and beard, there is no way he could have posed as an Israelite. We could not have led him through the cordon surrounding the city—even if we really had wanted to help him."

CONTACT INFORMATION

MOUNTAIN VIEW PRESS

To order additional copies of this book, please visit
www.mountainviewpress.com
Also available on Amazon.com and BarnesandNoble.com
Or by calling toll free (855) 946-2555